PRUE LEITH

Sisters

PENGUIN BOOKS

PENGUIN BOOKS

Published by the Penguin Group
Penguin Books Ltd, 27 Wrights Lane, London w8 5TZ, England
Penguin Putnam Inc., 375 Hudson Street, New York, New York 10014, USA
Penguin Books Australia Ltd, Ringwood, Victoria, Australia
Penguin Books Canada Ltd, 10 Alcorn Avenue, Toronto, Ontario, Canada M4V 3B2
Penguin Books India (P) Ltd, 11 Community Centre,
Panchsheel Park, New Delhi – 110 017, India
Penguin Books (NZ) Ltd, Cnr Rosedale and Airborne Roads,
Albany, Auckland, New Zealand
Penguin Books (South Africa) (Pty) Ltd, 5 Watkins Street,
Denver Ext 4, Johannesburg 2094, South Africa

Penguin Books Ltd, Registered Offices: Harmondsworth, Middlesex, England

First published 2001
3

Set in 10.25/13.25pt Linotype Palatino by Intype London Ltd
Printed in England by Clays Ltd, St Ives plc

Acknowledgements

Everyone warns that the second novel is harder to write than the first. It's true. So my thanks for help are heartfelt. My family, as before, have been consistently encouraging. If they shared my doubts, they kindly kept them hidden.

Then, as before, there is Julia Bell from The Literary Consultancy, who told me what was wrong with the first draft, editors Louise Moore and Harriet Evans at Penguin, who should be nannies for showing such belief in their charges, and Nicky Stonehill, who did such a great job in publicizing *Leaving Patrick*.

On the practical side, I must thank Tiny and Jan Barnetson and Judi Dyason for help on African game, geography and languages, Charlie Marshall and Roo Rogers on Italian colloquialisms, paramedics Graham White and Tina Flint on first aid procedure, and Graham King of Westminster Council for details of Paddington basin. But above all I must thank Kate Wiggins, not just for correcting the typos of endless drafts, but also for telling me what, true or false, I needed to hear – that she loved the novel.

For Li-Da

Prologue

Lucille lay in a deck-chair in the shade of the pergola and you could see she didn't want to be interrupted. Poppy stood beside her, fondling Sheba's ears and waiting for her mother to look up from her magazine. In the end she did, her eyes vague.

'What is it, darling?'

'I can't find Carrie. She said we could practise our concert. In the tree house.'

'She's with Hennie. His mom brought him over.' Lucille turned her head to look round the garden. 'They're somewhere about, I think.'

Poppy swivelled her toes in the dry sand where the grass had died. It was hot and gritty. She said, 'Hennie's a baby. He's even younger than Carrie. I wish he wouldn't come.'

'Why not, darling?' asked Lucille, putting an arm round Poppy's solid bottom.

'Carrie never wants me around if Hennie's here.'

Lucille slid her hand down and stroked her ten-year-old daughter's sturdy legs absent-mindedly, her eyes already back in the magazine.

'I'm sure that's not true, darling. Go and find them.'

Her mother was often like this, kind but somehow not there.

Poppy decided she'd see if the others were with Maisie. She sometimes had nice things to do. Like making ice-cream. If they turned the churn handle for her, which took ages and made your arms ache, she'd give them a scoop when it was done. Or shelling peas. Poppy liked shelling peas, the way the pods popped and the way the peas lay tight in their little green shells, like a fat crew in a canoe. And she liked Maisie. Maisie let you eat the peas. Only you weren't allowed to eat them out of the bowl. You had to shell your own.

The ridgeback bitch waddled after her, panting in the heat as Poppy zigzagged her way back to the house, leaping to patches of shade, dashing up the red-polished steps before her feet burned. When she gained the stoep the same red surface, now shaded, was smooth and cool under her feet. She pushed through the fly-screen door, letting it slap back behind her on its self-closing hinges. Sheba, shut out, flopped down where she was and lowered her head on to her paws, eyes closing.

Poppy wandered down the corridor, trailing her fingers along the wall in the way Maisie was always telling her not to. She could hear Carrie giggling.

At first she couldn't tell where they were. She opened their bedroom door but the room was empty. Then she heard Carrie's voice again. It was coming from their mom and dad's room.

She looked around quickly. Maisie would kill them if she caught them. They weren't allowed in there without a grown-up. Not since they dressed up with

2

Mom's necklaces and rings and her high-heeled shoes, and one of the rings had somehow got lost. It was even more of a rule since Carrie and Hennie had used Mom's make-up and Dad's shoe-polish to be Zulu warriors and afterwards the towels and the carpet were full of red and brown that wouldn't come off.

She opened the door slowly and looked inside. It took a second to see what they were doing. Then her heart somersaulted. They were sitting on the edge of the bed and Carrie was pointing a pistol – a real pistol – at Hennie's head. Carrie's voice was high and excited, and her hands, holding the gun, were shaking.

'Look, Hennie. This is the safety catch. When it's on I can't shoot you.' She held the gun in both hands like a cop on TV, pulling the trigger and saying, 'Bang, bang,' as she jerked the barrel upwards with each click. 'But nothing happens you see. The bullets can't come out.' She turned the barrel towards her and squinted down it, clicking the trigger. 'See – nothing.'

Poppy knew for absolute certain that the gun was real. It was Dad's. She'd seen it when he was cleaning his guns, and he'd told her he'd bought it when they'd lived in Zimbabwe during the Bush War. Even while Poppy was standing there, heart banging, the remembered scene flashed in and out of her mind: Dad saying that because no one was safe then he'd had to have a handgun. He said he'd never used it and he hoped he'd never have to.

Poppy swallowed. She must think. She heard the soft click as Carrie released the safety catch and aimed the barrel at Hennie again. She was saying, 'But look, Hennie, if I push this little thing here . . . the safety catch is off. If I pressed the trigger now, bang, you'd be dead. Brilliant, isn't it?'

Poppy knew she mustn't frighten Carrie. Was the gun loaded? She stood absolutely still, thinking only that she had to get the gun off Carrie.

Hennie reached up, trying to push the pistol away. His voice shaky, he said, 'Carrie, don't do that. It might go off.'

Poppy took a breath and walked into the room. She said, as casually as she could, 'Hey, Carrie, that's fantastic. Can I see? Where did you find it? I've been wanting to know where Dad kept that for ages and ages . . .'

Poppy could hear herself talking on, saying just anything. But it was working. Carrie had frozen at the sight of her sister, but when she saw Poppy was impressed and wanted to join in, she relaxed and smiled, pleased with herself.

Keep acting, Poppy said to herself as she walked towards them. You've got to pretend this is a game. She said, 'I'm older than Hennie, so I get the next turn.'

Hennie, now the gun was no longer pointing at him, looked less nervous and protested, 'But it's my turn. Carrie said . . .'

Poppy said, 'Okay, but you are too young to have it without the safety catch on,' and she reached out and took the pistol from Carrie, keeping the barrel

4

pointing at the carpet as she swung it away from Carrie's hand. Don't point at anything, she thought. Don't let it shake. Oh God, don't let it go off.

She looked carefully at the gun. The words ON and OFF were etched into the metal, and the catch was pushed to the OFF side. Poppy's heart thumped. For a moment she felt panic rising. Did OFF mean the gun was off? Or the safety catch? Then her mind cleared and she knew that ON was what she wanted. She slid the catch towards the ON. Her eyes closed briefly in relief.

Then she turned on Carrie, her voice rising, in danger of jetting out of control. 'Carrie, are you MAD? This is a real gun, you idiot. You could have killed Hennie. You could have shot yourself looking down the barrel . . .'

Carrie jumped up from the bed and cried, 'But you said . . .' Then she understood and her eyes flared with anger. 'You were just pretending, weren't you? So you could get the gun. You're mean. You cheated. You're horrible.'

Poppy was standing with the gun held over her head, out of reach of the two smaller children. Calm down, she told herself. It will be all right. In the most grown-up voice she could, she asked, 'Where did you find it, Carrie?'

Carrie's expression changed from outrage to sulkiness. 'I'm not telling. Anyway, it wasn't going to go off. I know about the safety catch.'

Poppy knew how obstinate Carrie could be. She

said, her voice softer, 'Carrie, you've got to tell me where it goes. Hennie, do you know?' But Hennie just looked up at her with huge round eyes and shook his head. 'Where was it, Carrie? In the drawer?'

Poppy could tell that Carrie was torn between refusing to tell her and wanting to show off, so she said, 'Carrie, I'm dying to know. Please tell.'

Then Carrie showed her the hook behind the bedside cupboard. 'I saw it when Maisie moved everything to turn the mattress.' She was boasting now, and it flashed through Poppy's mind that her sister's moods changed faster than anything.

Carrie's face changed again. She looked anxious, even frightened. 'You won't tell Dad, will you? You mustn't, you wouldn't.'

Poppy didn't answer while she hung the gun back on its hook. She felt calmer once she'd done it. Then she said, 'I won't tell if you promise that you will never touch it again. Ever, ever. You've got to swear on the Holy Bible. Both of you.'

She made Carrie get their mother's bible from her side of the bed, and then she told both Carrie and Hennie to put their hands on it and swear they'd never speak of the gun to anyone in their whole lives, and that they would never ever come near it as long as they lived. She made them say, 'So help me God,' and 'If I break this oath, may I be eaten by crocodiles,' and then they had to kiss the bible.

Afterwards Poppy climbed into the tree house and thought about it. She felt proud of being so calm. And she'd acted her part so well they'd believed her when she said she wanted to join in, and obeyed her when she'd acted like a grown-up. It was a great feeling.

And of course she'd never tell on Carrie. Carrie was so brave. And such fun.

But she was dangerous. I'll always have to look after her, she thought.

Four years later, Carrie lay on her bunk on the stoep and listened to the full-throated croak of bullfrogs in the dam and the incessant creak of crickets. She pulled the sleeping bag tight around her neck and smiled. She'd beaten her sister to the top bunk again. You could see the sky from both bunks, but not the veld. From this one you got everything. If she stayed awake long enough there'd be shooting stars; at dawn the sky would be a streaky mix of orange and aquamarine, and she might see dark outlines of zebras or even elephants trooping sedately to the waterhole. They looked like cut-outs against the light. The bottom bunk was useless. The stoep wall got in the way, and all you could see were the tops of the thorn trees and a strip of sky.

Though she'd won the bunk battle, she felt restless and sad, and didn't want to talk to Poppy. Usually they whispered for hours until Dad or Mom threatened to send one of them back to their bedroom. But there was pleasure in the sadness, a kind of sweet melancholy. She felt both romantic and lonesome. She liked that word, lonesome. I'm lonesome tonight. She wanted to snuggle down in the sleeping bag and think about Karl.

She was in love with Karl. She'd read enough stories in her mother's magazines, and enough Mills and Boon novels from the general store to recognize the symptoms: feeling sick, going weak at the knees and suffering mood swings, from miserable to ecstatic to angry and jealous, all in a morning.

It had started a couple of months ago, but it was a secret. She could never tell anyone. Not even Poppy. Poppy would, she knew, sound exactly like her mother. She would give her stuff about her being only twelve, about Karl being a grown-up, twice her age. Poppy would even say, which her mother never would, that you couldn't be in love with a *servant*. Which was ridiculous. Karl wasn't a servant. He was white, and he was a boss. He might work for Dad but he was the best game ranger and the best farm manager in the Transvaal. Everyone knew that.

From the bunk below rose the even sound of Poppy snoring. Carrie knew she'd be lying on her back with her mouth open, because she only breathed in that way – as if she had something heavy on her chest – when she was. Poppy said she'd snore too when she was grown up, but Carrie didn't believe her. And anyway Poppy was only fourteen, hardly more grown up than she was. Poppy snores, thought Carrie, because she's fat. Fat people snore, just like fat animals. Hippos snore. And so does Sheba.

She'd never get fat.

Above Poppy's breathing she could hear the murmur of conversation from the living room. On thick hot nights like tonight the windows between stoep and living room were hooked right back, which meant she could hear the grown-ups' voices inside. Carrie strained to distinguish Karl's from her father's. Occasionally she could, especially when he laughed. He had a younger, louder laugh than her father. Carrie wriggled up in the bunk, and leaned over the end so she could peer through the mosquito mesh. But she still couldn't see anything. They must still be at the dining table, round the corner in the bit she couldn't see.

If only Karl didn't think she was a kid, maybe he'd fall in love with her. Other people, especially the du Toit boys from the Steenbok Plaas, and the boys in the drama group at school, knew she was a woman.

Soon Karl would have to go home. He lived on the farm, but not in the house with the family. He had a thatched rondavel near the main gate on the Hazyview road. Carrie knew he'd come out of the living room and cross the stoep to jump into his jeep, and she was determined to stay awake. Make him notice her. Make him talk to her. Maybe make him kiss her.

As soon as the idea had entered her head, it wouldn't go away. If only he would kiss her. She must make him kiss her. But how?

It had taken a week of lying on the stoep, thinking and hoping, before she did anything. The first night

9

she had been too frightened by the thought, and he'd walked across the stoep before she'd got it together. The next night, a Saturday, he'd gone out with some friends and didn't eat with her parents. Then for two nights her sister had managed (by appealing first to Mom, and on the next night to Dad) to get the top bunk. Carrie knew you could not talk to someone, never mind get them to kiss you, if they had to stoop down to the bottom bunk. It had to be perfect, as she imagined it.

She imagined it lots of ways, but the best was that she'd have the sleeping bag pushed down and half off because of the heat, that her hair would be spread out in a dark tangle against the pillow, and she would look so beautiful and irresistible that he'd put his hands each side of her face and kiss her mouth while she pretended to be asleep.

But she knew this wouldn't happen, because Karl never looked across at the bunks at all. He just walked across the stoep, jumped down the steps in a bound, and strode across the lawn.

She'd have to attract his attention. But on Wednesday night, when she'd managed to get the top bunk, Poppy would not go to sleep and had insisted on talking about school and Michael Jackson for ages. Carrie had to pretend to be asleep to shut her up, but then Poppy had used the torch she kept hidden under her pillow to read. When Karl came through she'd even called out, ''Night, Karl,' and he'd called back, ''Night, girls,' as if they were five-year-olds.

And the next night, she could hardly believe it, she'd fallen asleep herself. She'd been all ready, and had even washed her hair with the posh shampoo from her mother's bathroom. But the grown-ups had talked and talked, and once Poppy was asleep she could feel herself slipping under, being sucked down into sleep. She forced herself to sit up, but her eyes kept closing. She got down quietly and reached underneath Poppy's pillow for her torch, then picked up Poppy's book from the floor under the bunk and climbed back.

The book was useless: tiny print and boring, a library book of plays by someone called George Bernard Shaw. She could not believe Poppy risked reading under her sleeping bag for anything so dull. And the awful thing was she'd fallen asleep with the torch on, and her mother had confiscated it when she'd come to check on them before going to bed.

Poppy was furious, of course, but the worst was her dad. At supper the next night he'd said, 'Well, young Carrie, I seem to have misjudged you. Bernard Shaw indeed. I'm astonished.'

She felt her face flush. Was he mocking her? She said, 'It's Poppy's book.'

'Ah.' Her dad seemed satisfied by this, as if it was what he'd suspected all along.

She burst out, 'Why are you always on at me about books? And anyway, I do read. You just don't notice.'

Her father said evenly, 'I'm glad to hear it, Carrie. What are you reading right now?'

And then, of course, she hadn't been able to think

11

of a single book, except last week's Mills and Boon, which was called *Warm Embrace*. Afterwards she realized she could have said *Pride and Prejudice*, which they were doing at school, or one of Wilbur Smith's books about the bush, which she'd read to impress Karl.

But finally, on the Thursday evening, everything was right. Poppy was safely asleep. She could hear her father whistling for the dogs on the front veranda, and her mother carrying glasses through to the kitchen. Then Karl was calling goodnight to her dad, and walking across the wooden floor of the living room in his soft veldskoen. She heard the creak as he opened the fly-screen door, and the crack as it slapped back, then he walked into view, heading towards the steps, swinging his old suede jacket over his shoulder.

'Karl.'

He turned at once, looking towards the darkness of the bunks.

'Poppy? Are you still awake?'

Why did he think it was Poppy? Couldn't he recognize her voice?

'It's me. Carrie.'

'What are you still up for, young lady?' he said, coming nearer.

'I wanted to speak to you.' She had no idea what she wanted to say. She didn't like the condescending 'young lady', though he sounded friendly. What should she say now?

Karl strolled over to her. 'Hiya,' he said, 'what's up, Carrie?'

'I . . . I . . . I just wanted to say goodnight.'

He stood beside the bunks, looking puzzled.

'Goodnight, Carrie,' he said, very matter-of-fact.

She was in too deep to back off. She leaned out of the bed towards him, and said in a determined, if shaky, voice, 'I thought you might kiss me.' When he did not react her courage failed her, and she added, 'For goodnight.'

He looked at her in silence for a moment, then smiled and bent towards her. 'Sure, kiddo,' he said. And he kissed her on the forehead, then rubbed her head, rumpling her hair as if she was a puppy. He pulled up her sleeping bag and tucked it round her neck, bouncing her slightly, playfully, as he did so.

'Good night, sleep tight, don't let the bugs bite.'

As she watched his headlights blare into the darkness, and then followed his red tail lights curling off down the track, hot tears of humiliation pricked her eyes.

I hate you. I hate you, Karl Van Reenen. I wish you were dead.

One

Angelina put her arms round her little brother's bottom and tried to hoist him into the upper basket of a luggage trolley. She staggered a few steps backwards, then lurched forward, her waif's face contorted with effort.

Poppy watched, a little anxious. Tom was fourteen months old and too heavy for a nine-year-old.

'Darling, don't do that. He can't sit in it. It's not a supermarket trolley – there's nowhere for his legs to go.'

Poppy took the child from her daughter and allowed him to stand in the top basket. One fat hand clutched her shirt and the other a hank of her hair as he swivelled this way and that, looking for diversion.

Angelina leaned into her from behind and threaded sly hands between the trolley and her mother's body, knotting them round her waist. How pale she is, thought Poppy, caressing Angelina's skinny arms with her free hand. 'Not long now,' she said. 'A few more minutes and you'll have a sister.' Angelina didn't respond, and Poppy thought, Please God, let her love Lorato.

Poppy was sure it was right to have brought Angelina and Tom with them. Angelina had been there (well, in the next room) when Tom was born. It had been wonderful. Both she and Eduardo had cried, relief and triumph and joy shared, just as at Angelina's birth. Maybe even more so: the first time some of the euphoria was because of the astonishment and wonder they'd both felt at the birth itself – the marvel of Mother Nature, you could say. But with Tom they had been conscious of their extraordinary and continued good fortune. Seven years on, her fame as an actress had reached the household-name level, which still astonished her. Eduardo's architectural practice was booming; they had money, they were still in love, they adored their daughter and they'd longed – well, she had longed – for another child. And there he was, healthy, perfect and bawling his head off.

Now she wanted a similar rite of passage for her soon-to-be-adopted daughter, a proper importance given to her arrival. They were all there to meet her, to share the first moments of the enlarged Santolini family.

Eduardo looked at his plump wife, unmade up, dressed in jeans and a sloppy jumper and hung about with children. He said, his perfect English modulated by an Italian cadence, 'Poppy Ferguson, I wish your fans could see you now. Do you think they'd recognize Cleopatra, or Ophelia, or Kate?'

Angelina stuck her head under Poppy's elbow and said, 'She's not Poppy Ferguson. That's only a pretend name. She's Mummy Santolini.'

Eduardo smiled at his daughter. 'Quite right, Angel.

She's Mummy Santolini all right. And we are here to collect another bambina. We must be mad.'

Perhaps we are, thought Poppy. Certainly everyone else seems to think so, the Harley Street psychiatrist more than anyone. He'd been adamant.

'It will be an enormous risk, Mrs Santolini. No one can suffer what that child has suffered without being scarred.'

'But she was only a baby.' Poppy had heard the pleading note in her own voice.

'Just because she may not remember doesn't mean she won't be damaged. With her history of loss, fear, hunger, etc., the change of languages could be one step too far for her.'

Poppy, clutching at the language question as the easiest to deal with, had said, 'But she's too young to speak. Why should it matter?'

'Because children learn almost all they need to know about their mother tongue before they speak a single syllable. She would have heard nothing but her own language until she was separated from her mother. Since then she will have been thoroughly confused by Afrikaans and God knows how many African languages before you came on the scene with English. I am not exaggerating, Mrs Santolini: that child will be traumatized. I would not be surprised if she doesn't speak a word until she is five, maybe longer. She may never speak.'

Eduardo's mother, Giulia, had been as negative and more forceful. She'd said, her thick Umbrian accent

16

becoming thicker with emotion, 'She is not of your blood, Eduardo. She is not Italian, not even European.'

Eduardo had tried to calm his mother, putting his hands on her small shoulders, trying to catch her eye, but she had silenced him with a click of her tongue. She'd demanded, 'Why you not make a bambino like everyone else?'

With a sharp shake of the head, she had turned her back to mop down the sink, a hairpin spinning out of her bun and making a tiny ringing sound on the marble tiles. 'Or okay, if you buy one, why not you buy a white one?'

'Oh Mama! Are you becoming a racist in your old age?' Eduardo had asked, bending over her shoulder to kiss his mother's angry cheek.

'Scemo!' the little woman had barked, confronting him again. 'It is not racist to see plenty, plenty trouble. For black children in this country it is impossible. Even for Italian child. But you want black child in Italian family, white parents. How can she be happy, eh?'

Even their family doctor had been less than supportive. 'It's not the girl that worries me. It's obviously a wonderful stroke of good fortune for her. But have you considered the effect on Tom? He . . .'

Eduardo had cut in, 'Why? It will be like having a twin sister. He'll love it.'

Dr Bartley had pushed her slipping glasses back into place and said with professional patience, 'He might. But all children find a new rival in the house

17

hard to cope with – even though the sibling is tiny, and can't do anything except demand attention. That's bad enough. But this child will be a serious rival: slightly older, walking. Tom isn't walking yet, is he?'

Poppy had laughed, 'No, but that's only because he's lazy and has sussed that if he curls his fat legs up someone will carry him.'

Dr Bartley hadn't smiled. 'There isn't much research on unnatural age gaps. It may be perfectly okay. But there is no denying you'd be giving Tom a real challenge.'

Poppy looked down at the little bruiser in the luggage trolley, pummelling her breasts and head-butting her neck, and thought they need not worry about Tom. He'd be fine.

Lorato's plane was late. Eduardo took the children off in search of Coca-Cola and a balcony from which to see the planes.

Poppy folded her ancient Barbour jacket into a cushion and sat on the luggage trolley. It wasn't very comfortable. Useless architects, thought Poppy, it wouldn't occur to them to provide seating in Arrivals. You were only meant to hang about in Departures.

Poppy was glad of the time to herself. She wanted to think, steady herself for Lorato's arrival.

Mummy Santolini, she thought, or Poppy Ferguson? Why had the choice not been harder? She knew that adding another child so soon after Tom wouldn't help her career. She'd taken almost a year off for Tom. If she really wanted to stay at the top, and maybe make the big leap into big-budget movies, then she should be riding the wave that her success at the National and at Stratford had brought her. She should be prepared to go to Hollywood, to go on tour, to be Poppy Ferguson more than Mrs Santolini.

But the decision had made itself. Six months ago she'd been sitting in the Green Room at the National between the matinee and the evening performance, eating a flavour-free sandwich from the vending machine while half listening to cast gossip. She was idly opening the mail she'd scooped up from the floor of the flat, putting the bills in one pile, the appeals to open fêtes and appear at events in another, the junk in the bin.

She had heard someone say that the new director wanted to cast a woman as Othello. How ridiculous, she'd thought, the whole point of Othello is his maleness. Then her mind had fastened on the letter she'd just opened. Maisie's letter, the one that had decided the Poppy Ferguson vs. Mummy Santolini contest.

Poppy shifted her bottom on the luggage trolley, and took the letter from her wallet, where she'd kept it like a sort of talisman during the long months of bureaucracy that had led so tortuously to this day.

Dear Miss Poppy,

I am writing to you because you will help me, God willing. You and Miss Carrie are always in my heart. I am old woman now, but I mind me of the good times when Master and your good mother was in Kaia Moya and I was your Honoured Cook.

I have picanin, one year old, Father he is being killed. Her brothers and sister all dead. Her Mother in Tzaneen prison. Soon go back Mozambique. Baby have Nobody. Not a one.

My husband say I must give her to the Police. But she is Good Girl. No cry. I no want to give her to Police. But I have no money. Agh, Madam, the poor mother. She just want one of her family stay living. She so happy when I keep Lorato.

You are rich lady. And your father was good man. Maybe you help. Baas Karl, he know about Lorato (she is Name Lorato). He say Also I must give to Police. But he say he say nothing while I write to you, my old family. He say if you telephone he explain better than poor old cook woman, knows nothing.

In God we Trust.

Yours with honour faithfully,

Maisie n'Tumalata

Poppy's mind went back to what she knew of Lorato's short history. Her parents had been among the thousands of Mozambicans, made destitute by war, flood and famine, who try to enter South Africa illegally. They believe that if they can just get across the border they will find work and food. Some are so desperate they cross the Kruger National Park on foot.

Poppy had seen the army patrols in the game reserve searching for 'illegals'. But they do not catch them all. A small percentage make it through to a life of misery in the squatter camps around the big cities.

An even smaller and unluckier percentage are killed in the park, mostly by lions looking for food or hippos protecting their territory. Occasionally by crocodiles. Karl had said Lorato's father had been killed by lions.

There was a gruesome example of natural adaptation going on in the park. A pride of lions, a large one of several lionesses and one heavyweight male, had learned to hunt under a line of pylons running hundreds of miles across the park from the Mozambique border to the western boundary. The Mozambicans, who travel by night to avoid the patrols, use the pylons as route markers to avoid the danger of wandering in circles in the dark. The lions use the pylon strip as their larder.

Poppy knew that once lions realize just what easy meat man is they give up the arduous business of catching buck and simply help themselves to people. Their victims included rangers, park workers, even the occasional tourist, but mostly they killed illegal immigrants. The rangers had already shot several previous families of 'pylon lions', but others soon moved in. As long as South Africa represented a Mecca to starving Mozambique, there wasn't an answer.

Poppy shook her head slightly, trying to banish the horror. She would not think about it. She wanted to greet her new daughter in calm and happy mood. But the images kept coming: of stick-thin shrieking women; of shouting men trying to fight off a lioness with branches or spears; of their gasping flight as the rest of the pride arrived; of Lorato's father's screams as the animals dragged off an arm, tore out his throat.

Poppy closed her eyes, tying to concentrate on the positive: Thank God for Karl. He now ran Kaia Moya as an upmarket game lodge and owned a third share in it, with Poppy and Carrie as equal but absent partners. It was not the first time desperate immigrants had arrived, exhausted, in the camp. He had done what he usually did, which was to tell Maisie to feed them all, allow them to sleep for eight hours, then turn them over to the police. But Maisie had hidden Lorato.

Poppy had known as soon as she read Maisie's letter, written in careful print on blue airmail paper (ironically bearing a picture of a snarling lion), that they would adopt Lorato.

She'd shown the letter to Eduardo, who'd guessed at once what she was thinking. He'd been typically generous, saying, 'If you want to adopt her, we'll adopt her. Why not? I like big families. And we can afford it.'

Poppy had thought Eduardo was too casual about it, as if he was giving her a present, not taking on a daughter. But she didn't argue. It wasn't as if they were making a decision today.

She rang Karl.

'Ja, Poppy, it's all true,' he said. 'I knew old Maisie was writing to you. I tried to stop her, but you know

Maisie. She considers you her family and me the hired help.'

Poppy smiled, an image of Maisie's not-to-be-thwarted face crossing her mind. 'But tell me about the child.' She found her heart was thudding. How odd.

Karl told her the story. 'Her mother persuaded Maisie to keep her. Poor woman, she'd seen the rest of her children die in less than two years: starvation, flood, disease. She just wanted to save her last baby.'

Poppy felt the anguish of that other mother. For a second she could feel someone tearing Tom or Angelina from her. 'Oh Karl, we've got to do something. What will happen to the mother? Isn't there a way to help them both? Can't we employ the mother? So she could keep the baby?'

'I'm sorry, Poppy,' said Karl, emotion flattened out of his words. 'There's no way. Believe me.' He paused, then said, more kindly, 'Poppy, we live with the immigrant influx every day. We cannot employ any more illegals than we do already. We have to give them up. That way, at least they get fed.'

Poppy heard the tiredness and the kindness, and understood. 'Okay.' Then she said, 'Karl, we could have her. You know Eduardo and I want another baby. We could adopt her.'

Poppy knew Karl would say this was a bad idea, and braced herself for his objection. He said, 'Poppy, you don't know what you are saying. For a start she's not the best-looking kid in the world . . .'

Poppy's voice rose. 'We're not buying a Barbie doll . . .'

'Sure,' said Karl, ignoring the outburst. 'But you haven't even seen her. She's not starving, but she's nearly so. Stick-thin legs, extended belly. Maisie says she's a good child, but she's silent because she's weak . . .'

Poppy made an effort to be unemotional. 'Karl, those are reasons for helping her, not for rejecting her. Besides, we do want another baby, and it took us seven years of trying to get Tom, and this seems like fate . . .' Poppy's voice trailed off. Karl would think she was an idiot, but she felt an extraordinary pull towards this unknown African child.

Karl waited to see if Poppy was going to continue. When she didn't, he said, 'Poppy, think about it. If you really want to adopt an African baby, maybe you should talk to the agencies. There are hundreds of deserving . . .'

But Poppy was only interested in Lorato. She would fly out, she said.

She took Tom with her, telling herself that her mind was not yet made up and she'd watch the children together first. Then, if she wanted to proceed, Eduardo would fly out too, and they'd decide together.

Her first sight of Lorato was a let-down. She was asleep on a blanket in a battered playpen in the rich-smelling gloom of Maisie's kaia. As Poppy's eyes adjusted to the dark, she made out the small lump of Lorato's blanket-wrapped bottom, sticking up uncomfortably over her folded legs. The little girl was sleeping on her knees, her face squashed sideways against the bars of the playpen.

Lorato was snuffling in her sleep, her mouth open. Poppy put Tom down next to the playpen, and knelt beside him, twisting her own head to see the baby's face. Though asleep, Lorato's lids did not quite close, leaving two thin white slips of eyeball showing under the deep brown skin.

Oh God, thought Poppy, could I love this child? She waved the flies away from Lorato's cheek, which was wet and shiny with childish dribble. Is what I feel pity? Or what?

As she crouched in silence beside the sleeping Lorato, Tom used the playpen rails to haul himself upright. Then he let out one of his piercing vocal experiments, half shout, half hiccup, right above Lorato's head. Lorato's eyes fluttered open. She shifted, and her bottom toppled sideways to roll her on to her back, releasing her face from the bars. She didn't cry, and she did not look at Poppy. Her eyes were fixed on the bouncing Tom, who was reaching through the bars to clutch her nose with his fat fist.

Poppy, kneeling up, reached into the playpen and lifted Lorato out. She looked deeply into the child's face as she held her aloft and brought her down on to her lap, but Lorato never glanced at her. On the whole up-and-over journey her solemn brown eyes were glued to Tom's dancing blue ones. As Lorato landed on Poppy's lap, Tom lurched forward and crash-kissed

Lorato somewhere between her broad flat nose and her wide round forehead.

Poppy put her arms round the two children, lowering her head to kiss the unfamiliar crinkly hair, breathe in the unfamiliar musky smell. Tom looked up at her, his face alight with pleasure. Yes, she thought. Oh yes.

When Poppy telephoned Eduardo that night, she tried to be detached and clinical, explaining how silent the child was. Should they perhaps get her looked at by a Johannesburg paediatrician before they made a decision? Eduardo had cut in, 'You want her, don't you?'

'Well . . . I . . . No. I don't know. You need to see . . .' A short pause and then, 'Oh Eduardo, how did you know? Yes I do. I want her, I think I'll die if we can't have her.'

'I'll catch tomorrow night's flight.'

Poppy was naturally law-abiding, and wanted to follow South African adoption procedure by the book. But Eduardo argued that Lorato would be grown-up before the combination of socialist bureaucracy and government incompetence would allow her to be handed over. He hired a Johannesburg lawyer not averse to distributing small bribes, and within a fortnight Lorato had an exit visa and adoption consent forms (presumably forged; Poppy dared not ask).

The English end had taken longer, but at last the Foreign Office was satisfied that the toddler would not take some Brit's job or cost the state anything, and had agreed to let Lorato in. Social services, in the person of an earnest young woman with a folder of forms, had gone through the Santolinis' life with a nit-comb. She'd found no reason for objection either. A guardian *ad litem* was appointed and adoption proceedings would begin as soon as Lorato was with them.

She'd be a paid-up Santolini before she was two.

When the airline rep arrived with Lorato in a push-chair, it was an anticlimax. The child was asleep, so there was no bouncing and hugging and laughing. Eduardo signed where the stewardess told him to. Angelina said, 'Can I push her?' and commandeered the buggy. Eduardo put Tom on his shoulders and Poppy picked up the Kaia Moya carrier bag containing Lorato's worldly wealth – half a packet of nappies and a baby's bottle filled with juice. They were on the Heathrow Express within five minutes and back at the flat in half an hour. Lorato was still asleep.

Two

Poppy was determined to win over her reluctant mother-in-law and her own mother that first evening in the Paddington flat. She had not yet managed to extract a word of approval about the adoption from Giulia, while Lucille could not retain any information for long enough to develop a view. Poppy hoped the physical presence of Lorato would somehow gain a foothold in her mother's muddled mind.

Poppy had planned her offensive with care. Giulia was coming up from the Oxfordshire farmhouse to inspect the child, and Poppy had suggested the best time would be early evening. That way Lorato could sleep all afternoon so she would not be grumpy; she'd be fed and watered to prevent hunger, drama and mess, then she'd be dressed in a white Italian lace dress and black patent leather shoes (Giulia had said Tom's baby-gro made him look like a Martian). Carrie would fetch Lucille and arrive in time for Lorato to wow them all for half an hour, then Poppy would tuck the two little ones up and park Angelina in front of *Pocahontas*.

Carrie had promised to cook the dinner. And, thought Poppy, she'd cast her usual happy spell. Poppy loved her younger sister, who was everything she was not: as captivating and beautiful as Poppy was bespectacled and dumpy. Carrie was carefree and confident, sometimes wild. People tended to stop talking when she came in, to stare at her at bus stops, look round when she swung by. Poppy would not have said so, but she was proud of having such a sister; she felt that her stock went up when Carrie was there.

So that was the plan: heart-warming family scene with enchanting children, followed by convivial family dinner.

But Lorato, who had slept all morning, refused to sleep at all in the afternoon, and cried instead. Poppy knew the little girl was exhausted, but every time she tried to lower her into her cot Lorato would curl up her legs as though she were being dipped in hellfire and scream blue murder. Tom, usurped as the centre of attention, screamed too.

Poppy gave up and decided food had better precede sleep. She knew Lorato had been weaned on African sour porridge and mielie meal, neither of which was available in the local M & S, so she'd opted for fish fingers, sausages and chunks of raw tomato.

The appearance of the food mercifully silenced the children. They sat in matching high chairs and ate with their fingers. Angelina helped Lorato, who opened her mouth, chewed and swallowed at an alarming rate. If Angelina did not immediately respond to the open mouth by putting something in it, Lorato would cram food into it herself with efficiency and concentration.

When Tom had reached the well-fed stage of trying to force his sausage into the spout of his tippy-cup, Poppy wiped his protesting face, hands and tray and lifted him to the floor. He plonked down on his Pampers-padded bum, and directed his energies to climbing the head of the long-suffering Great Dane, Olaf.

Lorato did not give up so easily. Her belly was tight as a drum, and she had a pouch of unswallowed food in her cheek, but she would not agree that supper was over. One hand held a fish finger, the other a sausage. It was clear she had eaten all she could, but when Poppy tried to prise food from her fists, she opened her mouth and wailed. Poppy used this opportunity to hook the wad of half-chewed food out of her mouth with a bent forefinger, which spurred Lorato to a higher pitch of protest.

Poppy's heart sank. Oh God, she thought, she's got an eating disorder. It wasn't surprising. She'd been hungry all her life until a few months ago.

'It's all right, darling,' she said, lifting the child and rocking her, 'you can keep the sausage and the fish finger. There, my baby, shush, shush.' But Lorato, perhaps fortified by the food, cried harder. Her yells and her distress intensified, tears spouting from her lower lids and running in small streams into her open mouth. No rocking or crooning or shushing could stop her. Tom, unsettled by the noise, climbed off the dog, and crawled to his mother's feet. He wrapped his arms round an ankle and joined in, his wails every bit as loud as Lorato's.

This was the scene that greeted Giulia.

'O Dio! What's this?' she asked, kissing Poppy, glancing at the yelling Lorato, hugging Angelina, lifting Tom. 'You have a very noisy new sister, eh?'

Tom stopped crying as soon as he was in his grandmother's arms. Poppy continued to bounce the struggling Lorato up and down, to no avail. Then Carrie came through the door, leading their mother by the hand. Poppy caught Carrie's eye and forced a laugh. Angelina said, 'Why is it funny, Mum?'

'It's not, darling. But I'd hoped to present your two grandmothers with a dream grandchild, and look what I've got.' She had to shout to be heard over Lorato's wails. She kissed the child's wet cheek, which prompted further writhing and crying.

Lorato smelled different, unfamiliar, not like Tom. The word 'alien' blew into Poppy's head and she suddenly felt unsure of herself. How could this wild and furious thing be her daughter? Tom would duck his head into her neck when he cried, but Lorato clearly wanted to get away from her.

'Oh Giulia, she won't stop.' Poppy was tempted to put her down and let her scream. She turned so her mother-in-law could see the bundle of rage in a smeared baby-gro, face streaked with tears and dribble, a lump of food in each hand. 'She stinks too. I was going to have her bathed and in a pretty white dress, smelling of Johnson's baby powder.'

31

'Heavens, who is that child?' Lucille asked Carrie, her face a picture of distaste.

Carrie answered, steering Lucille to an armchair, 'That's your new grandchild.' Lucille looked baffled, and Carrie said, 'I'll get us a drink.'

Giulia put Tom down on the sofa and turned to Poppy, 'I take her, poor little cabbage.' She whisked Lorato out of Poppy's arms. 'You look after Tom.'

Poppy watched as Giulia headed for the door, changed from imperious mother-in law to nursemaid in seconds.

'Con un bacino passa tutto,' she crooned, kissing the child's head.

Poppy sank down next to Tom, who promptly climbed into her lap. Almost at once Lorato's wails faded to whimpers then failed completely. Poppy took off her glasses to rub her eyes, put them back on and tried to smile. Her mother-in-law, as always, had proved herself superior on the domestic front. Well, at least she was cementing her relationship with her grandchild.

Carrie handed her a glass of white wine, and Poppy took a long mouthful, eyes shut.

'You look done in,' said Carrie.

Poppy, drifting exhaustedly, thought how nice it would be if, for just half an hour, Eduardo would fail to turn up, Carrie would entertain their mother, Giulia would stay with Lorato and Tom would fall asleep.

*

32

A week later, Carrie walked into the Paddington penthouse and followed the sound of Poppy's singing into the kitchen, where she found her sister bent double over the overcrammed rubbish bin, struggling with a bin bag. Poppy was trying to compact its contents with one hand so that she could tie the top, and was belting out 'Moon River' at full power as she did so.

Carrie watched her for a few seconds, thinking what a great rich voice she had. Poppy had always been able to sing, even before the lessons. When they were children it was mostly campfire songs and hymns in church, but even then Poppy had been the star, doing the solos and leading everyone else.

Carrie joined in, 'Mooooon Riv-er . . .' and did a couple of sliding dance steps across the marble floor.

Poppy stopped and lifted her face to Carrie's. She held her hands out stiffly, so as not to get any mess on her sister's clothes. Carrie put her arms round Poppy and hugged her, tight but brief. The way Poppy's face always lit up when they met was one of the chief reasons she loved her. Poppy was always glad, really glad, to see her.

'Hi, Popps. I thought I'd find you in despair, not singing your heart out.'

'Oh? Why?'

'Because you're turning down *The Controller*.'

For a second Poppy's face sobered and she made a resigned moue. 'Ah well,' she said, shrugging, 'can't have everything.'

'But Poppy, how *can* you turn it down? It's your first chance to direct.' Carrie persisted, 'Surely you *mind*?'

'Yes, I mind. A bit. Not too much. I want time with Lorato.'

'But the Theatre Upstairs! They may never ask you again.'

'Ah well, I expect I'll live.'

Poppy's plump body was again bent over the swing-bin. It was no good. It was too full. She started to empty some of the collection of nappies, passata cartons, banana skins and unidentifiable gunk into another bag. Carrie could never get over the insouciance with which Poppy did jobs like this. She cleaned up dog shit, baby sick, splattered food with the same easy competence with which she washed Angelina's hair or stirred pasta or with which she sang.

Even as a child on the Transvaal farm, Carrie had watched with a mixture of disgust and admiration as Poppy deticked the dogs, carefully getting her nails under their blood-bloated bodies so as not to burst them. It was Poppy who cracked fleas between her thumbnails, and happily helped in the bloody business of butchering game, cutting the meat into strips to dry in the wind and salting the skins.

Carrie knew Poppy as well as anyone could, but was still puzzled by her. Poppy seemed to have no difficulty making decisions that Carrie would have found anguishing – like not directing *The Controller*. She had also turned down a lucrative part in a TV soap being made in Newcastle, as well as a character part in a Hollywood film. It was unbelievable.

Carrie was not sure whether she thought her sister was a saint or a fool. Whatever it was, sometimes it grated a little. Poppy's easy acceptance that you can't have everything confused Carrie, who would have at least tried to bag the lot.

Also Poppy was so *competent*. So *capable*. Carrie considered how her sister had solved Lorato's two chief causes of misery (stopping eating and refusing to sleep) within days: Poppy now only spooned tiny amounts of food into a bowl, or placed only one or two pieces of bread or fruit in front of Lorato at a time – it was having to *give up* food that caused the child such distress; if she hadn't seen it, she was fine. And when Lorato cried from exhaustion and would not be put down, Poppy carried the child on her back, African-style, tied on tight round her bosom with a tablecloth. It worked like magic. Lorato would do the splits, her little legs straight out each side, and lay her head against Poppy's back. She'd be asleep almost as soon as Poppy had swaddled her in and tightened the cloth.

Poppy, bags tied and dropped down the chute, new bin liner installed, rinsed her hands under the tap. She gave them a shake, pushed her glasses back up her nose and took a bottle of Sauvignon Blanc from the fridge. She held it towards Carrie, 'Want a glass?'

'Poppy, dry your hands, they'll be rough as a bricklayer's. And yes please to the wine.'

Poppy clamped the industrial Screwpull on to the bottle and pulled the lever, over then back. The cork was out in seconds, and reminded Carrie that she'd taken ages to master that corkscrew. Same with deck-chairs. Poppy knew instinctively how things worked. She, Carrie, had to learn.

Poppy rubbed her hands together, and said, 'They're rough already.'

Typical, thought Carrie. Not a thread of vanity in her.

Carrie unhooked her long legs from the barstool, stood and reached up for two glasses. They hung upside down on a pegboard, as in a pub, except the board was gleaming stainless steel, the polished glasses reflected in it. Carrie loved this kitchen. Eduardo had designed it as an all-purpose living space: kitchen, dining room, bar, playroom, sitting room. One day she'd like a flat just like this, one big, open, informal space with real designer style.

The women took their drinks and the wine bottle on to the glassed-in section of the terrace, but they did not turn the light on. They sat in the dark looking at the light show beneath them. Red and green Christmas lights ran right up both sides of the great necks of the builders' cranes, and were reflected in the black water of the canal. To the left the Westway weaved away, a trail of red tail lights on the left, white headlamps on the right.

There were eight cranes on the site. It was to be a massive development, and it pleased Poppy to look down and know that Eduardo was largely responsible for it. As consultant architect to Westminster Council, he had designed the overall scheme, and as more of the buildings were started he was increasingly absorbed in it.

They had bought this warehouse on the wharf nine years ago, when Angelina was a baby and Eduardo had first started on the project. No one thought it would ever actually get built, but Poppy and Eduardo had both fallen in love with the area and bought the derelict warehouse for what now seemed like very little money. The first of the renovated buildings, it housed Eduardo's practice on the first two floors and their penthouse on the top.

Carrie, lighting a Marlboro, caught Poppy's flicker of concern. 'Yes, I know, Popps, I'll stop one day. Really. I will.' Poppy smiled, not believing her.

After a minute or two Poppy said, 'It is odd, I agree, my turning down work. The only thing that competes with the theatre is the children. Even Eduardo doesn't, really.'

'What do you mean?'

Poppy took a sip from her glass and frowned into it. 'I don't think he's ever quite got over having to cancel our honeymoon because I took a job at the Oxford Playhouse – do you remember?'

'Yes, I do. And those awful tours of awful plays you did before you hit the big time. You'd have done three years in *The Mousetrap* if there was nothing better on offer.'

Poppy laughed. 'So would every actress in the country. Anything at all is preferable to reading *The Stage* and waiting for the phone to ring. Once Giulia came to live with us, and Angelina was so happy with her, I was desperate to work.'

Carrie shook her head. 'But why?' she asked. 'Miserable digs, Equity rates, freezing theatres, rotten plays – I'll never understand it.'

Poppy laughed. 'Yup, that's all true, but it's a disease. Or a drug.' She slowly twirled her glass by its stem, ordering her thoughts. 'And for me there's the fact that I'm someone else on stage, someone quite unlike me. It's like being let out.'

'Who do you want to be?'

Poppy shook her head quickly. 'No, it's not that I want to be someone else, someone particular, or some special character. The addiction is *not being me*. Not being Sensible Poppy, solid and dependable. Ordinary.'

Carrie exclaimed, 'But you aren't ordinary! In fact you are extraordinary. Actresses are meant to be all ego and glamour, yet you couldn't give a damn. I don't know how you ever get a job. When you walk into a director's office or on to a stage for an audition, don't they just see Sensible Poppy standing there?'

'Of course not! I don't have to audition any more, thank God. But if I did, I'd do my homework and walk in as neurotic housewife, power-mad boss, nympho or whatever.'

Carrie looked unconvinced. Poppy went on. 'If I

go to a fancy movie premiere, I get out of the limo behaving like a star.' She put her chin up, and flashed an exaggerated eyes-and-teeth smile at the cameras. They both laughed, and Poppy said, 'Ditto if I'm speaking at Angelina's parents' day. And people duly ask for autographs. But I'm never recognized in Safeway or with Tom and Lorato in the park, because then I'm just me – the dumpy one.'

'Christ, Poppy, don't say that!' cried Carrie. 'You are not dumpy. You just have proper tits and a bum, which are fashionable now, anyway . . .'

'Okay, okay. But anyway, I don't mind. For some reason, right now I want to be me. Mummy Santolini, as Angelina said. She said, "Poppy Ferguson is just a pretend name." She's right.'

Carrie poured them both another glass, and said, 'Anyway, you should look after your hands for Eduardo's sake. Unless bricklayer's hands turn him on.'

'He wouldn't notice. These days sex is a bit of a distant memory.' Poppy spoke matter-of-factly, easily.

Carrie looked hard at her sister, but could not see her expression in the dark. 'But that's terrible, Poppy. I'd die without sex. It's what keeps me with Richard. It's as necessary as food.'

'Hardly. As wine perhaps. But you can live without it.'

'But are you sure Eduardo can live without it?'

Poppy laughed. 'Well, I certainly hope so! But he's exhausted too. He's got this Paddington thing, and

39

the conference centre outside Bilbao. The truth is, whoever's head hits the pillow first is asleep by the time the other arrives.'

Carrie could not imagine a relationship that did not centre around a man wanting to make love to her. Sure, there were other things: mutual interests, sense of humour and all that stuff. But sex was the point. Poppy must have hit middle age early, aged thirty-four. All those kids, and an older husband. That her sister could accept life without sex baffled her. She, Carrie, had only just begun. Thirty-two was the prime of life. 'Don't tell me you never . . . Is that why you adopted Lorato?'

'No, of course not.' Poppy smiled. 'Absolutely not. We adopted Lorato because she needed adopting.' Carrie didn't respond, and Poppy elaborated, 'We wanted another child but we felt we'd had our ration with Angelina and Tom.'

Carrie frowned in the dark. 'But how can you bear it? Without sex I mean? And here was I thinking you and Eduardo had the perfect marriage.'

'Oh Carrie, don't sound so mournful.' Poppy poured the last of the wine into their glasses. 'It is pretty perfect. I know I'll never be unfaithful to Eduardo. And if it wasn't tempting fate, I'd lay my life that he wouldn't be unfaithful to me. And we do make love. Just not so often any more, that's all.'

When Eduardo came in that night, Poppy was not asleep. She listened to his familiar progress through the flat: the click of turned-off lights, the high-pitched whine as he set the burglar alarm, the door opening and closing as he went in to kiss Angelina.

Then the baby alarm at her bedside amplified his goodnights to Tom and Lorato: Lorato's heavy snuffling was overlaid by Eduardo's murmured 'Goodnight, son, sogni d'oro' and 'Buona notte, bambina'. At last he came into his dressing room, and she listened to the thud of his shoes coming off, the laundry basket lid, the little squeak and click of the trouser press as he shut it and switched it on.

I wonder if other husbands have electric trouser presses? she thought. Or is it because he's Italian? Or a design freak? Eduardo liked knife-edge creases.

From the bathroom she heard in turn his electric toothbrush, the splutter and thrum of his shower, then the rattle of the aspirin bottle. He has too many headaches, she thought, dismissing the thought as he climbed, naked, into bed.

As he rolled towards her to kiss her, she reached up for a second and held on to him. He was still warm and damp from his shower.

'Hey, husband.' She looked into his face, her expression serious. 'You do love me, I trust?'

'Every bit of you.' He put his arm under her shoulder and hugged her to him. She thought how clean and comfortable, how familiar and safe he smelled.

'You smell of Badedas,' she said.

'I smell of whatever you hang in the shower.'

41

It occurred to Poppy that this showering at night was a hangover from the time when they made love every night. Eduardo could not bear her to wear perfume or to smell of scented soap. He wanted, he said, to breathe in the smell of her, not of some chemist shop. But he had to shower. Otherwise, he said, he'd smell like a navvy.

'Can't you sleep?' he asked. 'Why are you still awake?'

'Because Carrie has been preaching to me about the importance of sex. She says love isn't love without at least a nightly bonk. Or something like that.' Poppy looked up at Eduardo, her eyes half troubled, half teasing.

'Did she now?' He kissed her forehead, gentle, confident.

'And she says I've got bricklayer's hands.'

'I love your hands.' He reached under the bed-clothes and brought her hand up to his face. Turning it over, he kissed the palm. 'And your sister, cara mia, knows absolutely nothing at all about love.'

Poppy, held like a child against his chest, thought how right he was. Carrie had new lovers like other people have new jumpers, but she had never really been in love.

As Eduardo released her with another kiss and burrowed down into the bedclothes, she repressed a sharp stab of disappointment. She'd thought they might make love. The conversation had been so loving, and it could so easily have led to sex. But then she remembered the aspirins. And that he'd been up by six this morning. It was after midnight now, and he had to be at Heathrow in seven hours' time.

As his gentle breathing deepened into the steady rhythm of sleep, contentment replaced the momentary feeling of slight. My besetting sin is smugness, she thought. I have everything any woman could possibly desire. Eduardo's strong Italian looks seemed to improve with the years; he was educated and confident; he was an international architect with interesting and civilized friends, he spoke three languages, was liberal and tolerant, he adored the children, he was fun to be with, he admired her work in the theatre. And he loved her.

And then they had plenty of money, the farmhouse in Oxfordshire, this wonderful penthouse, and his mother to help with the children. The only fly in the ointment, and it was a very little fly, was her beloved sister. Eduardo was dismissive of Carrie. And that hurt, because Carrie was her best friend. Eduardo thought Carrie selfish and lightweight, but then Carrie was always at her worst when Eduardo was around. She liked to provoke him, but Eduardo always won.

What Carrie needed, thought Poppy as she drifted off to sleep, was a man like Eduardo – not the kind but slightly ineffectual Richard, whom Carrie alternately ignored and captivated. Pity Eduardo didn't have a brother.

Three

Poppy woke as the door opened. 'Happy Christmas, Mummy,' said Angelina.

For a split second Poppy wasn't sure if she was in London or Oxfordshire, but as she scrabbled for her glasses the realization of Christmas in the country settled round her. She pressed the light button on the alarm clock. 'Darling, go back to bed. It's two in the morning. Father Christmas hasn't even been yet.'

'He has, Mummy. He's eaten half the mince pie, and the stockings are full.'

Poppy, half asleep as she shepherded her daughter out, didn't have an answer to this. 'Sweetheart, it's too early for presents. You have to go back to sleep.'

Angelina craned over the balcony rail as they crossed the landing, waving her arm at the fireplace below. 'Look, Mummy, Father Christmas drank the wine. And he left a letter.'

Poppy ignored this. 'Shh, shh darling,' she said as she tucked Angelina in. 'You mustn't come into Daddy and Mummy until you count seven dings of the clock. Okay?'

Angelina nodded, her eyes wide awake and serious. 'I know it's you that fills the stockings. And Daddy drank Father Christmas's wine and wrote his letter. I saw you.'

Poppy felt a stab of dismay. She had checked the children were asleep before they'd started on Santa duty. Angelina must have been bluffing. She said, 'Oh darling . . .' but Angelina interrupted.

'Everyone in my class knows Father Christmas isn't true.'

'Oh dear.'

'I've known for years and years.'

Poppy brushed Angelina's hair from her face, stroking her head. Angelina's skinny arm reached out and her fingers gripped Poppy's nightshirt.

'It's okay, Mum, I won't tell Tom and Lorato.'

Poppy felt a flood of love for her solemn daughter. 'You are a good girl. I suppose you are a bit old for Father Christmas. But we'll all just pretend, shall we?'

As Poppy climbed back into bed, Eduardo mumbled, 'All okay?'

'Yes, fine. But she doesn't believe in Father Christmas any more.'

But he was asleep. Poppy lay on her back, thinking that her daughter had probably known the truth for years. While she couldn't be sure that the presents, the tree, the excitement, didn't depend on her believing, she'd hedged her bets. Poppy rolled on to her side, suddenly sad. Why did children have to grow up? Why couldn't they grow down?

Poppy couldn't get to sleep again, although she'd had an exhausting day. She loved Christmas. She'd loved it as a child in Africa when Christmas had seemed a wonderfully English thing: she'd imagined snowmen and robins in Hyde Park, reindeer and sleighbells among the red London buses. In the heat of the African summer they used to decorate the mopane tree with cotton wool for snow. And Dad had sweltered in a red woollen dressing gown and a sheepskin beard, handing out Christmas boxes to the servants, who always smiled shyly, hands together, not meeting his eye. And then the family sat down to the full English Christmas dinner, turkey, plum pudding, trifle, nuts and all. What a distant life that seemed now, almost surreal.

This year, as every year, she had made Christmas decorations out of last year's cards with the children, insisted everyone had a stir of the pudding, boiled and polished twenty-pence pieces to stick in it and taken Angelina and Giulia carol singing with the village. She'd also ignored Eduardo's objections to tawdry commercialism and taken the children to see the Selfridges windows.

But it was a tiring business. She missed the practical help of Giulia, who was spending Christmas with Eduardo's sister in Milan. Her own mother, staying with them for three nights, was more trial than help. She needed more attention and patience than the children.

Last night she'd insisted on laying the Christmas dinner table, which Poppy had had to redo once her mother was safely in bed. Lucille had rejected Poppy's

lace tablecloth in favour of a Teletubbies duvet cover
and set the table with a random collection of teacups,
mugs and kitchen utensils, including the garlic press
placed carefully on top of the bowl of nuts. When
Angelina had tried to replace it with the nutcracker,
Lucille had bitten her granddaughter's head off.

'Will you stop interfering! I am laying this table. If
I want that nutcracker, I'll have that nutcracker.' She'd
sounded like a child spoiling for a fight.

Angelina hesitated, dismayed, then held the garlic
press out to Lucille.

'But Gran, it's not a nutcracker. It's a garlic
press.'

To Poppy's relief her mother had taken the garlic
press, examined it closely and then burst out laughing.
'Oh dear!' she said, hugging Angelina. 'I'm so sorry,
dear. I must be going doolally in my old age. I won't
know my own name next.'

Replaying this scene in her head, Poppy thought
the time was not long off. Since Dad's death – how
long ago now? Three years? – her mother's mind had
grown a lot worse. Of course she'd been forgetful for
years, maybe fifteen or twenty. When she and Carrie
had been young teenagers, her mother's vagueness
had seemed like wilful lack of concentration. Or indifference. It had driven them both mad. But maybe that
was the start of Alzheimer's?

It was her mother's illness that finally transplanted
the family to England. Her father, with a British pass-
port and the right to live here, had scorned to take

47

advantage of it when they lost their Zimbabwe farm in the '70s Bush War – instead they'd moved over the border to South Africa, and started again – but in '82 he'd done so to get medical help for his wife.

Their dad had sold a third of Kaia Moya to Karl, who until then had been a salaried manager, and left him to turn it into a tourist game lodge.

Lucille's treatment hadn't worked of course. She'd become steadily, if slowly, worse, and her dad had hated managing a suburban golf club, Carrie hated doing O levels and Poppy doing A levels at a minor public school and getting more English by the minute.

By the time Carrie had finished her catering course and Poppy was through RADA, Lucille would forget appointments, lose things, get lost on the tube. Six years ago her dad gave up pretending that Lucille was just a little dilly. He quit his job and resigned himself to retirement in a tiny flat, 6,000 miles from his beloved Kaia Moya.

Poppy knew he longed to go back, but he thought it better for Lucille to be where her daughters were. Soon they'd be the only people she'd recognize. And Mpumalanga had no appeal for the girls. It could not provide a career on the stage for Poppy, nor bright lights and gourmet kitchens for Carrie.

Now Lucille did not know her grandchildren's names, and only intermittently remembered Eduardo's. Only Carrie and Poppy were truly familiar to her, though she made a pretty good stab at pretending. She phrased her sentences carefully to avoid having to say a name: 'How are you and yours?' or 'What are you all up to?'

Old age stinks, thought Poppy. There are no compensations. Widowhood, senility, frailty, death.

Then she remembered Woody Allen's phrase: *Age isn't so terrible, particularly when you consider the alternative.*

Smiling, she turned her head into the pillow and snuggled deeper under the duvet, resolving to enjoy God's good gifts while she had them. She pushed Lucille out of her brain, and ran through the day ahead. Eduardo would, with luck, take her mother off her hands, keep her out of the kitchen. The children would be absorbed by their presents. Poppy counted up the jobs she still had to do: turkey in, pud on, spuds, sprouts, bread sauce, cranberry jelly. Carrie would help. It would be a doddle.

Poppy relaxed as the familiar rituals of Christmas Day scrolled over her mind. She lost the place and started again, until the blissful slide into sleep engulfed her.

Carrie was sharing the spare room with her mother. She'd have preferred the little box room at the top of the house, or to bunk up with Angelina. She'd not have to bear her mother's snoring then, but Lucille could not be trusted on her own. She'd wander down in the middle of the night and set the burglar alarm off, or leave the taps running.

She should be in a home, that's the truth, thought

Carrie, but Poppy insisted it was worth taking the risk of her burning her building down or getting lost in the high street to allow her to stay in her own flat. She did have a rota of minders, led by the social worker Adrienne, who was adept at disguising herself as 'the gardener', 'the district nurse', 'the cleaner', 'a neighbour'. Poppy and Adrienne orchestrated Lucille's life, and Poppy paid for everything. A full-time, live-in minder was what she needed, but Lucille would have none of it. Help had to be disguised as a professional service or neighbourliness.

Poppy didn't say 'minders', of course. She said 'carers', or 'companions'. But Poppy's a lot nicer than me, thought Carrie, as she clapped her hands – softly at first, but getting increasingly loud – to wake her mother. She'd got this clapping business down to a fine art. If she woke her mother by calling or shaking her, Lucille would be livid, but if she surfaced gradually, and did not know what had woken her, she'd turn over on her side and, with luck, stop snoring.

Sure enough, Lucille gave a hiccuping garrumph and half sat up. Carrie at once stopped clapping, arresting her hands in mid-air. Then she heard the creak of Lucille's bed as she turned over, and, bliss, oh bliss, no snoring. Now the tricky part, thought Carrie: the race to get to sleep myself before she starts again.

Carrie, pencil and pad in hand, was trying to keep track of who gave what to whom. Poppy insisted on it, because she made Angelina write thank-you letters, and she did the babies' and Lucille's for them. Also, she said, it made Angelina read the cards and tags instead of just ripping into her parcels.

My sister, thought Carrie, is trying to give conspicuous consumption an acceptable face. The Santolinis are hugely rich so naturally there are all these expensive presents, but she doesn't really like it. She'd prefer everyone to have made their offerings themselves and hand-painted the cards.

Carrie called across the piles of discarded wrapping paper and presents, 'Angelina, who's that from?'

Angelina looked briefly at the book she was holding and dropped it on a chair without opening it. 'Gran,' she answered. 'It's a cookbook for kids. From Nonna.'

Lucille looked puzzled. 'Did I give you that, dear?' Poppy started to explain, wrong granny, but Lucille had changed tack, 'Yes, I remember, I bought it from my local bookshop.'

When Lucille realized what Carrie was doing she was indignant. 'I don't know why my daughters are so bloody bossy! Do you think I'm incapable of remembering who gave me things!'

Carrie, not without malice, said, 'Who gave you that, Mom?' She pointed at the pink pashmina in Lucille's lap, a present from Poppy.

'You did, of course.' Lucille stroked the fine wool, holding it to her cheek. Her irritation instantly forgotten, she stood up to kiss Carrie. 'It's lovely, darling. Thank you, thank you.'

Carrie caught Poppy's lifted eyebrow over their mother's shoulder. Damn, thought Carrie, I should have told her it was from Poppy. But the moment had gone, and her mother had turned away.

After the present-opening fest, Carrie went upstairs to put on the blue beach sarong and skinny knit silver cardigan Poppy had given her and didn't reappear. Poppy felt a stab of irritation. She'd hoped Carrie would give her a hand in the kitchen. Carrie, the professional chef, could make Christmas dinner with her eyes closed, and it would give Poppy a chance to spend time with her children.

When, an hour later, Carrie still had not come down, Poppy went in search of her. She found Carrie sitting on the bed, rolling a cigarette on the bedside table.

'Carrie,' accused Poppy. 'Is that a spliff?'

'Sure thing, sis. Want one? I've got lots.' Carrie's eyes fizzed with laughter as she waved a fat little plastic pouch at her.

'For God's sake, Carrie,' said Poppy, anger leaking out in spite of her effort to be calm. 'It's Christmas Day with the family, not a Chelsea rave. And I'd have thought you might give me a hand. It's bedlam down there. Lucille and the children underfoot. Eduardo's no help – he's deep in a book. And then you just disappear in a marijuana cloud. Honestly Carrie, you are about as selfish as it gets.'

Carrie listened equably to this long speech then immediately jumped up and flung her arms round Poppy. 'Oh Popps, I'm so sorry. Of course I'll help. I just got carried away with my sarong and top, and then I saw the ciggie papers and thought, why not?' Carrie let Poppy go and twirled about, saying, 'I *love* the clothes by the way. Aren't they great? I shall have to dye my winter belly brown though.' She pushed the short stretchy jersey up further to expose more of her midriff. 'Where did you get them? I'd never have thought . . .'

Poppy, instantly won over, interrupted. 'I know – you'd never have thought I had enough fashion sense to buy a present for you! Well, I don't, but I asked the girl in Gap.'

Carrie stuffed the joint-making gear into the drawer. 'Come on, then, let's go make Christmas dinner.'

Poppy was basting the turkey when Lucille walked in. 'It's Christmas Day, isn't it? I just saw it on the television.'

'It is,' said Poppy. 'We've just opened our presents. Don't you remember?'

'Never mind that now,' said Lucille. 'If it is Christmas, why aren't we going to church? We always go to church on Christmas morning.'

Actually, they didn't. Or not very often. But Poppy fetched the parish newsletter anyway. 'There's a Christingle service at 11.30. You could go to that if we get a move on.'

'Christingle? What on earth is that?' Lucille was suspicious. 'Not happy-clappy, guitars and kissing strangers, is it?'

'I think it's for children. You know, carols and candles and a crib, and so on.'

'Well, that's all right then,' said Lucille, smiling and decisive. 'Get your coats. We must get a move on.'

In the end Poppy stayed behind to mind her turkey. Carrie had whizzed around in the last forty minutes and everything was back on schedule: sprouts peeled, spuds and turkey in, giblet stock simmering, ice-cream balled, pudding steaming.

The others walked the half-mile to the village church. Lucille walked surprisingly briskly, her arm through Angelina's. Behind them Carrie, a sheepskin jacket of Eduardo's over her summer gear, led Lorato, and Eduardo carried Tom.

'This is crazy,' said Carrie, quietly so that Lucille and Angelina would not hear. 'Neither you nor I believe in God, and here we are going to church.'

Eduardo said, 'And why not? It's a great little Norman church. And it's a lovely day.'

'That's hardly a reason to join in a lot of mumbo-jumbo.'

Eduardo laughed. Carrie was struck, as she often was, by the burly good looks of her brother-in-law. He was a confident, even arrogant, man, but you had to admit Poppy had landed a catch. He had a broad dark face: dark hair, dark skin, dark eyes. The hooded eyes and sloping brows gave his face a serious, intellectual air, although the impression was contradicted by his mouth, with its small even teeth and full lips that stretched to a wide boyish grin. Eduardo smiled easily. He had a wonderfully relaxed love of life – of food, art, family – that Carrie could see was perfect for Poppy.

He said, putting his arm over her shoulder, 'My dear Carrie. We all need rituals. It doesn't matter if we believe in them.'

Carrie was slightly nettled by 'My dear Carrie'. He always patronized her. She was tempted to shake off his arm.

Christmas lunch was good. Carrie had returned from church in high spirits and got them singing nursery rhymes and carols, which Lucille enjoyed as much as the children. And Eduardo was indulgent with Lorato, cradling her in his lap while she crammed Smarties into her mouth.

Eduardo took snaps with his new digital camera (Poppy's present to him) and printed them out, enlarged to A4, through his computer. Angelina accumulated everyone's twenty-pence pieces from the pudding and most of the trinkets from the crackers. No one cried, and no one got cross.

Later, Carrie made turkey and cranberry sandwiches and fruit salad for an early supper and the exhausted children and no less exhausted Lucille were upstairs by 9.30. Poppy came down from seeing her mother into bed to find her sister washing up.

Carrie's arms were in the sink and she had to jerk her head to indicate the fridge behind her. 'Look over there,' she said.

On the fridge and freezer doors Eduardo had stuck his Christmas lunch photographs. Carrie dried her hands and followed Poppy to them.

Eduardo had exhibited only the best: Tom trying to put a paper hat on the dog's head; Lorato with her mouth so full her cheeks bulged like a hamster's; Angelina and Lucille singing. He'd caught Poppy's triumphant expression as she carried in the holly-decked turkey and Carrie rearing back as the over-heated brandy engulfed the pudding in three-foot flames. And he'd included the ones Carrie had taken of him, one hugging Poppy, one with the two little ones.

The sisters were exclaiming over the pictures when Eduardo came in. He put an arm round each of them, and said, 'Nice camera. Poppy. Thank you.' He squeezed her shoulder.

'Nice family,' replied Poppy, kissing his cheek.

Eduardo rubbed his great bear hands up and down the women's shoulders and arms. 'Are you two going to drool over happy families all night, or can I get to the fridge?'

He released them as they stepped back. He opened the fridge door and reached in to extract a bottle of Veuve Clicquot.

'Come on. A bit of La Grande Dame to celebrate the miracle of a stress-free Christmas and No Tears Before Bedtime.'

Poppy took this as a compliment, and kissed him again. Carrie smiled too, and did not make the remark that presented itself: 'No thanks to you, dear brother-in-law.'

But as she followed the Santolinis, arms now round each other, into the living room, the thought was replaced by a sharp stab of jealousy. Eduardo was such a thorough-going *man*. He might be arrogant, chauvinist and patronizing, but he wasn't wet, like Richard.

After Christmas Day, Lucille became increasingly restless, suggesting hourly that she went home. As soon as Adrienne was back from her break, on the 27th, Eduardo drove his mother-in-law back to London. He rang to say he'd stay in town until New Year's Eve, if Poppy didn't mind. She had her sister with her after all, and he'd be glad of the chance of a quiet few days in the office.

In truth, Poppy didn't mind. She and Carrie got on better when Eduardo wasn't there.

Carrie came upon her sister at the door of the playroom, standing very still. Poppy held her hand up to Carrie, signalling silence.

'Listen,' she whispered.

Carrie looked into the playroom. Lorato and Tom were sitting on their fat nappied bottoms, close together on the carpet, jabbering away like a pair of old women. The sounds were not regular or repetitive – not 'Dah dah dah' or 'Mum mum mum' – but as varied and complicated as a whole language.

Carrie looked at Poppy in astonishment. 'How

extraordinary,' she said, her voice low so as not to alert the children.

'I know,' replied Poppy. 'They've been doing it for two weeks now. Henson says twins quite often do it, but he's never met it in non-twins before.'

Carrie looked at her, puzzled. 'Henson?'

'Paediatrician at St Mary's.'

The first time Poppy had heard them at it, she'd wondered for a wild moment if it was Hwesa that had somehow lain dormant in Lorato's brain. 'It seems twins sometimes make up a private language, until their mother tongue takes over, when they drop it. Amazing, isn't it?'

From the door Poppy and Carrie saw Lorato and Tom clutching at each other, smooth brown arms against bright pink ones, chuckling and hiccuping with laughter. As they watched, Lorato swivelled her head to gaze for a second in silence at the two women in the doorway, then she said something incomprehensible to Tom. At this he waved his arms towards his mother and shrieked with laughter. The effort unbalanced him and he rolled over, legs in the air. Poppy darted forward and set him back on his bottom. Both children fell silent at this intervention.

Poppy said, crouching to hug the children in turn, 'Monsters. What's the joke then?' She tickled Lorato's belly. 'What did you say to him, Lorato?' Lorato looked at her in solemn silence, all trace of her former merriment gone. For a second Poppy felt hurt, excluded.

Carrie followed Poppy into the room and knelt among the toys. Tom bounced up and down on his bum and reached his arms wide, demanding to be picked up. Carrie said, 'No, sweetheart,' and compensated him with a purple Beanie Baby. He took it happily and chewed its head. Carrie turned to Lorato, who met her gaze without expression, and gave her a lime-green Beanie Baby, which she took and immediately dropped, her eyes not leaving Carrie's face.

Carrie tickled their feet. Tom curled his toes, jerked his legs in unison and giggled. Lorato moved her foot away, but otherwise did not react. Carrie blew gently into Tom's neck, and he squealed with pleasure. She did it again, and he shrieked and bounced in a paroxysm of delight. She tried it with Lorato, but the child bore it, Carrie thought, with fortitude. Certainly not with pleasure.

'I think she wants us to go, so they can continue the conversation,' Carrie said, smiling to cover her failure with her niece.

Back in the kitchen, Poppy jerked the espresso machine handle over the cups with a practised movement. 'I wanted you to see it. I don't think Eduardo believed me until I videoed them. He's home so little he's never caught them at it. I hardly believe it myself, so I'm glad of a witness.'

'It's amazing. Especially as she doesn't speak at all to us. Does she laugh or chatter with Angelina?'

Poppy shook her head. 'It's so sad. Angelina was

so excited by Lorato's arrival, and was determined to love her to bits and to mother her, but she's getting bored with her indifference.'

'When do children usually start talking? English I mean?' Carrie blew on her coffee, thinking that children were not all the blessing they looked.

'I suppose about now. Henson says Lorato may walk first, though he thinks the twin-jabbering is a good sign. And Tom already says "Mum". And "Lina" for Angelina, and "Dite" for Light.'

'How about Eduardo? I expect he's wonderful with her?' Carrie had a mental image of Eduardo carrying Lorato on his shoulders, mouth wide and laughing while he held Lorato's stubby legs each side of his face.

But Poppy replied, 'Not too good. I think her baleful stare gets on his nerves. He's getting ratty with her, especially when she cries and cries for no reason. He says he begins to understand baby-bashing.'

Instantly Poppy felt disloyal. Eduardo was a wonderful father; he'd never hit a child. She qualified her words: 'It's a bad time for him. He's working so hard, with Bilbao and the Paddington project going full tilt, and some new scheme in Manchester coming up. He could do with some peace at home.'

Poppy smiled at her sister, and gave a slight shrug, dismissing any problem. That's life, it said.

She regretted saying anything at all. She didn't want to discuss Eduardo with Carrie. She changed the subject. 'What about this photo shoot then?'

Carrie extracted a Hobnob and offered the packet to Poppy. Poppy shook her head.

'Thing is, Popps,' said Carrie, 'if I can do it here it will save me hours of searching for a venue, and for props and antiques, etc. And for happy family models – I can just borrow the Santolinis.'

Poppy knew that agreeing would get her in trouble with Eduardo. He would say Carrie was, as usual, exploiting Poppy's good nature. If Carrie came back for another three days, Eduardo would probably stay in London and work. He resented the mess and upheaval that Carrie's photo shoots or filming sessions produced.

Carrie's eyes were wide and frank. Poppy knew she'd not be able to say no. She stalled, saying, 'But who wants Christmas photos after Christmas?'

'It's for an American travel mag. For *next* year. Some promotion or other. They want to give away a pack of twelve Christmas cards with the November issue, with traditional English recipes on the inside.'

'Mince pies and brandy butter?'

'I guess. The Christmas cards are to be all holly wreaths on ye olde oake door and upmarket ivy garlands strung from the mantelpiece. Which you've already done.' Carrie waved her arm in the general direction of the drawing room.

'But why does a travel mag want to give away Christmas cards? Or English recipes?'

'The cards are supposed to make people buy the mag. And the recipes are to come from Cotswold hotels, and there'll be an article and a holiday offer in the mag.' Carrie grinned her wide happy smile. 'And with any luck I'll earn enough for a week in Antigua.'

Poppy shook her head in disbelief. 'From one photo shoot?'

'It will be a three-day shoot. But that's just the start. If I play my cards right, I'll get to ghost the hotels' recipes, write the travel piece and style the pics. And if you let me do it here, I can fiddle my expenses because they'd expect me to stay in all the hotels and I'd much rather stay with you.' She leaned back and flicked her hair off her face. 'And I'll charge them a location fee, hire charges for all the props, maybe even stylist fees for decorating everything.' She ended with a gleeful grin. 'Pretty neat, don't you think?'

Poppy frowned. 'But Carrie, the decoration's done. And you'd be getting the place and the props for nothing.'

Carrie put her arm round her sister. 'That's the point, Dumbo. It's money for old rope.' Then seeing Poppy's look of disapproval she added, 'I'll have to renew the leaves – the ivy will be dead by then.' She kissed Poppy lightly on the cheek and turned back to the espresso machine. 'Can I have another?' She set the machine going again.

Poppy didn't answer. The blithe admission of fiddling expenses worried her, but she knew Carrie thought she was old-fashioned and priggish. She was debating with herself whether to say anything.

'Well, can I, Popps?'

Poppy pulled her mind to the present and said, 'Of course. Help yourself.'

'Oh Poppy!' Carrie was more amused than vexed. 'I meant can I do the photos here? Took the coffee for granted, I'm afraid.'

'Yes, yes, of course you can.'

But something in her voice got through to Carrie, who said, perfectly cheerfully, 'Oh Poppy, you are not going to get on your moral high horse, are you? You can have the location fees and the hire charges if you like.'

'Don't be daft. We don't want anything.' Poppy turned to put her cup in the dishwasher, her back to her sister. Carrie, walking round to see her face, asked, with cheerfulness giving way to slight petulance, 'Well, what's the long face for then?'

Poppy caught the note of challenge. She hadn't wanted to change Carrie's carefree mood, but she forced herself to say, 'I suppose I think you should only charge what you pay for. Fiddling expenses, if I may be pompous about it, is dishonest.' There, she'd said it. She waited for the explosion, but to her surprise Carrie burst into laughter and put both arms round her neck.

'Oh Poppy, I do love you. You are such an innocent.' She stopped laughing with difficultly and said, 'Look, I work in Grub Street. Everyone understands about expenses. It's the system.'

Four

Angelina had gone to a friend's and Tom and Lorato were asleep. Poppy put *Aida* on the CD player with the intention of grabbing a rest on the sofa while she had the chance, but she found herself thinking about her conversation with Carrie. Or rather, conversations. The one they had half had about morality, and the one they hadn't had about Eduardo.

On the morality issue, she realized she'd done what she always did, and had always done: she'd let Carrie off. Her sister had made her feel prudish about the expenses, and she'd backed off.

And she'd let her have her way over the photo shoot, also as usual. She knew Eduardo would say Carrie was using her, that she took them all for granted. It irritated him that Carrie borrowed their books and seldom returned them; cried off for dinner at the last minute or turned up with uninvited boyfriends in tow; and frequently invaded their Paddington penthouse or Oxfordshire farmhouse for photo shoots.

He didn't know that she sometimes borrowed money too. Poppy felt a lump of unease in her diaphragm when she thought of that. It wasn't the money – the amounts weren't large – but she hated keeping things from Eduardo. She would mention it one day, but not now. For the first time in ten years Christmas had been as much stress as pleasure, and Poppy was tired.

The babies (she still thought of them as babies) were exhausting and Angelina had reverted to climbing into their bed at all hours of the night.

She suspected that Eduardo had found the enforced holiday idleness in the bosom of his family a strain. It would have been easier if Giulia had been with them. She spoiled Eduardo rotten, waiting on him hand and foot, and she was great with the children and shopped, cleaned, cooked and washed up like a machine. Poppy had been looking forward to Eduardo's mother being away for a change, giving her total access to her husband and children without competition, but now, as she thought of the mountain of laundry, the carpet of pine needles under the Christmas tree and the piles of newspapers and crates of bottles waiting to go to the recycling centre, she muttered, 'Come back, Giulia. I give in.'

No, it wasn't the moment to tell Eduardo about the latest £500. It was bad enough having to tell him that Carrie was coming back after New Year with a whole camera crew in tow.

How was she meant to say no to her sister? That's what families were for. Besides, Carrie was such fun: she'd go tobogganing on old teatrays with Angelina; she'd arrive with half of Harrods Food Hall in her boot and insist on fixing gigantic meals that might include the best sevruga caviar on buckwheat blinis and American hotdogs with ketchup out of squidgy bottles.

Most of the time she loved having Carrie around. Her sister could be maddening and selfish but she could always make her laugh, as unrestrainedly and incomprehensibly as she had when they were kids.

We are so different and yet so close, thought Poppy. I never tell her much, while she never stops gabbling. She'd always been the more reticent one. She thought that talking about relationships was an indulgence. Besides, she did not need a confidante. Only people with problems had to have someone to blab to all the time. Or people like Carrie, who just needed an audience.

Poppy closed her eyes and let the music wash through her. It would all be all right. Darling Eduardo, he would understand.

In the back of Poppy's mind, though, behind the door she was refusing to open, lay a fear that he didn't understand, or didn't want to. Especially about Lorato. Maybe she was becoming obsessed with Lorato. The child so absorbed and fascinated her that the thought of going back to work, taking a job in the theatre, where she'd have to obey a director's demands rather than Lorato's, was unthinkable.

She was intrigued and delighted at Lorato's relationship with Tom. The little girl patently adored her new brother, becoming anxious and fretful if he was removed from the room and instantly calming down if he was brought back. But there was still something wrong. Except with Tom, Lorato never smiled, never laughed. At the slightest sign of anger or impatience, a raised voice or a tone of irritation, Lorato would look up at the owner of the voice and make a small mewing noise, like keening, and wet herself. Lorato herself did not need to be the object of displeasure – anything could set her off: Poppy could chide Angelina for not putting the tops back on her coloured pens; Eduardo could snap at Tom for tormenting the dog; Giulia could even berate the British Telecom helpline; and Lorato's eyes would grow round and liquid, and she would pee.

Poppy found this deeply worrying, and she suffered for Lorato, but Eduardo was maddened by it.

'I'm being blackmailed, that's what,' he said. 'If my voice rises by so much as a decibel Lorato wails and pees, and you look at me as if I'm a criminal.'

'Oh, I don't, darling,' riposted Poppy, hurt. 'She just needs time.' She put a placating hand on his arm. 'It will be all right, I know it will.'

'Well, it better be all right soon. This is an Italian family, and Italian families don't go around talking in tones of holy hush.'

Lorato could still bawl for hours. She seldom cried if she hurt herself, but she became desperate if Poppy tried to take something from her that she wanted to hang on to (especially food), or if she didn't want to be put down at bedtime, or if anyone tried to lift her out of her bouncy swing. She would stand stock-still, her

67

mouth open so wide it seem to occupy her whole face. You could see her tonsils. Tears would run in streams from her tightly shut eyes, and she would yell. Unremitting, high-pitched wails of such distress it broke Poppy's heart. With Eduardo it broke his patience, and he would sometimes yell back at her. Then Poppy would yell at him. And he'd slam out.

Poppy made a determined effort to stop thinking and to listen to Verdi. She'd just managed to disappear under the music when the telephone wrenched her back.

It was Lucille, giggling down the line.

'Too silly,' she said. 'I'm stuck in the bath. Can't for the life of me get out.'

Poppy's mind whirled about. Someone must have forgotten to put the bathplug on the top of the medicine chest. They hid it so Lucille could not have a bath when there was no one around to haul her out. And why was she in the bath in the middle of the day?

Her mother sounded perfectly cheerful. Thank God she's mad, thought Poppy. If she knew I was an hour and a half away . . .

Lucille went on, 'Just as well I've got your telephone number on the wall, isn't it?'

Poppy blessed Eduardo's good sense. He'd put up laminated notices all over Lucille's flat in numbers large enough for her to read without her glasses and installed a telephone (with huge numbers on the buttons) next to the bath.

'Oh God, Mom, are you on your own?'

'Of course I'm on my own, you silly girl. Your father died years ago . . .'

Poppy's mind raced round her mother's circle of helpers. It was Adrienne's day, wasn't it? Poppy looked at her watch: 3 p.m. Adrienne would have given her mother some lunch, and wouldn't be back until 5.30. Maybe Carrie was in town. Trying to keep her voice casual, Poppy said, 'Darling, I'll ring round and find someone. I'll ring you back. Don't worry now.'

She dialled Carrie's number but only got her maddening message: 'Hi, Carrie here. If it's boring, please send a fax. If it's fun, here's my mobile . . .' She tried the mobile – it was switched off – and the two other women on her mother's rota. There was no reply from Mary Roberts, and Joy Black had gone out and taken Lucille's door key with her, although her husband Eric was instantly helpful. 'Poor Lucille. I'll go and chat to her through the bathroom window. I can be there in five minutes. Stop her panicking. What do you think?'

'Oh, thank God for you, Eric. I'm so grateful. I'll get the fire brigade or the police or whatever you do, but it would be wonderful to know you'll be there.'

Poppy rang 999 and was impressed. Old ladies obviously get stuck in the bath a lot. 'No problem, madam. We'll have her out in no time.' They said they'd send the fire brigade and the police.

This seemed a little like overkill to Poppy, but she

gratefully accepted and rang her mother back to tell her help was on the way.

Her mother answered at once.

'Hi, Mom. You okay?'

'Yes, of course I'm okay. I'm having a bath.'

Poppy's relief at her mother's lack of distress was tempered by irritation at her indignant tone. 'Mom, you just rang me to say you couldn't get out of the bath, so I was calling back to say help is on its way.'

'Goodness, you do talk nonsense. Of course I can get out of the bath. I get out of the bath every day of my life.'

Poppy took a breath and said steadily, 'Mom, if you roll round on to your knees, you will get up better than trying to pull with your hands.'

Poppy could hear swishing noises. 'Mom. Are you there? Are you on your back, or sitting up, or what?'

'I'm going to have to stop chatting, darling,' said her mother, her voice now as friendly and sweet as seconds ago it had been sharp. 'It's such a luxury having a phone in the bath so I can chat to you. But I'm getting chilly, and I must get out.'

'But Mom, that's the point. You can't get out.'

'Of course I can get out. That's just what I must do. I will ring you back after breakfast.' And the telephone went dead. Poppy shut her eyes. Breakfast! It was 3 p.m.

Poppy dialled again. It took a couple of rings before her mother answered, and she sounded out of breath.

'Oh Poppy, is that you? What a bit of luck you rang.

You'll never believe this. Too silly. But I can't get out of the bath . . .'

'I know, darling, but I've rung the fire brigade and they are going to come and rescue you.'

'The fire brigade? You've rung the fire brigade? But I'm stark naked. I can't let the fire brigade in here.' Lucille laughed. A relaxed merry laugh. 'Still, it will be the first time for God knows how long any man has seen me in the buff. What a joke.'

Suddenly Poppy could hear Eric Black shouting through the bathroom window. 'Lucille, are you okay? Hear you are stuck in the bath!'

Poppy held the telephone a little away from her cheek as a shouted conversation between her mother and Eric ensued, then her mother was talking to her again.

'Hello, who is this? Oh, it's you, Poppy, is it? I must go. I have to get out of the bath and let someone in. I haven't a clue who he is, but he seems to have come to see me and I'd better let him in.'

Poppy had a fleeting thought that her mother would let in absolutely anyone. Another of the multiple risks of senility. She shelved the thought for later and started to tell her mother once again how to get out of the bath, but Lucille had already put the phone down.

In the end, according to Eric, it was quite a party. The fire brigade arrived but as Lucille wasn't panicking they were reluctant to stave the front door in and waited for the police, who tried, without success, to pick the lock. Lucille repeatedly declared herself about to get out of the bath and let them in, and then found to her astonishment that she couldn't.

Eventually the smallest of the policewomen burgled her way through a narrow skylight into the bedroom and opened the front door. At this moment Adrienne appeared and she and the policewoman hauled Lucille out of a now tepid bath.

And then three firefighters, two police officers, Eric, Adrienne and Lucille had tea and toast together. Lucille responded to Poppy's call with, 'Can't talk now dear, I've got guests for dinner.'

Oh God, thought Poppy as she put the telephone back in its cradle, what am I to do with her? Carrie's no help, though she lives round the corner. She thinks because our mother doesn't know if it's Tuesday or Belgium she needn't bother with her. Pretends she visited yesterday, and promises to visit tomorrow. And sometimes Lucille is not as daft as she seems and is hurt.

If only Lucille would have someone live with her. But she sniffed at the idea of a companion. Once, when she'd forgotten Dad was dead and Poppy had again suggested live-in help, she'd said, 'What would Bill think? He doesn't want to come home to find a lodger in the house, does he?' Poppy hadn't had the heart to remind her she'd been a widow for two years, that she'd kissed her husband's cold, dead cheek, still showing the downward pull of the stroke that had killed him.

Sometimes Poppy felt like a sponge, with everyone – Eduardo, the children, her sister, her mother – sucking at her.

And would she ever get back to the theatre? There were moments when she felt that this domestic life would capture her, that she'd never again feel the glorious lift of a standing ovation, the heady triumph as the curtain comes down, the delirium of giving an unassailable performance.

Maybe, if she didn't accept something soon, she'd never work again? She shouldn't have turned down *Bogside*, a new play by a young Irish writer that her agent had insisted she read. The part of Sinead was made for her: a passionate young woman brought up in a revolutionary family, who sees the ceasefire as a betrayal and ends up killing her brother and destroying her world. It was a bleak story, but Poppy had seen at once how she would play Sinead: light-hearted as well as passionate, sympathetic as well as bigoted, the audience on her side one moment, hating her the next.

But even before she put the script down she'd known she wouldn't do it. Lorato wasn't ready yet.

Poppy rang Carrie's number again. She left a message, her voice a lot brisker than normal, 'Carrie, why is it ME our mother rings when she's stuck in the bath? Go round and hide her bathplug, will you?'

Five

Carrie liked the Eurostar. The food was awful, of course, and the service not much better, but there was a pleasant pinkish thirties feeling about the decor, and the champagne was free. She felt great. She was wearing a new cream suit from Nicole Farhi and had recently spent a fortune in the Tanning Shop standing in a ring of ultraviolet tubes: it had taken six twelve-minute sessions to make her look as if she'd just returned from St Moritz. And her tan was all-over, which wasn't true of her skiing friends in Momo.

Carrie looked over the top of her copy of *Tatler*, checking for talent. A few boring and bored couples. Most of the passengers were men, but none of them were on their own. Pity. A mild flirtation would pass the time.

She felt a bit guilty about ditching Richard at the last minute, but since she was now committed to interviewing four chefs and eating at each of their restaurants, it wouldn't have been much fun for him. Besides, his absolute adoration was beginning to be a drag. He never stopped talking about love.

Richard worked for Eduardo. He'd left the Cambridge School of Architecture at twenty-four, backpacked for two years, and worked for her brother-in-law ever since. Carrie had met him at an office bash given by Eduardo. Eduardo and Poppy gave great parties – on their terrace in the summer, in the flat in the winter. Carrie always went because she liked the mix of creative successful people. They were mostly the right age too, late twenties to early forties, with a few older grandees thrown in. There was almost always someone there she fancied. Either young and beautiful, or old (well, not too old) and famous.

It was a hot evening last summer and Richard had been helping Poppy ladle out the risotto when Carrie first saw him. She wanted him at once. He had a bony thinness she found really sexy, and deep dark eyes behind rimless oval glasses. His dark hair was very short, almost shaved, and he wore the designer's obligatory collarless black shirt, open at the neck.

'Richard,' said Poppy, 'meet my sister, Carrie. Now, she really is a cook. She does it for a living.'

Richard looked up at her, and Carrie knew at once that she'd landed him. She just kept very still, looked unblinking into his eyes, then smiled slowly.

Richard said, 'Sisters? You can't be sisters. You look so . . . You sound so different.'

Poppy laughed. 'It's okay, you can say it, I don't mind. She's the stunner.' Her eyes teased Carrie. 'But I'm the one who's been taught to speak posh, while Carrie here still displays her bushveld background . . .'

Richard interrupted, his eyes on Carrie, 'Is that what it is? I was listening to you – eavesdropping actually – earlier. I thought maybe you had a trace of down under . . .'

Carrie still hadn't said anything. Richard changed tack. 'You're a cook?'

She nodded. 'I cook for a living. For mags and books, you know? And for rich people who give parties. Carrie's Catering. I write stuff too.'

From then on it was easy. Richard dished up the risotto and she carried the bowls and forks to the guests. As she moved around the room, she was conscious of Richard's gaze. She was wearing a short black mini and a lacy black dévoré top through which her black bra was clearly visible. When she'd bought the top she'd wondered, just for a second, if at thirty-two she was too old for such teenage fashion, but she looked great in it, and what the hell?

She was at her most vivacious when she was furthest from Richard. A little jealousy did a lot to cement desire.

After supper, Carrie allowed Richard to waylay her, and they talked about her latest project – styling the food for a film about Mary, Queen of Scots. She was careful not to spend too much time with him, though. Nonetheless she kept an eye on him. She didn't think he'd disappear, but you never knew. Some guys headed for safer ground when they felt the pull of the current.

When one of Eduardo's assistants, an amateur DJ, set up her decks and put on some dance music, Carrie said, 'Come and dance. It's great music.' But Richard shook his head. Carrie joined the dancers anyway, and for a while forgot about him. She loved dancing. The music got right into her head, took her over, made her forget everything else. And she knew she moved well.

She didn't forget Richard entirely. She was aware of his tall frame slouched against the door to the terrace. He was watching the dancers. Watching her.

Then suddenly he was no longer there. Carrie stopped dancing and, flushed and gasping from the exertion, staggered on to the terrace. It was cooler out there, but still warm. She was sweating and she could feel her hair sticking to her neck.

Poppy emerged from the kitchen with fizzy water and a tray of tumblers filled with ice. Carrie filled two, took a couple of gulps from one of them, then carried them over to Richard, who was standing on the far side of the terrace, looking down into the canal.

'Here,' she said.

Richard took the proffered glass. 'Thanks. Good idea. It could help with the hangover.'

'You pissed then?'

'I guess. Do you mind?'

'No.'

Carrie put her glass down on the ledge. She was still panting, and hot. She leaned on the terrace wall, feeling the cool stone against her bare arms. She could feel Richard studying her, looking at her face as if he had to draw it from memory. She liked him looking.

Straightening up, she breathed in deeply and

77

linked her hands, interleaving her fingers, and then stretched her arms out in front of her. She turned her palms to the front, exhaled a long breath and shut her eyes. Her shoulders rounded and flexed under the gauzy top. As she prolonged the movement she thought of Richard's eyes on her narrow black bra straps each side of her armholes. As she lifted her arms over her head, she knew he'd watch her hair swing round her shoulders and flow down her bum as she arched her back. She knew his eyes would be fixed on her neck, offered like a sacrifice as her head fell back in an exaggerated yawn. Then he'd see the two-inch strip of bare belly, warm and damp from dancing.

She took her time, luxuriating like a cat, enjoying the display. The mating game. She wondered if he'd take the bait. She wanted him to. She didn't want to have to pretend she was yawning because she was tired.

Of course he took it. She felt his hand slip into the gap at her midriff and slide round her body to encircle her waist. Then he seemed to stop, hesitating. She heard him put down his glass. He was giving her time to say yes or no.

Without straightening up, without opening her eyes, Carrie shifted her feet very slightly apart and turned her body fractionally towards him. She heard Richard's quick intake of breath as he moved his knee between her legs and pulled her to him, dropping his head to kiss her neck.

He smelled divine, a mix of alcohol and aftershave, or maybe shampoo. Whatever. She raised her head and opened her eyes to look, unfocused because of the nearness, into his. She held his gaze as he brought his mouth down on hers. He kissed her and she again closed her eyes, letting her mouth relax, willing and soft.

It was a deep sexy kiss, and Carrie could feel it in her legs. When he pulled away, she took her glass, tipped the remaining icecube into her mouth and slowly used her tongue to push it into his. His eyes locked hers as he passed it back to her.

Then Richard tipped a handful of icecubes from his glass into his hand and ran them down her hot neck, over her bare shoulders, round the exposed rim of stomach, back to her face, into her mouth. Carrie's breath came faster. It was an amazing turn-on: her supercharged skin, the hot desire and freezing ice.

As Carrie thought of that first meeting, she felt a pale reflection of the original desire. That night, at Richard's flat, they had had controlled, then uncontrolled, sex. And drunk or not, they'd come back to each other twice more in the night, and again in the morning. Sore, hungover and weary, they had finally risen at noon with the unspoken knowledge that this was not a one-night stand. They were an item.

Since then Richard had fallen in love with her. They still had passionate sex, but the passion, she thought, was born of desperation rather than lust, the roughness more of jealousy than desire. And it was pretty irritating to be telephoned at 6 p.m. to be asked when you'd be home, or to feel your lover's eyes on you every minute you were together.

She needed a bit of time away from him. That was the truth. She'd told him her editor was too mean to pay for them both, and before he could say he'd pay his share, she'd said, 'I guess it's better anyway. I don't work as well with you around. We eat and drink too much, and fuck too much.'

Richard smiled. 'We could try not to.'

'No, really, I don't want you to come. My deadlines are hell. I have to file the first piece from Paris the day after I meet the guy. And the other three within a week.'

'Okay, sweetheart. But no jumping into bed with the boys in white.' He was trying to joke, but Carrie knew he was jealous of her chef friends. He was probably right to be worried. Some of them were pretty tasty. But still, why did he have to say it in that proprietorial manner? She'd never made him any promises.

The theme of the series was the takeover of posh Paris kitchens by the British. It would be fun to write, because all four chefs (one Irish, two Scottish – one a woman – and one English) were good. They could give the gastronomic frogs a run for their money. She'd tried hard to find a Welshman, but as far as she could see there weren't too many Welsh chefs outside Wales, and none in Paris.

Her first appointment was for lunch with Kevin O'Hearne. Thanks to the Eurostar being late and taxis at the Gard du Nord being non-existent, she hadn't time to drop her luggage off at the Hotel Berkeley. Even so, she didn't arrive at Kevin's restaurant until 1.45. Le Relais Irlandais, in the unfashionable 18th arrondissement, was somewhere between a brasserie and a bistro, and there was nowhere to store her Gucci holdall, which became a hurdle for every waiter passing her table.

But the food was good. Kevin O'Hearne was a big simple guy and he served big simple plates of Irish food. Carrie had worked for him once, years ago, when he'd been head chef of a Belfast hotel and she'd been hired to help him do the food for the hotel's brochure. What she remembered most about his cooking was how awful it looked and how wonderful it tasted, which is why he'd needed her. She also remembered that they'd gone to bed together and, full of Guinness, he'd fallen asleep during the trailer. What she couldn't remember was what happened when he woke up. Main feature or a blow-out? It was mildly embarrassing not to know.

His cooking was quite as good as she remembered. A great steaming lump of mutton (curiously called hoggit) came with a giant wedge of Savoy cabbage and waxy boiled potatoes in a bowl of broth. It looked like peasant fare, but the broth showed the skill of a master. It was crystal clear, completely free of fat, with a deep, aromatic, meaty flavour worthy of Escoffier.

The mutton fell from the bone, and the cabbage was emerald green, fresh and tender.

When she was on the pratie apple (a deep-fried apple dumpling made with potato pastry and served with treacle and thick Irish cream – heart attack food, but divine), Kevin joined her. He was red-faced from the heat of the kitchen, his ginger hair in damp points round his face, his apron filthy.

'Hi, me darlin',' he said, wiping his face with his torchon before kissing her. Carrie knew Kevin's real accent had only a hint of Ulster in it, but for some reason he liked to play the bog Irish yokel. He dumped two bottles of Murphy's on the table and sat down, tripping over her Gucci bag.

'Be-jasus, woman, what's this? Are you after staying for a week or somep'n?'

Carrie rubbed the fine tan leather where his chef's clogs had marked it. 'Clumsy bastard. You haven't changed, I see.'

Kevin grinned and dropped the stage Irish. 'Hope not. Hope you haven't either. You look as edible as ever.' His green eyes, shiny and round in his shiny round face, flashed at her. 'Any chance of a replay? I seem to remember I screwed up last time. You were a touch hostile at breakfast.'

Carrie smiled, unfazed. 'Forget it, friend. This time it's your cooking on trial.'

'Okay, fair enough. But if you change your mind . . . If you need a squire in Paris, I know some good haunts.'

It flashed through Carrie's mind that she might like an evening with him. His rough looks still attracted her. He had lovely eyes, hazel-green, the lashes much darker than his hair.

'Okay, Kev, thanks. I might take you up on that.'

Kevin put his great bearpaw over her hand, and she noticed the half-moon purple burns on the side of his wrist, and the black outlines to his fingernails.

Chefs generally had battered hands like this, the burns from the oven shelves as they slammed in trays and pans, the stained fingers from chopping mushrooms or onions, stoning cherries or peeling beetroot. Maybe that's why she found chefs so attractive: the combination of artist and artisan; the mix of style with a bit of rough.

Six

At 4 p.m. Carrie was back from the third of her Michelin Star restaurant sessions. As she rode the gilded lift to the third floor she thought how good a vodka and Coke in the bath would be. In the last two days she had interviewed three of the chefs, eaten their food, and supervised the photographing of their dishes, their restaurants, and themselves. She was knackered. Only one to go, the Englishman, and he worked here in the hotel.

Somehow she'd managed to file her copy on Kevin, and had been cheered by an e-mail from the food editor: 'Great piece. Kevin sounds as tasty as his hoggit. Pics perfect too.'

She'd drafted her articles on the two Scottish chefs, though they were not done yet. She wanted to finish them before the meals blurred into one great gastronomic binge.

She was exhausted. Eating that much was hard work, and because the chefs always wanted her to try half a dozen other dishes she had not ordered it took forever. Then, with stomach tight as a drum, and not exactly sober, she had to supervise the shoot, before going back to the Berkeley to write her copy and ring Lulu, her assistant-cum-head chef, left behind to cope with Carrie's Catering party clients. At least she didn't have to take the pics too. For some of the kitchen catalogues she worked for she was writer, stylist, cook and photographer.

She pushed open her bedroom door, and her heart sank. Her room was a total tip.

She walked to the telephone and dialled house-keeping. She spoke French, smiling into the handset. Could someone possibly come and service Room 21? Yes, she understood that the maid had not wanted to disturb her papers, but she'd sort them now. 'You are most kind, madam. I am very grateful.'

Carrie ordered a Diet Coke and a large vodka from room service, then whirled into action, scooping up menus and papers and stuffing them into the dressing table drawer, flinging dirty chef's whites and shoes into the cupboard, swinging into the bathroom to turn on the taps full blast. She stood on her trainers to force them off her feet, hauled her clothes off and kicked them after the others into the cupboard. She shrugged into the hotel's towelling robe, and again lifted the telephone. She dialled Kevin's mobile.

When he came on the line, she could hear the roar and clatter of his kitchen in the background. She said, 'I thought you had Thursday nights off?'

'I do. Just leaving. Why? Do you want to party?'

'I want you to come to the Berkeley and help me eat my way through Robert Hanlon's food.'

'Sounds good to me. What time?'

'Nine? In the bar?'

'You're on, lady.'

Carrie pressed the TV remote until the radio delivered some timeless French torch singer. Juliette Greco, she thought.

The maid and room service waiter arrived together. She overtipped them both, then carried her drinks into the bathroom, leaving the maid to do her best with the room.

Carrie sank into the blissful combination of warm water and music, groaning pleasurably as the ache of exhaustion receded. She tipped the vodka into the Diet Coke, and took a mouthful. God, this was good. And the job was nearly done. And she was earning a packet, getting three fees: for writing the article, for the food styling, and for supervising the photography. She had negotiated a decent whack because it was a rush job to replace a feature that the egomaniac magazine editor had suddenly taken against, and Carrie could deliver both copy and pictures. She knew the Paris restaurant scene, she spoke good French, and she could work fast.

This little burst of overwork would pay, she hoped, for a new van. The old Renault hatchback had carried so many copper saucepans, crates of silver and heavy-weight props that it was down to its axles, and no amount of scrubbing seemed to lift the faint smell of spilt food and olive oil. What Carrie wanted was a decent van and a separate car. Preferably a sports car with no room to carry any catering gear or props. A Porsche would be nice.

As she lay in the Givenchy bubbles and Piaf took over from Greco, Carrie examined her arms and hands, stretching them out before her in the steam, admiring them with narcissistic attention. Her skin was good, golden and smooth with not the slightest sign of wrinkly armpits or sagging upper arms. She looked as good as she had at twenty-two, ten long years ago. Maybe better, due to all that torture in the gym. And her hands, for all she was a cook, were pretty good. One bad scar, from years ago, where the boning knife had slipped. Of course cooking meant she had to keep her nails pretty short. Maybe she'd treat herself to a manicure. Metallic silver perhaps?

Her mind drifted back to Monday, after lunch, when she'd been helping Kevin make his great lumpy portions of food look camera-worthy. He'd looked with distaste at her surgical gloves and said, 'What the hell are you wearing those for? Do you think I'm going to poison you or something?'

'No. But I don't want hands like yours.' She'd held his fingers in her gloved ones and said, 'How do you get these clean, presuming you ever do?'

'Neat bleach.'

'Yeah. That's my point.'

Carrie took a lot of trouble with the way she looked, even to work. She wore chef's whites, but not any old whites. She ordered her trousers made-to-measure from the French chefs' supplier, Braggart. They had a tiny black and white houndstooth check, smart enough not to be recognizable as chef's pants at all.

They fitted snugly round her bum, and the straight narrow cut emphasized her long legs. And Bragard's jackets for women were double-stitched and perfectly cut.

But she didn't obey all the sartorial rules of the professional kitchen. If she'd worked for a hotel or a catering company, jewellery would have been out. She liked the glimpse of a single pearl on a silver wire, visible where she left the top button of her jacket undone. And she generally wore pearl stud earrings, or gold hoops.

I may be untidy, she thought, but I mostly look okay. And my hair's always clean. Which Poppy's isn't.

The thought of her sister clouded Carrie's face. Poppy was mad. She had the dishiest husband in the world and she didn't mind how she looked. She never dieted, she washed her hair in the shower and let it dry as it liked, she only wore make-up for the stage or when filming, and she was systematically tidy. She tidied up as their parents had taught her, and had failed to teach Carrie: as you went along, automatically, and all the time.

By five o'clock Carrie was feeling fine, and she decided she'd earned that manicure. Maybe a blow-dry too. The hotel salon was still open, and she spent a couple of hours in its perfumed calm. She emerged with her hair two inches shorter, the ends in soft seventies flick-ups, and her fingernails painted Cruella de Vil.

Carrie knew what she was doing when she invited Kevin to dinner. She didn't pretend, even to herself, that they would not end up in bed. As she walked down the marble stairs to the bar, her thoughts flicked uneasily to Richard, but only for a second. He didn't own her. She'd never made him any promises. And she wasn't proposing to fall in love with Kevin, just have a good time. Sex was like food. If you thought it was important, you took trouble to see that you got the best. And you couldn't live on the same food forever, however good it was. A bit of exotica made home fare the more welcome, anyway.

Kevin looked out of place in the plush and panelling of the Victoria Bar. The other customers were all middle-aged and upper-crust. Most were British – the Berkeley prided itself on its Englishness – or the sort of cosmopolitan French who shopped in Bond Street rather than the Rue du Faubourg-St-Honoré.

Carrie thought he looked good, even in imitation Armani worn with black sneakers and a collarless shirt. His strong square face, burly figure and explosive red curls had a dynamism she liked.

His eyes were impish as he asked the barman for a Black Velvet. The barman was nonplussed. Carrie translated, 'Guinness and champagne, half and half.' The barman's face registered first disbelief and then distaste.

'*Mais oui. C'est vrai,*' she said, and then, by way of explanation, '*Il est Irlandais.*' The barman smiled at Carrie, shrugging almost imperceptibly, and reached into the fridge for a can of draught Guinness. She turned to Kevin. 'You did that just to get him on the hop, didn't you? No one drinks Black Velvet any more.'

'Doubt if they ever drank it in Paris. But this place looks too rarefied to drink Guinness in, so I thought I'd cut it with the posh stuff.'

Kevin swallowed a mouthful. 'Aagh,' he said with exaggerated satisfaction. He wiped the foam from his top lip with the back of his hand and grinned at her. 'He's lucky. Where I come from Black Velvet is Guinness and cheap cider.'

They had a good dinner, Carrie taking care to stay sober enough to make notes on the food. Kevin had the foie gras. He said it was the true test of a great chef. You had to know what you were buying, then you had to clean it with infinite care, getting rid of every piece of membrane and thread of vein. Cooking it was a nightmare: too much heat for too long and all the fat ran out of it, not enough heat and it stayed raw and slimy.

Carrie didn't like the idea of geese being force-fed to make their livers fat, but Kevin just laughed. 'They love it. They are French geese. Very greedy.'

Carrie had poached turbot in a beurre blanc sauce flavoured with fresh ginger and green coriander berries, topped with an explosion of finely shredded and deep-fried spring onions. It was a triumph of 'fusion' food, the marrying of classic French cuisine with Eastern flavours. Such muddling did not often come off, but this was perfect.

'Try some,' she said. Kevin leaned over to scoop up some of her sauce with a piece of bread.

They continued to reach for each other's food and feed each other mouthfuls of their own with the concentration and appreciation of the professional. It was friendly and casual, and they both knew it was a prelude.

Then Eduardo walked into the dining room.

Carrie's first reaction was of amazement. She'd no idea her brother-in-law was in Paris. Then she thought that since he never stopped travelling it was hardly surprising. He'd be more surprised to see her. She said, 'Kevin. Guess what! My brother-in-law has just come in. Shall we ask him to join us?'

Kevin turned and looked at Eduardo, still talking to the maître d'hôtel, and said, 'That him at the desk?'

'Yes.'

'Well, if you want my vote, it's no. We've finished and we'd have to sit through him eating forever . . .'

Carrie, pleased and excited, interrupted. 'But he's really great. You'd love him . . .'

'And I think we have other things to do.' Kevin put out his big hand and touched her cheek. 'Look, I put them in bleach for you.'

Carrie glanced down as Kevin displayed his hands, holding them out over the table. They were perfectly clean, not a cut or wrinkle edged in grime. Carrie took one of his hands in hers and turned it over.

'You must have *scrubbed* them in neat bleach.'

'Sure I did.'

Carrie laughed and said, 'Yup, and they feel like it. Pure sandpaper.'

The brief distraction of Kevin's hands had taken Carrie's eyes off Eduardo, but now she looked back towards the entrance and saw Eduardo step forward to greet a thin tall young woman with a cloud of blonde hair. She looked vaguely familiar.

Eduardo kissed her cheek. Both cheeks. Then the first cheek again. Three kisses, French style. Then he reached to take the pale fox fur from her shoulders. Carrie registered her practised swirl as she turned her back to Eduardo for him to take the coat.

Carrie's thoughts came thick and muddled. No one would wear real fur in England. God, what a beautiful woman. And so *young*! Looks like a Botticelli angel. I'm sure I know her. Why is Eduardo with her? She adores him – you can see it in the way she tilted her face for his kiss. That blonde hair can't be natural.

Kevin was saying something, but Carrie's mind was on Eduardo's big familiar hand steering the girl through the small of her back. As the space narrowed between the tables, Eduardo dropped behind her and they followed the waiter single file. The blonde had a model's gait – bum tucked under, bony hips stuck forward and non-existent stomach to the fore.

They passed Carrie and Kevin's table but Eduardo didn't see them. Carrie's instinctive move to waylay him died as she caught his look. His eyes followed the gentle gyrations of his companion's bottom under the silk of her short skirt. That's lust, Carrie thought. His tongue is practically hanging out.

She stared in disbelief, and with mounting distress. It couldn't be . . . Eduardo would never . . .

When the couple arrived at their table, and the woman bent her head to hang her bag on the chair arm, Eduardo put his hand on the back of her neck, in the space between her round neckline and her froth of pale hair. Then Carrie knew for certain. It was a gesture so intimate, telling of such ownership and desire, that you couldn't misread it.

Kevin's voice made it through to her.

'Carrie, what's up?'

Carrie looked away from her brother-in-law and back at Kevin, her face unfocused, blank. And then she felt the prick of tears behind her eyes and looked away.

'Nothing.' She shook her head as though to clear it. 'It's nothing.'

Kevin looked across at Eduardo. 'That's one hell of a woman he's got there. Isn't it Michelle Ward?'

'Michelle Ward?' Even as he said it, Carrie knew he was right.

'The supermodel. You know. I'm sure it's her.'

'It can't be.' Even to Carrie, her statement sounded too final. Rude. But Kevin didn't notice.

'She comes into my place with the young movie crowd. Or sometimes with ageing rock stars. All sorts, but rich.'

Carrie said nothing. She was having trouble concen-

93

trating. She was suddenly angry. What the hell did Eduardo think he was doing playing away from home? She had a clear picture of Poppy with Lorato on her back, baking home-made focaccia because Eduardo didn't like the shop stuff.

She said, her voice hard, controlled, 'Let's have another bottle.'

'Sure.' Kevin signalled the sommelier and gave the order. Then he leaned back in his chair and said, 'C'mon, Carrie. Give.'

Carrie looked across at Eduardo's table. She could not see his face, but the woman was in semi-profile. Her straight nose, wide mouth, dark eyes and flawless complexion were right out of a glossy mag. Her fuzzy curls were turned into a halo by the light behind her, and she was laughing, relaxed and happy.

'Tell, Carrie,' insisted Kevin.

'That bastard is cheating on my sister,' Carrie said.

'Lucky guy. Who wouldn't with a number like that?' Then he looked into her face, blank with pain. He tried again, 'You don't know that. Could be a business associate.'

Carrie jerked her head, impatient. 'No chance.'

The waiter poured them both another glass, and Carrie took a couple of large, slightly uncontrolled gulps. 'I can't believe it. He's always on the moral high ground. Always at Poppy about how I have no "moral core". That I sleep around. That I'm selfish. That I'm vain. Jesus, what a jerk.'

'Hey, Carrie, you are over-reacting a bit here. Your

94

brother-in-law has a bit of posh totty on a trip to Paris. What's the big deal?'

Carrie was drinking fast, her face flushed with a combination of alcohol and anger. 'You don't understand.' For a moment she looked as though she might cry, then she shook her head. 'But why should you? Let's forget them.'

For the rest of the bottle – and it didn't take long – she tried not to look across at Eduardo's table. She tried to talk about other things, whether this place deserved its star rating, whether she could get the photographer to give Kevin a few prints of the pics he'd taken at Le Relais Irelandais, but it was hard work. The fun had gone out of the evening and she'd have liked Kevin to go home.

Carrie signed the bill and they stood up. She had decided she'd leave the dining room without alerting Eduardo to her presence at all, but that table across the room drew her attention like a magnet. Suddenly she changed her mind and walked fast towards the table.

Kevin tried to stop her, 'Hey Carrie, give the guy a break . . .'

'Fuck that.' By now she was almost on them. 'Eduardo!' she said. The blonde model looked up, surprised, her perfect mouth open. Eduardo swung round.

If she'd needed any confirmation of her brother-in-law's infidelity, his face provided it now. He opened his mouth. Shut it again. Said, 'Carrie!' Stood up so hurriedly an empty glass fell over. Then he said, 'Good Lord.' And, 'This is . . . er . . . What a surprise.'

Carrie didn't answer. She didn't know what to say. She didn't know why she'd come over.

Eduardo rallied, regaining composure. 'Carrie. How amazing. What are you doing in Paris?' He stretched his arms out to take her shoulders, intending to kiss her, but Carrie jerked back.

While he'd been trying to right the glass, stuttering and confused, Carrie had felt almost sorry for him, but the speed with which he resumed his charming in-control self infuriated her. She felt her face flush red and hot, and she had a burning feeling, a lump of fury, in her chest. She said, her voice hard and loud, 'More to the point, brother-in-law, what are *you* doing in Paris?'

Neighbouring diners looked up, curious. Carrie was having trouble staying upright. I'm drunk, she thought. Well, too bad. Kevin tried to put his arm round her, but she flung it off with an angry jerk.

Eduardo's voice was low and steady, 'I'm on business. Let me introduce you. This is Michelle Ward, an old friend.'

'Old friend?' mocked Carrie. 'Not very *old*. Seventeen, is she?' Carrie swayed over the young woman, pushing her anguished face into the model's perfect heart-shaped one. 'Like older men, do you? Other people's husbands?'

Michelle Ward's brow furrowed and her eyes, at first wide with alarm, narrowed. She looked scornfully at Carrie, up and down, then turned her eyes, cool and questioning, to Eduardo. She did not say a word.

Carrie was very drunk, but not so drunk that she did not know she was making an idiot of herself. Or rather this . . . this . . . juvenile was making an idiot of her. The girl's composure was worse than her beauty or her youth.

She could not stop. 'Well, I guess this non-speaking babe is a few years older than Angelina, anyway.'

By now Kevin had both his big arms round Carrie, pinning hers to her sides. 'Sorry mate, we're leaving.' Two waiters appeared to hustle Kevin and Carrie towards the door.

In the foyer, Kevin said, 'C'mon, lass. Bed now. You're pissed.'

But Carrie was still angry, burning with the humiliation of what she'd done and her fury at the super-model's refusal to speak. She shook free of Kevin and walked fast – to disguise the unsteadiness – to the reception desk. Resigned, he followed her.

The young man looked up from his computer. 'What can I do for you, madam?'

Carrie, steadying herself on the mahogany desk, said very carefully, 'Can you tell me if Mrs Eduardo Santolini has checked in yet?'

The young man tapped his keys, looked up and said, 'Mr and Mrs Santolini. Yes, they are in the hotel. Would you like me to ring their suite for you?'

So it was true. A suite too. What a bastard. The

receptionist looked inquiringly at her, and asked again, 'Shall I try Mrs Santolini for you?'

'No, no thanks.' Carrie felt her throat tighten and a great sob collect in it. With a wobbly intake of breath she turned to Kevin. 'What's the matter with me?' she asked.

'You're drunk as a fiddler's fart,' he said.

Seven

Carrie was having a fraught morning. She'd overslept, and Lulu was on holiday. Her mother had rung three times in ten minutes, each time to say thank you for the birthday flowers. They had, of course, been sent by Poppy, though the gift tag bore both their names. After the third call Carrie rang Adrienne and asked her to throw away the card. If it stayed where it was her mother would read it anew every time she passed the vase and ring one of her daughters with thanks.

Then the shower head had come apart in Carrie's hands. And she'd had to do without toothpaste because for the third day running she'd forgotten to buy any, and even stamping on the tube would no longer produce a smudge of paste. And when she got downstairs Richard announced that he'd dropped the answerphone and it was now kaput. Carrie clenched her jaw in irritation. She said, 'Don't you have work to go to?'

He'd looked up, surprised at the snap in her voice. 'I'm only due on site at ten. And since I'm away tonight, I thought we'd have a civilized breakfast for once.'

Carrie grabbed a tray and started banging the cafe-tière, Richard's cereal bowl, half-full mug and toast plate on to it. 'Did you now? Well, sorry, I need the table.'

Carrie shoved the sugar basin on to the tray, and added the milk carton, setting it awkwardly on the cereal bowl. Then she swung away. The movement was too fast, and the milk carton fell over, spouting an arc of milk over her arm and on to the floor.

Richard, still sitting with a piece of toast in one hand, lunged for the carton, catching it with his free hand and righting it as it hit the floor. He looked up at her, pleased with himself. It had been a spectacular save, and most of the milk was still in the carton.

Carrie dismissed his boyish look. 'Could you just go, Richard? Please. I need you out of here.' She wiped her arm and the floor with a J-cloth, and turned her back on him to stack the dishwasher.

'Okay, okay, I'm going. But Carrie, what's up?'

'Nothing.' She was making no effort to disguise her impatience. 'Nothing. And anyway I've no time to discuss it. Not everyone can start work at ten.'

Richard frowned slightly, his expression a mixture of hurt and concern. 'Okay, but darling, I'm not an idiot. You've been snapping my head off ever since you got back from Paris.' Carrie didn't answer. She drummed her fists on the sink edge, glared at the ceiling and let out a clenched-teeth moan.

Richard walked out of the door, saying, 'If you want to discuss it, I'll see you tomorrow night. Or you could ring me in Manchester. The number's on the pad.'

When he'd gone, Carrie felt a small cloud of

remorse. She watched him through the kitchen window, zapping his car with the electronic key, throwing his overnight bag into the back seat. His face was set, hurt and offended.

But what did he expect? Archetypal bloody male. Men always assumed their work was important and yours wasn't.

By nine the table was strewn with soft fondant roses, lace ribbons, icing tubes, greaseproof paper, a bowl of icing, pencil, ruler and compass. The three tiers of a Victorian wedding cake were covered in smooth white icing. You'd never guess they were made of polystyrene.

The cake – due at the studios for some long-frock drama tomorrow – was starting to take shape. She held the paper icing cone in her right hand and steadied the tip with her left forefinger. Thin even lines of white icing quickly built up to make the delicate half-moons of trellis spaced round the edges of the cakes. The tiers were different sizes and Carrie adjusted the sizes of her decorations, and the distances between them, with mathematical precision.

As she worked she kept the bowl of royal icing covered with a doubled damp J-cloth to prevent it forming a crust. When her icing cone was empty, she took another square of greaseproof paper from the stack and, working fast and expertly, folded it into another one. She extracted the metal writing nozzle from the spent icing bag, and dropped it, point first, into the new one. Snipping off the paper point, she shook the nozzle down so that its tip protruded, then spooned a tablespoon of icing deep into the bag. She held the bag tight round the spoon so she could drag it out clean, then folded the paper edges down to seal the top. Finally, she squeezed a test length of icing on to the marble slab. Perfect. Moist enough not to break, dry enough to hold its shape. She lifted the top tier on to the turntable. She was proud of the shiny smoothness of its final coat, which had gone on liquid. It was rare to get the surface so faultless: smooth as silk, and not a bubble.

Royal icing was more trouble than fondant, which you could buy ready-made, but for tiered cakes, with the layers separated by columns, she preferred the reliable concrete of royal.

Cake icing was calming. She could do it on auto-pilot. It required just enough concentration to stop her thinking of Richard, or of Eduardo and her sister. She worked quietly, feeling a lot better.

When the telephone rang she thought, Damn, I can't stop now, and went on to finish the last lines of trellis. The ringing stopped, and Carrie started carefully to position the fondant roses between the crescents of trellis, glueing each into place with a blob of icing. The telephone rang again, and this time she picked it up.

It was Richard. 'Darling, I'm so sorry.'

'What about?'

'About being so off with you. I know you are frantic this morning. I should have thought.'

Carrie's reaction was an instant return of irritation. What was with the guy? Why was he so wet? All he'd done was get an earful from her, and *he* was on the phone apologizing to *her*.

'Yeah, well, I'm sorry too. But I've got to go now. I'm in the middle of icing this cake and I can't stop.' She put the telephone down.

As soon as she'd picked up the icing bag in one hand and a fondant rose in the other, it rang again. She dropped the icing bag, snatched the phone up and barked, 'Richard, for Christ's sake. I told you. I'm busy.' And she slammed back the receiver.

Almost at once it rang again. Carrie lunged for it, picked it up, and banged it down. The next time it rang she pressed the ansaphone button, then remembered Richard had wrecked it. She yanked the telephone lead out of the wall, then reached into the open basket that served as her work handbag and switched off her mobile too.

The calm mood instilled by the therapy of cake-icing had gone now. She was worried that one of her customers might want to get through, and she was beginning to feel bad about Richard. She restored the two telephones and finished icing the cakes, then carried them carefully into the dining room. They could dry out on the big table, where no one was likely to damage them. She'd deliver them early tomorrow and assemble the tiers at the studio.

By noon she had a severe case of guilty conscience. She'd been a right cow. She telephoned Richard's office, but he was still on the building site. She dialled his mobile.

'Richard, it's me.'

'Oh, hi darling.' His voice was cheerful, his normal self. A flicker of irritation overlaid her contrition. Why wasn't he cross with her?

'Look, I'm sorry, but every time you telephoned I had to stop icing that damn cake.'

'What do you mean every time? I only rang once.'

'Only once!'

'Yes.'

'Oh no!'

'What? Why "Oh no"?'

Carrie started to laugh. She had a mental picture of one of her truly grand customers, the overbearing Duchess of Oakhampton perhaps, as the telephone was slammed down on her.

She told Richard about switching off the telephones, and said, 'I guess it serves me right if I miss a load of good business. But I am sorry I was so ratty.'

'Oh Carrie, I do prefer you laughing to growling. See you tomorrow.'

'Fine. And good luck tomorrow.' He was going to see the Manchester city-planning department about Eduardo's plans for the new leisure centre.

She restored both mobile and landline and started on the pile of veg. She chargrilled slices of courgette on the lava-brick grill while simultaneously tossing chunks of orange pumpkin in cinnamon oil in a giant wok. She'd been hard at it for half an hour when the telephone sprang into life again. Good, she thought. Thank God for persistent customers.

'Carrie, it's Eduardo. I've got to see you.'

Her stomach did a flip. Eduardo. Carrie did not want to talk to Eduardo. She was still angry with him. She resented the need to keep his secret, having to be cagey with Poppy. She'd avoided going round to see her, and had only spoken to her once, briefly, since she'd got back. She'd said nothing of seeing Eduardo in Paris. Which might not be lying, but it was close.

'Hello, Eduardo. Why so urgent?' She knew the answer of course. Eduardo was into damage limitation here. He wanted her to promise to keep quiet.

But Carrie wanted him to suffer a bit. She'd no intention of telling Poppy what she'd seen, but that was for Poppy's sake, not Eduardo's. A bit of begging would be good for the arrogant sod.

Eduardo said, 'What are you doing tonight? Can I come round?'

'No. I'm working. I've got a photo shoot this afternoon, and I don't think we'll finish early.'

'We? Who is we? I thought you took your own pics?'

He sounded as if he didn't believe her. He thinks I'm fobbing him off, thought Carrie. Good. Let him sweat. 'Not always. I only take pics if the client is too cheap to hire someone better.'

'Fine. That's perfect. I'll come round at 9 p.m., and if you aren't finished I'll wait.'

'But Eduardo, it may be much later . . .'

Eduardo cut her off.

'Look, Carrie, I'm coming to see you. Okay?' And he hung up.

That evening, working on the shoot, Carrie mostly forgot about Eduardo. Nick, the photographer, was the best, and they worked well together. His pictures had a magical quality, something that made you gaze at them for longer than you'd usually look at pictures of food.

Gastroporn was how he described it.

He took enormous pains, fussing over the tiniest detail. Lighting his subject took forever, and by the time he was happy with his sunlight streaming through the kitchen louvres or with the soft glow of tallow candlelight, Carrie would be dissatisfied with the lack of shine on the grilled edge of tomato or the plumpness of a chicken breast, or she'd want to redo the salad because the curled fists of lamb's lettuce were looking tired. One way and another, it took a long time.

By 9.15, when the doorbell rang, they were only halfway through the last set-up.

Carrie opened the front door. Eduardo kissed her on both cheeks in his usual way, and she let him, thinking she would embarrass them both if she made a thing about it. She led him into the kitchen and said, 'Nick, this is my brother-in-law, Eduardo.' Nick ducked under the giant silver umbrella and a spotlight on a tripod to extend his hand. Eduardo had to lean over the jumble of photography equipment to shake it.

'Nick, Eduardo can sit on the sofa and watch, can't he?'

'Sure. No problem.'

Carrie gave Eduardo a bottle of red and a glass, and went back to tipping browned pumpkin into the cast-iron karahi. The shot was going to be good. It was for an Indian cookery book and was of a half-made pan of kaddu mulai, set on a trivet on her battered wooden table. She'd added slivers of cooked onion, shiny and brown, shreds of fresh green and red chillies, and a handful of coriander leaves. Then she'd turned the ingredients carefully to look as though they'd been tossed and stirred in the pan, not carefully positioned.

Nick took test shots with his ancient Polaroid, warming them in his armpit to speed up development, peeling off the backing, consulting with Carrie. At last they were both happy with everything: lighting, food, props, design. The actual shooting of each set-up took less than two minutes: click click click, in three different exposures.

'That's it,' said Nick. 'It's a wrap.'

'Thank God for that,' said Carrie. 'Here, have a jar.' She picked up the bottle from Eduardo's feet, and poured two more glasses.

In half an hour Nick had packed his gear and gone, and Carrie had cleaned up the kitchen. Now she'd have to let Eduardo have his say.

For a minute she stalled. She was tired. The wine was sending relaxing messages from inside out. She'd really like to order a pizza and pig out in front of the television for an hour, then fall into bed.

'Shall we go into the sitting room?' she said.

'I like it here,' said Eduardo. She followed his gaze round the familiar room. Since she worked in it almost every day, and she and Richard practically lived in it, she had ceased to look at it, but now she saw it afresh.

It was a big space, made by knocking the front and back rooms together. The two halves were furnished in distinct styles. The cooking end, with windows that gave on to the street, was all stainless steel efficiency, with the latest in commercial kit. This end, with French windows on to the garden, was country-cottagey, with pine dresser, Spanish plates, sofa covered in an Indian throw and a big old table that had once been in a Victorian dairy. There was an Aga cooker with a double wrought-iron pot rack above that housed copper pans of every size and shape, and from which hung various old-fashioned skimmers and strainers, whisks and ladles. The Aga wasn't on. Carrie cooked in the modern end, but the old stove was useful for photography backgrounds or when she was so busy she needed all the ovens. In the corner was a stink-wood chest she'd brought from Africa. It had claw and ball feet and ornate brass handles and hinges.

Carrie sat at the table and said, 'Have you eaten? I'm up for a pizza, if you are.'

'Can't we eat some of that lovely stuff you were photographing?'

'You can. I've been smelling and tasting it all day, and I'd rather bin it.'

'Carrie, you can't.'

In the end they had a sort of picnic, Eduardo eating the curried pumpkin with two fried eggs on top, and Carrie eating cream cheese spread on bread with a dollop of pesto and a lot of salad. They ate at a corner of the big table, and opened another bottle of red wine.

Carrie knew she should summon up her previous anger, ready to do battle for her sister, but the food and wine had this mellowing effect and Eduardo was at his most charming. He said, admiration in his voice, 'Carrie, I've never seen you working before. You're really good.'

'Of course I'm good!'

'Okay, okay, but I've never seen it! Of course I know you're a good cook. But watching you is something else.'

'Why?' Carrie knew that this was a charm offensive, but she liked it. To have impressed the ever critical Eduardo was something.

'It's the way you go about it. So economically. Never a move wasted. You carry things this way and that, change this, fix that, toss the next thing, all in an apparent whirl but with no sense of muddle.' He half patted, half stroked her shoulder. 'You are a well-oiled cooking machine.'

Carrie laughed. 'Cooking machine maybe. Well oiled, not enough.' She reached for the bottle. Partly she wanted to fill her glass, but she also wanted to make him drop his hand from her shoulder. She wasn't going to let him get off scot-free. She took a breath and plunged in, 'So why are you cheating on Poppy?'

Eduardo looked as if he was ready for that. He gave a fractional shake of his head. 'Carrie, that's why I wanted to see you. I know that's what you thought . . .'

Carrie interrupted, her tone cynical 'Oh. And I thought wrong?'

Eduardo turned to face her more directly, his forehead creased, dark eyes earnest.

'Yes, you did. I've known Michelle Ward for ages. She's just a friend.'

Carrie wanted to believe him. He looked so believable, his eyes troubled and sincere, but she knew he was lying. She opened her mouth but he got in first.

'Carrie, I love your sister. We have a great marriage. I wouldn't do that to her.'

Carrie began to get angry. It was obvious he thought she'd be a pushover. 'Don't give me that crap, Eduardo. Do you think I'm blind or something?'

'Carrie, she is . . .'

'Bollocks.' Carrie could feel control going out of the window. She stood up and leaned over the table. 'And that's why you were registered as Mr and Mrs Santolini, I suppose? In a suite?' Her voice was rising.

Eduardo's face went blank. She'd hit home there all right. She waited for him to say something, but he didn't. Now she was shouting, 'That's how you treat all your old friends is it? With champagne in a bucket by the bedside?' Anger made her fluent. The words came out slick and perfect. 'With fancy dinners for two in Michelin Star restaurants? When did you last give Poppy dinner at Pizza Express, never mind a weekend in Paris?' She spun away from him, then back again.

Eduardo stood up. He put his arms out as if to take her by the shoulders, but she dodged back, face on fire. He said, voice steady, 'Carrie, try to understand . . . Poppy is so busy with Lorato and . . .'

Carrie cut him off, shouting, 'So you have to screw some bimbo because Poppy is a good wife? A good mother? Is that it? Next minute you'll be telling me your wife doesn't understand you.'

Eduardo's expression hardened. So did his voice. 'Carrie, I do not have to account to you. I came to see you because I hoped you would not make trouble with Poppy. But I see you are determined to play the righteous sister.'

'Well, that makes a change from your being the righteous brother-in-law, doesn't it? Always preaching about my life. At least I'm bloody honest about it. Not sneaking off "on business" so I can have a bit of rumpy pumpy on the sly.'

'Oh no? So that Irish muscleman you were with was an old friend too, was he? Old friend of Richard's perhaps?'

For a second Carrie stood nonplussed, then she took a breath to shout at him again, tell him that she wasn't married to Richard, that she hadn't slept with Kevin, that she wasn't the slag he thought she was, but Eduardo didn't give her time. He turned and headed for the door.

Suddenly that was exactly what Carrie did not want him to do. She cried out, 'Eduardo!'

He turned back, eyes weary, questioning. Then he shook his head ever so slightly, and put out his hand to touch her sleeve. It was a gesture of resignation and tenderness. I can't explain, it said, and you don't want to hear. Then he turned away again.

Carrie knew she was going to cry, and that made her furious all over again. How dare he refuse to explain? How dare he walk out now? She ran at his back, fists flailing at his body. Even as she was doing it, she thought how childish and how ineffectual. Eduardo was a big man, and his body was hard and impervious under the cotton shirt. He just stood there at the door, not even facing her, while she let fly at his back and shoulders. When all energy had gone from her punches and she was sobbing out loud, he turned round and put his arms round her, clamping her arms to her sides.

'Carrie, Carrie, stop now.' He spoke to her as he might to a wild animal, his voice deep and calming. She tried to pull away, but he wouldn't let her.

She was still sobbing and yelling at the same time, 'How could you? Eduardo, how could you? Poppy lives for you.'

He didn't answer, just said, 'Shhh, shhhh, it's okay,' and pressed her head into his chest.

Carrie fought away from him, lifting her face to

stutter, 'I thought you were different. I worshipped you, you bastard.' She was still crying, her face distorted with anguish.

He just held on to her, very close. Gradually she stopped snivelling. She could feel the dampness of his cotton shirt where she'd been crying, feel the warmth of his body, breathe the soapy smell of him. It flashed into her mind that it would be nice to just stay like this, leaning on him, smelling him.

And then she realized that what she was feeling was desire. Oh God, no. I can't, she thought. That's evil. She leaned back, looking up at him in distress.

He let her back away enough to see her clearly, then said, 'It's all right, it's all right.' His eyes held hers. She couldn't look away, trapped like a rabbit in the headlights. Then he dropped his face slowly on to hers, his mouth on her hot cheeks, kissing her tear tracks. She thought, Oh God, this is all wrong. Jesus, it feels so good. Maybe it's all right, he's just comforting me like a brother. Maybe it's just me that's randy. He kissed her eyes, first one, then the other. Her insides dissolved with longing. Then he was kissing her mouth, which felt divine under his, swollen from crying and lust. Oh Jesus.

Then they went at each other as if it was a fight. As soon as Carrie responded to his kiss, as soon as her arms went up around his neck and her mouth opened, Eduardo unfastened the strings of her big white apron, tied in front, unwound them and yanked the apron away. His mouth was on hers as he undid the buttons

113

of her chef's coat. They were stud buttons in a double row and his violence sent a couple of them clicking across the floor. Then he pulled the cuff of one sleeve and she spun round so he could pull the jacket off.

She undid the top two buttons of his shirt, and glued her mouth to his neck. She lost patience with the other buttons and pushed his shirt up so she could kiss his chest. He pulled the shirt off over his head, and she had a clear run at his body. Her hands were everywhere, exploring him, caressing his armpits, biceps, his belly. She pushed her body against his, and he forced his hand up under her bra. The feel of his big hand on her tit and the way the bra elastic tightened round her other breast and round her back forced a groan of longing from her. He undid her bra, dropped it on the floor and led her to the sofa.

Within seconds they were both naked, his trousers lying on top of her chef's checks on the floor. He pushed her back on the sofa with the words, 'Christ, Carrie, you are beautiful.' She felt beautiful, beautiful and powerful. She arched her back, her arms behind her head, then stretched towards him, an open invitation.

But the sofa was too short, and they slid together to the floor. It was a swift, unceremonious coupling. When it was over they lay together, heaving, and Carrie felt a great wave of content. As Eduardo rolled off her, and sat leaning against the sofa, she felt nothing but lassitude and fulfilment. He's right, she thought, I'm an immoral cow. But I don't care.

Eight

'Do you mind if we go through the carwash?'

Carrie craned forward to look at the old Espace's bonnet and said, 'No problem. You do seem to have collected half the mud of Oxfordshire.'

Poppy headed for the filling station. 'I know. Who would have thought I'd become a Pony Club mum?'

'Is that what you've been doing? Pulling the pony trailer?' said Carrie.

'I have. I can even reverse in a field without jack-knifing the thing now, which means the other horsey mothers deign to talk to me. I tell you, the Heythrop Pony Club is more of a challenge for me than for Angelina.'

Carrie looked at her placid, no-make-up sister with affection and thought that it would take more than a county squire's lady to put Poppy down. Poppy went on, 'Angelina wants to marry a horse when she grows up. In the meantime, she's content to drool over fences at them, plait their tails, oil their hooves and spend weekends camping with them in muddy fields.'

Carrie turned round to look at her niece in the back seat, but Angelina had her earphones on and her eyes shut. Her lips were moving and her head nodded to the beat. On each side of her Lorato and Tom were strapped into child seats. Tom was asleep. Lorato met Carrie's gaze with her usual unflickering stare.

Poppy swung the car into the filling station forecourt. 'Remember those Basuto ponies we had? Mafuta and Thabili? That was fun, wasn't it?'

'I don't think we'd have won any Pony Club rosettes though,' said Carrie. 'As I remember we hardly ever groomed them, we didn't clean their tack and we mostly rode them bareback.'

Poppy smiled at the memory. She drove into the carwash and turned to check that Angelina was still lost to her Walkman. She dropped her voice and said, 'One day I'll buy myself a horse so I can ride with Angelina. She longs to have her pony at Manor Farm instead of at the riding stables. I'd love to do it now, but there's talk of a big West End part. Eduardo thinks I should take it.'

Carrie's immediate thought was that Eduardo had said nothing to her. And why was he encouraging Poppy to take a job? It was much better when Poppy stayed at Manor Farm, leaving London and Eduardo to her. 'What's the part?'

'Filumena. At the Gielgud. Great role. Not bad money. It's tempting.'

'Filumena?' Carrie had never heard of it, but while she asked the question her mind was dashing along its own track: with Poppy in town it would be hard for her and Eduardo to get any whole nights together. He'd have to invent more trips abroad. On the other hand, Poppy would be safely at the theatre six nights out of seven. Carrie hauled her thoughts back to what Poppy was saying.

'Italian comedy by de Felippo. Filumena is a feisty ex-whore who tricks a rich old boy into marrying her. It's a wonderful part. Perfect for me.'

Carrie smiled. It was true. Poppy had this extraordinary power on stage. She could be anything she wanted to be: beautiful, mad, whacky, wonderful.

Poppy swiped her credit card through the carwash slot and punched the Full Wash and Wax button. There was a low roar, then the great pink and purple brushes of the carwash began their predatory progress up the sides of the car.

Carrie snuggled back into the passenger seat and said, raising her voice over the noise of the machine, 'I love carwashes, don't you? Reminds me of hail on our tin roof at Kaia Moya. Quite a turn-on really. Imagine being trapped in here with Brad Pitt.'

She was interrupted by a scream from behind. Both women swung round to see Lorato cowering in her seat, her hands flailing. She was yelling and crying, her eyes wide and filled with horror.

'Oh my God! I didn't think,' said Poppy, frantically trying to undo her own seatbelt so she could get to the child. But Carrie was quicker. Unencumbered by a steering wheel she knelt up, leaned through the gap between the front seats and released Lorato. She hauled the little girl into the front and handed her to Poppy.

By now Tom was crying too. Angelina pulled off her

117

headphones and said, 'Mummy, what's the matter? What's happening?'

Carrie caught the anxiety in her voice and, raising her own voice to be heard above the din, said, 'Lorato is frightened of the carwash. Can you look after Tom? Let him out and hold him, okay?'

Angelina did as she was told. She let Tom climb on to her lap and shouted, 'Why don't we stop it, then?'

Poppy looked round wildly to see how to stop the machine, but she couldn't find a stop button. And you couldn't just drive out of the tunnel, because now huge roller brushes were bashing the bonnet, steadily and inexorably rising to the windscreen.

Lorato saw them too, the great pink strings flailing the screen, flying in the wind, beating the car. She screamed and plunged her face into Poppy's neck, then immediately jerked her head back and swivelled round to watch the brushes, her eyes wide with terror. She screamed, 'No, no! Go 'way.'

Poppy said, 'I've got to get her out of here,' and opened her door. Clutching the child to her front, Poppy ducked under the giant roller, now raping the roof, and ran through a deluge of water and out of the carwash.

Carrie leaned over and pulled Poppy's door shut, just as the side rollers descended again for another onslaught on the sides. Through the soapy-streaked windscreen she could see her sister, her hair in sodden strings, walking back and forth on the sunny forecourt, rocking Lorato like an infant, one hand over the child's head, the other round her bum.

It wasn't the first time Lorato had freaked at loud noise. Carrie remembered the scene in Hyde Park when a helicopter had come over to land in the grounds of Kensington Palace, and Lorato had cowered, whimpering, between Poppy's legs. And the time she, Carrie, had been unable to get Lorato past a pneumatic drill making a hole in the pavement. Lorato must have some subliminal memories of war in Mozambique, thought Carrie. Or maybe the noise triggered memories of her father's death. She watched as Poppy crouched down, set the child on her feet, talked to her.

As the great roller brushes were hoisted out of sight and the noise quieted, Angelina said, 'Carrie, did you hear? Lorato spoke.' But Carrie wasn't listening. She was shuffling across to the driver's side, and wondering if she should wait for the wax and hot-air dry programme, or whether to just drive out and collect Poppy and Lorato.

Angelina repeated, 'Carrie, Lorato said, "No, No," and "Go away." In English.'

This time Carrie heard and turned to Angelina. 'Good Lord, you're right. She did, didn't she?'

Carrie looked out again. Poppy was now sitting on the low concrete wall that ran round the perimeter of the filling station, and Lorato was standing between her jean-clad legs. Poppy was drying her glasses on a hanky and Lorato was hanging on to Poppy's shirt as she pressed her face into her stomach.

Carrie watched as Poppy looked up at the approach of a man in filling station uniform. His face was anxious, fearing a complaint. Hers was shining with relief, happiness and a drenching.

Richard was becoming a pain. Once she'd fallen in love with Eduardo, Carrie had dumped him, but she hadn't told him why.

For weeks he had telephoned, come round, written e-mails and faxes, even letters. But finally he'd given up. Must have realized, thought Carrie, that the more he pleaded the more I went off him. Poor guy. It would have been easier for him if he'd known there was someone else. Being ditched with nebulous excuses about needing more space must be pretty hurtful.

But now he'd rumbled the truth, and Carrie was both ashamed of herself for lying to him and also frightened. Who knew what Richard would do? A man scorned might be quite as dangerous as a woman.

The cat had got out of the bag one day at Eduardo's office. She'd met Richard on the forecourt as she was coming out and he was going in.

His face brightened at the sight of her. Oh God, thought Carrie, he thinks I've been looking for him. She said quickly, 'Hi, Richard. I thought you were in Manchester.'

His face clouded. 'I was. Just back.' He stood still for a second, confused, then said, 'Did you want something? Here, I mean?' His head jerked at the studio and offices behind her.

'No, no. Or rather I did. I've just come to collect something from Eduardo.'

Richard looked puzzled. And Carrie realized she was carrying nothing except a minuscule handbag on a long leather thong over her shoulder – not much more than a purse. She said, rather too hastily, 'A credit card,' and patted the bag. Then she thought that Richard would think Eduardo giving her a credit card was very odd. She added, 'For Poppy. I'm meeting her for lunch.'

Richard, frowning, said, 'Aren't Poppy and the children in the country?'

Oh God, thought Carrie, I'd forgotten that. She said, walking towards her car, 'Yes, they are, I'm going down there now.' She fished her car key out of the bag and turned to wave.

Richard walked after her. 'But it's 12.15 now. You'll be much too late for lunch . . .'

Carrie, out of plausible responses, snapped. 'For Christ's sake, Richard, what is this? The Inquisition?' She clicked the electronic key and yanked the driver's door open with a jerk.

Richard put out an arm to stop her sliding into the driver's seat, and said, 'Hey Carrie, I'm sorry. What's the matter? I was only asking . . .'

'But it's none of your business, is it?' said Carrie, making an effort to keep her voice down and speaking through locked teeth. Richard dropped his arm at once and stepped back to make way for her to get into the car. She flung herself behind the wheel and shut the door with unnecessary force, then drove off, eyes straight ahead. Richard looked after her, perplexed.

Two streets away, Carrie stopped the car. She fished out her mobile phone and keyed in Eduardo's direct line.

'Eduardo Santolini.'

Relief flowed like cool balm through Carrie. 'Oh darling, I am so glad I've got you. I've done such a dumb thing.'

'Oh?' His voice was unruffled, rather distant. 'What then? Did you forget something?'

Carrie dashed at her story about meeting Richard downstairs.

Eduardo interrupted her: 'Calm down, Carrie. I'm sorry, I wasn't concentrating. Can you start again? You need a credit card? Or Poppy does? But what has that got to do with Richard?'

Carrie's voice rose, 'Eduardo, please listen. He'll be in the office by now. Just remember you've given me a credit card for Poppy and I'm setting off for Oxfordshire . . .'

But he interrupted her again, 'Oh, Richard has just walked in, Carrie, so he can explain . . . Richard, Carrie's on the phone . . .'

The fingers of one hand clutched at her scalp as Carrie, torn between shouting to make Eduardo understand and whispering to prevent Richard hearing, hissed into her handset, 'No, Eduardo. *Don't* talk to Richard. Don't. Do you understand? I've got to explain first.'

Suddenly there was a change in the quality of Eduardo's voice. He sounded much clearer, less echoing, and Carrie knew at once he'd been talking to her with the loudspeaker on, and had just turned it off. He said, 'Richard's just walked out again. How odd. Carrie, what's going on? Is there something between you two again?'

Carrie saw it all. Eduardo, who still sometimes liked to draw in the old-fashioned way with a pencil and drawing paper on an architect's drawing table, must have kept his private line on 'hands-free'. Which meant Richard had heard everything she said. Of course he'd walked out.

'Carrie? You still there?'

Suddenly she felt weary and tearful. She repeated her tale, feeling more foolish every second. Eduardo said, which hurt, that maybe she should stay away from the office. Sure he liked seeing her, but she came more now than when she was with Richard and had a legitimate reason. He also thought she was drama-mongering. He said Richard had probably been as confused as he was. Just forget it, he said.

But she couldn't forget it. Eduardo obviously thought she'd created the situation unnecessarily. And it was true. Why had she felt obliged to tell Richard anything? She should have just given him a cheerful wave and left him standing.

She crouched over the steering wheel, hugging her stomach and rocking in the confined space between wheel and seatback, her mind spinning from one unpleasant thought to another, buffeting about, trying to find a way out, a solution.

She wasn't cut out for adultery: she hated the secrecy, the plotting, the inevitable tangled web. If only she and Eduardo could just vanish together. Or if only Poppy didn't love him. If only Poppy wasn't her sister. If only she didn't love Poppy.

She hated what she was doing to everyone. She had hurt Richard more than he deserved. He was a good guy, and he loved her. But did Eduardo love her? He'd seemed so nonchalant about the credit card, as if it was trivial.

Carrie rummaged for her cigarettes and lit one with shaky hands.

He doesn't take me seriously, she thought, anger winning the fight with self-pity. Blast him to hell, I was only dropping off a couple of leftover carrot cakes for his staff, hardly a crime.

But she knew it wasn't true. She'd delivered the cakes because she needed an excuse to see Eduardo, even for a few minutes in the lift while they rode up and down escaping the two floors of glass-walled drawing office. Just to have him torment her with his hand down the back of her jeans, or her chin gripped in his fingers as he kissed her quickly and hard and sent her out weak with longing.

With sudden resolution Carrie straightened up, tossing her hair off her face as she turned the key in the ignition. She could not, she would not, exist forever on the crumbs from Poppy's table.

Nine

Carrie knew she made Eduardo feel young and care-free. There was a new energy about him, a greater willingness to joke or laugh, and she was responsible.

She took him to all her haunts. At first he'd been reluctant in case they were seen by some friend of his or Poppy's, but Carrie had pouted and said, 'Don't be wet, Eduardo. If we are seen, so what? I'm allowed to go out with my brother-in law, aren't I?'

He'd replied, sardonic, 'Allowed by whom?'

She'd snapped then, 'Oh Eduardo. You know what I mean. We can invent an excuse – my date let me down, and I invited you to fill in . . .'

'Hardly likely if we are lunching *à deux* at the Mirabelle . . .'

Carrie's eyes glittered at him as she interrupted, 'So, I'm reviewing the place for the *Dispatch*, and you are along as camouflage. Or you are taking me to lunch to discuss your birthday present for Poppy.' She shrugged. 'Or your firm wants mine to arrange a party to celebrate the start of the Paddington project . . .'

'Stop. Stop, Carrie. Good God, your talents at instant deception amaze me.'

Carrie looked at the ceiling in a pantomime of

patience, then said, 'I seem to remember you aren't too unpractised yourself.' She exaggerated Eduardo's Italian accent to quote: '"Meet Michelle Ward, an old friend of the family." You didn't seem too concerned about discretion then, did you?'

'True,' he replied. 'And look where it got me.'

Of course Carrie had won the argument about going out. Poppy had at last gone back to work, accepting the part of Filumena. She didn't leave the theatre until 10.15 so Eduardo and Carrie had supper together most nights. And sometimes they'd manage a late evening, or – best of all – a whole night, when Eduardo would tell Poppy he'd be out late with clients, or away on business.

They went to clubs he'd never heard of, where there was little chance of running into his friends or acquaintances. One night, when Eduardo was meant to be in Manchester, they went to Hanover Grand. The bouncer looked Eduardo up and down, wondering, Carrie supposed, what anyone in his forties was doing there, but he knew Carrie and must have decided her over-the-hill date looked cool enough in his mustard Armani to be admitted. They danced for hours, sweating and swaying with the crowd, drunk on the beat and the strobing lights.

The next day Eduardo complained of calf muscles that felt as if he'd climbed a mountain, but Carrie just laughed. She bustled about, clear-eyed and energetic, while he sat, drained and foggy, over strong black coffee.

She took him to a salsa dive off Kensington High Street. Carrie liked Bar Latino for its seediness and for the fact that you didn't need to know anyone. Drinks were cheap, and every age, shape and race turned up and danced. The music was too loud for talk even if you'd wanted to, the floor shook to Cuban rhythms and the air was thick with sweat.

As soon as she and Eduardo were in the room, a grey-haired burly guy took Carrie's hand and led her on to the floor. He danced so well that Carrie felt like a pro, following his every step with ease and enjoying the attention as most of the room stopped to watch them.

After that she'd danced with Eduardo, who wasn't bad, but he didn't seem to enjoy it, so at the next break she left him and danced with a young black guy. He was great, so they kept dancing until she felt Eduardo's hand on her shoulder.

She turned to him, trying to hear what he was saying, then shrugged her apologies to her partner as Eduardo took her wrist and pulled her out. He'd already collected her jacket from the cloakroom, and he hustled her up the stairs.

'Christ, Carrie, how can you dance like that with complete strangers? That black guy was practically screwing you.'

She laughed. 'Oh Eduardo, what a party pooper. It's salsa for Christ's sake. That's how it's done.'

There was satisfaction in the thought that he was jealous.

Sometimes they went to more traditional night-clubs, so Carrie could dress up and show off. Eduardo took her to Annabel's, and she felt great – being with him in public, in his space – but she noticed that he seemed wary, a bit on edge lest he be caught with her.

But he said he liked the classy mix of raffish old Etonians and overfed businessmen, and that she was more beautiful than Annabel's famous crop of stylish Sloanes. He also said, as he prevented her from slithering to the pavement at 3 a.m., that she got plastered so charmingly.

Carrie didn't like the music at Junk, but Eduardo, who was more relaxed in the knowledge that no one he knew would ever darken its doors, seemed to enjoy the tawdry glitz of the place. He liked the half-naked lap-dancers, and the amazingly good-looking women, both staff and customers. Carrie supposed its vulgarity appealed because it was so far from his civilized existence.

There was nothing remotely vulgar about Eduardo's life with Poppy: the penthouse on the canal was an essay in restrained minimalism; the Oxfordshire house, a mixture of good English antiques and Conran, was equally restrained *Country Living*; he bought designer suits and Italian shoes; even his cigarette lighter was an expression of quiet good taste.

Carrie congratulated herself on providing an anti-dote to all that.

She hoped – no, she prayed – that it wasn't just a

holiday, a diversion from real life for him. She had to be his real life.

But she wasn't sure of him. If he lied to Poppy, might not he lie to her? And then she thought how often she'd lied to *her* lovers, and winced. But that was before she fell in love. It *must* be the same for Eduardo.

On a rainy May evening Eduardo was again at Carrie's house. He was sitting at the kitchen table in his shirt-sleeves, a packet of Rizla cigarette papers, his old Zippo lighter, a saucer and pack of Marlboro in front of him. He was laughing. Carrie thought, not for the first time, how good his teeth were. Not a filling in sight, and bright white. She said, smiling in response to his laughter, 'So what's so funny?'

'You. You are. No one else in the world would conceal marijuana between the dried thyme and the oregano.'

'Why not?' She grinned, pleased with herself. She liked surprising Eduardo. 'Best place for it. It's a dried herb after all.' She reached the jar down from a row on the dresser and placed it in front of Eduardo.

Eduardo picked it up, read the label, BASIL, unscrewed the top, and smelled the contents.

'But won't someone think it *is* basil and put it in the pesto or something?'

Carrie chuckled. 'Might make interesting pesto.' Then she shook her head. 'No, Lulu knows what it is. And the junior cooks don't get to invent recipes. They follow instructions. Besides, dried basil is disgusting.

We'd never use it.' She moved behind him and put her arms round his shoulders, dropping her head to smell his hair and mumble his neck with her lips. Over his shoulder she watched him tear open a cigarette and loosen the contents. 'Don't put in too much tobacco. I'm trying to quit.'

'Stop smoking?'

'Uhuh, well, stop smoking tobacco.'

Eduardo turned his face to brush her warm bare arm with his mouth. 'When I was as young and wicked as you, we used to smoke hash in a pipe, without tobacco.'

Carrie came round and sat at the table, close to Eduardo but diagonally across from him. She answered, 'Yeah. But that's such a hassle. Keeps going out.' Then she said, 'What do you mean "used to"? When did you last have any?'

He lifted an eyebrow at her. 'Last night, remember?'

'No, I mean, before me. Don't you and Poppy ever have a joint?'

She didn't like mentioning Poppy, but she kept doing it. Poppy kept getting into the conversation.

'Not any more. We used to, years ago, but Poppy stopped when she was pregnant with Angelina. She thinks it messes up your brain.'

Carrie leaned back in her chair and wound her bare feet round Eduardo's ankles, sticking her toes up inside his trouser legs to rub his hairy calves. 'She's right. But what the hell?'

He wasn't managing too well: he'd overfill the

cigarette paper and then get tobacco on his tongue as he tried to lick the edge, or he'd put the mix in unevenly and the filter tip would fall out of the loose and lumpy spliffs. Carrie let him struggle a bit. It amused her that there was something he did badly – he did most things so competently. And she liked watching his hands. His fingers were big and brown, with dark hairs in little patches on the back, between the joints. Pretty soon she couldn't stand it and took the gear from him, saying, 'You clumsy great lump. Let me.'

She unravelled his half-made cigarette and tipped the contents into the saucer, then started again. She cupped a new paper lengthwise, dropped the filter tip from the Marlboro into one end, carefully sprinkled shredded pot and tobacco along the length of the joint, tamped it down, rolled the cigarette up, licked the paper's edge, sealed it, and twisted the end. Then she repeated the process and made another.

She reached for the Zippo and tried to light one of her joints. 'How do you work this thing? It should be in a museum.'

'I know. It used to be my dad's.' He took it from her and lit her cigarette. 'I keep it because it's a design classic.'

'Is it now?' she said, teasing. 'A design classic indeed!'

'Yes,' he said, 'like the Eames chair and the Dualit toaster.'

She took a deep drag, holding the breath deep in

her lungs to give it time to do its magic, then she passed him the joint.

He took it between finger and thumb and smiled into her eyes. She was supremely, hugely happy. Right now she had no doubts at all.

'You won't believe me, I know, but I've never been in love before,' she said.

'You are not in love now, baby.'

Her face clouded for a second, then she said, putting a hand on his wrist, 'I am, Eduardo.'

Eduardo looked at her with a slight, indulgent shake of the head. 'Whatever.'

She repressed a wash of disappointment. If only he'd say he loved her. She'd noticed before that such talk embarrassed him, that he changed the subject if she talked about the two of them at all. It was understandable. It had only been six weeks, and it must be hard for him. He and Poppy had been together for eleven years, and they had three children. The guilt trip must be awful.

Tonight she felt no guilt at all. Carrie was so happy there wasn't room for any other emotion. She was working harder and doing better work for her clients than ever. And she had more energy, felt healthier, and was more patient with her kitchen staff. That's what love does for you, she thought. Just like they say, it makes you a better person.

They sat in near silence and finished the joints, then Carrie said, 'Let's eat,' and they carried the pumpkin ravioli and two bowls into the sitting room. They ate it with fresh Parmesan, grated, not shaved. Carrie thought the fashion for shaving Parmesan was a style-led mistake: you didn't get the same depth of flavour, and it took forever. She grated the stuff in a machine, and it took seconds.

'This is delicious, Carrie. Wonderful,' Eduardo said, his mouth full.

'Good. Courtesy of Fratelli Franco.' Carrie ladled two more giant ravioli, slippery with tomato and tarragon sauce, on to his plate and added a heavy sprinkling of Parmesan.

'Who is, I mean who are, Fratelli Franco?'

'Chilled pasta company. They've asked Dominic Antoni to produce twelve pasta recipes for keen cooks who want to stuff their own ravioli or be more adventurous, but he's too grand to test anything, and it turns out he can't write, can't spell, can't add.'

'Is he the chef at Mansoni's? The one who throws people out, and beats up his kitchen staff?'

'The man himself. He gets three grand for each recipe, and his face on the pasta carton.' Carrie cut into one of her ravioli and tested the texture of the pumpkin filling with the back of her fork, then took a careful mouthful, concentrating for a moment. Satisfied, her attention switched back to Eduardo. 'Thirty-six grand for having your picture taken isn't bad, is it?'

'Doesn't he do *anything*? Do you write the recipes, everything?' He looked sceptical.

'Yup, I do, but he has ideas. Mostly useless. Here,

look.' She stood up and fished among the papers on her desk. She found what she was looking for, and passed it to Eduardo. It was a single sheet of Mansoni letterhead, scribbled in pencil:

Dear Carrie,

Ideas for the pasta thing. Can't think of any more. So do what you like.

Rigatoni with wild boar sauce

Pumpkin ravioli (tarragon jus?)

Canneloni with pig's trotter farce, pinenuts on top

Soft-shell crab tortellini, basil and olive oil dressing

Pasta salad with chunks of spicy fresh tuna – keep the tuna raw

Tagliatelli with double-smoked air-dried Cumbrian ham, cream sauce

Farfalle with flageolet beans, wilted rocket and garlic

XXX DOM

Eduardo said, 'Sounds delicious to me.'

Carrie nodded and said, 'Sure. In his restaurant. Only trouble is, the recipes are for home cooks who shop in a supermarket.' She reached for the letter and looked at the list. 'How are they going to get wild boar, pigs' trotters, soft-shell crab, Cumbrian air-dried ham?' She tossed the sheet back on the pile. 'The man's an idiot.'

'So what do you do?' Eduardo looked at her with admiration.

135

'I try to stick to his ideas, if they'll work. Like this pumpkin thing. It's simple to do, pumpkin isn't too hard to find.' She flopped down beside him on the sofa, and snuggled against him. 'But otherwise I just do something else. Use things people have heard of, and can buy. Like spinach and ricotta, minced pork rather than pigs' trotters, crabsticks and prawns rather than soft-shell crabs, and so on.'

'Doesn't he mind?' Eduardo had put down his empty bowl and was caressing her forearm. Carrie stopped listening and closed her eyes. God, it felt good.

Eduardo repeated his question and Carrie made an effort to ignore the stroking.

'Mind? He doesn't notice. He's too busy being a superstar.'

'Does he pay you, or does the pasta company?' He leaned over and kissed her forehead. One hand was on her knee, moving up her thigh, disappearing under her short denim skirt.

Carrie wriggled back on the sofa, away from him, trying to concentrate on the conversation, but the marijuana had got to her. She was floating, feeling the power and the beauty of it. 'They both do. He pays me for the recipe development. When I think I've got them right, I send them to him, all neatly typed on Mansoni paper.'

Eduardo took her bowl off her lap and put it on the floor. He undid the zip of her skirt, and his cool hand explored the silk of her boxers, felt the firm small roll of her belly. Carrie's breathing was speeding up. He said, 'Keep talking. I want to know about the business.'

Carrie was drifting divinely now. She didn't want to talk about recipes. She wanted to stretch out on the sofa and make it easy for Eduardo to put his hands wherever he wanted to. But she also liked him controlling her, telling her what to do.

She took a wobbly breath and tried not to think about his hands. 'Fratelli Franco don't know I write Dom's recipes. They think I just test them and do the food for the photography, so they pay me for that.'

'How much?' The pitch of Eduardo's voice had dropped, and Carrie knew his desire matched hers. She put her tongue in his ear, but he said, 'Answer me. How much?'

'I do all right. About £600 a recipe, altogether.'

'Quite the little businesswoman.' Carrie knew he was patronizing her, but he could have been crooning to her. Who could believe the sound of a man's voice could be such a turn-on?

Eduardo gently pulled her tee-shirt over her head. Her bare breasts jiggled as she lowered her arms. He stroked her body very slowly in an upward movement, pausing with his hand on the underside of her left breast, holding it as though to weigh it.

'And beautiful too,' he said. 'A design classic if ever I saw one.'

Ten

Carrie and Lulu surveyed the buffet table. It did look good, thought Carrie. Tiered pineapple shapes were covered with diamonds of apricot, lime and violet marzipan and stuck with ornamental skewers, every bit as elaborate as hatpins. There were turreted blancmange castles, and sugar follies of ruined pillars garlanded with cherubs. Frosted grapes and crystallized dates were piled in formal pyramids or captured in lacy caramel cages. There were silver epergnes of fruit made of clear hollow sugar, so realistic it was hard to believe the oranges, pears, figs and apples were not the real thing. Carrie had gone to a specialist confectioner for them, and had watched him blowing the liquid sugar like glass.

They'd cribbed the tiered buffet idea from a Carême design for the Prince Regent at the Brighton Pavilion. Not that they'd been able to follow his recipes. His moulded jellies and mousses needed so much gelatine or starch to keep them from collapsing they'd have been disgusting. They had compromised with edible but less dramatic versions on the bottom tiers and inedible *pièces montées* on the upper ones, safely out of reach.

Princess Alice and her husband, a City financier,

came in. The banker, round and fat, was convincingly dressed as George the Fourth, his thin and beaky wife miscast as the voluptuous Caroline. They were checking the arrangements for after the concert. Guests were to listen to Handel's *Water Music* by the pond, then come back to the house for dinner.

'It is quite, quite perfect,' she exclaimed, fingering the garlands of flowers and gathered silk swags round the buffet.

'It was fun to do,' Carrie replied. She felt a curious urge to curtsey, as if she were in a play. Get a grip, she told herself, she's only a very minor royal even if she's dressed as a queen and lives in a grace-and-favour house in the middle of Richmond Park. Leaving Lulu to handle the oohs and aahs and 'However do you do it?', she went through to the kitchen to supervise preparations for the dinner. Both Kitty and Jamie were casuals, provided by the Chef Centre, and they needed watching.

She found them gawping through the window at the arriving shepherdesses and Regency bucks, exclaiming as they recognized movie people and rock stars, politicians and royals. As the guests stepped out of modern taxis and chauffeur-driven cars, some younger ones were loud in their self-conciousness, shouting and hooting to each other across the gravel. The soberer and older guests were quieter and more mild-mannered, putting out a gloved hand to be helped from the car, smiling and decorous. They hardly glanced at the bewigged and liveried servants standing in lines either side of the path to the garden. They took glasses of champagne off the proffered trays, as if from a table.

'God, I'm glad I'm not a waiter,' said Jamie. 'I'd toss it in their faces, I would.'

Carrie thought he had a point, but said, 'But since they pay our wages, how about you two getting back to shining up those flats? I don't want silver polish, fingerprints or tarnish anywhere. Okay?'

Carrie wondered when Eduardo and Poppy would arrive. Poppy would know how to handle herself in costume. She'd know to gather her dress to climb steps, but not to do so when descending. She'd smile her thanks to the immobile waiter; she'd know the depth of curtsey required for every rank of aristo.

Carrie admired her sister's ability, once in costume, to assume a beauty and dignity she did not have in real life, but when she thought of Poppy's gloved hand resting on Eduardo's arm, a needle of jealousy went through her. Of course she loved them both. But she resented being in the kitchen while the two of them stepped into this Regency house, in Regency clothes, to eat her Regency food. Poppy and Eduardo were invited everywhere, while she slaved in the kitchen, doing her Cinderella bit.

Turning from the window, she looked at her check-list, taped to the fridge door, and mentally ticked it off. The oysters had been shucked and were waiting on ice, the soup was made and only needed reheating, the soused mackerel fillets were ready to go, the accompanying mustard potatoes and grape relish were already in their bowls.

In truth a Regency banquet was easier to manage than a modern one, because you didn't individually plate each guest's food. The dishes (except the soup, which was served to everyone) were put down the middle of the table and the diners ate what they could reach or persuade their neighbour to pass them. The courses came in waves, the 'removes' replacing spent platters. She'd cheated a bit of course. Modern tastebuds required a lot less spice and couldn't cope with partridges hung to the point of stinking.

She glanced at her watch. Eight o'clock exactly. Dinner would not be served until ten and she was well ahead. She was down to the bread.

8 p.m.   Bake the rolls
         Prep the partridges
         Dress salad
         Prep parsnip cakes
         Fry croutons
         Soup on to heat

She went through to the larder and lifted the box of partridges down from the slate shelf and carried it back into the kitchen. She picked up the saucepan of melted butter from the Aga, and used the large paintbrush to swiftly grease two giant baking trays. Then she laid out the partridges, twenty-five to a tray, and slapped her butter brush over each bacon-barded bird.

She tested the bread dough with a finger. Perfect. Puffy and risen. She sprayed a fine mist over the balls of dough with a water-gun, then slammed the two baking sheets into the electric oven.

She stamped fifty perfect small ovals out of the baked parsnip and potato mixture and arranged them on small trays. They could go into the bottom of the Aga at 9 p.m. to warm through.

She set young Kitty, nervous but keen, to deep-fry the heart-shaped croutons, instructing her to drain them on kitchen paper. Then she flipped the switch behind the soup cauldron, lifted its lid, used one of the teaspoons in her chef's jacket to taste it, and flung the spoon into the washing-up water. She said to the lad up to his elbows in the sink, 'Jamie, give the soup a stir every few minutes, will you? That cauldron sticks.'

'Yes, chef,' he said.

Carrie turned to the salad. Using her fingers to turn the leaves she thought, as she always did, of the French phrase '*Elle tourne la salade avec les doigts*'. It implied youth and innocence, virginity, the idea being, she supposed, that if you were a virgin you would be so squeaky clean that you could put your hands in the salad. Well, she, thirty-two and no virgin, tossed the salad with her fingers because it was the quickest way to do it, and it didn't bruise the leaves.

She lifted the dressed leaves into the three salad bowls, taking care not to streak their sides with

142

dressing. She rinsed her hands under the tap, dried them on the torchon hanging from her apron strings, and turned back to the time plan. Her eye ran down the familiar list. She liked catering at this stage, when everything was organized and you were working to a schedule, on time and in control. And then something further down the list caught her eye:

9.15 p.m. Sorbet from freezer to fridge to soften

Oh my God. The sorbet. She'd forgotten the sorbet. It was still in the freezer in Primrose Hill.

She stood immobile, her eyes closed, her mind racing. It didn't matter. No one would miss it. They could just skip the course altogether, and go straight from fish to partridge. Then she thought, But what if it's on the menu? She turned to Jamie. 'Get me a menu from the dining room, will you?'

He reached to the windowsill and handed her one. 'There's one here, chef,' he said. 'What's up?'

Carrie opened the menu and studied its cherub-infested print. There it was: 'Sorbet of lime and pomegranate' in filigree writing with a swag of limes and green leaves tied up with trailing ribbons each side of the statement.

'Get Lulu, will you?' she said, yanking her towel out of her apron ties and reaching behind the door to fish in her coat pocket for her keys.

'Lulu,' she said as her second chef appeared. 'I've forgotten the bloody sorbets. I'm going to get them.'

'Oh shit.'

'It's okay,' Carrie grinned at Lulu. 'You know I like a crisis. We'll be fine. They aren't due to eat until ten. Just follow the timeplan. Don't be tempted to put the partridges in too soon.'

Lulu nodded. Thank God for someone who never flaps, thought Carrie. I must give her a raise, that's what. 'Everything's on time. The bread is in. Better keep an eye on it in case the top tray cooks faster. David knows what he's doing out front. Just make sure the waiters march in in line. They are meant to look like Regency servants, not like a bunch of out-of-work actors.'

'Got it,' said Lulu. 'See ya.'

Carrie ran out of the back hall, past racks of shooting sticks, tennis racquets and every size of royal wellie.

As she drove fast out of Richmond Park, through the great iron gates, the thought that someone might lock them at sunset flicked into her brain. Maybe the few posh people who lived in the park had keys? No, if they closed the gates at all it would be at 1 a.m., like Hyde Park.

There was no traffic, and no one stopped her as she broke speed limits and jumped lights, and the return journey was trouble-free too. As she swung up to Richmond Gate, the box of sorbets beside her on the passenger seat, it was just past 9.30. The guests would still be at the concert.

She accelerated into the park entrance, and came bang up against the great gates, shut. She skidded to a stop. Oh, God, I don't believe this, she muttered, jumping out of the car. They were locked. She dived back into the car, arms flailing around for her handbag behind the seats. She needed her mobile phone.

No handbag. Christ. She'd come with only her keys.

Cool it, she said to herself. I'll drive to the next entrance. One of these gates must be open.

At Ham Gate the gates were closed too; she drove blindly on with a vague idea there was a keeper's lodge at Kingston Gate.

There was. She saw with relief that there was someone at the front window of the lodge.

She jerked to a stop, leaped out and ran up the little path. She rang the bell and knocked on the door simultaneously. Almost immediately it opened and a small offended woman said, 'All right, all right.' Then she looked suspiciously at Carrie and said, 'What is it?'

'I've got to get into the park. It's urgent,' said Carrie, trying to keep her voice steady.

'Sorry. I don't live here. I'm just babysitting.' She looked pleased, nodding with satisfaction.

'But this is the lodgekeeper's house. He must have keys to those gates.' Carrie waved her arm in the general direction of the park.

'Well, if he does, I don't know anything about them.' The woman smiled, her face smug. 'And if I did,' she ended, 'I couldn't just let you in, could I?'

Carrie repressed a desire to push past her and ransack the house. She ran back to the car, jumped in and slewed back on to the road.

She drove as fast as she dared, swallowing her rising panic. Christ: 9.50. Dinner was due to start in ten minutes.

At Robin Hood Gate there was the sound of television from the front room. Carrie banged the brass knocker, up and down, hard. She waited a few seconds then did it again.

God, they'll never hear above that racket, she thought as a burst of canned laughter assailed her. She stepped into a flowerbed, and knocked hard on the window.

Thank God, she thought, as the TV died. Then the curtain flipped open and a man, bearded and angry, mouthed silently at her through the glass. The curtain dropped back into place and the next minute the door swung open and there he was, shouting, 'What the hell do you think you are doing in my flowerbed? Them's new petunias in there . . .'

Carrie stepped back on to the path. 'I'm so sorry, but there was no answer . . .'

'Too bloody right there's no answer. It's sodding night-time and I'm off duty.'

God, he's going to close the door, thought Carrie, and she stuck her foot in the gap.

He banged the door on it.

'Ow. That hurt,' she yelled, hopping up and down but trying to keep her leg in the door. 'Look, I'm sorry about the petunias, but you've got to help me. I'm cooking Princess Alice's dinner. It's her fiftieth birthday and she's got Prince Charles and all sorts to dinner, and I've got locked out . . .'

'Princess Alice! Prince Charles!' His mouth curled. 'Fucking toffs.' He opened the door a little and for a second Carrie thought he was going to come out and assault her, until she realized he was opening it only to bang it the harder. She jumped back as he slammed it inches from her face.

Carrie's blood was now up. Her foot hurt. She had had, she thought, just about enough of unco-operative or non-existent gatekeepers. She hammered again on the door, shouting, 'If you've got a problem with royals why the hell are you a gatekeeper in a royal park? And anyway, why take it out on me? I'm only the cook, comrade. And I'll lose my job if you are too bloody-minded to help. How about some solidarity for the bleeding worker?'

There was no reply, but she knew he was behind the door. She raised her voice and shouted, 'What is it with you anyway?' Suddenly she knew he wasn't going to help, and she turned away, saying loudly, 'What a bastard.'

She heard the door open behind her. Christ, he's going to clobber me one, she thought, trying not to run down the path. But he shouted, 'I don't have a key, lady. The police have them. Ring the cops.'

Carrie swung round. 'Oh, thank you,' she said, forcing her voice to be civil. 'Could I use your telephone? I haven't brought my mobile . . .'

The sneer returned. 'Don't push your luck, lady. There's a box over there.'

Carrie rubbed out threatening tears with the back of her fist. The unkindness of the babysitter and the aggression of the man had unpicked her. And it was now ten o'clock and the guests would be being seated at the long refectory tables. Poor Lulu.

Carrie ran across to the phonebox, which was yellow and announced itself as an emergency telephone connected to the park police.

Oh, thank God, she thought. She jerked the door open and picked up the handset. Dead. Nothing. No dial tone. No friendly park copper.

Carrie let out a scream of frustration and banged the set down, then flung herself back in the car and drove on, trying to calm herself, until she found a BT box. It was getting dark, and the light fitting had been vandalized. It was hard to see the buttons, but at least the telephone was working. She rang 999.

But the police did not regard her problem as an emergency and told her to ring the Richmond police station. They gave her the number. She hadn't a pen and had to memorize it.

She dialled.

'Richmond police station'.

She started to answer, then beep beep beep. Oh God, it wasn't a free call. And she had no money. No handbag. She needed coins or a phone card.

She dashed back to the car. There were three pound

coins, two twenty-pence ones and a ten-pence in the parking money dispenser.

She dialled again. Thank God. A ringing tone. As soon as the efficient female voice answered, Carrie launched into her story about the royal party, no sorbets, locked gates and unhelpful gatekeepers.

There was a pause. Then the woman said, 'I'm terribly sorry, dearie. I do feel sorry for you, but I don't see how I can help. I'm a housewife in Hampton.'

Carrie put her head against the windowpane and closed her eyes. Now what? She thought.

She dialled 192, asked for the Richmond police number, and accepted the offer to connect her. They put her through.

Once again she told her story.

'Okay, miss, we'll send someone round to Richmond Gate with the keys. Meet you there, okay?'

She hurtled round the rest of the perimeter road – she'd now driven right round the park – to get back to Richmond Gate, where she'd started.

And then she waited. And waited.

It was agony. Had they come before she'd arrived and gone again? Should she risk leaving to find another telephone box? Should she go through the open pedestrian gate and *carry* the sorbets? No, ridiculous. Must be at least a mile. Why the hell had she not brought her mobile? Poor Lulu must be frantic.

Finally she could stand it no longer and knocked on the door of a big double-fronted house, its garden overlooking the park, its elegant front rooms facing the road. The woman who answered was wearing a silk shirt tucked into well-tailored wool trousers, pearls at the neck, and buck teeth. She did not open the door very far.

'Could I possibly use your telephone?' said Carrie. As she spoke she thought she heard a car, and thinking it might be the police, glanced back over her shoulder.

'Why? Who are you looking for?' asked Buck Teeth, her voice firm, peremptory.

'The police,' said Carrie and immediately wished she hadn't. She was going to have to explain the whole story or this woman would never let her in.

Even when she'd finished her tale, her troubles were not over. Carrie wanted the woman to stay at her front door so that if the police came she could call her, but Buck Teeth, looking at Carrie's tear-streaked face and the smears of partridge blood on her apron, was not going to leave her unguarded in her house. She insisted on coming with Carrie.

Carrie had the satisfaction of seeing the woman's suspicion turn to curiosity, even to sympathy, as she once again repeated her tale to the police. The officer was apologetic. The panda had just left. It would be with her in ten minutes.

Carrie dropped the phone into its cradle and ran back to the front door, the house owner on her heels. It was now almost dark, and as they emerged into the street she saw the tail lights of a car disappearing into the park, beyond the once more locked gates.

'Oh, God, no . . . oo,' cried Carrie, all control finally

evaporating. She ran forward and heard herself shouting, 'Come back, come back,' as she shook the massive gates. She felt tiny, like Alice in Wonderland, and utterly despairing.

'That's Tommie Fenton's car. He lives in the park too. He could have let you in. Oh dear,' said Buck Teeth.

At precisely 10.30, the police arrived, keys in hand.

Carrie burst into the kitchen in time to see the last of the red tunicked waiters disappearing through the swing door, huge silver trays of soused mackerel with mustard potato salad and grape relish carried shoulder height.

'Oh God, Lulu, I'm so sorry.'

Lulu straightened up from the oven with a roasting tray of gleaming partridge. Her round face was crimson from heat and exertion and she staggered slightly with the weight. She banged it down on the central table and smiled. 'No sweat,' she said.

'Oh Lulu, you are a star,' said Carrie, giving her a quick hug before she dashed her hands under the tap and stuffed the corner of a tea towel into her apron strings. 'But "No sweat" doesn't quite describe the look of you.' Lulu's dark curls were stuck to her neck and forehead.

'Did you get the sorbets?' asked Lulu. 'We should be plating them now. They won't be long with the fish.'

'Oh God, I'd forgotten them. They'll probably be

soup by now, it's taken me so long.' Carrie hurried out to the car and brought in the box.

They were perfect. The hollowed-out lime shells she'd used as containers had provided good insulation, and the sorbet was soft but not melted. They arranged them in silver eggcups set on mirrored trays, and decorated them with twining ivy and halved pomegranates.

'There aren't enough for everyone to have both kinds,' said Lulu, counting.

Carrie nodded. 'I know, but they won't want them. It's a mad idea eating sorbet in the middle of a meal anyway.'

Once the waiters had been dragooned into an orderly line and sent in with the sorbets, the four of them worked fast and furiously but in near silence, with only an occasional barked 'Gravy, Kitty' or 'Two more flats, Jamie' from Lulu or Carrie.

As the stress mounted, Carrie felt the familiar adrenaline high. This was what she liked about catering – the danger of the whole thing going pear-shaped, the team effort to ensure it didn't. The kitchen was very noisy. From the children's playroom next door, which had been commandeered for the 'clear', came the clatter and ring of cutlery tipped into boxes, plates sorted and stacked, silver flats flung on to piles.

It was also very hot. Carrie wasn't wearing a chef's hat and she had to wipe her face with her apron to stop the sweat running into her eyes.

They dished up the veg first, then covered each dish with a layer of foil and a couple of tea towels to keep in the heat while they did the partridges. Five flats were lined up on the central table. Jamie held the hot partridge trays as Carrie, using a fish slice under and her fingers on top, rapidly put ten birds on each flat, in a circle, breasts out, feet in. Lulu followed her with a catering-size bag of Smith's crisps and poured a pile of them into the middle of the birds – Carrie had long since decided making game chips wasn't worth the effort. Kitty came next, twisting the stalks off water-cress, and planting little bunches of leaves between each bird. Carrie then ladled gravy over each partridge to give it a last-minute shine.

The waiters lined up, partridge bearers alternating with vegetable waiters. Carrie stood at the door and waited until David signalled. As the waiters passed her Carrie scattered parsley liberally on the parsnip cakes.

When they'd gone, the cooks, with one accord, disappeared to the back yard for a smoke. Their job was pretty much done. The desserts were already on the buffet, and coffee was David's problem.

It was blissfully cool out here, and Carrie leaned against the back wall, eyes cold, suddenly completely knackered. She was usually elated, on a high, if a job had gone well, but the adrenaline rush had faded and now all she wanted was a cigarette. Then a whisky. Then bed.

'I thought I'd find you here.' It was Eduardo,

dressed as a highwayman, looking ridiculously hand-some.

'Have you got a fag?' asked Carrie.

'I thought you'd given up.' He spoke mildly, putting a cigarette between her lips. He lit it for her, his hand sheltering hers as she bent her head to pull on it.

She flicked her hair out of her face.

'How did you escape?' she asked.

'Everyone's fighting over the desserts on that great construction of yours. They'll be ages at it.'

Eduardo's eyes travelled up and down Carrie. She forestalled any comment with 'I know, don't tell me. I look incredibly fetching in a cook's apron, no make-up and a sweaty face.' The cigarette seemed to revive her, and she grinned. 'And you look a complete prat in that rig.' She twitched his lace jabot and poked the shiny buttons of his jacket.

'Actually, you look like Little Orphan Annie – have you been crying?' He touched the mascara smudges under her eyes with his thumb.

Carrie started to tell him her adventures with the park-keepers but they were interrupted by the appearance of Poppy, emerging from the kitchen. Carrie saw, with a burn of jealousy, that she looked sensational. Clever corseting and a wonderful low neck empha-sized her narrow waist and high plump breasts, and the flawless expanse of her neck and shoulders was pink and creamy. She was wearing her contact lenses, and theatrical make-up made her already wide eyes huge. Carrie felt both baffled and cheated. Poppy always wore her glasses and seldom wore make-up except on stage. Her sister was meant to be a comfortable mum, not a glamorous courtesan.

Poppy kissed Carrie's cheek. 'Eduardo, I knew you'd be slumming it in more interesting company. Carrie, that dinner was a triumph.'

Carrie thought, Madame Bloody Bountiful. She smiled and touched her forelock in mock subservience, 'Thank'ee kindly, m'lady.'

Poppy put her arm through Eduardo's and said, 'Everyone's back at the table eating pud. We'll be missed.' Eduardo nodded, and she led him away, round to the front of the house. Back to the bright lights, back to the ball.

When they'd gone Carrie remained standing against the wall, miserable. It was Poppy's ownership of Eduardo that hurt, the authority with which she had claimed him, and the obedience with which he'd gone. Carrie did not know what she expected Eduardo to do. He could hardly say, 'Sorry, Poppy, I'd prefer to stay here with my lover.'

Jealousy and anger took turns with self-pity. She hadn't even been able to finish her tale of the park gates. And Poppy and Eduardo both looked so stunning, the epitome of fashion's beautiful people. Come to think of it, they looked noticeably happy and relaxed these days. Was that her function? To service the husband so he'd be nice to the wife?

Eduardo had practically said as much. He'd certainly said that because Carrie made him so happy, he was a less ratty father and a more considerate husband. Bloody hell, thought Carrie, why does she have to be my sister? If it was anyone else I'd just march in there and blow her out of the water.

Carrie dropped her cigarette butt on the gravel and ground it out with a vicious foot. Stuff them both, she thought, going back to help with the clear.

Eleven

Poppy pushed the dog away from Lorato, saying, 'Out, Olaf, out.'

Olaf, abandoning hope of a breakfast titbit, lumbered off to a respectable distance and sank down, his mournful eyes fixed on Poppy's face.

'Good dog,' said Poppy, kissing the soft carpet of Lorato's tight curls. She moved her thigh so the little girl could get her arms round her jean-clad knee. Lorato's favourite position, if she could not be spread-eagled on Poppy's back, was clinging to a leg. Poppy stretched for the marmalade and said, 'Guess what? We're coming off on Saturday.'

Eduardo's slice of toast stopped before his open mouth. 'What! Why? I thought the play was a sell-out.'

Poppy shrugged. She did not seem the least put out. 'I know. It's mad, but the theatre is booked for yet another Lloyd Webber musical. We were supposed to transfer to the Lyric, but the deal wasn't watertight and the Lyric's decided to keep that gay dance thing they've got.'

Poppy reached down and picked up Tom as his unsteady dash across the floor ended with a collision into Lorato. Poppy stood him on her lap and buried her face in his neck. Her voice muffled, she said, 'So Mummy will have the summer off. What about that, Tom-Tom?' Tom shrieked with pleasure and echoed, 'Tom-Tom, Tom-Tom.'

Poppy stroked Lorato's head. 'What about that, Lorato?'

Lorato lifted her solemn eyes to Poppy's and said, 'Tom-Tom, Tom-Tom.'

Eduardo watched the familiar breakfast scene without seeing it. 'Summer off? Does that mean you've got another job lined up already?'

Poppy shook her head. 'Not exactly. They want us to reopen with *Filumena* in August or September. Same cast.'

Poppy hoisted Tom over to Eduardo, who had to put down his toast to take him, then reached down and picked up Lorato.

Eduardo asked, 'Surely the cast will all have drifted off? They can't hold you all summer without paying you, can they?'

Poppy smiled. 'No pay, I'm afraid. But I don't think we'll lose anyone. We're such a tiny company and the others feel like I do: nice to have the summer off.' She handed a segment of orange to Lorato, who crammed it, whole, into her mouth. Juice ran down her chin, then her eyes rounded and bulged and she started to choke. Poppy hooked a finger into her mouth and extracted the orange. She caught Eduardo's look of mild disgust as she cut the mangled segment into two and handed Lorato half of it. 'We'll get a week's rehearsal before we reopen,' she said.

While Lorato devoured the second bit of orange, Poppy poured more coffee. She liked filter coffee in the morning, in great French bowls, with full-cream milk. To hell with the calories. 'The management would have liked us to go on tour to fill the gap, so they're fed up with me.'

'Do you mind? Them being mad, I mean.'

Poppy shrugged. 'Not really. They've known all along. I said I'd only go back to work at all if I could sleep every night in my own bed. It's been in my contract from the beginning.'

Tom plunged his fist into the sugar bowl and Eduardo moved it out of reach. 'Hey, basta, keep your hands out of there,' he said, handing Tom a finger of toast from his neat pile of discarded crusts.

Lorato immediately set up a wail, reaching towards Tom's prize. Poppy said, 'Oh Eduardo, now you'll have to give her one. She'll be as fat as butter at this rate.'

Eduardo reached over with a crust, holding it just out of her reach. 'What's this, Lorato?' The child stopped crying at once, and looked anxiously at Eduardo. 'Say "Toast," Lorato. "Toast."'

'Toast,' she said. She said it perfectly, without a lisp.

'Well, I'll be damned,' said Eduardo, giving her the crust. He turned to Tom, 'Say "toast", Tom.'

'Shosh,' said Tom, beaming with pride.

'Shosh, shosh,' continued Tom as he wriggled off Eduardo's lap and made for the French windows in a rapid crab-wise crawl. Poppy set Lorato down and went up to open the doors. Lorato walked fast ahead of her and, when she caught up with Tom, stood in front of him, sturdy as a rock, blocking his path. She commanded, 'Up, up, Tom.' Pulled by Lorato, Tom obediently stood up and finished the distance at a wobbly walk.

'That's right. You tell him. Lazy little devil,' said Eduardo, laughing.

Poppy held Tom's hand to help him negotiate the step, but Lorato took it in her stride and made straight for the sandpit, saying, 'Cover off.'

'Please, Mummy,' admonished Poppy.

'Please, Mummy,' said Lorato, pulling at the plastic cover. Poppy rolled it back and lifted the two children into the sandpit.

Olaf, who had followed them through the French windows, rested his head on the edge of the pit. Tom immediately poured a beaker of sand on his nose; the dog simply shook his head and stared dolefully at the children.

'Watering can,' said Lorato. Poppy, on the point of going back inside, turned and looked at her, impressed that she'd remembered the words.

'Watering can, please Mummy,' said Lorato.

Poppy filled the little plastic watering can from the terrace tap and gave it to Lorato, waiting for her to say thank you before she handed it over.

'Did you see all that?' she asked Eduardo as she stepped back into the kitchen, but he was back in his newspaper.

Poppy was tempted to insist. She would so love Eduardo to share her pleasure in the children's every word and step, but, conscious that domestic details bored her husband, she thought better of it and set about clearing the table.

As she reached under Eduardo's newspaper to wipe the crumbs from the table, he lifted the paper to the side and said, 'You *could* go on tour, you know.'

Poppy frowned, confused. 'But I don't want to.'

'Lorato is fine now. Look at her. She's gabbling away much better than Tom.' His eyes rested on the two small figures on the terrace.

'I know. It's marvellous isn't it?' Poppy's round face was pink with pleasure. 'She can say watering can . . .'

'Why don't you do the tour?' Eduardo interrupted, folding his paper along its original creases and turning to look at Poppy.

'Oh, all sorts of reasons. I'd rather be in the garden than in a sweaty theatre. But mainly because I want to be with the children.'

Eduardo did not look convinced, and Poppy felt compelled to add, 'Besides, maybe Lorato is fine now precisely *because* I've been at home all day. Maybe she'd go back to wetting her pants and refusing to talk if I disappeared.'

Eduardo shook his head slightly but said nothing.

161

Poppy noticed the gesture and, provoked, said, 'You don't *want* me to go on tour, do you?'

Eduardo said quickly, 'Of course not. But you shouldn't sacrifice your career for the kids. It's not as if they don't have me and Giulia.'

Poppy said, 'I'm not. I told you, I'll be back on the boards in September.' She picked up a bottle of sun block from the window-sill and changed the subject, 'I'll put some sun cream on those two. I've no idea if Lorato would burn, but Tom will, for sure.'

As she brushed sand off the children's pudgy arms, she thought of what she hadn't said to Eduardo: that he wasn't much use because he was hardly ever at home, and anyway the children spent the summer here in the country, not in Paddington. And that she did not want her mother-in-law as a permanent stand-in either.

And that she had a plan, half formed, for a family holiday in Mpumalanga.

Poppy spent the whole day weeding Lucille's garden in the rain. She grubbed out the grass from between the paving stones with an old knife, hacked back the canary creeper and ivy and planted the tubs with a hundred pounds' worth of instant bloomery.

She didn't mind the physical labour, or even the rain making the tools slimy. It allowed her to feel she was doing her duty by her poor old mum without having to talk to her too much. Circular conversations were fine for an hour, but Poppy found trotting round the same loop ten times hard going.

Besides, she would be away in South Africa for almost a month and she felt she should do her bit to make up for that. Not that Lucille noticed her visits or the lack of them. Carrie didn't agree, but Poppy was sure that somehow, in some subliminal recess, her mother was glad of the attention, of the evidence of love. And she did love Lucille. Indeed she felt fonder of her mother now than before she'd lost her memory.

Today Lucille was driving her mad, appearing every few minutes to demand, 'Darling, what are you doing out there? Come and have some lunch.'

'Mother, we've just had breakfast. It's 10.30.'

'Good Lord, so it is.' As always her mother was genuinely astonished at her own forgetfulness. 'How odd. My mind is getting very odd, you know.'

Sometimes her interventions were less cheerful. She'd lean out of the French windows and snap, 'Poppy, do leave that. I'll have a go at it tomorrow.' Poppy forbore – what was the point? – from replying that Lucille had not been up to planting a petunia for five years. She tried distraction: 'Mom. It's tipping down. Why don't you cosy down and watch the telly? I'll join you in a minute.'

She wouldn't of course, but Poppy figured her mother, once hooked by the Teletubbies, would forget about her. But Lucille wasn't playing.

'*Will* you stop bossing me about? Anyone would think I was senile.'

And then, two minutes later, 'Darling, do come in. We'll have some lunch.'

Mercifully, Adrienne turned up in the guise of a beautician and thoughtfully elongated Lucille's pedicure for an hour and a half, and then made lunch, drawing Lucille's attention away from her daughter's efforts in the garden.

After lunch her mother fell asleep to the drone of the stock-market report, and Poppy managed to finish the job and assemble the garden table and four chairs she'd bought at B&Q, But she failed to spirit away the old ones. Just as the heavily bribed taxi driver finally managed to unscrew the rusted table legs to get the thing to fold flat, Lucille appeared at the front door. 'And what may you be doing?' she demanded.

Poppy's heart sank. She knew that duchess tone.

'Mom, I bought you a new table and chairs, and I've put them on the terrace. Go and look.'

Lucille stood where she was, indignation fizzing.

'There is nothing wrong with these ones. All they need is a lick of paint. I wish you wouldn't interfere, Poppy.'

'Mom, they are rusted to holes. Look.' Poppy pointed to the tabletop, the metal edge rusted away from the top. 'It's dead. Beyond rescue. Dangerous even.'

'Nonsense. I am not having this man take away my things. Besides,' she said, suddenly looking plaintive, 'I feel sorry for them. You cannot just dump them. I'll take them to Oxfam. When I've painted them.'

Poppy suspected she was beaten, but made a last attempt, 'Mom, come through to the garden, please. I want to show you the new table and chairs I've got you. They are really . . .'

'But I don't want *new* things. I want my old things. Why can't I just have my own old things, Poppy?' Lucille looked so forlorn. Poppy thought, Oh God, she's going to cry. Putting an arm over her mother's shoulder and kissing her cheek, she said, 'Okay, Mom, you win.' Lucille's face cleared at once.

Poppy turned to the taxi driver, who was beginning to look as though he might report her for mother-abuse.

'I'm really very sorry,' she said, 'but could you put this thing back together again?' She dropped her voice so Lucille would not hear and said, 'I'll pay you, of course.'

'What are you two whispering about?' said Lucille. 'I'm not deaf, you know.'

The taxi driver reassembled the rusty table and he and Poppy carried it and the chairs back through the flat and into the garden, where her mother supervised their reinstatement beside the new ones.

As Poppy drove back to Paddington she thought crossly that the beautifully revamped little garden now looked like a furniture store. Poppy told herself that Carrie could damned well deal with the defunct table and chairs.

This thought set Poppy brooding on Carrie's relationship with their mother. Carrie was altogether too casual about Lucille. She was forever cancelling intended visits, or rushing off as soon as she'd swallowed a cup of coffee or a glass of wine. She maintained that, as her mother didn't know if she'd been there yesterday or last month or stayed for minutes or hours, it didn't matter. All that was important was that Lucille had a good time when she did come. Which she did, Poppy had to admit. Carrie made her mother laugh, and they'd giggle together like schoolgirls.

But Poppy felt a knot of resentment. I'm forever cast as the sensible nanny, and Carrie as the princess, she thought. Carrie takes no part in trying to keep Lucille's flat, or even Lucille herself, half decent.

Poppy could just hear Carrie, 'Oh Poppy, sweetheart, stop worrying! If Mom doesn't care about the threadbare carpet or the spring-free chairs, why should you? Just leave her be. She's happy. Why bully her into a clean jersey? Or frog-march her to the hairdresser? Just go with the flow, sis.'

The next day Poppy returned with a bottle of Pathclear. The label promised if she applied it to the terrace slabs, she'd not have to grub around with a penknife for at least another nine months. She hadn't been able to apply it yesterday because of the rain, and she hadn't dared leave it in the flat in case Lucille drank it, fed it to the cats or added it to her bath.

As soon as she knocked on the door, Lucille was there, her face flushed with excitement. 'Come and see what your wonderful sister has done,' she said. 'She is such a wonderful girl, that Carrie. I don't know what I'd do without her.'

Bemused, Poppy followed her hurrying mother through the kitchen and out into the little garden. Lucille advanced a few paces on to the terrace. Turning round, her arms swept over the little garden. 'Look,' she said. 'Your sister has weeded the whole place. And planted the tubs. Aren't they beautiful? And she bought me these lovely table and chairs. Isn't she wonderful?'

Poppy opened her mouth to protest, then thought better of it. What was the point? Lucille said, 'We just need to get rid of these rusty old chairs now. And this horrible table. Will you take them to the recycling centre for me, Poppy?'

Twelve

Poppy found the condoms when she was packing their bags for the plane trip. They were in the bag Eduardo used for short trips.

At first she looked at the two slim black packets with elegant gold lettering VIVA L'AMOR in puzzlement. One of them was unopened, but the sticky flap on the other was crookedly resealed.

Poppy sank down on the bed, and sat very still. She looked at the packets in her hand, mentally distancing herself from them, not allowing her mind to pursue any train of thought. Then, almost absently, she opened the resealed pack and registered that two condoms were gone, one still there.

After a full minute she stuck the little flap down again, lining it up neatly and smoothing out its wrinkles between her finger and thumb. Carefully she tucked the envelope back in the bag, and stood up. She collected Eduardo's washbag from the bathroom, then his book from his side of the bed. It was Tom Wolfe's *A Man in Full*, which even in paperback took up more than its fair share of the carry-on bag. She'd have to stuff her own book in her handbag. She walked through to Eduardo's dressing room for his cashmere cardigan.

She put the book in the bag and folded the jersey neatly. Condoms did not mean an affair. Sleeping with someone did not mean love.

Her spirit crouched inside her, afraid. She would not think about it. She couldn't face it. Couldn't face what? There's nothing to face. These are Spanish condoms. Eduardo spends weeks at a time in Spain. One-night stands in Bilbao don't count.

Poppy went into the bathroom to get her things, resolving to take the minimum. They'd give them those washbags on the flight. Her mind leaped to a lifeline: perhaps Spanish airlines put condoms in their toilet bags?

This brief escape route fizzled out: two of the condoms had gone. And anyway, Eduardo always refused the washbags. Unnecessary tat, he said. Why don't they just reduce the airfare by a fiver?

She reached inside the medicine chest for aspirins. In case Eduardo had one of his headaches. And sleeping pills, so he'd get at least some sleep on the plane. And her Microgynon.

She looked at the row of little broken blisters on the card. She'd dutifully taken a pill every day for eighteen days, since her last period.

And for what? She shut the medicine cupboard door and sat down on the loo seat. Think, she told herself. Think. She and Eduardo had not made love for weeks. Could it be months? Yes, months. She'd been stuffing her body with drugs day after day while he made love to someone else.

But they had a wonderful marriage, didn't they? Sex wasn't everything. Her mind went back to a conversation with Giulia, about a month ago, when as Eduardo left the flat late one Saturday morning, his mother had said, 'Poppy, you should be more loving for Eduardo. Men are same as children. They need a *coccola* also.'

'*Coccola*? A cuddle?'

Her mother-in-law said, 'Eduardo, he takes children to the park. When they come home, you hug and kiss all the bambini like you no see them for a year, ask plenty plenty questions. But Eduardo, he get nothing. No kiss. No thank you. No questions.'

'Oh Giulia, you don't understand. Eduardo and I talk to each other when the children aren't around. It's impossible with them underfoot . . .'

Giulia pulled her apron off and sat on the kitchen stool. 'You sit down, Poppy, I tell you.' Poppy did as she was told, half irritated and half amused. Giulia was so wonderfully old-fashioned.

'Eduardo is same like his father. Everyone love him. Wonderful man. But he must be in the middle. How you say? The centre of attention. His father want always beautiful things all round. Beautiful clothes, beautiful buildings, beautiful food. Sometimes beautiful women.'

Eduardo had told Poppy that his father, like most of his class and generation in Milan, had had a succession of mistresses, and that Giulia had never reproached him but waited on him hand and foot, exactly as she now did for Eduardo.

Poppy said, 'Eduardo loves those things too – except, I hope, the beautiful women. But he doesn't expect me to run around him. Eduardo's attitudes are the same as mine . . .'

Giulia tapped her forehead with her fist. 'In his brain. His brain agrees with you, but . . .'

'But what?'

For a few seconds Giulia hesitated, then she answered indirectly, 'Eduardo's life has been too easy. Still too easy.'

As Poppy reran the little scene with her mother-in-law, she wondered if Giulia had been trying to warn her, trying to say that after a dozen years of marriage men, anyway Italian men, got tired of their wives.

Poppy stood up again and stared at her face in the mirror, seeking an answer. Was she unattractive? Was it her fault? Her reflection stared back, pale, eyes wide and worried behind her lenses, mouth set and unhappy.

Unblinking, she watched her eyes fill with tears. And then she couldn't see any more, and she ducked away and reached for a towel. She lifted her glasses and rubbed her face, then restored them. She folded the towel carefully lengthwise. She dropped one end behind the towel rail, the other in front, adjusted the towel to align the ends and smoothed it neatly on the rail. She stood for a moment, not knowing what to do next, her hands gripping the rail through the towel. She pulled on her arms and leaned her brow against the marble wall. What shall I do, what shall I do?

The telephone rang and she went to it, unthinking. It did not occur to her to ignore it or to let the machine pick it up. She took a breath and pushed her chin up.

'Hello.' Her voice sounded normal. Fine.

It was Carrie. 'I've done it. I'm coming with you!'

Poppy didn't get it. 'You're what?'

'I'm coming with you to Kaia Moya. I've swung two commissions. One for *American Gourmet* on bush cooking. You know, braais in the boma and potjies round the lapa fire. And a safari piece for *Tatler*!'

Poppy said, 'But Carrie, we leave tonight . . .'

Carrie's excited voice interrupted her, 'I know. I'm just trying to translate my two Economy tickets into one Club so I can sit with you.'

Poppy found her spirits lifting slightly. 'Oh Carrie, I'm glad. That's . . . that's wonderful. You . . .' As she spoke her voice caught and faltered.

Carrie interrupted. 'Poppy, what's wrong? You sound . . . Popps, are you okay?'

'I'm fine,' said Poppy, fighting not to cry. 'Really.' She gave a barking little laugh. 'I'm fine,' she said again.

'Poppy, are you sure there's nothing wrong?'

Poppy forced her voice into normality. 'Carrie, everything's fine, I promise. But I have to go. Where will we meet? At the Paddington check-in?'

'Why don't I come over to you? Then I can help you with the kids and the gear. Bags and that. I'll come about four. Okay?'

Poppy wanted to say no, nothing's okay, but she said, 'You needn't. Really.' Poppy knew she didn't sound convincing. Besides, she wanted her sister with her. She'd be a buffer between her and Eduardo. She didn't know what she'd say to Eduardo.

Carrie said, 'See you later then,' and hung up.

As Carrie drove along the canal down Blomfield Road, skilfully swerving to minimize the effect of the speed ramps, she dialled Eduardo's number with her left hand.

When Eduardo answered he was, as usual, unconcerned. Carrie insisted, 'But I know there is something wrong, Eduardo. Poppy's upset about something.'

'Carrie, she's fine. You're imagining things.'

'Are you sure she doesn't suspect you? Us?'

No, he was sure not. Poppy had been fine when he'd left, with all the kids' stuff packed, and just theirs to do.

How arrogant men are, thought Carrie. He's quite sure he's in the clear. And why can't he do his own packing?

Carrie frowned at the road. She was about to say goodbye and ring off, when he said, 'Carrie, are you sure you should come?'

Her heart sank. 'Why? Don't you want me to?'

'Of course I do. You know I do. But Poppy isn't blind. You'll have to behave yourself.'

Carrie felt a little streak of anger. She fired back, 'Christ, Eduardo. I've never given Poppy a second's anxiety. I've played the dutiful mistress, haven't I? You know that I've never . . .'

Eduardo interrupted, his voice emollient, 'You're wonderful, cara mia. But with Poppy and the children around all the time, it could be tough for us both.'

Carrie said, her voice tight, 'Eduardo, I can't go without seeing you for three weeks. I've got to be with you.'

Eduardo caught the near hysteria in her voice. 'Okay, okay . . .'

'And I've bust a gut to get a reason to go. Poppy won't suspect.' She ended bitterly, 'She's far too nice.'

'Yes,' said Eduardo. 'She is. You're right. She's much too nice for her own good.'

Carrie pulled into the forecourt of Eduardo's building and turned off the engine. 'I'm here now. If I find out what's troubling your perfect wife, I'll let you know.'

She turned off the mobile before he could answer and tossed it into her bag. The gears crunched as she jammed the stick into reverse to back into a parking place.

Carrie let herself in and walked through to the bedroom. Poppy was just putting the telephone down, looking fine, normal.

'Hi, Popps.'

'Oh Carrie, you are an angel to come.' Poppy put her arms round her sister and hugged her, fractionally harder and longer than usual. Carrie felt a wash of relief. Poppy did not suspect her.

The women looked at each other for a prolonged second, and Carrie noticed the reddish lids and over-bright eyes behind Poppy's lenses. 'You've been blubbing, sis. What's up?'

'Oh, it's nothing,' said Poppy, shaking her head and smiling. 'And anyway, it's over. Come, let's go and find the children. They'll be so excited you are coming with us . . .'

Carrie put out a hand to stop her heading for the door. 'Poppy, this is me. Carrie. I'm your sister – remember? The one you tell things to?'

Poppy gave her a wan smile and put her hand up to her forehead, shading her eyes as she rubbed. 'Okay. But Eduardo just rang and I'm fine now. It's funny, he hardly ever telephones, but he said he wanted to check I was all right, and ready for tonight.'

God, thought Carrie, that was quick. He must have rung her the minute I rang off. She said, 'So, what was the matter then?'

Poppy said, 'Of course I didn't tell him. I mustn't jump to conclusions. I should . . .'

Carrie interrupted, 'Poppy, start at the beginning. I don't know what you are talking about.'

They sat on the bed, and Poppy took her glasses off and polished them on her skirt. 'I feel such a fool. But you see, I was packing our bags and I found these condoms. Eduardo and I don't use condoms. So he must be . . .'

Carrie put her arms round her sister. 'Oh Poppy, Poppy, is that all? I thought the sky was falling in!' Carrie's relief was genuine, though for herself rather than for Poppy. Her concern for her sister was real, though. Poor Poppy. She was such an innocent.

Poppy let out a curious snuffling sob, and burst out, 'Oh Carrie, I can't bear it! What if he's got a lover in Spain? He's been to Bilbao every month for a year. I checked. Sometimes he stays all week. Maybe there is no conference centre. Maybe it's all lies . . .'

'Poppy, Poppy, stop. You are letting your imagination run riot here. Of course there's a conference centre, you stupid cow. You've seen the brochure, haven't you? And the model in Eduardo's office?'

This stopped Poppy's headlong plunge into the worst-case scenario. She nodded, looking gratefully at Carrie, who went on, 'Darling sis, the truth is that all men are to some degree bastards. Their moral intentions might be in the right place – chastity in the absence of the loved one, etc. – but their instincts are stronger. They can't help screwing around.'

Poppy shook her head vigorously. 'I don't believe it. Eduardo isn't like that. He's too fastidious to ever go with . . .'

'Sweetheart, posh hotels are full of high-class whores. Eduardo would not have to go kerb-crawling or visit a brothel. Just a tip to the concierge, that's all. It's not love, Poppy. It's trade. Just be glad he wears a condom.'

Poppy's eyes registered alarm, then distaste. She was silent for a moment, then said, 'But how do I know it's not more serious than that? If he can be unfaithful to me, why would he tell me the truth? Oh Carrie, I still don't believe it. Maybe the condoms aren't his? Maybe there's a simple explanation.'

Carrie shook her head. 'They all do it, Popps, what-ever they say. They need to. Like eating and drinking. Don't you remember Beryl Bainbridge's line about women being programmed to love completely, and men being programmed to spread it around? She says we are fools to think any different.' Her arm rocked Poppy's shoulder.

Poppy hung her head, and Carrie felt a rush of love for her. Poppy said, 'How humiliating to be thirty-five and the mother of three before you learn these things. How come you are so much wiser than me, Carrie?'

'You are one of nature's innocents,' said Carrie. Her arm and hand trailed affectionately over Poppy's shoulder as she stood up. 'And I am a streetwise spinster.'

She took Poppy's hand and pulled her to her feet. 'Come on, Popps, let's have a glass to celebrate my horning in on your holiday. You could use a drink anyway.'

As they drank a toast to three good weeks Carrie

marvelled at what a first-class cow she was. I'm the actress, not Poppy, she thought, and a bloody good one too.

The thought did not depress her. Happiness ran through her. And something of triumph. She'd averted Poppy's suspicions, she'd lifted her sister's gloom, she was going on holiday with the Santolinis. And Eduardo slept with her, not with his wife.

Thirteen

'Do you *mind*?' Carrie used her elbow to give the man in the next seat a vicious jab.

'Whassa matter?' he said, opening his eyes and trying to focus.

'Every time you fall asleep, half of you ends up in my seat,' replied Carrie, picking up his arm with both her hands and trying to fling it back where it belonged.

'Sorry, darling,' he said, pulling himself upright and leering at Carrie. 'Why don't we have a drink then, hey? Then I won't fall asleep. We can get to know each other.'

'In your dreams,' retorted Carrie, turning away from him and closing her eyes.

But she couldn't sleep. A child in the seat behind her was trained in the art of torture. Every time she nodded off he kicked her seat or cried.

She hadn't managed to get into Club. When Poppy had suggested that Angelina swap with her, Angelina had looked so forlorn at the prospect of ejection from the family that Carrie refused. No offers of his seat from Eduardo, she noticed. She had an uneasy feeling that Eduardo would have preferred her to stay behind. He liked his life simple, she suspected.

Wife and kids in Box A. Lover in Box B. And yet Eduardo loved her, she was certain of that.

Oh, no, she thought, not again. She felt the steady pressure of her neighbour's thigh against hers. She shifted away, bouncing in her seat and jerking her leg so that he'd wake and realize what he was doing, but this only gave him more room and his horrible fat leg followed hers, once more pressing against her.

Carrie sat up and looked at him. God, men can be disgusting, she thought. His open mouth emitted warm beery breath, his legs were spread, one hand was on his crotch, and the other was flung over the back of his seat.

Carrie heaved herself out of her seat, kicked the blanket out of the way and walked to the back of the plane. She could kill for a cigarette. She asked the steward for some water and he gave her a plastic bottle of Volvic. She leaned against the loo wall, drinking the water and thinking.

Maybe she should not have come. She was apprehensive about Poppy. They had always been so close, no secrets, no lies. Now it was secrets and lies in spades. And if her sister realized Eduardo was not the faithful husband she'd believed, would she rumble the whole truth?

Eduardo was right, she'd have to be careful. But I'm never careful, thought Carrie. And do I really want to be? Or do I want to bust things wide open?

Carrie's overnight miseries were forgotten the minute she stepped on to the airport steps. Johannesburg airport was huge and international, but it could not quite blot out the smell of the highveld. Carrie felt her spirits lift as she narrowed her eyes in the glare of the winter sun, and breathed in the unforgettable smell of bone-dry air and parched grass. Just to be in Africa again was a joy. She would have a good time, come what may. And it would be wonderful to see the old lodge again. And Karl. And Maisie.

They hired a Volkswagen combi and Eduardo drove. Carrie felt a stab of jealousy as Poppy climbed into the passenger seat. She'd sat in the back with the children a million times as Poppy's sister, both in England and here. The Santolinis came to Kaia Moya every year, and this would be the fifth time she'd joined them. She always sat in the back, but now she resented it. She wanted to be beside Eduardo, to feel his hand on her thigh as the lion-coloured plain and sparse kopjies rolled by.

Two days after their arrival, Carrie had her first photo assignment, a picnic photo shoot outside one of the camp's safari tents. Carrie wanted to give it a colonial look and the props were mostly borrowed from Karl's ninety-year-old grandfather, Piet.

Piet, grizzled now but still upright, had been a big game hunter when safaris meant guns not cameras, and he knew the bush as intimately as his son. He lived in a whitewashed bungalow at Kaia Moya in return for entertaining the guests at the bar with stories of man-eating crocs and ivory poachers.

His roof space and living room were stacked with stuff, some of it inherited from his own father. Carrie spent the morning cleaning and polishing. There was a mahogany travelling chest with brass corners, a set of leather suitcases, a hinged 'butler's tray' table, two hardwood deckchairs with slung seats made of faded green leather, a wicker hamper complete with china plates, and cut-glass decanters in a tantalus.

The weather was perfect: clear and sunny to give the deep shadows Carrie needed for the long shots, but not hot enough – at least in the shade – to wilt her salads or make the cheeses sweat. She set the food out on the tent's veranda, arranging the dishes casually on the stacked suitcases, butler's tray and travelling chest. It all looked wonderful, bathed in diffuse light from the green canvas awning.

She had just added a basket of guinea fowl eggs, still in their shells, to this artful still life, when Karl appeared.

'Carrie, this looks fantastic!'

Carrie was pleased. She stood back to better judge the scene and said, 'Yeah, it's coming on.'

Karl studied the tantalus, examining the gleaming stand and intricate lock. 'I haven't seen this since I was a child. I still think it was a mean trick to lock up the spirits but leave them visible. Like saying to the servants, "We know you are thieves and drunks," and at the same time, "You can look, but hah! You can't have."'

'I should think the lock was as much to stop the

wives and daughters as the servants,' said Carrie. 'But it looks good, doesn't it?'

Karl continued to inspect his grandfather's antiques and Carrie's food. Carrie put a hand on his shoulder and said, 'Karl, I need a gun for the background, but your oupa won't let me near his gun cupboard. Do you think he's got some sort of ancient hunting rifle or blunderbuss or something?'

Karl took a step back and Carrie dropped her arm. 'I am sure he has. He's never sold a gun in his life.'

Carrie stuck her fingers into the back pockets of her jeans and flexed her shoulders. The gesture brought her elbows up and stretched her chef's jacket across her breasts. She smiled into Karl's eyes and rocked lightly on her trainers. 'And could you persuade him to lend me one?'

'Sure thing. When do you want it?'

'In an hour? Sam's coming at two. The photographer.'

Karl nodded slowly, considering. He said, 'Oupa won't leave a gun unattended, even without any ammo. You'll have to put up with him being here for your photo session.'

Carrie cut a slice from the end of a raised game pie and angled it to display the pink meat inside. She said, 'Won't you do?'

'What do you mean?'

'I mean, I'd rather have you as a gun sitter than your grandfather.' She flashed a confident, mischievous smile at him.

Karl was unmoved. 'No can do, Carrie. I'd love to learn a few photography tips from a pro, but I've got work to do. It's Oupa or no gun.'

Carrie was bending over the picnic basket, extracting the china plates from their leather straps. As Karl left he patted her lightly on her denim-clad bum.

'Bye, kiddo,' he said. Like dismissing a horse, thought Carrie crossly. It still got to her that she'd never managed to impress Karl. Even as a child she'd get her way with almost everyone, even sometimes with her father, but not with Karl. He thinks he sees through me, she thought, and he's concluded I'm shallow and useless. Well, who cares?

Carrie was sweating. They'd done the open-fire shots, and she'd had to baste the kebabs over the fearsome coals. Her face was flushed and her hair clung to her forehead and neck in wet shreds. The shoot was going well, though. They only had the close-up cold food shots to do.

At four o'clock, she heard Poppy's voice behind her.

'Carrie, here.'

Carrie looked up from cutting yet another slice off the game pie – the air turned the meat grey and she wanted it fresh and pink – to take the glass Poppy offered.

It was Maisie's lemonade, made as she remembered from twenty years ago, by steeping lemons with fresh ginger and mint.

'Mmmm, wonderful,' she said, drinking half the glass at one pull. Eduardo and Karl were there too. Karl was helping himself to lemonade, but Eduardo, she was pleased to see, was watching her.

Her gratification was short-lived. Eduardo was soon in deep conversation with Sam about DV cameras. Annoyed, she said, 'Sam, are we going to photograph this sodding pie, or what?' Her tone came out more bad-tempered than she'd meant, and she quickly pasted a smile on top.

Sam looked up, puzzled. 'Sure, Carrie. Won't be a sec.'

Carrie joined them. 'Thought you were too busy to bother with us,' she said to Karl, pushing her hair off her forehead with the back of her hand. He smiled and lifted his shoulders in a casual shrug. 'Just thought I'd check up on the old boy.' He nodded at Piet, who was dozing bolt upright in a plastic chair. Karl picked up Piet's straw panama, and returned it gently to his head.

She turned to Eduardo. 'Don't you want some lemonade?' She injected her voice with as much intimacy as she dared.

'Thanks, no,' he said. Then he looked at her with a small frown and said. 'You look hot.'

'It's called work. Some of us have to do it, even on holiday.' She immediately regretted this, and offered, 'Sorry. But I feel really ugly. Face of boiled beetroot, and I expect my hair smells of smoke.' She stood close up to Eduardo, and said, 'What d'ya think?' bending her head and standing on her toes so he could smell her hair.

'It's fine,' he said, without dropping his head or sniffing her hair. He immediately returned to his camera conversation with Sam.

Carrie felt put down. He hadn't denied, as he was meant to, that she was ugly and red. It was humiliating, especially when she looked up to see Karl watching her. He caught her eye and turned away abruptly, his face hard and disapproving.

Put out, she returned to her trestle table under the mopane tree and started to toss the wild spinach in French dressing with her fingers. Oh Eduardo, she thought, do you want me or not? Or is humiliation your bag?

Suddenly the heat was unbearable. She had to shed some clothes. Emboldened by seeing Poppy carrying the lemonade tray back towards the lodge, Carrie walked up to Eduardo with her hands, oily from the salad, out at her sides.

'Eduardo. Help. Can you get me out? Undo the apron?' Eduardo, puzzled at first, complied, pulling the strings at her waist. Carrie wondered if he even realized that she was trying to remind him of that first time, when he'd unwrapped her apron and they'd been on the floor seconds later.

The apron fell open and Carrie turned so he could pull it off her. As he rolled it into a ball, she came up close, intending to give him a playful kiss, as she might her sister's husband, but when she was close enough to smell the deliciousness of him she sensed his resistance. For a second she did not know whether she wanted to kiss him or head-butt him. She said, 'Thanks, brother-in-law,' and licked him. It was a long, chin-to-cheek, very public lick, and he started back, protesting, 'Carrie, lay off.' His eyes, she noticed, immediately looked for Poppy, and registered relief that she was gone.

Carrie laughed, and turned to Karl. 'Karl, Eduardo is squeamish about helping me out of these things for some reason, but you'll help, won't you?'

'Sure,' said Karl. 'At your service.'

Conscious of Eduardo's eyes on her, she gestured with her greasy hands at her double-breasted chef's jacket. 'The buttons are rubber. You have to bend them to get them through the holes.'

'Sure,' he said again. And did so. He did it quickly and efficiently, and without looking up to catch any signals from her.

'There's another row,' she said, ducking her chin at the second line of six buttons from shoulder to hem. Karl looked at her for a second then turned to Eduardo. Taking the rolled-up apron from him, he pushed it at Carrie and said, 'Why don't you wipe your hands on your apron? Then you can do them yourself.' She had no option but to take the apron and do so.

And then she had to take the jacket off: otherwise it would be obvious that her motive had been more about wooing Eduardo, or flirting with Karl, than getting cool. She undid the rest of the buttons and slipped out of the jacket, her eyes on Eduardo. She was wearing a black bra, edged with lace and with narrow lace ribbons for shoulder straps.

'That's better,' she said, too brightly. She undid her jeans, then sat on the corner of the travelling chest to pull them awkwardly over her trainers.

'If the strip tease is over,' said Eduardo, 'I'm off.'

Karl gave a general wave too as he followed Eduardo. 'See you.'

Working in her bra and pants was a lot cooler, and she told herself it was no different from wearing a bikini. Eduardo and Karl were just too old: they had the puritan attitudes of her grandparents. No one of her age would have looked so po-faced at someone taking off a few clothes. For God's sake, this was the African bush, not Knightsbridge. They'd not have been so boring if they'd been by the pool. It was illogical and bigoted. Her bikini was a lot skimpier than these knickers, for a start.

And besides, Jannie, Sam's assistant, was only wearing shorts. Why one rule for the boys, another for her?

While she cleared up the debris of the shoot, and organized a couple of the kitchen staff to lug Piet's possessions back to his house, she was still arguing her case to herself. She knew she'd somehow made a fool of herself, but she wasn't quite sure why. She found she minded Karl's disapproval as much as Eduardo's.

*

'Poppy, for God's sake, it's not much money. With the rand so weak, it's nothing in real money. A couple of hundred quid.'

Poppy looked at the assortment of intricate baskets, heavy clay pots, wooden salad bowls, cast-iron potjies and woven tablecloths on the floor of Carrie's rondavel.

'But they'll cost a fortune to crate up and ship home. And there'll be duty on them.'

Carrie put her hands on her slim brown hips, in the gap between her cropped top and her bikini bottoms. 'No, there won't. They'll be used by then. I'll say they're the tools of my trade.'

Poppy ignored this. She went on, 'And the pots will arrive smashed – if everything isn't stolen by the baggage handlers, which is more than likely.'

Carrie was only half listening. She twirled around, admiring her tan in the mirror, and said, 'What a little ray of sunshine you are, O sister mine!'

Poppy frowned. Carrie's sarcasm hurt, and for a second she was nonplussed.

Carrie pulled her eyes off her mirror image, and pursued her advantage. 'Why do you both have to be so critical? Eduardo went on as if I was asking him for a mortgage, not a measly few hundred.'

Poppy, nettled now, said, 'Maybe he's rumbled that you aren't too good at paying back the money you borrow.'

'What money? I don't owe him anything.' Carrie jutted her chin at her sister.

'Oh, come on, Carrie, I've been signing cheques on and off for . . .'

Carrie interrupted, 'Poppy, for Christ's sake, you're my sister. That's nothing to do with Eduardo . . .'

Poppy saw she had Carrie's attention now. More than attention. Carrie's eyes had a slightly desperate look. Her voice softened. 'Carrie, darling, grow up. Eduardo's my husband. His money and mine are the same thing.'

'But he doesn't know about the money you've given me, does he?'

'Lent you. And yes, of course he does.'

'Why? What did you tell him? What did he say?' Carrie clutched a fistful of her hair on the crown of her head, then let it go. 'What does he think?'

Carrie's distracted air and earnest questioning puzzled Poppy. 'Look, Carrie, you know what Eduardo thinks. He's told you often enough. He thinks you're extravagant and unreliable.' Poppy smiled, trying to soften her words. 'He's probably right.'

Carrie could not help herself. She said, 'Not any more. I don't believe it. Eduardo wouldn't say that. He . . . he . . .'

Poppy tried to put an arm round Carrie, but Carrie swung away. Poppy said, 'C'mon, sis, why so upset? You know Eduardo. Nothing's changed. He just thinks you're a bit self-centred . . .'

Carrie cut in, accusing, 'When did he say that? When?'

Poppy didn't want to have this conversation. She

could see Carrie's mounting distress and, though she did not understand it, she sought to mitigate it. 'Oh Carrie, I don't know. He's always saying it. Nothing's new.'

Carrie changed tack with an effort. She waved her hand at the African artefacts and said, 'Well, he'll get his precious money back as soon as I can sort out my bank. I wouldn't have asked him at all if my Visa card had worked.'

Poppy's big sister act was maddening. All that patronizing calm. It had taken a real effort not to tell her that Eduardo, far from being the censorious, respectable paterfamilias, was in fact sleeping with Poppy's unreliable, extravagant, self-centred little sister. But she had just enough control not to. She would tell her, but calmly, and not until she was sure of Eduardo.

'Come, darling, out now,' said Poppy, standing by the pool with a towel. Lorato was determined not to hear. She was kicking her powerful little legs behind her like a frog, and dog-paddling with her arms. She was making impressive headway across the pool.

The child was fearless in the water. She was wearing armbands of course, but her bravery astonished Poppy. She would run headlong from the grass, over the crazy paving, and leap into the pool with such momentum that she'd go right under. Then she'd pop up like a cork, shrieking with pleasure.

Poppy watched her with a sense of awe. Lorato was

a miracle. Two months ago the child would not speak, clung like a limpet, peed hysterically. Now she chattered non-stop, was sturdy, determined and emphatically happy. Poppy had been vaguely uneasy that the smell and sound of Africa might somehow set her back, that long-buried memories of terror and loss would resurface to cloud her confidence. But no, Lorato had turned a corner and she wasn't going back. She was a joyous child, that's what she was.

Poppy called again, 'Lorato, out now.' Lorato had now reached the floating child's rubber ring she'd been aiming for, and was bashing it happily with her fists, splashing and shouting.

Poppy could not reach her from the edge, and jumped in. She lifted Lorato and sat her bottom in the ring. 'Got you, young lady,' she said. Lorato bounced up and down in the ring. 'Mumm . . . eee, Mumm . . . eee.'

Poppy, laughing and averting her face from Lorato's splashing, pushed the ring towards the shallow end.

Suddenly she heard Maisie's shout behind her, and turned to see Tom running towards the pool. He was not wearing armbands.

'No, Tom,' shouted Maisie and Poppy together as Tom slithered without a splash into the deep end and disappeared, sinking like a stone.

Poppy was with him in two fast strokes. She ducked under the water and put her hands round the child's body, but Tom was greasy from sun cream and flailing in panic. He slipped from Poppy's grip; for a second

Poppy saw his open mouth belching bubbles, eyes wide with terror.

Poppy took a breath and went under again, this time grabbing Tom round one wrist and by his trunks. She pulled him above water and in seconds he was in Maisie's arms.

That evening the sight of the sleeping children undid Poppy. Lorato, as usual, had crawled into Tom's bed and the pair were curled up like puppies, Lorato's snuffling face against Tom's bottom, Tom's elbow cradling a plastic tipper-truck. Angelina slept silently, her face unwontedly pink in spite of Poppy's diligence with the sun block.

The thought that these children's happiness depended on her, on her and Eduardo, suddenly scared Poppy.

What if Tom had drowned? It happened. Children died. Or what if Eduardo left her for the condom woman?

For nearly two weeks she'd been trying not to think about Eduardo's condoms, but she did it all the time. It must mean, she thought, that his love was shallower than hers, his commitment less.

She thought she could live, maybe, without the theatre, but she couldn't live without Eduardo and the children.

Eduardo found her sitting on her heels by Tom's bed, her head in her hands.

'What's the matter, mia cara?' he said, putting his hands under her elbows to help her up. 'What is it?'

Poppy put the back of her wrist against her mouth to hide its trembling. Her eyes were dark and shiny. She said, 'Oh darling, it would kill me if we lost one of them. Or if I lost you.'

Fourteen

Eduardo had stayed in bed. He'd said he didn't share the sisters' enthusiasm for dawn drives: for rising at 5 a.m., struggling into jeans so glassy-cold they raised goosebumps on warm legs, drinking milkless coffee round the remnants of last night's fire, then trawling the bush for four hours before breakfast. He had barely stirred as Poppy and Angelina dressed, and was soon fast asleep again. The 'babies' hadn't woken either.

Carrie drew the rough Basuto blanket across her face, trying to exclude the freezing wind as the jeep bucketed along the track. In spite of gloves and a fur-lined anorak, icy air blew into every crack and gap. As Karl accelerated out of a sandy skid and over a narrow bridge, Carrie needed both hands to hold the handrail. She grinned at Poppy as she abandoned the attempt to keep the blanket round her ears.

Reflected in her sister's face she saw the exhilaration that she felt herself. Poppy's cheeks were flushed, her eyes glittery with excitement. Karl's assistant, Danie, driving the other tourist jeep, had radioed with news of a cheetah sighting. If they went flat out they'd be there in ten minutes.

Angelina, her nose blue with cold and pale eyes streaming, was huddled close to Poppy, their striped blankets enveloping them both in one family parcel. Carrie felt the old twinge of envy as she watched Poppy duck her head to press her cheek against her daughter's.

When they arrived, Danie's jeep was in poll position, its occupants leaning this way and that to take pictures of the cheetahs. The extended body of the jeep allowed four rows of seats, each one higher than the one in front to ensure unimpeded views without anyone having to get up. Standing was not allowed. Karl said the animals were used to the outline of the jeeps, but a different profile might make them nervous – and dangerous.

The male cheetah was sitting upright on a concrete switch-box beside the road, eyes blinking as he faced the weak morning sun. His mate lay in the sand of the road just ahead of them, her dappled coat gleaming as her belly rose and fell with her breathing, her small neat head perfectly still. They take your breath away, thought Carrie. Is there anything so beautiful?

After ten minutes, during which the cheetahs hardly glanced at the jeeps, the male poured himself elegantly off his perch and ambled down the road, followed by his mate, long tails just clear of the ground, legs liquid in a high undulating gait.

The tourists followed at a respectful distance. After a while, and with no apparent excitement, the cheetahs peeled off the track into the brown grass and began to hunt: they split up, their paths slowly diverging until they were 300 yards apart, both approaching the same scattered herd of zebra, one from each flank.

At first the herd grazed unconcerned, round fat bottoms striped like Bridget Riley paintings, short black tails spinning, then suddenly their heads shot up and they began to trot in all directions, noses held high, their manes rigid hedges along their necks. One cheetah broke into a loping run to separate a group of mares and foals from the rest, but they circled back to the thick of the herd and the play began again. It was like watching a wildlife movie, thought Carrie, except that your own heart beat faster.

They didn't see a kill. After another forty minutes of cat and mouse, with the action getting more difficult to follow as the herd trotted further away, the tourists began to get bored and think of breakfast. Karl drove to a waterhole and they drank thermos coffee, dunking chunks of sweet mosbolletjie rusks into their mugs. It tasted wonderful, thought Carrie, their childhood distilled in a flavour.

'Look,' said Karl, pointing. Carrie took the binoculars from him and watched the jacana birds stepping delicately on the lily pads, a brood of little ones under their parents' long legs. Karl picked up a pebble and tossed it to land a few feet from the waterlilies, and immediately one of the adult birds squatted low and spread its wings to scoop up the chicks huddled below. The bird straightened up and looked about, daring the world to suggest any babies were hidden anywhere.

'Wow,' said Carrie. 'I've never seen that.'

'It's the male,' said Karl. 'Men can be fierce protectors of the family too.'

There was something in the way he said it. Carrie looked sharply at him, but Karl was repacking the thermos jugs and the mugs and did not look up. Carrie studied his sun-lined face, not sure whether to challenge him. Karl sensed her eyes on him and turned to look at her.

Carrie looked about her for Poppy and Angelina. They were the other side of Danie's jeep, out of earshot. She asked, 'What did you mean by that? About the male?'

'Why? Didn't you understand?' His voice was steady and gentle but matter-of-fact.

'Of course I understood what you said. But it sounded as if it was intended to mean more.' It didn't come out as cool as she wanted.

Karl swung the picnic basket into the back of the jeep, slammed the trunk shut, and walked round to the driver's seat. Carrie followed and climbed in behind him. As he sprang lightly into the jeep he said, his voice low so no one else would hear, 'I was just making the point that few males really want their nests torn to bits. Most of them, in nature anyway, go for the quiet family life.'

Mercifully the noise of the engine stopped the conversation. Carrie was silent as they drove on, looking at the back of Karl's head, thinking vicious thoughts. How dare he? What business was it of his? She knew he was referring to her and Eduardo, but how dare he imply that *she* was trying to shred Eduardo's nest, as if Eduardo had nothing to do with it?

As they drove on some degree of shame overtook her anger. Was it so obvious? It was true that ever since they'd got here, she had been desperate for Eduardo and he had seemed more concerned to play happy families than the ardent lover. He was attentive and loving to Poppy and affectionate to the children, while his attitude to her seemed to have reverted to his old, pre-love stance of big brother: sometimes indulgent or affectionate but mostly irritated.

She had tried everything. She'd even resorted to asking him to rub suntan oil into her back by the pool, but he'd obliged as if she was made of wood, smearing the stuff on fast then wiping his hands on the grass as though he'd just rubbed flea powder into a dog. She twice suggested an evening game walk at the time she knew that Poppy would be busy bathing the younger children and putting them to bed. Once he'd agreed, and when she'd whispered that they could go to her cabin instead, he'd said no, he thought a game walk would be great, and he had called Karl and Angelina, and they'd gone . . . walking. The other time he'd just said no, he didn't feel like it, and he'd sat drinking Castle lager at the bar with Karl.

The truth was that they'd only made love once in the fifteen days they'd been here, and that was when Karl had driven Poppy into Nelspruit to do some shopping, taking Angelina with them and leaving

Carrie in charge of Lorato and Tom. Carrie had seized her chance and asked old Maisie to look after the children. Maisie had been sitting on the stoep step, dehusking mielies. Carrie tipped a pile of toys on to the floor, and left them to it.

It had not been like London, though. Eduardo had looked trapped and uneasy when she'd appeared in his and Poppy's rondavel. She'd undone her sarong and, letting it fall to the floor, stood there, sun-burned and naked. But he'd not moved to her. He'd sat at the desk and said, 'Christ, Carrie. Not here, for God's sake. What have you done with the children?'

She'd moved in on him then, putting her arms round his head so that his face was between her tits. She knew she smelled of Giorgio. It was a perfume he'd given her, and it worked. His arms came up round her bottom and caressed her waist, her back, down to her thighs. Then he said, his voice a tone deeper, 'Not here. I'll come to you.'

And she'd had to wrap up in her sarong again, and go along the raised wooden walkway to her rondavel. She passed the security guard, posted there to keep a look out for elephants or lions, and wondered if he'd guess she had nothing on, and if he'd tell the other guards and trackers that Eduardo had followed her.

She lay naked on her bed, under the mosquito net. There were no mosquitoes in midwinter, but she thought she'd look good half hidden behind white tulle.

When Eduardo failed to appear at once she feared

he'd had second thoughts, but in five minutes the door opened and he was there, a dark silhouette against the blinding light of the doorway.

He shut the door and stood looking through the netting at her. Then he slid out of the towelling dressing gown, pulled the mosquito net aside and pushed her back on the bed. He fucked her hard and fast, missionary style. Her first thought was that it was unfair; he was skipping the loving rituals of mutual arousal. Then suddenly she found his grabbing urgency a turn-on, and she was up there with him. His roughness excited her. And when he put his big hand over her mouth to keep her from crying out and she bit his hand and struggled, it was fantastic.

In ten minutes he was gone, leaving her feeling bereft and with the faint suspicion that she'd been used, not because he loved her but because she'd asked for it.

The next evening Carrie sat on her veranda watching the soup-plate sun setting between the thorn trees and feeling an old melancholy, familiar since childhood, the sadness of evening. In the east the purple wash of dusk was taking over, the colours deepening then merging. What was she doing here, lusting after her sister's husband, making a fool of herself in front of Karl?

As she thought about it, her will hardened. She wanted Eduardo, and she hardly cared about Poppy. She wanted Eduardo to leave Poppy and marry her.

She knew Poppy bored Eduardo. Look at him now, en famille; he was so middle-aged. In London he'd dropped twenty years when he was with her. He'd laughed more, lived more.

And Poppy had her career. And it wasn't as if Eduardo would desert her. Of course they would all stay friends. They'd be very civilized and grown up about it. And Poppy would keep the children.

Children. The word slid into Carrie's heart like a thief. Carrie bent over double, hugging her stomach and rocking to and fro on the wicker chair. She wanted children too, Eduardo's children. Eduardo had to leave Poppy and she and Eduardo had to start a family.

And it had to be soon. She was thirty-three, and she could not bear being alone any longer.

Carrie straightened up, her eyes dark and desperate. She would confront Poppy. Tell her. Eduardo wasn't going to force the issue, so she'd do it. She couldn't go on like this, pretending to be just the best friend and loving sister.

She stood up abruptly and walked swiftly towards the old house. The bar was on the old stoep, where as children she and Poppy had slept on hot nights. Climbing the old red steps she had a sudden longing to be a child again, interested only in animals and climbing things.

She'd have a couple of drinks. Tomorrow she'd tell Eduardo what they had to do.

*

In the morning, as always, her courage failed her. She didn't dare force Eduardo to choose. What if he chose Poppy?

The next five days were not good. Carrie felt she was losing it. She received four e-mails from *American Gourmet*, desperate for copy she had not delivered. Never mind not delivered; she hadn't written a word, if they but knew. And she cocked up big time with the photo shoot for *Tatler*. The picture editor, photographer and his assistant arrived at 10 a.m. to find Carrie still asleep and nothing done in the way of preparation. She'd had to scramble round, her head thick from last night, getting the lapa fire going and borrowing some wide-eyed children from the staff compound. She'd had to bribe them to forego their trainers and Nike tee-shirts and revert to ragged shorts or a belt of beads.

Thank God for the stuff she'd bought at the craft market. The pots and wooden bowls, salad servers with beaded handles, baskets and napkins did wonders. And the *Tatler* crew were impressed by her ability to work fast, producing mielie bread in cast-iron pots, bread dough twisted round sticks, and perfectly charred kebabs of eland, sweet potato and aubergine. Her triumph was a whole fish in a salt crust, baked in hot sand. The fact that the fish was a mummified one, borrowed from its glass case above the bar, delighted the photographer, who lit it and photographed it with dedication.

'What is it, anyway?' asked Amy, the assistant. 'A trout?'

'God knows.' replied Carrie. 'Does anyone else?' No one did. She laughed, eyes alight. 'Hope someone does. And that it's edible. I've got to write the recipe to go with the pic.'

That night Carrie got seriously drunk. It was, she knew, the relief at having busked through the day and winning over the picture editor. She deliberately ordered another bottle of wine because Eduardo said they did not need one. Fuck it, she thought, why should I care? His disapproval was upsetting. The way Karl said nothing but watched her made her want to scream.

The following morning Carrie was again hungover. She stayed in her rondavel, working on the overdue recipes on her laptop. By mid-afternoon the power it took was too much for the solar panel on her roof and the computer died. Carrie crawled into bed. Maybe, she thought, Eduardo'll come looking for me. But he didn't. No one did.

In the evening Karl sang Western ballads to his guitar, and the mood was gentle and soft. Poppy sat between Eduardo's knees at the campfire, with Angelina between her own. What do they think they are, Carrie thought, Russian dolls?

Some of the rangers joined them after supper and sang along. Karl's repertoire was impressive. His tenor voice had a mellow, seductive timbre. He sang country and western, then sea shanties, then old English folk songs.

Then he got up and walked towards the African compound, carrying his guitar. Carrie thought he must be going for a pee in the bush, but then she heard voices in Shangaan, and presently he returned with Maisie, two of the lodge staff and two trackers. The black staff looked pleased, but shy. Karl insisted they sit on the heavy logs that served for benches round the fire, and he passed them some beers. Striking a few chords, he said, 'This is a Tsonga ballad. It's about drought and rain.' He sang the first verses on his own, his voice deep and his accent, to Carrie, indistinguishable from native Tsonga. After a while the black Africans joined in, their voices haunting and mellow. Carrie shut her eyes, letting that rhythmical rich African sound thrum through her like warm honey.

Then they were singing a lullaby, a Shangaan lullaby Maisie had sung to them as children. Carrie had not thought of it, or heard a note of it, for nearly thirty years, but suddenly she could smell the clean starch of Maisie's cotton apron, breathe in the warm brown smell of safety and love. Carrie burst into tears, a loud hiccuping sob breaking into the gentle melody.

The singers faltered, trailing, but Karl lifted his voice and kept singing, and the others rejoined him. Carrie stood up hurriedly, one hand over her face. Poppy started to struggle up, but Carrie said, almost viciously, 'No, don't move.' She stumbled up the stone steps, and ran down the walkway to her rondavel.

When she reached it the light would not work – no

more power until the solar panel got some sunlight – and for some reason this seemed the ultimate tragedy, an excuse to fling herself into the wicker chair by the door and weep in earnest. After ten minutes she stopped. She was exhausted, but the sensation was not unpleasant. The cold evening air on her face was soothing, and there was something satisfactory about her sore, dry throat. She wiped her face on her sleeve and tilted her head back against the wall, eyes closed.

'There, there, Miss Carrie, don't you fret now.' It was Maisie, holding a glass of hot milk, laced with honey. 'You 'member when you and Miss Poppy was sick, your mama she make me give you hot milk and honey? Good for sleeping with no worries.'

Carrie, touched, stood up and hugged her. 'Thanks, Maisie. I don't know what's the matter with me.'

'You not happy in your skin, Miss Carrie. Wanting Poppy's husband not good. Makes you sick. I go now.'

She handed Carrie the milk and was gone, her kerchiefed head held proudly, fat buttocks rolling. Carrie looked after her in astonishment.

God Almighty, thought Carrie, does the whole camp know? She carried the drink through to the bathroom, feeling her way along the walls with her free hand. There she tipped out a good inch of the milk, felt for her half jack of whisky and used it to refill her glass. Then she carried it carefully to bed, climbed in and drank it in the dark, waiting for the blessed blanket of anaesthesia.

*

The next day Carrie set out to provoke Eduardo by flirting with Karl.

Karl was a challenge. Even when she was a teenager and they had been close, she'd never been able to dent his big brother stance.

Once, when she was fourteen and home from school, she and Poppy and a bunch of boys had gone to the local cinema to see the new Bond movie. They were sitting towards the back when Poppy reached over the two boys between them and hissed, 'Carrie, Carrie. That's Karl in front, isn't it? Look! With a girl! Who is it?'

'Where? What?' whispered Carrie.

Poppy half stood up and leaned towards Carrie, pointing across her to a couple sitting close together, four rows in front.

'Over there. The two lovebirds. Look, he's kissing her!'

'Sshh!' came from behind, and Poppy muttered, 'Sorry,' and sat down. She faced forwards again and was soon absorbed by the film.

But Carrie had followed Poppy's pointing hand and seen Karl pull the girl towards him and kiss her. Then she'd put her head on his shoulder, and snuggled into him.

Carrie felt her face on fire. She couldn't bear it. She wanted to shout at Karl, furious. For the rest of the movie she'd watched them, feeling progressively less angry and more miserable.

She'd never said anything. And now she didn't care

about Karl at all; he was just a friend. But it would be satisfying to topple him from his cool high horse. And he was very attractive. A flirtation? Why not? A holiday affair would be good for everyone. It would restore her confidence, and make Eduardo realize he couldn't have it all his own way. And besides, Karl must want a bit of sex. He lived on his own, with only, she thought, the odd randy tourist to satisfy.

As he was climbing into the pick-up, she ran up to him. 'Karl! Stop, I want to come. Where are you going?'

'Hazyview. To collect some fencing. But I can get you anything. What do you need?'

She put her arm up to act as a sunshield and squinted at him from under it. 'No, I just want the ride. Small-town childhood memories. Is the ice-cream parlour still there? You can buy me an ice-cream.'

At that moment, Nelson, one of the trackers, arrived.

'Carrie, I'm sorry,' said Karl. 'I'm giving Nelson a lift into town.'

'Well, he can go in the back, can't he?'

Nelson immediately went round to the back of the bakkie to drop the tailgate and climb in, but Karl stopped him.

'No, Nelson. The back is full of cement dust. And you're in your best gear. You will sit in the front. If Carrie wants to come, she can get dusty.'

Nelson looked uncomfortable, but Karl clapped

him on the shoulder and opened the passenger door. 'Nelson, get in. I insist. Carrie is probably not coming anyway.' Nelson climbed in and Karl shut the door. He walked round to the back of the truck and said, his voice low, 'Carrie. This is the new South Africa. You do not order black people into the back of trucks like sheepdogs. Now, are you game for a ride in cement dust? I wouldn't recommend it.'

Carrie smarted at the tick-off. She was ashamed at her assumption that she took precedence over Nelson too. She said, 'Sure, I'm game.'

Karl said, 'Just a minute,' and disappeared behind the lodge. When he returned he was carrying some sacking and an old cot mattress under one arm and shepherding Angelina, who was clutching two old cushions, with the other. He said, 'As it's to be an ice-cream outing I've invited young Angelina to the party.'

He spread the sacking on the floor of the truck, and laid the mattress on it, then he dropped the tailgate and lifted the excited Angelina into the back. He waited for Carrie to climb in, and slammed the gate shut, fixing the bolts in place.

He smiled at Carrie. 'Don't stand up. And hang on to the sides.' Carrie smiled back, acknowledging round one to him. He'd succeeded in putting both Nelson and Angelina between them. But he'd not get away that easily.

It was fun but uncomfortable as they bucketed about in the back. Once they got off the pot-holed and corrugated dirt roads and on to the tarmac, it was easier, and Carrie relaxed. She liked the combination of wind and sun, and the cosiness of her niece tucked between her knees, the cushions at her back. Carrie watched the dun-coloured grass and the marula trees flash by in the foreground and, far away, the blue of the mountains intensifying as the mountains receded. She counted six matching ranges, in wavy steps to the horizon. Above that, limitless faded blue.

Little kids, sometimes as young as two or three, walked in groups along the edge of the road. Older children carried smaller ones piggyback, and they all waved. I love this country, she thought. Maybe one day I'll live here again. When I've calmed down. When I'm grown up and conservative, like Poppy.

Once they got behind a bakkie belching black diesel smoke, and she banged on the cab window to signal to Karl that they were choking in the fumes. He gave a thumbs up and accelerated fast past the pick-up. They dropped Nelson at the coach stop – he was catching a bus to visit his parents fifty miles away. Carrie and Angelina squeezed in beside Karl and they collected the roll of wire fencing, did a few errands in the high street, then swung into the forecourt of the ice-cream parlour.

The shop was on a corner, in what had once been a house, with a garden to the side. The owners had put out a few tables, children's swings and a trampo-line.

They carried their double-headed ice-cream cones

to the garden, intending to sit at a table, but the well-watered kikuya lawn drew Carrie like a magnet. She kicked off her flip-flops and pushed her toes into the springy turf, feeling the coarse runners scratching the soles of her feet. She sat down on the sloping bank, and the others joined her.

When they'd finished their ice-creams, Angelina went to play on the trampoline. Carrie lay back on the grass, eyes shut against the sun, luxuriating in the warmth. She liked the thought that her long brown legs stretching from the shortest of shorts and the exposed slice of belly under her crop-top might be a turn-on for Karl. Assuming he was looking. She opened her eyes a crack, and saw that he was sitting up, arms between his knees, watching Angelina.

Carrie shut her eyes again and said, 'Karl, do you like pierced belly buttons? Or do you think I'm too old for one?' She spoke lazily, just making casual conversation, and without looking at him. That way she could not be accused of a come-on. If he did not reply, she could pretend she'd been talking to herself, but she knew the question would force him to look at her stomach, which she now stroked lightly with one hand.

She could hear him moving next to her, and her mind raced to the idea that he would put his hand on hers, slip his fingers from her belly into her shorts or up to her tits. She wriggled down the bank a little and stretched like a cat. Maybe the first signal she'd get was his head blocking out the sun as he leaned over to kiss her mouth. Sleepily, she said, 'This sun is bliss, isn't it?'

But Karl did not touch her. She realized as soon as he spoke that, far from lying back, or rolling towards her, he'd stood up. Her eyes shot open as he said, 'Carrie, you are completely beautiful, sexy, desirable, everything you want to be.' He spoke mildly, but his voice had an emotional charge to it. She knew at once this was going to be awful. 'But you are a raving nymphet. Have you no conscience?'

Carrie sat up, her face indignant. 'What do you mean?'

He interrupted her, his voice hardening. 'Don't you give Poppy, the sweetest woman in the world, a thought? She's your sister, for God's sake.'

'How dare you . . .'

He leaned down and grabbed her wrist. 'Get up,' he said. 'I dare because I'm an old family friend. Do you think I don't know what your game is? The only reason I'm getting the come-on is to make Eduardo jealous. And the only reason you want Eduardo is because he belongs to your sister.'

Karl hauled her to her feet and took her roughly by the shoulders. For a second, a split second, Carrie thought he was going to shake her, or slap her. His fingers dug into her shoulders as he glared at her.

Carrie wanted to shout at him that it was none of his bloody business, but her mouth opened and closed without a word. Then his shoulders dropped and his fingers relaxed. He held her gaze as he sighed and said, 'You did the same when you were kids. Anything she had, you had to have one too, or have hers. Anything *you* had stayed yours.'

He let her go, and turned away. Carrie started to protest, then felt her composure go, and stopped. Karl said, 'It's not going to work this time, Carrie. Eduardo won't leave Poppy. So give it up now.' And he walked off to collect Angelina from the trampoline.

Fifteen

Two days after their holiday, with the English summer temperatures even hotter than Africa, Poppy was in the Acton Community Hall, rehearsing.

She stuck her chin up, proud and taunting, and sang, '*I am teaching some tricks to a monkey: he is learning to do what I say.*' She jerked her head like a flamenco dancer at Domenico, flashing contempt.

'Fine, Poppy. Just right.' The director turned from the group of actors on the stage and lifted his voice to encompass the rest of the company. 'Okay, everyone. That's it for tonight, and thank you. Tomorrow's call is for 10 a.m., 10 a.m. sharp tomorrow, please.'

Poppy walked down the few wooden steps to the grey plastic chairs clustered a few yards in front of the stage. Scrambling under the bags and scripts she extracted her holdall and made for the door. As Filumena she could have gone on provoking Domenico all night, even in this heat; as Poppy she was suddenly tired to the bone.

'How about a quick one, Poppy?' asked Ramon, her co-star.

Poppy had known and liked Ramon for years but she wanted to get home. She kissed his cheek and said, 'I'd love to, but I'm pooped. Rain check?' She waved at the others as she made for the door, scrabbling in her handbag for her keys.

Filumena was one of the most demanding parts she'd ever played, and they were due to reopen in a fortnight. She had hoped it would be easy, because the cast was to have been the same as before, but the male lead had decamped for Hollywood. Ramon was going to be an excellent Domenico, maybe better than his predecessor, but it took so long.

Thank God we get into the theatre next week, she thought. She knew her performance lifted on a real stage. These dreary community halls and poxy rehearsal rooms depressed her.

It was after 10 p.m. when she entered the central lobby of their Paddington building and felt the welcome blast of air-conditioning. The lights of Eduardo's offices were on, and she glanced through the clear-glass panels that alternated with the frosted ones. A few architects still crouched over computers in the big open office beyond reception, and Richard was at the espresso machine in the bar area. She waved to him and he lifted his elbow in the 'Do you want a drink?' sign. For a second she was tempted. It would be nice to wind down with a glass of wine, like she used to in the old days, when Eduardo's office was a cramped floor in Soho, and more like a club than a workplace. She'd turn up after rehearsals with her actor friends and they'd all have a few jars and then go out to eat.

Maybe she'd go in, have a drink with Richard and

see if Eduardo was ready for supper and home. But then she remembered Eduardo was in Spain. Or was it Manchester? She frowned. She should remember where her husband was. The thought flashed into her head that maybe she didn't think about where he was because she didn't want to think about who he was with. Did he buy Manchester condoms too?

She shook her head and put her hands together under her tilted cheek, signalling sleep. Richard gave her a thumbs-up of understanding and Poppy waved again and stepped into the lift. She liked Richard. The little incident was pleasing. A whole conversation in age-old sign language.

Riding up the two floors, she wished that at least the children, or even her mother-in-law, were home, but it was school holidays, and Giulia and the children were in the country.

She had a slight headache. Must be the heat. She swallowed a paracetamol, had a shower, and settled down in her pyjamas to watch the 11 p.m. news with a bowl of cornflakes on her lap and a glass of wine at her elbow. Being on one's own had its compensations.

When the telephone rang she thought it would be Eduardo. He usually rang late when she was working. But it was Carrie, ringing to see if she'd like to come to supper one night, or catch a movie. 'I bet you aren't eating proper food on your own.'

'You must be psychic,' returned Poppy. 'I'm eating cornflakes in front of the box. And how did you guess Eduardo was away?'

'Oh, I . . . I don't know. You must have told me. Or maybe he said he was going to Manchester.'

So, thought Poppy. It is Manchester. 'He'll be back at the weekend,' she said. 'We'll go to the country. Or rather he will, and I'll follow on Saturday, after the first dress rehearsal. Do you want to come?'

'I'd love to. But what about this movie then? How's tomorrow? If we don't do it soon, you'll have opened and we'll have no chance till the end of the run.'

Poppy explained about the never-ending re-hearsals. They agreed she'd go to Carrie's whenever she got off, early or late, and they'd decide then on movies or dinner, or scrambled eggs and a video.

In fact Poppy arrived early, and the sisters carried tall glasses and big bottles of Pilsner Urquell into Carrie's little garden, laying the bottles down on the unmown grass.

Carrie made a half-hearted attempt to wipe London grime from a plastic chair, but Poppy waved her away and collapsed into it, saying, 'Don't bother, Carrie. I'm absolutely filthy. You have no idea how dirty a community hall can be. And I'm sweaty as a racehorse. Probably stink too.'

Carrie poured a glass and handed it to Poppy, who looked at the pale beer and foamy head then held the cool glass to her hot cheek. 'Oh Carrie, I shouldn't drink beer, but what the hell?' She swallowed a mouthful, eyes shut. 'Heaven in a glass.'

Carrie lay on the grass and stretched. Poppy

noticed, as she always did, how lithe and beautiful Carrie was, even wearing chef's checks and a thread-bare tee-shirt. Carrie looked up at the overhanging tangle of greenery and said, 'You wouldn't like to look after my garden as well as our mother's, I don't suppose?'

'Dead right, I wouldn't.' Poppy turned her head to take in the overgrown borders and moss-covered paving. 'Why isn't it all dry as a bone? We're in the middle of a heat wave. And I don't see you out with a watering can every evening.'

Carrie sat up with a gleeful snort. 'Too right. But next door have this massive watering system that comes on every night at 2 a.m and includes my little patch by mistake.' Carrie grinned at Poppy. 'They're mega rich, but they're such mean bastards they'd go ape if they knew they were giving away water.'

Poppy said, 'But isn't there a hose pipe ban? I thought sprinklers weren't allowed either?'

Carrie laughed, 'Oh, my law-abiding big sister! Yes, there is. If it wasn't that I'm a beneficiary, I'd report them, just to see their toffee noses out of joint.'

Poppy closed her eyes and let the Pilsner seep into her. Wonderful how alcohol could turn one kind of exhaustion into another: from fraught and miserable to pleasantly languorous. And Carrie's nonchalance always cheered her.

They talked about Poppy's rehearsals, and then about Karl's plans for Kaia Moya: he wanted to join

a marketing consortium to sell bush holidays in the States. After a while they lapsed into silence, enjoying the cool of the shade and the lager.

Carrie poured them both another glass. Shouldn't, thought Poppy, it's going to my head.

'So,' said Carrie suddenly, 'are we going to the movies?'

'Oh, let's not, Carrie,' said Poppy. 'It is so divine here. I don't think I could bear the effort, all those bodies in a queue, and hot furry seats, and maybe no air-conditioning . . .'

'Okay, okay, Popps. It's not obligatory. We'll stay in and get plastered. I've got *Cat Ballou* on video. Or *Shakespeare in Love*, which I've still not seen.'

'*Cat Ballou*,' decided Poppy. 'I don't want anything about actors and plays.'

Poppy let the back of her hand caress the top of the uncut grass, swinging her arm gently. I must be drunk, she thought. It feels so good. 'Do you remember the bit when Lee Marvin is pissed as a newt and the Indian kid says, "Your eyes are all bloodshot. They look awful," or something, and he says . . .'

'"*You should see them from my side!*"' Carrie and Poppy said the line together, already laughing.

Once they started laughing, they couldn't stop, and it launched them down a path of telling each other old chestnuts.

'Do you remember your Standard Two science exam?' Poppy asked.

'Of course I do. Mom and Dad told everyone who

219

came to dinner for years afterwards. I used to die of embarrassment, but it's funny now.'

The sisters again quoted together, their faces alight with amusement, eyes on each other's, '"The abominable cavity contains the bowels, of which there are five – a, e, i, o and u."'

Carrie, her eyes streaming, said, 'And who put "To keep milk from going sour, keep it in the cow"?'

Poppy, wiping her eyes with the back of her wrist, said, 'Or "For fainting, put the head between the knees of the nearest medical doctor"? If Eduardo saw us now, Poppy spluttered, 'he'd think we were drunk.'

'We are drunk,' said Carrie. 'Well, mildly drunk. Which you do not get often enough, Popps. Your life is too serious. Serious work. Serious family.'

Poppy heaved herself out of the chair and said, 'Carrie darling, can I have a shower? I'm so filthy, and if we watch a video I'll be too tired to have a bath when I get home.'

Carrie gathered up the glasses and empty bottles and said, 'Sure, Popps, you know where everything is. Grab a clean towel from the landing cupboard. I'll make cheese on toast or something.'

Poppy dumped her bag and kicked off her shoes at the bottom of the stairs. Walking up to Carrie's bathroom she peeled off her clammy shirt, and started to undo the buttons of her jeans.

She helped herself to a towel, dropping it on the cane chair in the bathroom, then pulled off the rest of her clothes, tossing them into a pile in the corner. She would borrow something cool and baggy from Carrie. Poppy turned on the shower, and was about to step into it when she realized there was no soap or shower gel.

She looked across at the bath, but there was only an empty mini-bottle of some hotel shampoo. Damn, I really want some nice smelly soapy bubbles, she thought. She opened the little mirrored cabinet above the basin with a jerk. Several flat boxes of medicines fell out of it, cascading into the basin.

Blast, she thought. Why can't they be proper bottles like they used to be? She started to gather the packages up: sore throat lozenges, antihistamines, Rennies. And then her hand stopped. As if touching the next package would burn it.

Suddenly she was completely sober. Horribly sober. She stood immobile, her brain whirring, her eyes fixed on the packet still lying in the basin. She wanted to stop thinking. This train of thought was taking her somewhere she did not want to go, but she couldn't stop. Click click click. A plus B equals C.

It was a condom pack. The condoms were Spanish: VIVA L'AMOR. She had seen them before. She'd found them in Eduardo's washbag. They were not available in England.

Poppy picked up the pack. Click click click. No English lettering. Only Spanish. Carrie did not go to Spain.

Her husband was sleeping with Carrie.

That's why she knew he was in Manchester.

She walked out of the bathroom, still holding the condoms, and sat on the bed. She must think. Must decide what to do. But her brain, so inexorable before, was now stuck in a groove.

Her husband was sleeping with Carrie. He was in love with her sister. Her best friend. The woman she had just spent an hour laughing with. The two people she loved most in the world were sleeping together, deceiving her, betraying her.

She stood up. What was she to do? Then she sat down again.

Carrie was at the door, a glass of red wine in each hand. 'Did you find the towel?' She held out the glass, but Poppy did not take it. Poppy seemed to look past her, her round face pale, distraught.

Carrie said at once. 'God, Popps, what's the matter?' She put the wine glasses down on the bedside table and said, 'What's happened? Are you all right? Why are you sitting here with no clothes on?'

Poppy took her glasses off and put them back on again. Her eyes for the first time met Carrie's and they were hard as nails. 'You're sleeping with Eduardo,' she said. 'You're having an affair with my husband.'

Carrie's mouth opened. There was a tiny pause and then she shouted, '*What?* What? You're mad.'

Poppy held up the condom packet. Carrie took it, and said, too quickly, 'So what does that mean? I agree I sleep with guys from time to time. But Poppy, what's got into you? How can you think I'd sleep with

Eduardo?' Carrie's earnest eyes were wide and pleading, concerned and hurt.

For a second Poppy was tempted to believe her. It would be so nice to believe her. But she knew Carrie was lying. She'd heard her plead her innocence throughout their childhood. She stood up, and tossed the condom packet on the bed.

Her voice was stone. 'Then how come your condoms come from the same chemist in Bilbao as Eduardo's? The ones you told me not to worry about, because all men were weak and unfaithful, and it didn't mean anything serious? Well, I hope you are right about that. I guess we are both about to find out.'

Suddenly her being naked in front of her sister was unbearable. She stood up and walked swiftly into the bathroom, shutting the door and sliding the bolt, as if she thought Carrie might insist on following her.

Poppy rooted in the pile of clothes for her knickers and bra. They were damp from sweat, and she struggled to get them on. All the time she was dressing, she avoided looking at herself in the big mirror. She mustn't let her mind dwell on Carrie naked in front of that mirror, of Eduardo peeling off his shirt. Right now she had to just get away. Get away from Carrie. Get out of her house. Go. Go.

When she came out of the bathroom Carrie had left the bedroom. Poppy was relieved by this, even though her mind told her that if Carrie was innocent she'd have banged the bathroom door down. But then she already knew Carrie wasn't innocent.

As Poppy walked steadily down the stairs, a part of her brain congratulated herself on a perfect exit, even without her shoes. I'm doing what I do best, thought Poppy, I'm acting. She held the banister rail, treading carefully. At the bottom of the stairs, she was conscious of Carrie in the kitchen. She did not look at her. No point in adding to the melodrama. She put on her shoes, picked up her bag and walked out into the street.

Carrie's first instincts were to barge into the bathroom after her sister, stop her, tell her it wasn't true. Put her arms round her and comfort her, make the pain go away. But something in the straightness of Poppy's plump bare shoulders, in the carriage of her head, prevented her. Besides, Carrie was frightened. She did not know what to do.

She went downstairs, saying to herself that she needed time to think. She'd stop Poppy before she could leave. But when Poppy came down and calmly donned her shoes, picked up her bag, went out and turned to close the door quietly behind her, Carrie found she could not move.

Carrie clutched her hair each side of her temples, pulling hard, then she ran into the study and got her Filofax from her bag. On the inside cover was a yellow sticker with Eduardo's Manchester hotel number.

Her hands were shaking so much she had to have

three goes at it, but at last she heard a brisk, 'Good evening, Hotel Manchester.' She gave Eduardo's room number, her throat tight and her heart banging, her eyes staring wide but unseeing at the dresser shelves, laden with cookbooks.

He wasn't there. She knew it as soon as the long buzz had sounded three times. She remained frozen, listening to the sound of distant ringing in an empty room, until there was a click and a recorded voice told her that her party was unable to take the call but she could press One to leave a message, or Two to return to the operator, or Three to . . . She pressed One. More clicks, and then a different recorded voice: 'This is the guest-messaging service. Please record your message now.' Beep.

When she finally spoke her voice had vanished. What came out was a small squeak, and then a gasping, 'Eduardo. Poppy knows. Shit.' She swallowed and tried again, her voice stronger, almost angry. 'Christ, Eduardo, where the hell are you? I need you, for God's sake.' She tried his mobile then, but it was switched off. She left a calmer message on that, and put the telephone down.

Carrie longed for comfort. For Eduardo to burst through the door and put his arms round her. For Poppy to ring her and say . . . say what? That she believed Carrie: of course she hadn't stolen her husband. Or that she was glad really: it was okay. She and Eduardo had been strangers for years . . .

But Carrie knew none of this would happen.

Eduardo was out, and miles away. And Poppy's eyes had been full of hatred.

When she thought back to that look of Poppy's, it was like an action replay. More clearly than the first time, she saw Poppy's eyes, dry and slightly narrowed behind her specs. How could that one look have carried so much? Accusation, disbelief, scorn. Contempt for a sister who could so betray love, and who then denied it. Even loathing.

The thought shook her. Poppy hates me. She actually hates me. But Poppy *couldn't* hate her. Poppy had always loved her. Defended her to their parents, stood up for her to Eduardo, helped her out of a thousand scrapes, loved her and comforted her every time she'd been shipwrecked by some man. Believed in her and encouraged her, been there for her.

As she said the trite phrase to herself, *been there for her*, she realized just what she was losing. She was losing her mainstay, her best friend, her sister. Her mind kept turning, from long habit, to the thought that Poppy would know what to do. More than anything she wanted to do what she'd always done in a crisis, and pour her heart out to Poppy, who would give her wise advice and make her feel better.

But now she couldn't. She lay curled up on the kitchen sofa, every now and again writhing from one position to another.

'Fuck it. I need a drink,' she said aloud, and fetched the bottle she'd opened for Poppy all those years ago. She looked at her watch. It was less than an hour ago. She poured a large glass at the sink, and drank it like medicine, in one go. She tipped the rest of the bottle into the glass and carried it through to the living room.

Automatically she aimed the remote control at the television and a football match sprang to life. She crouched in an armchair, her feet under her bum, and watched the little figures running about the screen. Like Subbuteo, she thought, or play people.

She didn't follow the game – she had no idea who was playing whom – but she didn't switch channels. She stayed in a ball in front of the screen, her eyes glued but unseeing, drinking steadily. When the glass was empty, she fetched a fresh bottle and went back to the television. It was a game show now. She did not follow it, but she watched the screen as before.

By nine o'clock she'd finished the second bottle, but she felt entirely sober. She'd hoped the booze would ease the anguish, but if anything it was worse.

Tears started to run down her face. She was completely alone, abandoned by the two people she loved most in the world, Poppy and Eduardo. Poppy didn't understand how hard it had been for her. Poppy, the plain one, the dull one, had everything. She was a successful actress. She had children. A house – two houses – money, Eduardo. She had bloody everything.

Carrie pulled a cushion on to her knees and hugged it. She thought, I'm the one everyone said was lucky. The pretty one. The vivacious one. And what have I got? A sodding great overdraft, no husband, no children. It will be baggy tits and cellulite next. She buried her face in the cushion, wiping tears and mascara on it in equal proportions, and sniffing. Oh, why didn't Eduardo ring? Maybe he was on a flight right now. Or a train. Maybe he'd got her message and was flying back to her. This thought sustained her for a little, but in fact she knew he'd have telephoned if he'd got her messages. And she doubted if planes and trains ran that late.

She tried his hotel, but he still wasn't in. She called his mobile to hear again the clipped, 'Eduardo Santolini. Please leave a message.' She was very tired. Bed. She'd go to bed. As she locked the front door she looked into the little hall mirror. Her face was red and puffy, streaks of make-up under her eyes. Ugly. Ugly.

Still sobbing slightly, she went up the stairs. Why aren't I drunk, she thought? I'm usually drunk on a bottle.

She pulled her clothes off, but didn't do her teeth or wash. Good, she thought, seeing the two untouched glasses of wine at the bedside. Maybe if I drink them?

But she knocked one of them over while reaching for the television control. She used a handful of tissues to mop ineffectually at the table, but didn't bother with the carpet. It's a dark carpet. It won't show.

The little TV at the end of the bed must be on the blink, she thought. Its vertical hold has gone. The newscasters kept rolling up and being replaced by another identical pair. She drank the remaining glass of wine, while she watched the uncontrollable telly. It was the same on all channels. In fact the whole room's vertical hold was dicky.

Must be drunk at last. Good. Sleep now.

Sixteen

When Eduardo entered their bedroom at seven the next morning, Poppy had barely slept. She felt dreadful. Her skin was pasty and tight, her eyes puffy and lids leaden.

Eduardo pulled a chair up near the bed and put the tea tray down on it.

'Do you want some tea?'

She nodded. 'Please,' she said. She thought how odd to be talking about tea. In fact the whole thing was like a play. Eduardo never brought her tea in bed unless she was sick. And he didn't turn up at 7 a.m. if he'd been away. Carrie had called him then, so he knew that she knew.

He handed her a cup and she wriggled up to a sitting position. She fumbled for her glasses and put them on. She examined her husband, sitting on her bedside like an anxious family doctor. He looked strained too, she was glad to see. She felt oddly reluctant to say anything more. If only they could just sit here and drink tea.

With a kind of weary inevitability, she started the conversation, which could undo her life completely. 'Are you leaving me then?' she said.

'Leaving you?' His eyes widened in alarm and

disbelief. 'Leaving you? Darling, do you want me to?'

Poppy shook her head, more a gesture of confusion than a no. 'I don't want you to stay with me if you'd rather marry my sister.' There, she'd said it. All the night as she lay churning and gnawing at it, that had been the worst scenario. That he would leave her and marry Carrie.

'Marry Carrie! Oh darling, I'd never marry Carrie.'

'What is it then?' She had to put the cup and saucer down because her hand shook so badly they rattled. He didn't answer, but reached out to take her by the shoulders.

She snapped. 'No, Eduardo. Let's get on with this. How long have you been sleeping with my sister?'

Eduardo had the grace to look ashamed. He was on a hook and didn't like it. He looked at his highly polished Italian shoes and said, 'How do you know? Did Carrie tell you? She threatened . . .'

Poppy interrupted him. 'Haven't you spoken to her? Hasn't she sent you to say this thing is bigger than the both of you, that you couldn't help yourselves, that your wife doesn't understand you . . .'

Eduardo stood up. 'No, no. Listen, Poppy. You've got to listen . . .' He picked up the tray and set it on the dressing table. She looked at his back as he did so with something very like loathing, then he turned back and sat down on the chair, facing her. 'But finish your tea first.'

Poppy knew he was playing for time but she needed

the tea. She held the cup in both hands so she would not spill it, and then drained it. Eduardo took it and said, 'More?'

She shook her head, and said, 'I'm listening.' Her voice told him she would not believe him anyway, but it had to be got through.

'It just happened, Poppy. I didn't plan it. Carrie is such a flirt, and I fell for it.'

'So it's Carrie's fault?'

He gave a slight shrug. Six of one.

'Where?'

She knew that he understood the question, but he pretended not to. 'Where? What do you mean?'

'Where did you first sleep with her? In Kaia Moya? Here in this bed? In our bedroom at Manor Farm?'

'Poppy, you don't want to know the sordid details. I had an affair with Carrie. A brief affair. And it's over.'

'Who says so? Carrie? Does Carrie know it's over?' She knew her eyes were gimlets, boring at him. He shifted uneasily, opened his mouth to say something, but she was merciless, 'And I *do* want to know the sordid details. I want to know the whole lot. When, where, how long, is this the first? How many affairs have you had while I've so dumbly thought you loved me . . .' She stopped abruptly. If she went on about love she'd cry.

'Poppy, I swear to you. I am so, so sorry. I would not have had this happen for worlds. I cannot believe

I could have . . .' His voice trailed off, dried up by the coldness of her stare.

She said nothing and he asked, the fingers of his right hand fiddling lightly with the very edge of the lace of her sleeve, 'Poppy, how did you find out? Did Carrie tell you?'

She wouldn't give him the satisfaction of telling him anything. She said, 'I think it's for you to explain things, not me.'

'I can't explain it. I can only say I regret it. Which I do. I really do.'

For a fleeting moment Poppy felt her heart soften towards him, but she denied herself any such weakening. She pulled her legs up and said, 'Well, in that case, could you shift now? I've got to go to rehearsal.' He stood up and pulled the chair out of the way as she swung her legs over the side of the bed. 'I'll be back at eight. That gives you a whole day to tell Carrie it's all over, or pack your things and get out of here.' She picked up her watch from the bedside and stood up, a small, round, determined woman, her chin high.

'And you should know, Eduardo, that those are your only options. I know you both too well for you to get away with any more screwing behind my back.'

Eduardo didn't like the phrase, she could see. Too bad. She went on, 'I may have been blind up to now. Trust makes you blind, I guess. But you've blown that. I'd notice now if you waved at her from a mile away.'

233

She headed for the bathroom, ending with, 'And if you decide to stay, fine, but tell Carrie a mile away is not enough.'

Carrie came to the flat three days later. She used the key she'd had since the Santolinis moved in, and she was in the kitchen before Poppy could prevent it.

'What the hell are you doing here?' said Poppy. She had a bucket of plant debris in one hand and a pair of secateurs in the other. She swept into the kitchen from the terrace, anger in her every movement, and dumped the bucket in the sink.

Carrie hesitated, then came towards her sister. 'Poppy, I have to talk to you . . .'

Poppy interrupted her at once. 'Carrie, I've nothing to say to you, and I don't want to hear anything you've got to say to me. So go, please.'

'Poppy, how can you be so horrible? Can't you see I'm in hell?' Carrie tried to touch Poppy's arm, but Poppy backed out of reach, flinging off Carrie's hand with a jerk.

'And who made the hell? You did.'

Carrie tried again to reach for her sister, but Poppy stepped back and raised her voice, 'And you dragged me and Eduardo in there with you. But then, you always did that, didn't you? Made other people suffer for things you did.'

Carrie's head came up at this. Stung, she said, 'What I did? I suppose you think I seduced Eduardo? Do you? Well, I bloody didn't. I don't suppose your inno-cent husband told you he insisted on coming to my house, did he? Or why? And I suppose you think I'm the first? Well, sis, I'm not. He's been cheating on you for years. Ask him about Michelle Ward, for a start. The only difference is that this time he . . . he loves . . .' Carrie faltered and stopped.

Poppy suddenly felt on treacherous ground. She had wanted Eduardo to tell her everything, and he wouldn't, but she did not want to hear it from Carrie. Carrie jerked her chin higher and said, 'He loves me, Poppy, and I love him.'

Poppy folded her arms across her bosom and faced her sister, face drained of all colour, all expression. 'He said so, did he? That he loves you?' Carrie didn't answer and Poppy gained momentum from her advantage. 'Did he? Then why won't he see you? Why doesn't he return your calls? Why is he staying with me?'

Carrie's shoulders suddenly fell. 'That's what I don't understand. I know he loves me. No, don't shake your head. He does. He's just frightened of you, Poppy, and he loves the children. But you could let him go . . . You could tell him . . .'

Poppy's eyes widened and she let out a gasp of astonishment. 'What? I don't believe I'm hearing this. Carrie, are you asking me to give Eduardo leave to screw you? Tell him to go ahead and shove his dick where everyone else does?'

Carrie, taken aback by her sister's crudeness, said

nothing, and Poppy went on, 'You are as immoral and selfish as you were at ten years old. You think you can just do what you did then, turn on those big beautiful eyes and you'll be forgiven, and be given exactly what you want, whether it's yours or anyone else's. Well, for once, baby sister, it won't wash.'

For a second there was silence, as the red of Carrie's flush climbed her neck and burst over her face. Then she yelled, '*Me* get everything I want? That's rich! Who got to go to RADA when there wasn't enough money to send me to Switzerland? Who got all Dad's books?'

Poppy frowned, then a dry little laugh escaped her and she said, 'Don't be ridiculous, Carrie. I got the books because I read books. You don't. And I went to RADA on a scholarship, as you know perfectly well. And the hotel school was way beyond Mom and Dad's means. Though I expect you'd have been happy to see Dad spend what he had on you rather than on looking after poor Mom. You don't give a damn about Lucille.'

'And what exactly do you mean by that?'

For a second Poppy struggled to regain control, to be her normal, reasonable, accommodating self, but then, with a feeling of pure exhilaration, she let go, releasing years of resentment in a river of fury. She stuck her face into Carrie's and shouted: 'I don't think you even visit her when you say you do. You know she can't remember, so you just don't bother. When did you last take her out to lunch? Or do a jigsaw with her? Or do anything at all other than steal her silver and china for photo shoots?'

Carrie took a step back. Then, her mouth twisted and ugly, she spat out, 'Well, why should I bother when little Miss Goody Two Shoes, wearing her halo and waving her fairy wand, does it so well? Who needs Carrie when Perfect Poppy is at hand?' She drew a breath and said, 'Except Eduardo of course, who finally couldn't bear another day of domestic perfection and opted for some fun instead.'

'Fun. Yes. That's exactly what you are good at. I expect half of London has enjoyed your idea of fun. What's the recipe, Carrie? Other than sex, drugs and rock and roll? Well, get this. You cannot have Eduardo. And he does not love you.'

Carrie turned away, then flung herself into a chair. She pulled out a packet of Marlboros and lit one, her hand shaking. 'You hate me, don't you?'

Poppy drew a breath, and said with more control but still forcefully, 'Are you surprised? Doesn't sleeping with my husband warrant hatred? Christ, Carrie, grow up! You aren't ten years old now, helping yourself to the best bike, or best pony, or top bunk. You can't just help yourself to Eduardo and expect me to forgive you. I'll never forgive you.'

Carrie's face was still flushed, but now her eyes filled with tears.

'Okay, Poppy, I came here wanting to be friends. I thought we could talk about this. Whatever I've done, or Eduardo's done, we are all in it together, and you don't hate me.' She hesitated. 'We all love each other . . .'

Poppy exploded, 'Love each other? Love? What I feel for you, little sister, is not love. Eduardo is right – you don't know the meaning of the word. Love, real love, is for grown-ups.'

Carrie was reeling under Poppy's onslaught. She had never seen her remotely like this, but while Poppy's venom astounded her, it fired her once more to retaliation. She dashed the back of her hand across her eyes and shouted, 'Oh yes? Like you and Eduardo, I suppose? Is that why Eduardo spent more nights with me than he did in Bilbao or Manchester? Because love with you was so all-consuming?' Carrie glared at Poppy, wanting only to hurt her as deeply as she could. She went on, 'Maybe Eduardo has run home to Mummy now, but don't think he won't miss the recipe, as you call it. He said I was the best fuck he'd ever had. He said being with me was an undreamed-of liberation. He said I made him feel twenty years younger . . .'

Poppy had a childish desire to cover her ears. For a second her hands fluttered in distress round her own face, then she ran at Carrie, swinging her right arm as hard as she could. The slap made a sharp crack, jerking Carrie's head to the side.

The sisters stared at each other in silence.

Then Carrie righted herself in the chair, and put both hands up to her cheek, now suffused with purple. Her eyes brimmed with tears as the stinging pain spread. 'Hitting me won't change the facts, sis. Eduardo hasn't the bottle to leave you, but that doesn't mean he loves you.'

Poppy looked at Carrie's face in horror. Horror at her own violence. For a second she wanted to fall on her knees and put her arms round Carrie and say I'm sorry, I'm so sorry, but she just stood there, and then the thought occurred to her, No, I'm not sorry. I'm not sorry at all.

Poppy swung away from Carrie and took a few paces, then turned back and said, quietly now, 'Do you think I want to be the sensible one? Do you think I like being the dependable wife who always does the right thing? While you gad about looking beautiful and getting exactly what you want from everyone?'

Carrie looked at her in disbelief. 'Me, get everything I want? That's rich coming from you. Who has fame? And a fantastic career? And money? And children?' Her voice faltered as she said, ' . . . And Eduardo. Forgive me if I'm a bit short on sympathy.'

Carrie stood up, picked up her bag and made for the door.

Poppy heard the bang of the front door and the whirr of the lift as Carrie pressed the button. Her palm was still ringing from hitting her sister.

Poppy was sustained by her new cynicism. Bitterness helped her get through the days, but she would have preferred to have remained a dupe. She'd been a fool to have so innocently believed in love and truth and happy ever after, but she'd been happy then.

Until the first night of *Filumena*, Poppy mostly managed not to think. She concentrated all her efforts on the play, escaping with relief to the feisty life of Filumena, ex-prostitute, who tricks her long-time lover into marriage. Pouring invective on her stage husband, organizing the lives of her sons, dominating the other characters, the play and the audience, Poppy felt each night the adrenalin rush of power.

They opened to few reviews since this was a second run, but the *Guardian* gave them a rave, declaring Poppy's performance magnificent. After that the steady routine of domestic life and the heavy demands of a great leading role helped her to avoid a descent into misery. But she felt ten years older, the age of the role she played.

When she had first read the play, Poppy had seen it simply as a strong character part, with no relevance to her own life. Now she understood Filumena's rage and desire for revenge. Because she'd so loved Domenico, Filumena had spent twenty years as his mistress, only to wake up to the knowledge that while she'd been keeping house and running his business for him Domenico had been travelling the world and cheating on her. Poppy knew every performance was a kind of catharsis. Sometimes she felt she might spit out the name Eduardo instead of Domenico.

The play was funny rather than dark, though. On the first night Poppy was glorious, powerful and captivating. The audience wept with laughter, and the bravos and curtain calls went on and on. Poppy could not help comparing the esteem and love that the audience seemed to bear her with the tired duty of Eduardo's attitude. She was now inclined to believe he did not love Carrie, but she thought the less of her husband for so readily abandoning his lover. What kind of a man sleeps with his wife's sister and then ditches her at his wife's say-so?

As Carrie and Richard climbed the stairs to the star dressing rooms they heard Eduardo behind them. Richard turned and said, 'Hello, Eduardo, I knew you'd be here. I suppose you got the house seats, you lucky dog. We could only get the back of the circle.'

'Hi, Eduardo,' said Carrie, her heart pounding. 'She was wonderful, wasn't she? Even better than before the summer?'

Eduardo did not answer, and Carrie was pleased to see he looked uncomfortable. She had made some serious decisions since her row with Poppy, and one of them was that if Eduardo was such a wet as to crumble because his wife issued an ultimatum, then fine. It had only been a week since she'd been utterly in love with him, believing she could not live without him, but now she knew she could get by.

Only she could not afford to lose Poppy. She'd talked Richard into coming to the *Filumena* first night, when her sister's dressing room would be full of friends and Poppy would not be able to turn her away.

She felt bad about Richard. She'd treated him so appallingly. It was time they were friends again. Why couldn't they be friends? He was the only person who had known about Eduardo, and he'd been wonderful, telling no one. She'd make it up to him.

When they went from the gloom of the corridor to the bright lights of the dressing room, the first thing Carrie noticed was how old her sister looked. Forty, at least. She'd appeared magnificent on stage, glamorous and confident and very sexy. Now, in spite of first-night elation, she looked pasty, her stage make-up accentuating the exhaustion of her eyes. There were already four or five people in the dressing room and in the hubbub of congratulation the fact that neither Eduardo nor Poppy said a word to Carrie went unnoticed, except by Carrie.

Poppy was buoyed up by the audience's reception of her, on a high, so when a gay couple she'd known since RADA days suggested supper at the Ivy, saying they'd booked a table for four on the off chance, she turned to Eduardo, 'Do let's, I could do with a bit of fun. It's been a tough couple of weeks.'

As they trooped out of the theatre, Eduardo turned to Richard to say, 'See you at the office then.' Carrie said, 'Bye Poppy, bye Eduardo,' but neither answered.

As Carrie followed Richard out of the stage door into the piss-soaked alley behind the theatre, she was close to tears. She felt like a child told to go to bed at a party, a child no one was allowed to talk to.

'Are you going to tell me what's going on?' asked

Richard. 'Has Eduardo dumped you?'

For a moment Carrie's throat hurt with the effort not to cry. She said, 'In a word, yes.' She was tempted to tell him the whole sorry saga, but she was ashamed. 'Oh, Richard, you don't want to know. And anyway, it's over.'

Carrie put her arm through Richard's and leaned in close. She smiled up at him with visible strain. 'What I need,' she said, 'is a few drinks and a line of coke.' Seeing his frown, she amended, 'Okay, some good weed.'

Sunday was the one day Poppy had off, and she was tired after the week's performances. She'd driven down late last night after the show, crept into bed next to the unmoving Eduardo, and slept until the arrival of Tom and Lorato at seven. She wished Giulia had kept the children at bay, even for an extra hour, but she suspected her mother-in-law disapproved of her working, especially as an actress. In truth she sometimes disapproved herself. She would have preferred to be with the children more, and sometimes thought she'd be happy to give up the stage, yet she knew the desire to act would gnaw at her, pull her back to this dual life.

Now she was pushing slivers of garlic and needles of fresh rosemary into a leg of lamb. Preparing Sunday lunch was no longer the pleasure it used to be. Perhaps she was just exhausted after the emotional upheaval of the past few weeks. She'd found the two shows yesterday particularly draining, partly because of the heat, but also because she felt so marooned in London while the rest of the family were out of town. It never occurred to Eduardo to stay up with her and drive her down.

She used to like Saturdays. In the past, when she'd been working, she and Carrie would sometimes drool round Harvey Nicks on a Saturday morning, or meet at the Fifth Floor restaurant or the sushi bar for an early lunch. Or Carrie might turn up in her dressing room between the shows with a picnic, or they'd walk round Neal's Yard. Or if Carrie was coming down to Manor Farm she'd collect Poppy from the theatre and they'd drive down together. Such sisterly jaunts were out of the question now.

Poppy wiped her hands on the tea towel and leaned against Olaf to push him out of the way while she shoved the lamb into the top oven of the Aga, then she went through to the larder to get the potatoes, the dog padding after her.

'I don't bloody believe it,' she said aloud, looking at the potato box, where one wrinkled potato lay in a bed of dusty earth.

'What's the matter, Mum? What don't you bloody believe?' It was Angelina, barefoot and in shorts, at the larder door.

'I don't bloody believe,' said Poppy, 'that neither your daddy, nor your granny, nor the bloody gardener has dug up any bloody spuds. So guess who's got to?'

Angelina said, 'Hey, Mum, wicked. You never say

bloody. That's really cool.' But she looked more anxious than admiring.

Poppy looked at her skinny daughter and laughed. 'Oh darling, you are not meant to be impressed. I am not meant to say bloody. And certainly not in front of you. Come on. You can dig up the spuds.'

They collected a fork and a bucket from the potting shed – Poppy was mildly irritated that the spade wasn't where it should be – and set off for the vegetable garden. As they went through the little gate in the hedge, Angelina exclaimed, 'Look, Mum, Daddy's digging up the potatoes, and he's got the spade!'

Eduardo smiled broadly at Poppy. 'You thought I'd forgotten, didn't you?' He shook a clutch of potatoes free of soil and scooped them into his bucket. 'Angelina, would you like to do your old dad a *huge* favour?' Angelina nodded solemnly. 'Will you finish this job for me? I want to talk secrets to your mother for five minutes. Then we will come back and admire how many spuds you have managed to dig up.'

Angelina took the spade eagerly. Eduardo went on, 'If you have filled both buckets, without putting the spade through any of the potatoes, I'll take you to the stables after tea. Is it a deal?'

Angelina hopped about, 'Yes, yes. It's a deal. Cool, Dad.'

Eduardo put his arm over Poppy's shoulder and steered her towards the lane that ran down to the river.

Poppy was mollified by Eduardo remembering the potatoes. She was even a little gratified at his wanting to talk to her. But she felt so drained by the misery of the last couple of weeks that she almost wished he would not say anything at all. Maybe they could just walk down to the river and watch Olaf fail to catch squirrels or rabbits.

He said at once, 'Poppy, I know I have put you through the mill. And I won't go over everything again. But I just want to make a speech, which I want you to listen to without interrupting. Okay?'

Poppy started to protest, 'Oh Eduardo, let's not . . .' but he cut in, 'Darling, all I want to say is this. You are the most astonishing and wonderful woman. To have managed to go through the last two weeks, to give a truly great performance as Filumena and to behave to the children and to Giulia as though nothing has happened proves what I have always known. You have more character, more good sense, more talent and more love than any woman on earth, and I am a complete bastard to have lost sight of it for a single second. I love you, Poppy. And that's the truth.'

Poppy could not help being touched by this. Eduardo, though physically affectionate, was not given to emotional talk. But she would not let herself melt so easily. She kept her voice even and detached and asked, 'Carrie says you love her. And have told her so.'

Eduardo walked in front of her and put his arms

on her shoulders, forcing her to look at him. He said, 'I don't. And I have not.'

It's odd, thought Poppy, but at this moment, anyway, I do believe him.

After lunch Angelina ran and the toddlers staggered backwards and forwards through the spray of the lawn sprinkler. Poppy lay on the grass under the walnut tree and Eduardo slept in the hammock, the *Independent on Sunday* on the grass beside him. Giulia had gone upstairs for a proper siesta on a bed.

Poppy looked at the idyll before her, but it did not lift the bleakness. Eduardo's speech before lunch had helped, but she could not forgive him easily. She feared she'd never forgive him.

The spray caught the sun and refracted it into a rainbow over the greenest of lawns. The shrieking children ran under the water and danced about with unselfconscious excitement. The three naked bodies were the picture of health and happiness: Angelina's milk-white and skinny, her blonde hair darkened into rat's tails; Tom's burly and pink; Lorato's round, brown and shiny. They haven't an inkling of how close we all came to shipwreck, she thought. Or that we may founder yet.

Eduardo drove up to London on Sunday night after supper and Poppy had to will herself not to accuse him of going up to see Carrie. He said he had to be up for an early plane for Bilbao.

She didn't say that it was almost as quick from here to Gatwick as from London. She had to stop accusing him all the time. Over the last fortnight she had run the gamut of accusation, hurt, hate, misery and fear. Somewhere she had lost the mastery she had had that first morning when he'd appeared in their bedroom and brought her tea and contrition. Now, only on the stage did she feel in control and confident.

If I become a neurotic wreck, even if it is his fault, she thought, he'll leave for sure. He's not the type to nursemaid a feeble wife.

In truth she didn't think he was seeing Carrie. She suspected that Eduardo was secretly relieved to have the decision about Carrie made for him. For her it was more complicated. She both mourned the loss of Carrie, as if she had died, and hated her guts. One thing was for certain: she was never going to let her back into her life.

Seventeen

Poppy pressed the play button and stiffened as she heard Carrie's voice: 'Poppy. It's Carrie. The only communication I've had from either of you is Eduardo's e-mail telling me not to write as you won't open the envelopes. So I'm going to have to say it all on this thing.' Carrie's voice faltered and then was suddenly very loud. 'Don't switch it off, Poppy. *Don't*. If you are there for God's sake pick it up and let me talk to you.'

There was a pause, and then Carrie's voice resumed. 'Okay, if you won't, at least hear me out. Poppy, I need you. I can live without Eduardo, but not without you. I've been either drunk or high on coke or knocked out with sleeping pills for weeks. There's nothing stable in my life. I've just lost a job for the *Sunday Times* because I failed to turn up for a meeting. I know it's all my fault. But for Christ's sake, Poppy, help me. Lucille asked me what was wrong and I started crying and . . .'

The mention of their mother electrified Poppy. She snatched up the receiver and said, 'Carrie, for God's sake, you haven't told Mother . . .'

Carrie said, 'Oh, thank God.' Poppy could hear her

wobbly intake of breath and then she said, 'Don't hang up, Poppy. Please. Just talk to me, okay?'

There was a pause, then Poppy said, 'All right, I won't hang up. But Carrie, what's the point?'

Poppy could hear the break in Carrie's voice, could tell she was crying. 'Please, Poppy, just let me come and see you.' Another pause. 'I'm begging you.'

Poppy felt a tug of angst, even sympathy, but she said, 'Carrie, I'm trying to get over what you did. I'm trying to stop being angry with Eduardo. I'm trying not to become bitter as hell. I've nothing left for you.'

Carrie put the phone down then, and Poppy felt a tiny flash of triumph, of satisfaction in hurting Carrie.

Within an hour, though, she was miserable, a hard ball of guilt in her chest. What if Carrie OD'd on some awful drug? What if she drank herself stupid? She picked up the telephone.

Carrie answered immediately. Poppy spoke fast, her voice flat, 'Carrie, it's me. Look, I don't think it can ever be right between us, but you are my sister. Come round if you like.'

When Carrie arrived they sat each side of the kitchen table, as if at a meeting. Poppy poured tea, then sat down and began. 'Look, I've got enough troubles without you becoming a pothead or drinking yourself out of employment. If you think it will help to see the children and me, I'm okay with that. But if you ever get within a mile of Eduardo, I'll kill you.'

She said it so unemotionally that for a second Carrie could believe the threat. Carrie tried to smile and said,

'It's okay, Poppy. I can't pretend it doesn't hurt – his dumping me after all that we ... Sorry.' She swallowed, then shook her head and cleared her voice. More firmly she said, 'But I don't think I want to see him anyway. I just don't want to be cut out of *your* life, okay?'

Poppy said, her voice not quite as cool as before, 'Carrie, how can it ever be okay between us? After what you did? That night, before I found the condoms ... I thought we were so close ... laughing about when we were kids. How could you be so loving while all the time deceiving me? How am I to ever understand that?'

Carrie just shook her head, her eyes on her lap. When she looked up, they were wet with tears. 'Poppy, I don't know either. It was as if the two things were separate. I suppose I told myself they were. It doesn't mean I didn't love you.'

They agreed a sort of wary truce. Carrie promised to lay off the drugs and the booze, at least most of the time, and Poppy agreed to resume family relations.

Poppy didn't believe either side would keep to the bargain. Carrie was incapable of saying no to anything. As to sisterly relations, that was blown. She felt only anxiety for Carrie now, not love.

With what seemed to Poppy dizzying speed, Carrie was back in her life. It wasn't the same though. Both she and Carrie were careful with each other, which they had never been in their lives before. Neither mentioned Eduardo. Poppy had to admit that it was nice to have Carrie arrive with a video for the children or a plan to go rowing on the Serpentine. And she was grateful that Carrie was obviously avoiding Eduardo. She came to the flat only when she knew he was in Spain or Manchester.

At the end of September, Carrie asked if she could do a photo shoot at Manor Farm one weekend. She wanted, she said, to get a few pics of the children eating scones and jam tarts for an article in a South African magazine. 'It's for *My Mag*. Do you remember it – fat upmarket glossy? They want a piece on English teatime, as if that still existed. I think the ed has a vicarage lawn in mind with silver teapots and bread and butter before cake.'

Poppy sounded reluctant, 'Oh Carrie, I don't know. You know Eduardo hates the children being used as models.'

Carrie interrupted, 'But it won't take long. And no one in England is ever going to see the photos, so being child models is hardly likely to go to their heads. And it will be a doddle to do.'

Carrie paused to give her sister time to say yes, but when she didn't immediately do so, she forestalled a refusal with, 'Say yes, Poppy. You'll get the silver cleaned for free and end up with a freezer full of white walnut cake, treacle tart and Victoria sponge. And I'll be a Saturday babysitting service.'

Poppy laughed. 'Okay,' she said. 'But I'll hold you to the babysitting bit. Giulia has hardly had a break since *Filumena* reopened.'

*

252

Carrie was pleased with herself. She hadn't expected Poppy to agree to the photo shoot. Previously her using Manor Farm for pictures had annoyed Eduardo quite as much as her borrowing the children.

Carrie suspected her sister would not have agreed if she'd known the whole deal, and she was quite certain Eduardo would have blocked it. The truth was that the article was not going to be exclusively recipes. It was also to be a 'lifestyle' piece about the Santolinis.

The family was perfect celebrity fodder for *My Mag*. Eduardo's company had recently won an international competition to design the gigantic new South African Sports and Arts Centre, Poppy was a well-known actress brought up in South Africa, and the icing on the cake was their adoption of a black African child. A triple hook. *My Mag*'s editor had first approached Eduardo directly, but had been told by his office that he never agreed to personal publicity: they were welcome to a handout on the Santolini architectural practice, or drawings of the proposed centre in Natal, or even a head and shoulders of Eduardo. But no family stuff.

So *My Mag* had contacted Carrie, who assured them she could swing it under the guise of a food piece. She'd let on later about the 'famous family' angle. Carrie reckoned Eduardo would not really mind. He had occasionally consented to be photographed with Poppy to promote her career or her latest play, and Carrie intended to write only flattering things about them all, so how could they mind? It would help atone for the last months, make Poppy forgive her. And it would make Eduardo ... Carrie shied away from what she hoped of Eduardo.

The family snaps were not a problem either. She had some good shots taken before they went to Mpumalanga in the summer: Eduardo playing croquet on the lawn with Angelina, and everyone eating lunch under the pergola. If she cropped them right she could cut out the grilled salmon and wine bottles. Maybe if Nick, who was a bit of a computer nerd as well as a photographer, scanned them into his PC he might be able to replace the salmon with scones and the wine with a jug of lemonade. Anyway, they'd manage, and she'd end up with some great pics, a few good recipes and an article that would restore her relations with the Santolinis.

As she drove across the humpback bridge over the Windrush and turned into Manor Farm's poplar-lined drive, Carrie studied the sky. Some of the leaves were just beginning to turn, but the light was similar to the day she'd taken the photos in June, with scattered cloud, not blazing sun. If she got the kids into the clothes they were wearing then, and made sure the background was green lawn, she'd be away.

Giulia did not seem pleased to see her. She was stringing runner beans at the wooden table outside the kitchen and she nodded at Carrie without pausing in her task. I wonder if she knows about Eduardo and me, thought Carrie. Old witch, she probably knows by instinct. But the children were excited to see her, dancing round the car as she unloaded the food, props and white string hammock.

Neither Eduardo nor Poppy was there. Carrie wasn't surprised – she'd guessed Eduardo would avoid her, and Poppy was only due home late after the theatre.

All the same, she was disappointed.

'Where's Eduardo?' she asked Giulia, hoping her voice betrayed no eagerness. 'I thought he was coming home last night.'

Giulia shrugged without answering. Rude cow, thought Carrie.

Angelina helped Carrie string the hammock between the ancient walnut and the apple tree and Carrie left the children playing in it while she set up. By the time Nick arrived at noon, with his usual vanload of aluminium camera cases, tripods and lighting umbrellas, the lace-covered table was just about ready.

It boasted a triple-tier cake-stand of cake, sandwiches and scones, all for the moment swathed in clingfilm. A stemmed stand sported a pyramid of strawberries, unhulled and almost plastic in their perfection. Poppy's Royal Doulton teacups and saucers clustered round her silver teapot and sugar basin, now gleaming from Carrie's attention with toothbrush and silver polish. Orange juice glowed in a fat-bellied glass jug. A mahogany tea tray, inlaid with ivory, was propped against one deckchair, and a wooden tennis racket and white cable-knit sweater lay on another.

Angelina eyed Carrie's jamjar of buttercups and wild scabious with all the scorn of a ten-year-old. 'We've got proper vases for flowers, you know,' she said.

'Ah, but you see, you are going to hold the jamjar, as if you'd just picked the flowers in the orchard. You are supposed to be innocent flower-loving children.'

Angelina rolled her eyes to heaven, gave an exaggerated sigh, and did a cartwheel on the grass.

'For God's sake, Lina. Not so near the table. I don't want your feet in my strawberries.'

Angelina laughed, and cartwheeled to the hammock, which she commandeered from her protesting siblings. 'My turn,' she said, tipping Tom and Lorato out on to the grass.

Giulia put her head out of the drawing room window and called the children. She spoke in Italian, which Carrie knew was intended to exclude her. Giulia wanted the children to go shopping in Witney, but Carrie protested, 'Giulia, please. I need them. Nick has to get some pics of them in the hammock, and they are happier here than in a hot car. I'll look after them. You have a break.'

At first Giulia tried to insist, but she gave up when the children added their objections to Carrie's. In that case, she said stiffly, she'd not be back for lunch. She'd take the opportunity to go to the cash and carry in Oxford.

So much for having a break, thought Carrie. If the

woman wants to be a martyr, fine. The longer she's gone, the better.

Carrie felt childishly pleased to see her go. She immediately handed round slices of treacle tart, which they ate in their fingers.

'Is this our lunch?' asked Angelina. 'Granny made soup for lunch.'

Carrie thought about the pot of potato and leek soup sitting next to the Aga. 'Which would you prefer? Treacle tart or soup?' she said.

Tom and Lorato looked up at her, baffled.

'We could have the soup after the treacle tart, if you like. A backwards lunch.'

'No soup,' Tom said. 'Don't want soup.'

Carrie laughed and scooped him up. 'Okay then. We'll fill up on strawberries and ice-cream. What do you think, Lina?'

Angelina looked worried. She smiled hesitantly and said in her grown-up way, 'Of course we'd prefer treacle tart and strawberries, but won't Nonna be hurt? Or cross? If we don't eat her soup?'

Carrie put down the squirming Tom and put an arm round Angelina's shoulders. 'You are a lovely girl, Lina, and you are right. We'll throw away her soup, then she won't know we didn't eat it.'

'That would be a criminal waste,' said Angelina, sounding exactly like Poppy. 'And dishonest.'

For a second Carrie was put out. Even ten-year-old Santolinis lectured her on her morals. Then she laughed. 'Okay, Goody Two Shoes, we'll put it in the fridge and confess. You can have it for supper.'

Carrie rummaged in the children's cupboards for the clothes they'd worn when she took the photographs in June. She found Tom's Nike sweatshirt and Angelina's sundress and denim jacket, but she couldn't find Lorato's dungarees. Carrie pulled out her swimming things. She can wear these, she thought, as if she's just shed the dungarees. She carried the clothes downstairs.

Lorato wriggled into the bottom half of her swimming costume, demanding help with the bikini top. Carrie tried to persuade her to abandon the top – bikini tops for infant girls were a naff idea – but Lorato was insistent. 'Go swimming. Go swimming,' she shouted.

As soon as the top was done up, Lorato ran to the linen cupboard and came back with a towel. 'Go swimming,' she repeated.

'Not today, darling. But you can go under the sprinkler. Come on.' Carrie tried to take Lorato's hand, but she flung herself on the floor and yelled. 'Go swimming in the river. In the riv . . . ve er.'

Angelina appeared, stepped over her screaming sister with barely a glance, and said, 'It's really boring. They both do it. Only Tom has tantrums on his back, and Lorato on her front.' Lorato was by now hitting the carpet with her fists and her forehead.

Carrie bent to try to pick her up, saying, 'C'mon,

Lorato, don't be an idiot. You can swim under the sprinkler.'

Lorato's screams went up a scale, and Angelina said, 'It's best to leave her. She'll stop soon. Mum says it's the terrible twos.'

Carrie showed her photographs to Nick. He was impressed, asking, 'Is there no end to your talents?'

Carrie was pleased. 'I learned the rudiments years ago so I could get the photographer's fee as well as the writer's. Papers and mags pay you guys more than us hacks, so I figured I should be able to do both.'

Carrie had been nervous that Nick would refuse to have anything to do with pictures he had not taken, but the challenge appealed to him and he promised to fiddle around with them so no one would notice that Angelina's dress was looser and longer in some shots, and that Tom's complexion varied from deep South African tan to English pallor.

Lorato reappeared, tantrum forgotten, and by 2 p.m. Nick had taken all the shots round the tea table and in the hammock, and the children were released. The sky had cleared and the early autumn day was surprisingly hot. Carrie left the children playing in the hammock while she and Nick did the kitchen photos: flapjacks in an oven tray, drop-scones being flipped on an iron griddle, lemon curd thickening in the pan.

By 3.30 they were through, and Carrie left Nick to collect up his kit and load his van while she cleaned up the kitchen, then took some lemonade into the sitting room, where the children were now watching *The Lion King*. Or rather Angelina was watching and at the same time cleaning her pony's saddle, Tom was playing with Eduardo's chess set, and Lorato was fast asleep in Poppy's armchair.

Carrie felt an uneasy squeeze of guilt. The little ones were supposed to have a nap after lunch, which had gone by the board. Both Lorato's face and the sand-coloured leather chair were smeared with jam and Angelina's leather dressing stood on the floor only inches from the pale Tabriz carpet. Carrie remembered there was a Santolini rule about no children in the drawing room on their own – presumably to protect such things as Eduardo's chess set and the furnishings.

Carrie fetched a cloth and wiped Lorato's face and the chair, saying, 'Lina, I'm going for a quick shower. Look after these two, won't you? Don't knock over that leather dressing and don't let Tom spill his lemonade, or we'll all be for the high jump.'

Angelina did not respond. She was deep in Disney.

Carrie heaved herself upstairs. She was exhausted by the heat of the Aga and the pace at which they'd been working. She hoped Giulia would not get back just yet.

As she passed the open door to Eduardo and Poppy's room, she suddenly reversed her steps and went in. She walked straight to the wardrobe and opened one side. Poppy's clothes. She shut the door and opened the other side to see Eduardo's jackets in a neat row. She pushed her face into the cupboard and breathed in. His smell was overwhelming and she felt the tears form in her eyes and throat. She opened one jacket without removing it from its hanger and buried her face in its smooth silky lining. It felt good against her hot cheeks and she stayed there for half a minute.

She pulled away, shut the cupboard doors and went into her sister's bathroom. It was large and modern, with white marble tiles, glass shelves and stainless steel fittings. The only old-fashioned thing in it was a great Victorian bath on legs, standing almost in the middle of the room.

Why not? she thought. It's much nicer than the spare room's shower. She turned the catch that released the great brass cylinder into the plughole and turned on the taps. They gushed with gratifying force.

She lay back in her sister's Givenchy bubbles and closed her eyes.

She woke with a start. Someone was pounding up the stairs. It was Angelina, shouting, 'Carrie, Carrie. Quick. Where are you?' She heard Angelina run past the bedroom door and into the spare room, still shouting.

'I'm here. Angelina, what is it?' Carrie leaped out of the bath, her heart pounding. She knew with absolute certainty that something terrible had happened. Angelina crashed into the bathroom, her face contorted with fear. 'Lorato's in the river. She's drowning.'

Eighteen

Carrie thought, Four minutes. She was sure you had to get them breathing in four minutes. How long since she went into the river? You could run across the garden and the field in a minute. With shoes on. The paddock's too stony for bare feet. Put some shoes on.

'It's okay, Lina, I'm coming.' With the calm of panic Carrie pulled her sneakers from the tangle of clothes. Her mind, clear as morning, raced down a straight logical path: Dry your feet or you won't get them into the sneakers. Do up the laces or you will trip.

Angelina was desperate. 'Carrie. She's drowning. She's going down the river. We'll never catch her. Oh please, *please*. Hurry, Carrie, come *on* . . .'

Tying her laces with rapid precise fingers, Carrie said, 'I can run faster than you but I need you to show me where she is, so you start now, and run as fast as you can to the river. I'll catch you up.'

Angelina bolted out of the door and down the stairs, three at a time. Carrie was behind her within seconds, but ran into the living room to grab her mobile phone, its earpiece and lead still attached, from the coffee table. Tom, asleep on the carpet, didn't stir. Carrie raced after Angelina, 100 yards ahead of her, across the garden.

Carrie, her mind still extraordinarily focused, punched in 999 as she ran naked across the back yard. At the end of the garden was a rough stony paddock, with the dried clay in hard ridges and lumps from the passage of tractors and horses. Carrie leaped like a goat across the uneven ground, concentrating on landing securely, on not twisting an ankle.

It seemed an age before she was through to the more even field and had caught up with Angelina. The child was sobbing and gasping as she ran downstream along the riverbank.

Carrie pulled Angelina to a stop. Putting her hands on the child's thin shoulders, she forced her to look at her. Her voice was hard and urgent, 'Lina. Stop crying. You have to be brave. Where did she go in, darling?'

Before Angelina could answer, Carrie saw her.

Lorato was in the middle of the river. Face down. She wasn't moving and her body twisted slowly in the eddying water.

Carrie thrust the mobile phone and lead into Angelina's hands. 'Take this,' she said, her urgent face a few inches from Angelina's. 'When they answer, ask for an ambulance. Tell them your address and what has happened, okay?'

Angelina, her bottom lip trembling and her eyes wide and fear-filled, nodded and held the telephone to her ear.

Carrie scrambled through the wire fence and ran full tilt at the river, diving into the weed and striking out towards Lorato. She was with her in seconds. She grabbed her under the arms and pulled her upright. Her head flopped forward. She was lifeless, and her face and neck were a dark purple-black.

Carrie had some memory that you did backstroke when lifesaving, but the river wasn't deep, and she simply held Lorato out of the water and somehow scrambled to the bank.

She could not remember what she'd once learned about resuscitation. She held the child upside down and squeezed her, then thought she'd been told this was wrong and stopped. She could not tell if any water came out of Lorato's mouth. Water was dripping everywhere.

She laid Lorato on her back, remembering to tip her head back, chin up. Oh Christ, how do I know if she's breathing? Or find a pulse? Carrie put her cheek against the child's mouth, and looked along at her round inert chest. Nothing. There was nothing, no movement, no breath. Oh God, oh God, she thought, what next?

Then suddenly her brain cleared and she knew what to do. She put a finger into Lorato's mouth and peered inside. The child's tongue was relaxed and she could see down her throat. Carrie pinched her nostrils closed with one hand and put her mouth over Lorato's to blow into her, but she could not get a grip on the small wet nose and her fingers got in the way of her own mouth. It was hopeless. Carrie let go of the child's nose and opened her own mouth wider to cover both

Lorato's mouth and nose. She blew steadily for a few seconds. While she did so, she squinted down Lorato's body and saw her chest rise. That's right, she thought, that's right. Now let her breathe out.

She waited while Lorato's chest subsided then breathed into the child once more. Lorato's skin felt cold and her lips blubbery. Nothing happened. She did not cough into life, as in the movies. Oh Jesus, she's dead. She's dead. Her heart must have stopped. Oh, why don't I know how to find a pulse?

'Lorato, Lorato, breathe darling, breathe.' She pinched Lorato's cheek, quite hard, hoping the pain would jerk her into life. Still nothing. Lorato's eyes were half open, but unseeing.

Carrie shifted her knees slightly to kneel up next to the child. She put her hands on her chest. She pressed down, not sure if you did this to start the heart or expel the air. Then she again breathed into Lorato's mouth and nose. Is this what you do for people full of water, or only for electric shocks and heart attacks? Why don't I know?

'The man says I must put you on.' It was Angelina, holding out the mobile phone.

Carrie knew she'd need her hands. 'Is the lead pushed into the phone? Lina? Give me the earphone end.'

Angelina did what she was told, and Carrie put the earpiece in her ear. 'Hello,' she said.

She heard a male voice. 'You are Carrie, is that right? My name is David.'

'Yes, yes.' She felt pathetically grateful that he knew her name. Angelina must have told him. Funny, she had not heard her talking on the phone at all. 'Yes, I'm Carrie. I don't know what to do. I . . .'

'Stay calm, Carrie. You are doing a great job. You will do better if you take your time. Is Lorato on her back or her front?'

'She's on her back.'

'Is her throat clear? No weed in it? Will you check for me, please?'

'Yes, it's fine. I checked. There's nothing there.'

'Good. Now Carrie, I want you to hold Lorato's nose shut with one . . .'

Carrie interrupted, her voice urgent. 'Her nose is too small. I tried. But I can do it over mouth and nose together.' Oh God, he's not going to waste time quarrelling over technique, is he?

But his voice was reassuring. 'That's fine, Carrie. Just breathe into Lorato's mouth and nose, putting your own mouth right over hers and blow gently for two seconds, okay? Count, "And one and two," okay? Then wait until her chest subsides.'

Carrie did as she had before, then, as she took her mouth away, said, 'Now what? What now? Nothing's happening!' Now there was a paramedic in charge, Carrie could feel the panic rising.

'Keep calm, Carrie. You are doing great. Now keep going, exactly as before.' She obeyed, but in the gap between breaths, while Lorato was breathing out, she said, 'But don't I have to do the chest thing? She's not breathing. Maybe her heart . . .'

'Just do as I tell you, Carrie. We need to do a minute of this first.'

Carrie did as she was told, making an effort to count slowly, not to hurry, but afterwards Lorato was as still as before. 'It's not working. Nothing's happening. She's . . .'

'Okay, Carrie. Now, I want you to get your own knees close to Lorato's chest, so that when you straighten up you are over her, okay? Now put one hand low down in the middle of Lorato's chest, with the heel of your hand on her breastbone. Your arm should be straight.'

'Only one hand? I thought . . .'

He interrupted. 'You only need one hand, Carrie, she's only little.'

Carrie said, 'Yes, yes. Do I push slowly, or in jerks?'

'Press firmly, like a bounce. You want to press the breastbone down about an inch. Do it five times for me, okay? You are squeezing Lorato's heart to make the blood flow in and out.'

Carrie pressed down on Lorato's chest. She was surprised how easily Lorato's ribs squashed. She released the pressure then pushed again, counting three, four, five, then said at once, 'What now? What do I do now?' She seemed to have been here forever, powerless with the inert Lorato.

'Okay, Carrie. Now do another breath, then another five compressions. One breath, five compressions.'

'Oh God!' Carrie could feel the swell of panic again, but the paramedic seemed to sense it, and steadied her with, 'Carrie, you have lots of time. Don't think about it. Just do what you have to do.'

Carrie could not answer because she was blowing into Lorato's mouth again. She swapped from blowing to pressing and back again, and kept it up without speaking.

David's voice cut in, 'The ambulance is on its way, Carrie. They'll be with you very soon. Tell me each time you press her chest, so I can monitor your speed, will you?'

'I can do that,' said Angelina. 'I'll tell you when she's pressing and when she's blowing.'

And she did. Even as Carrie breathed and pressed, and searched Lorato's face for a flicker of life, she registered Angelina's clear high voice, 'She's blowing. She's pressing. One ... two ... three ... four ... five. Now she's blowing and counting, "And one and two."' A rush of love for both these children threatened to overwhelm Carrie. Don't think, she told herself, don't think.

Carrie kept up the steady blow, press, press, resisting the desire to speed up or blow and press harder. She tried not to think, but now her brain was released from decision-making, it would think. Lorato is going to die. Maybe she's already dead. It feels like ten minutes at least since I got her out. But maybe it's only three. Please God, can it be three? How long can you live without breathing? How long for the brain not to be damaged? How long before full cardiac arrest? Is this cardiac arrest? Oh Christ, how did she get to the river? I have killed my sister's daughter.

Lorato coughed. Her eyes flickered open, then shut again. She vomited feebly, the water and sick running down one side of her chin. Carrie pulled her upright and bent her head between her knees, thinking that she must not choke. She coughed again, then drew a gasping breath, and started to cry. A tiny, mewing, wail.

Carrie's face crumpled. She reached to pull Lorato to her. The little girl's wail strengthened and she turned into Carrie, arms lifted in appeal.

Relief and happiness enveloped Carrie, and she started to cry too, her blubbering mouth uncontrollable. She held Lorato tight against her wet and naked skin. She was smiling and crying and she thought, I will always remember this moment. It is the best moment of my life.

David was talking in her ear. Something about the recovery position.

'Is she all right?' Lina's frightened voice brought Carrie to her senses. She looked up and reached for the girl's arm, pulling her down beside them.

'Yes. Yes, she is, darling. And you saved her.' Carrie kissed the side of her niece's head, and wrapped her arms round both the children. The three of them sat huddled on the grass, Lorato cocooned between Carrie's chest and her sister's. All three of them were crying.

The paramedic's voice got through to her, 'Are you okay, Carrie? I gather you've done it?' He sounded excited now, released from calm professionalism.

'Oh, yes, yes. We're all fine.' She was blubbering and ecstatic. 'Thank you, David. Thank you. Thank you.'

'That's okay, Carrie. You did it, not me. The ambulance must be almost there. Shall I stay on the line?'

'No. It's okay, We're okay,' she said, more calmly.

He said, 'Fine, but you need to wrap Lorato up warmly. Can you get a blanket?'

Lina, who still had the phone clamped to her ear, struggled up at once and pulled off her denim jacket. 'Here,' she said, wrapping it round her sister. 'I'll go . . .'

Carrie said, 'Lina, you are an angel. Check on Tom too, will you? If he's still asleep, leave him. If he's awake, bring him . . .'

And then, wonderfully, came the distant wail of the ambulance siren. Carrie, lifting a face luminous with triumph and relief, said, 'Run into the lane, darling, and tell them where we are.'

Carrie sat rocking Lorato, who seemed sleepy now, as she watched an advancing posse of hurrying people. Angelina danced beside them. Soon this will all be over, thought Carrie, and we will be a family again. She dropped her head over Lorato's, exhaustion seeming to take over every limb as she waited for them to get to her.

Then, really near, she heard Angelina's voice protesting, in high-pitched distress, 'But she *saved* her . . .'

She looked up to see Giulia, her face set, mouth zipped shut, swooping down on them. In seconds she had reached down and yanked Lorato from Carrie's lap. Other people were running towards them.

Suddenly she felt hunted, terrified of the advancing crowd. She put an arm up as if to defend herself.

'She's alive,' she said, trying to smile, trying to recapture the triumph and relief of a few minutes ago.

But no one came near her. They surrounded Giulia and Lorato. A paramedic was checking Lorato; another was tucking shiny silver foil around her. One of them said something about running some checks in hospital, and Giulia, without a word to her, carried Lorato away across the field with Angelina at her side.

Carrie's teeth started to chatter. She was gibbering and shaking with cold. She looked down at her mud-streaked body. Wet blades of grass stuck to her arms and belly and there was a long bloody scratch along one thigh where the barbed-wire fence had caught her.

'Here.' It was an ambulanceman with a blanket. He put it round her shoulders. 'You saved that child's life, you know.'

He shepherded her towards the house. As they reached the ambulance he said, 'Do you want to come with us? You're in shock. They'll give you something at the hospital.' He led her round to the back doors.

Grateful, Carrie nodded, but when she looked into the ambulance she was met by Giulia's gaze. Stony-faced, she looked at Carrie with a mixture of hostility and contempt, even hatred. She held Lorato tight against her breast, one arm round the foil-wrapped bundle, as though she expected Carrie to wrest her from her. The other arm clutched a bewildered Tom to her side. Angelina stood by the open doors, looking scared.

Suddenly Carrie's calm and exhaustion vanished. She felt the hot swell of rage rushing to her face, the relief of letting go, of losing it. She jumped on to the ambulance step and shouted at Giulia, 'Do you think I did it on purpose? Do you think I *wanted* her to drown?' Grief and desperation contorted her face.

Lorato, as always distressed by shouting, started to cry again, and Tom joined her. Giulia turned her head away from Carrie without responding, soothing the children with 'Calma, calma. Tranquilla, bambini.'

Carrie fell back from the step and turned towards the house, shaking off the paramedic's arm. She saw Angelina's look of bewilderment as, called by Giulia, she climbed into the ambulance. Carrie half ran, half staggered to the kitchen door. She fumbled with the handle and fell into the house and on to a chair. Immediately she felt a hand on her shoulder.

It was the paramedic. 'If you won't come with us, miss, WPC Jones, that's Karen here, she will stay with you. She'll make you a cup of tea, I'm sure.'

'Yup, that's right,' responded the policewoman, her voice both matter-of-fact and kind.

Carrie didn't reply. Her outburst at Giulia seemed to have emptied her of every last ounce of energy. She could not say a word.

There was a silence. Then he said, 'I'm sorry, miss, but do you think I could have the blanket? It belongs to the ambulance. And it will be a nuisance for you to have to return it. Can Karen get you a dressing gown or something?'

Carrie started to laugh. She had a vision of the man having to account for the loss of a blanket. 'Yes, sir, I realize it is Health Authority property, but the woman was stark bollock naked.' Can women be bollock naked? The more she thought of it, the funnier it seemed. Soon she was laughing so hard her eyes were streaming and she could barely breathe.

Suddenly a stinging heat exploded down one side of her face. Her mouth and eyes shot open in astonishment. Karen had slapped her cheek.

The WPC said, 'Sorry about that, but you'll exhaust yourself if you get hysterical. Just sit there for a minute and I'll get you something.' She was back almost at once with the mohair rug from Poppy and Eduardo's bed, which she held up like a screen to shield Carrie from the paramedic's gaze as she shrugged off the blanket. Carrie felt the mirth rising again. What a farce: the man had already seen her in the buff. Another glimpse would not constitute a social crime. She bit hard on her lip, and managed to change blankets without guffawing.

The ambulance man made a final attempt to get Carrie to go with them to the hospital. 'You could do with a check-over. And I bet you'll all be back tonight. The little girl is fine. She looks better than you do.'

Carrie shook her head. 'I'm fine. Really. Please go. You're holding them up.'

At last the policewoman went too. Carrie had stopped shaking, and was now deadly tired. Wrapped in the mohair rug, she carried the mug of tea the woman had made for her upstairs to the little spare room over the kitchen. She drank it sitting on the bed, then rolled over and buried her face in the pillow. I should have a bath, she thought, I smell of the river. But I'm too tired. I should go home. I should telephone Poppy. I should telephone the hospital. Later, I'll do it all later. Her thoughts drifted in a semi-conscious cloud between sleeping and waking, then slid away altogether.

The sound of wheels on gravel beneath the window woke her, and for a second her mind spun in panicky confusion. As her eyes focused on the mohair rug, the horrible pieces of the jigsaw fell into place with the inevitability of a nightmare. Oh Christ, she thought, I should have gone home before Giulia came back with the children. She leaped up and looked out of the window, but it wasn't a taxi or ambulance returning the family. It was Eduardo.

Carrie's first thought was what a mess she looked.

She looked down at her naked body, still streaked with mud and grass stains. She turned her gaze to the dressing table mirror to register puffy eyes, tangled still wet hair, pale face.

Heart banging, she watched Eduardo climb fast out of the Range Rover and make for the kitchen door. She pulled the rug round her and ran down the stairs and into him.

'Eduardo, I'm so sorry, I'm so sorry,' she said, forcing him to put his arms round her as she plunged into him.

He smelled so familiar, so wonderful. He said, 'Carrie. Carrie, what's up? You look so . . . What's happened?' She jerked her head back to look into his face. Could it be that he didn't know? That Giulia had not told him? That he hadn't been to the hospital?

'Don't you know?' she asked

'Know what? What, Carrie?'

'I . . . I . . .'

'For Christ's sake, Carrie, tell me.' Eduardo held her away from him, shaking her roughly by the shoulders. 'Is Poppy all right? What is it?'

She tried to tell him, but it all came out wrong. She wanted him to realize that she and Angelina had saved Lorato's life, but he wouldn't listen. As soon as he'd understood that Lorato was in the John Radcliffe Hospital, he left her standing in the hall and rushed into the kitchen. She heard him dial the hospital and ask for casualty.

Carrie leaned against the passage wall and listened.

She heard the relief in Eduardo's voice as some distant staff nurse got through with the good news she had been trying to give him.

'But is she okay? Are you sure? I mean, is there brain damage? – Oh, thank God . . . I'll be there. Thirty minutes, max. Thank you, thank you.'

He strode past Carrie, and headed back towards the yard. She was crying again now, her face ugly with exhaustion and misery. She reached for him, gripping his jacket sleeve with the tenacity of desperation.

'Eduardo, for Christ's sake, speak to me.'

But he shook her off, only pausing at the door to say, 'Carrie. I've nothing to speak to you about. Other than to tell you to get out of my life. Out of all our lives. You're a wrecker, Carrie. Or a witch. Go haunt some other family.'

Nineteen

A week later, Carrie sat at her computer, but she was not working. She was churning. She would never forgive the Santolinis. The cruelty with which they had simply shut her out was breathtaking.

She had, bloody hell, saved Lorato from drowning. She knew she had acted with sense and courage, and you would have thought at least Poppy would have acknowledged that. That there would have been a word from her. A phone call, a note. But no, nothing.

And how could Eduardo, who a few months ago had been so in love with her, not even want to know that she was all right? And she was not all right. How could she be when her erstwhile lover, by way of thanks for saving the life of his daughter, kicked her out of the house, calling her a witch? Condemning her to a nightmare drive back to London, in which she'd had to stop twice because she couldn't see for the tears, and after which she'd had to drag her shaking body to bed. Alone.

Anyone with half a heart would have tended to her scratches, run her a bath of healing herbs, tucked her up in bed with a whisky, a sleeping pill and a hug.

As always when she went over the events of that day, self-pity welled into tears. Pushing abruptly away from her desk, she walked into the kitchen and yanked off a piece of kitchen roll to bury her face in, then jerked the fridge door open. She poured a glass of white wine and stood drinking it with her back to the Aga.

Her mind made an inventory: this table is where he rolled our joints; over there he first kissed me and unwound my apron; that sofa is where he first saw me naked; that patch of floor is where we first made love.

But when her thoughts wandered upstairs, and to Poppy discovering the condoms, she hauled her mind away and went back to her *My Mag* article.

It wasn't easy. When she'd agreed to do it she'd been determined to ingratiate herself back into the Santolinis' life, and she saw it as a means to please them. Now she hated both Eduardo and Poppy, and she wished she could write an altogether different article. One about infidelity and lies, about ingratitude and indifference.

But *My Mag* was in the hagiography business. And she was to receive three fees, one for the article, one for her photographs and a bit extra for getting the Santolinis to agree.

Not that they ever had agreed, and it was too late to tell them now. It was also too late for them to object, since she had the pics: Nick's had been beautiful, and he'd done a great job doctoring hers, especially a close-up of Eduardo, head back, glass in hand, laughing.

All Nick had had to do was change the red wine in the glass to lemonade.

Carrie shuffled the prints on her desk until she found the one of Eduardo. Looking at the deep-set eyes, the clear olive skin, the whole energetic animal health of the man, she felt again the lunge of longing. She still wanted him, still loved him.

No she didn't. He was a shit, like most men. Only too willing to cheat on their wives for a bit of totty, then dump the totty if it became inconvenient.

At 5 p.m. she'd done the piece. She'd managed it by pretending she was writing about some other couple, unknown to her, who just happened to have all the accoutrements of the Santolinis: four of the five big F's – fame, fortune, family and friends.

But no fucking, she thought with a little shaft of malice. I get the fucking, and they get the rest.

Not that sex with Richard was anything like as good as with Eduardo. She needed someone who cared about her, though, and Richard did.

Getting Richard back had been easy. A fortnight after their trip to the theatre, she'd just rung him up and asked him over. She had to talk to someone, she said. Any shame at her own actions had, since that night, turned into anger at Eduardo, and she wanted someone on her side, someone who would comfort her. Besides, Carrie needed sex. It had been a month now, and celibacy withered her, made her feel ugly.

At first Richard had been stand-offish and hurt.

'But were you *in love* with Eduardo?' he wanted to know.

'Oh Richard, how do I know? I thought I was. But now I think I hate the bastard.'

Richard looked unconvinced and Carrie put her arms round his neck. 'Look, I know I was a cow to you. I must have been mad to think that Eduardo was a better bet.'

He put his arms round her, and dropped his head, rather wearily, on top of hers. 'He's not a bastard, Carrie. He's just Eduardo. And you are difficult to resist, you know.'

Carrie pulled back, indignant. 'Are you saying *I* hit on *him* then?'

'No, I'm not, but it would be difficult not to come on to you. You radiate pheromones. It's like diving into honey. And Eduardo could never resist a honeypot.' He kissed her forehead, and went on, 'It killed me, watching you falling for Eduardo. I knew you'd end up hurt. They all do.'

Carrie didn't want to be alone. She knew she was drinking too much, and smoking too much dope, but at least Richard confined her to marijuana and wine, which couldn't be too bad. He wouldn't do coke. Sometimes he behaved like a maiden aunt, like the time he'd taken down the poster on her bedroom wall. She still thought it was funny, but he'd said it was childish. It was a picture of a skull and cross bones with the slogan: 'Don't Drink and Drive. Have a Spliff and Fly.'

*

With professional detachment Poppy examined her puffy eyes and dull skin mercilessly lit by the fifty bare bulbs that ran like fairground lights round the dressing room mirror. Condemned veal, she thought.

She took her glasses off to smooth the foundation over her face. Without them she looked softer and mistier. Pity Eduardo didn't wear them. If he did, at least she'd look okay to him when he took them off.

Not that it mattered now. Eduardo had regarded her as a comfortable but undesirable wife for years. And he was right.

Oh God, she thought, I'm thinking those thoughts again. I must not do this. She put her hands each side of her forehead and pressed her temples hard. But, as in a bad dream, she could not drag herself away. She knew her mind would now take her one of two ways. Lorato's near drowning, or Eduardo's betrayal.

Carrie's words plagued her. 'He's just frightened of you, Poppy, and he loves the children.' Her taunts said that Eduardo strayed 'because life at home was so satisfying, so exciting'.

I'm completely outclassed by Carrie. I'm a boring, unsexy, spent mother of three.

Poppy let out a thin moan and bent double to put her forehead down on the dressing table. The thought 'mother of three' had triggered the other nightmare. Oh God, imagine if Lorato had drowned! After all that little girl had been through in her short life. What kind of a mother lets her child fall in the river? Me, Poppy Santolini, that's the kind.

She shook her head slightly as if to clear it. Why am I obsessing like this? Carrie saved Lorato. I must remember that.

But then the thought of Carrie again twisted in her gut. Please God, Eduardo is not seeing Carrie. I know he's not. But is he faithful? Where is he this minute? Where is he every night I'm at the theatre?

For the thousandth time, repeated images of Eduardo making love to Carrie slammed into her mind. It was always the same scenario: Eduardo's muscled back with Carrie's long slim legs wrapped round him, her thighs pressed to his sides, her head thrown back, her mouth open.

Poppy stood up with a jerk and went to the basin for a glass of water. She filled the glass and drank it in one breath.

The grown-up thing would be to put it all behind her, move on, look forward, let things mend. But oh, how could she?

Eduardo, who had made such a passionate speech of love and commitment two weeks ago, was now, she thought, indifferent. It was as if he'd said his penance and now expected to be forgiven, everything back to before. But she was ratty and quick-tempered, and kept weeping, which irritated him, though he tried to hide it. They had hardly ever quarrelled before and now they did it all the time. And the oddest thing was the way she missed Carrie. How can I hate my sister and miss her too?

Her mobile's ring jerked her back to the present and

she dived under the dressing table for her handbag.

'Poppy, is that you? It's Karl. I'm in London.'

Poppy had completely forgotten that Karl was coming to the UK to attend a trade exhibition. Kaia Moya and several other game lodges were being sponsored by the South African Tourist Board to promote safari holidays.

'Karl, how wonderful.' Poppy straightened up, looking at her half made-up, desperate face in the mirror. 'How are you? How's business?'

'Ja, everything's good. Very busy. Booked solid through to April. Though God knows why tourists want to be in Mpumalanga in summer.'

Poppy listened to the soft South African voice. Usually she disliked the flat vowels and slack-jawed diction of her childhood, but somehow the accent suited Karl.

She said, 'Maybe they're escaping the European winter?'

'Ja, and into temperatures in the 90s, and a good chance of malaria. And they can't see the game because the grass is long and the leaves are out. They're nuts.' He chuckled. Poppy had a mental picture of his worn tanned face, clean white teeth with a front one chipped. 'And thank God for that, since it pays my wages.'

While he was talking, Poppy began to worry that he would mention Carrie. He'd expect to see them together. Sure enough, he said, 'I thought I'd give Carrie a ring, and maybe we could visit you in the country on Sunday. If you'll be there. Will you?'

Poppy hesitated for a second. It would be so good to see him, but she knew Eduardo would not want Carrie at Manor Farm. And she didn't either. She could not face the inevitable exposure of their sorry story.

She stalled. 'Have you seen her?'

'No,' he said. 'I only got in this morning, and I have been at the exhibition all day. But I'll ring her now. Maybe if the weekend is no good, we could come to your play.'

'Carrie's seen it,' Poppy said quickly. 'I don't think . . . But . . . but you must come. We could have supper afterwards.'

'Poppy, is something wrong? Maybe this is a bad time?'

'No, no, nothing's wrong. Why?' Poppy watched herself smiling determinedly into the telephone. Lousy performance, she thought.

'You sound so formal. Sort of tight.'

She gave an unconvincing little laugh. 'Must have caught it from the English.' Then she thought, Oh, the hell with it. We've got to see Carrie again sometime. 'Sunday would be lovely. Come for lunch.'

Eduardo wasn't pleased, and breakfast on Sunday was a silent affair. Poppy was tired from yesterday's two performances and the late-night drive home, and Eduardo's polite unfriendliness hurt. It was a relief when Tom had a tantrum over which cup he'd drink from, and Eduardo picked up his coffee cup and the *Observer* and walked out.

Then, two hours later, when Poppy asked her mother-in-law if she'd dress the salad, Giulia had declared she would not cook for a putana, lay the table for a putana, sit down with a putana. Her back ramrod stiff, she'd set off for the laundry room, spray-starch in hand.

Poppy, shaken, went in search of Eduardo. He was on the terrace, now reading the *Sunday Times*. 'Eduardo, Giulia says she won't join us if Carrie is here. She says she's a whore. You've got to talk to her.'

Eduardo looked up from his paper. 'Why? Joining us is not compulsory, is it?'

Poppy made an effort to keep her voice neutral and light and said, 'If I can be civil to my sister, surely she can?'

Eduardo turned his handsome face squarely to her, and Poppy knew they were in for another quarrel. He said, 'That's probably because you blame me for what happened while my mother blames Carrie.'

Poppy, already close to tears from the argument with Giulia, felt a wave of misery. She wanted to say, As it happens, I blame myself. Instead, she said, 'Well, whatever her reasons, if she's going to go on living with us, she'll have to put up with who comes to lunch.'

Eduardo laid the paper aside and stood up. 'But she needn't have lunch with them, need she? I've half a mind to bugger off myself.'

It was so unlike him to swear that Poppy was taken aback. It was as if he'd cheated, taken an unfair advantage. She said, her voice cool, 'Oh, and why is that?'

'Because, to tell you the truth,' Eduardo replied, 'I'm with Giulia on this. It is all very noble of you to forgive us, Poppy, but being forgiven is hard work. Like living in a penitentiary. It will be worse with Carrie around. Much better for us all if she stayed away.'

As he spoke, Poppy's emotions flared and faded in quick succession. Anger that he should side with his mother; indignation at his accusing her of piety, remorse that she'd made him feel criminal. But finally outrage at his easy sacrifice of Carrie.

The colour flooded her face as she replied, 'God, Eduardo, your selfishness takes my breath away. Carrie is to be banned because it might make *you* uncomfortable!'

Eduardo made for the terrace steps. 'I'll be in the pub. Back at 1.30.' But Poppy was too quick for him. She blocked his path and said, 'Oh no, Eduardo! You can't just bugger off, as you put it. Why should the children lose their aunt, and why should I lose my sister, just so you needn't be reminded of rumpy pumpy in her bed?'

He still refused to answer, just put his hands on her shoulders to move her out of the way, then walked down the steps in the direction of the drive.

Am I going mad? thought Poppy. One day I'm

determined never to see Carrie again, the next I'm pleading her cause with Eduardo.

Karl was driving. He was such an unreconstructed male chauvinist he'd just assumed he should, even though it was Carrie's car. But she didn't mind, just as long as he didn't suss the trouble between her and the Santolinis. She couldn't bear that he'd seen it coming, warned her that Eduardo wouldn't leave his comfortable nest. She'd die if he knew.

Carrie was silent as they sped along the M40. The obvious friendliness of Karl's hug that morning, the pleasure of being with someone who accepted her – even liked her – for what she was (or in spite of what she was?) was so good.

Her thoughts drifted from present upheavals to past ones, long ago in Mpumalanga. Things were at their worst when she was about fourteen. Her father thought she was useless, only interested in pop music and fashion, and that had made her more determined to play her tapes at maximum volume, paint her toenails blood red and dye her hair. She remembered one tiny scene as if it were yesterday.

Her father had said, his voice carefully patient, 'Carrie, surely you know who Joshua Nkomo is?'

But she didn't and she had to shake her head. He turned to Poppy, his eyebrows questioning. Poppy said, 'He's the leader of the Zim opposition party, ZAPU, and he was defeated and outmanoeuvred by Mugabe and his ZANU party.'

Her father nodded, then smiled at Carrie and said, 'You'll be telling me next you don't know who Mugabe is.'

She'd felt her face on fire with humiliation and anger. It was true she was useless at history and politics and stuff, but she wasn't a complete dumbwit. He obviously thought she was too thick to join in a conversation. Also, her sister's neat recitation maddened her. Poppy was always using big words like outmanoeuvred.

Carrie fired back, 'Maybe if you occasionally talked to me like you talk to Poppy I *would* know something about politics.' She marched out of the room and slammed the door.

She crossed the stoep and walked fast across the lawn to the clump of trees on the far side of the drive. Their childhood swing was still there, suspended from the gum tree, like an old friend waiting. Its blue nylon rope was pale with age, the rubber tyre at its end full of fallen leaves. Holding the rope, she stepped through the hole in the middle and sat on the hard inner rim, then walked back a few paces, until she was on tiptoe. With an angry jerk she threw herself back, lifting her feet from the ground, and the swing went into ponderous action. As it swung, Carrie kept her eyes wide open, staring at the leaves above. She was not going to cry. She gave the ground the occasional kick to keep up the momentum.

Keeping the swing going required effort, so after a while Carrie let it slow down and sourly considered her plight. The fact was, she was sick of her family.

A shaft of loyalty interfered with this thought. Mom was all right, she supposed, even if she did always back Dad up, right or wrong, but her vagueness and forgetfulness drove her mad. Sometimes she looked at you as if you were a surprise, someone else's daughter who'd just walked in. But there was no meanness in her. She just didn't count.

But her sister and her dad were truly horrible. Poppy was such a goody-goody: top marks at school, nose forever in a book, getting the part of Juliet in the school play when Carrie was obviously prettier. Whoever heard of a dumpy Juliet with glasses, for God's sake?

And her dad would not leave her alone. He never stopped. Nag, nag, nag, like some old woman. 'Pick up your trainers.' 'Get your hair out of your eyes.' 'Don't you ever read a book?' 'Turn that noise off.' On and on.

He upset her a lot, her dad. Not because he disliked her music, her clumpy shoes, or her watching TV soaps. Those things were normal, what grown-ups did. They were meant to disapprove of everything you liked. But her father seemed to disapprove of *her*, dislike *her*. Like now. Why had he been telling *Poppy* the story of why they'd had to leave Zimbabwe when they were little, abandoning their farm? Why couldn't he tell her, or both of them? She'd only interrupted to ask who Joshua Nkomo was to get into the conversation, and he'd just squashed her flat.

Poppy couldn't do a thing wrong, and she, Carrie, couldn't do a thing right. He'd talk to Poppy about things she liked, like plays, which was a joke since they only ever got to the local pantomime, in Afrikaans. Dad thought plays were art, or literature. Carrie liked films, but they didn't qualify. He'd say, 'Photography isn't an art, it's just aiming a machine at something and going click.'

She knew he was wrong, but she couldn't win an argument. She'd get in a muddle and end up crying. And then she'd be mad at herself. And at Poppy. Last time she and Dad had this silly argument about movies – they had it at least once a week – she'd shouted, 'Poppy, you are on my side. I know you are. Why didn't you help me?'

Poppy had said, 'Because there's no point. Dad's not going to change his mind. So let it go.' She tried to put her arm round Carrie, but Carrie spun away.

'But that's so dishonest. You like pop music, but when Dad says it's nothing but thump thump thump and noise, you never say a word.'

Poppy said, in that placid reasonable voice that drove Carrie mad, 'Because I don't mind what Dad thinks. He's old. Anyway, why should Dad agree with us? People can love each other without agreeing about everything.'

'No, they can't,' Carrie had yelled.

Carrie turned the swing round in circles, winding it up like a top, then let it go and trailed her sneakers in the dirt as it unwound itself, spinning her round.

She saw Karl when he was halfway across the lawn. She pretended she hadn't, though. He sat down on the grass beside her and pushed the swing with the toe of his veldskoen.

'Don't,' she said, looking away, her mouth grim.

'What's up, cookie?' he said, catching hold of her foot to steady the swinging tyre.

The kindness in his voice undid her and she bit the inside of her lip to stop her mouth wobbling. 'Oh, everything.'

He raised his eyebrows at her slightly, inviting her to go on. She blurted out, 'I hate it here. We are in the middle of nowhere. And Dad goes on as if the sky's fallen in because I had my ears pierced without his bloody permission. And Mom won't stand up for me although I know she thinks pierced ears are fine. And of course Poppy is some sort of bloody saint. She wouldn't dream . . .'

Karl interrupted, sharply, 'Carrie. Don't swear. Just tell me.'

She glanced at him, then pulled in a shaky breath and said, 'Sorry.' Her eyes filled with tears and she burst out, 'Poppy's Dad's favourite. Anyone can see that.'

He didn't protest as she'd expected. He seemed to consider the idea, then said, 'Maybe. But things change. When I first came here, and you were little – How old? Nine? Ten? – you were his favourite.'

Carrie stared at the ground, reluctant to consider this. It was true it had been different then. On the old farm, in Zimbabwe, she'd gone everywhere with Dad. She'd ride next to him in the hot cab of the pick-up if they were going to town, and next to him in the open jeep if they were going through the bush. If she was barefoot and there were thorns, he'd carry her on his shoulders. She knew he liked her along.

And even when they came to Kaia Moya, he'd spent more time with her than with Poppy. He'd taught her to ride and to shoot, and to love the bush. Poppy mostly stayed at home with Mom, so Carrie had got used to their father being more hers than her sister's, but she still wasn't ready for Karl's next question.

'Why shouldn't fathers have favourites anyway?'

The thought shocked her. 'Because they are not meant to. They should love all their children the same.' She could feel her eyes prick at the soppiness of her words.

'Who said anything about love? You can love someone who drives you mad just as much as someone you get on with. You love your dad, don't you?' He peered up at her face, ducking his head to look under the tangle of hair, and ended, 'And he drives you ballistic.'

Now, years later, Carrie felt as childishly misunderstood as she had then.

Karl changed down as he swung the car off the motorway. He said, 'You are very quiet, Carrie. Heavy night last night?'

'No, as it happens,' replied Carrie, sounding frostier

than she'd meant to. 'Why does everyone assume all I'm good for is parties?'

'Whoa, whoa, Carrie! What have I said?' laughed Karl.

'Sorry. It's just that I was rerunning childhood quarrels with Dad. And resenting all over again that Poppy was cleverer than me. Pathetic, isn't it?'

Karl glanced across at her and grinned. 'Yup. Especially as you had a pretty perfect childhood, and you're still the best of friends.'

Best of friends, thought Carrie. Oh, I wish.

Twenty

Karl and Carrie came round the side of the house to find the Santolinis on the garden terrace, Eduardo cursing as clouds of barbecue smoke enveloped him, Poppy whacking a cloth-wrapped bundle with a rolling pin on the terrace steps.

'What on earth are you doing, Popps?' said Karl, hugging her.

'Crushing ice for mint juleps,' she said. 'Allows one to drink whisky in the middle of the day without a conscience.'

Karl was in khaki shorts, a bush shirt and trainers with a small backpack, doing duty as overnight bag, slung over one shoulder. Carrie wore a loose linen dress of pale peach, slit-eyed dark glasses and white espadrilles.

From now on, thought Poppy, looking at Carrie's flawless skin and full unmade up mouth, I'll always notice Carrie's beauty. But she said, 'This is October in England, Karl, not summer in the bush. You'll freeze.'

Karl laughed. 'I'm fine. I've been wearing trousers and jacket – even a tie, would you believe – all week and I couldn't stand another day of it.' He looked across the paddocks, down to the river and the smiling landscape beyond. 'God, Eduardo. How can you bear to ever go back to London?'

Carrie put a basket of yellow figs on the terrace table, and Karl produced three furry toys for the children. There was a lurid green frog, a mustard-yellow lion and a striped zebra, all with magnets in their feet.

They were a great ice-breaker. As the children contorted the floppy creatures into every position, glued them to a drainpipe and made them link arms or ride each other by dint of their magnetic feet, Carrie could ooh and aah about the garden, and Poppy could ooh and aah about the figs and toys.

Eduardo and Karl walked, drinks in hand, down to the river with the children dancing around them. Carrie did not want to go. She didn't want to retrace the route she'd run down to save Lorato and stumbled up again with the ambulanceman. She knew that Eduardo would tell Karl about Lorato's near drowning, and she didn't want to feel his disapproval.

Although she was relieved no one pressed her to go with them, she felt a little forlorn as she watched the group enter the meadow and saw Karl hand his drink to Eduardo so he could pick up Lorato, settling her easily on his shoulders. The long grass hid Tom from view, and they were almost out of earshot, but Carrie correctly surmised Tom's outstretched arms and demands for equal treatment: the next minute Tom was on his father's shoulders. Angelina, skinny with her white blonde hair down her back, walked between the two men. As so often, Carrie felt on the outside, looking in.

Left alone with her sister, Carrie was grateful that Poppy said nothing of consequence as they laid the table and brought out the lamb steaks and sausages.

'This fire is altogether too much of a good thing,' said Carrie. 'It is going to incinerate everything.'

'I know,' replied Poppy. 'What is it with men and barbecues? They know nothing about cooking, but make a fire outside and suddenly it's their domain.'

Carrie laughed. '"Me Tarzan," I guess. "You Jane, stay in the cave."'

She peered at the six-inch layer of coals in the great red Weber barbecue. They were covered with a fine grey ash, glowing orange underneath. 'There's enough charcoal in here to cook for the army.'

Poppy shrugged, the indulgent wife. 'Two bags of it. And costing more than the lamb and sausages.'

Carrie was right about the fire. Eduardo's first batch of sausages were inedible: black and cracked on the outside and red raw inside. And he was not a happy host. He burned his hand, got smoke in his eyes and kicked over the pan of honey and soy marinade.

Poppy's attempts at helping and Carrie's offer to take over irritated him, so Poppy made two huge mint juleps for herself and Carrie and they left him to it. Karl stayed with him, too wise to offer advice or comment. The women sat on the swing seat and Lorato crawled up between them. She climbed on to Carrie's lap and said, 'No swimming in the river now.'

Carrie looked into her solemn face and pulled it into her bosom. Her eyes met Poppy's over Lorato's head. 'Oh Poppy, I am so, so sorry.'

'It's okay,' said Poppy, touching her sister's wrist. 'We'll get over it eventually. We are already. The thing to remember is you saved her life.'

After that, it was better for both the sisters. Carrie read Poppy's conciliatory words as the chink in the door. It would all come right. It would just take time, that's all.

As Poppy saw her sister's expression go from anxiety to relief, she recognized Carrie's old ability to shake off gloom and head for the sun. But Poppy knew it would never be the same. How could it be? The sense of betrayal would never leave her. She smiled at Carrie. What else could she do? And a part of her did want Carrie in her life, a part of her still loved her.

Carrie sprang up, her face cloud-free, and swung down the terrace steps to play croquet with Angelina and make a fuss of Tom's angora rabbit.

Eduardo, irked by Karl's gaze and his own incompetence, took it out on Olaf, who was standing immobile, his nose lifted to the smell of charring meat. Eduardo took a run at the startled dog, shouting at him, 'Beat it, you great brute. Go on. Off.'

Olaf shambled hastily down the terrace steps, baffled but obedient. This seemed to irritate Eduardo further and he handed his barbecue fork and the tea towel to Karl. 'Here. Do your African ranger thing then,' he said.

'Sure,' said Karl, putting the fork down and picking up a roasting tin. 'Do you mind if I rearrange the fire a bit?' He scooped hot embers from the barbecue into the tin and set it down on the stone paving. Then, crouching on his haunches, he used this inauspicious little fire to expertly grill the lamb steaks and the rest of the sausages.

Poppy, appearing at the kitchen door, watched him take a sausage from his grill and put it, without benefit of plate, on the terrace floor. He was talking to Lorato, 'Smells good, eh Lorato?' he said. The child's eyes, anxious and solemn, flicked from his face to the sausage and back again. Karl took his claspknife from his pocket and split the sausage accurately down the middle. Picking up one half, he blew on it and handed it to Lorato. Her face opened into relief and pleasure.

An assortment of thoughts streamed through Poppy's brain. How typical of him to carry that knife, even in England; that grease is going to stain my expensive encaustic tiles; should I care that he's feeding my daughter food from the floor?

He looked up at her. 'Have I broken the rules? Giving her an advance tasting?'

'Of course not,' said Poppy, although in truth she didn't let the children eat between meals. She watched his brow furrow as he concentrated on wiping Lorato's greasy cheek with a tea towel and thought, he'll look like Clint Eastwood one day. Maybe Carrie will marry him and leave Eduardo alone.

For some reason this last thought did not bring her the comfort it should. She pulled herself together and went in search of Tom and Carrie, calling, 'Lunchtime, everyone. Lunch.'

The next day dawned sunny. Poppy felt, for the first time in months, a flicker of happiness. She found herself singing in the shower. It must be months since she'd done that. Carrie had gone home to London last evening, but Karl had stayed the night and was going with her and the children to Donnington Castle. It would be a half-term treat for Angelina, and give her pony a day's rest. The child would live at the stables if she could.

As soon as breakfast was over and Eduardo had gone, Poppy began the pleasurable business of assembling a picnic. She sent Angelina to the cellar for the ancient wicker hamper and the quilted bedspread that had been born again as a picnic rug. She sent Karl to the larder for mineral water and orange squash, and then to the orchard to pick the last of the apples. She filled vacuum flasks with coffee, jamjars with sugar, plastic bags with wet J-cloths for messy faces and sticky fingers.

Poppy had long since abandoned gourmet picnics. She didn't even make sandwiches. She just packed the hamper with whatever she could find. Today this turned out to be granary bread, butter, tomatoes,

Marmite, cheddar, a packet of salami, fish paste, lemon curd and jam. The freezer contributed a squashy rhubarb cake Carrie had made months ago. Poppy added breadknife and board, a tray for laying out the spread and a clutch of buttering knives.

At the castle they set up camp in Poppy's favourite spot – a grassy enclosure inside a ruined stone. Poppy felt guilty relief that Eduardo wasn't there: he fussed about their picnicking in the castle grounds – you were supposed to use the picnic area. But Poppy hated the rows of wooden benches and strategically placed litter bins, and she liked to be out of sight of other families.

While Poppy set up her sandwich-making operations, Karl took charge of the drinks, pouring half an inch of orange cordial into their glasses and the children's mugs and topping them up with water. He handed a mug to Angelina, who gulped thirstily. Suddenly her eyes shot open, wide and horrified, and she sprayed the picnic spread and her mother with a mouthful of orange. Spluttering and gagging, she held the mug out to Poppy.

Poppy smelled it. Orange. She tasted it, and then burst out laughing. She took the bottle from Karl and turned the label to show him.

'It's gin.'

'Oh God,' he said. 'I thought it was water. Angelina, I am sorry.'

Angelina, enjoying the drama now, said, 'But what can we drink?'

Karl gave her money to buy drinks at the castle, and she set off. The two little ones, delighted at the prospect of Coca-Cola, went with her.

As she watched her ten-year-old daughter walking between her two youngest, holding their hands, Poppy was assaulted by a wave of love.

'That's such a lovely girl.'

'It's in her genes,' said Karl. 'You were just like that at ten. You put up with merry hell from Carrie.'

The flattery pleased her, but she didn't want to pursue the subject. Smiling, she said, 'And what are *we* going to drink?'

'Neat gin,' said Karl. 'Can't waste it. And besides, we need warming up. Your idea of a perfect day for a picnic is my idea of a perfect day for log fires and booze.'

It was true. The sky had clouded up and it was breezy and cool. They pulled on their coats – Poppy's cracked and discoloured old Barbour, and Karl's khaki bush jacket – and sat eating salami sandwiches and slowly sipping gin. The children came back and Poppy made sandwiches to order.

By the time they'd repacked the picnic stuff it was unpleasantly cold, but Poppy's suggestion of home was loudly countered by Angelina's clamour for the adventure playground.

They had the playground to themselves, and Angelina undertook to push Tom and Lorato on the swings.

'When you are sick of them, darling,' said Poppy,

'bring them back to us, and you can ride the mini-bikes.'

'Where will you be?'

Poppy's eyes searched for somewhere out of the wind. 'In the Wendy house.'

She and Karl crawled into the little cabin, and Poppy spread the quilt on the floor. They sat cross-legged upon it, facing each other with mugs of orangey gin between them.

I mustn't drink too much, thought Poppy. I'm driving.

There was something both cosy and daring about sitting knee to knee with Karl. She felt insulated from the world and safe. At first they talked of Kaia Moya, of Lorato's progress, of Lucille.

Then suddenly Poppy found herself telling Karl about Eduardo's affair with Carrie.

'It's so awful,' said Poppy. 'It's screwed things up with both of them. I want to trust Eduardo again, but I can't. And I want to forgive Carrie, and I can't do that either.'

Karl put out a hand and gently shook Poppy's jean-clad knee. 'You will, Poppy. Give it time.'

Poppy, once started, couldn't stop.

'And then I get furious with Eduardo for wanting to cut out Carrie. I keep thinking he wants to keep her at bay because he's in love with her. You saw them yesterday. Is he in love with her?' Poppy pushed her finger up under her glasses to rub out incipient tears.

Karl held her gaze and shook his head. 'No. He's not. No question.'

Poppy sniffed, rubbing her nose with the back of her hand, 'If he wanted to see her I'd kill him I think. But when he refuses I give him hell too.' She tried to fish a tissue out of her jeans pocket, but it was difficult to extract sitting down, and it emerged in bits.

'Here.' Karl handed her a red-spotted handkerchief. It smelled clean and soapy. She blew her nose and said, 'And it's all my fault. I . . . I just thought he'd love me forever, even though we hardly ever . . . I've just taken him for granted. I got so absorbed in Lorato. And I kept working, left his mother to do the chores . . .'

Karl put his mug down and reached forward between his knees to take both Poppy's wrists in his hands. 'Stop, Popps. What you need to keep in your head is that there are no villains in this story. You are the same beautiful, wonderful woman Eduardo married . . .'

'Beautiful?' Poppy shook her head.

'Yes, beautiful. Every bit as beautiful as Carrie. She's stunning of course. But you are lovely too.' He scrutinized her features as he described them: 'Huge eyes, hidden behind glasses, but so what? Nice straight nose, wide high cheekbones, perfect even teeth, big smile, square jaw, dimples, wonderful pink and perfect skin . . .'

Poppy shook her head, pleased but disbelieving. 'Stop, stop.' But she wanted more. Eduardo had never said she was beautiful. Sexy, yes, but not beautiful.

'And apart from all that, you have the sexiest, richest voice, and you are generous, warm, loving. So you are not to blame, okay?' Karl dropped her wrists, and handed her one of the mugs between his feet. 'Here.'

She took a gulp, allowing the thought that she should go in search of the children to glance, unrecognized, off her mind.

Karl went on. 'You could blame Eduardo. But only for weakness, or for being stupid. He doesn't love Carrie. He loves you.'

The words were like balm. 'Oh Karl, thank you,' she said, 'thank you.'

Feeling restored and only very slightly drunk, she said, 'And Carrie isn't to blame either?'

Karl said, 'No. Poor Carrie. She loves you, but jealousy gets in the way.'

'Jealous? Carrie jealous of me?' Poppy's voice rose and her eyes were wide with disbelief. 'You're crazy.'

'You've got everything she wants. Security, career, fame, house in the country, children, marriage.'

Poppy shook her head vigorously. 'No, no. Carrie doesn't want any of that. She wants excitement, fun, all-night parties.'

'C'mon, Popps. Carrie's never been able to live up to you. You were better at school than her, better at coping, better at acting. Now you are kinder, steadier, nicer. It's tough for her.'

'But she's so vivacious. And everyone loves her.'

'Just as well,' said Karl. 'Since I don't think she loves herself too much.'

They sat in silence for a few minutes, Poppy feeling curiously content, as if a boil had been lanced. Suddenly a small boy plummeted through the door, and stopped in horror. He turned tail and ran, shouting, 'Ma, Ma, there's witches in the Wendy house.'

'So much for your beauty,' laughed Karl. 'He thinks you're a witch.'

Twenty-one

For the next four days Poppy saw Karl every day. At first he'd wanted to include Carrie, but she was working. And anyway, Poppy said it was too soon – she'd made an effort on Sunday, but she did not feel easy with her sister. So Karl would have supper with one sister and spend his days with the other. Poppy, for so long stoical and brisk with herself, enjoyed the days spent out of her usual groove. Karl managed to give the simplest activity, like riding on a bus, a charge. Being with him felt like bunking off, illicit and exciting.

On the Tuesday she left the children with Giulia and was at Karl's hotel by 9 a.m.

As he bounced down the steps she was conscious of two young women, out for a quick puff in the porch, eyeing him. He turns heads like Carrie does, she thought, feeling childishly proud that it was she he kissed when he landed on the pavement.

They went down the Thames for Karl to see the changes along the riverfront. They looked at Canary Wharf and the Dome from the water, then took another riverbus upstream to Bankside.

After an hour in Tate Modern – only long enough to be bowled over by the spaces – they did the guided tour of Shakespeare's Globe. The tour guide, an out-of-work actor, recognized Poppy and persuaded her to demonstrate the acoustics with a speech from the stage. At first Poppy had protested, but she gave in when Karl said, 'Go on, Poppy. Today has been a revelation. It will be the icing on the cake.'

So Poppy recited 'Shall I compare thee to a summer's day?'.

When she stopped there was that moment of silence, the tribute of an audience to something magical – as if no one can bear to break the spell. Then everyone was clapping and asking for her autograph.

Poppy felt proud and proprietary that Karl was so knocked out by the new buildings, as if she was responsible for the regeneration of her adopted city.

And then, at the Pont de la Tour, Poppy knew the manager and he gave them free champagne. Poppy wondered if he thought Karl was a lover or a movie director.

It was a wonderful day, right outside Poppy's normal life.

On Wednesday Karl went to Poppy's matinee. Afterwards Poppy stopped to sign half a dozen autographs for some drama students at the stage door and then they walked to the Ritz.

'Are you a guest of the hotel, sir?' The doorman's eyes ran up from Karl's soft veldskoen via his jeans to his collarless neck and down again.

'No, I'm not. Is there a problem?'

They were saved by an American couple who descended on Poppy, brandishing their *Filumena* programmes. Embarrassed but determined, they gushed their congratulations and Poppy smiled and signed.

The doorman waved them through, followed them in, and whispered to the head waiter. They were bowed to the table.

'I like you being so famous,' said Karl. 'That grandee on the door was squaring up to put me back on the pavement.'

Poppy thought Karl had the sort of authority and style that would have won the battle, tie or no tie. He also had an unabashed appetite, accepting a succession of sandwiches, scones and fancy French cakes.

Poppy watched him with admiration. 'You'll be sick,' she said.

He shook his head. 'I'm not paying thirty-two pounds for a cup of tea and a biscuit.'

The forty minutes in the gilded prettiness of the Ritz foyer went too fast. Poppy had slight back-to-school blues as Karl left her at the theatre.

On Thursday afternoon they took the children to the zoo. Karl had discovered you could get a barge a few hundred feet from the Santolini flat right to Regent's Park. The canal trip was fun, with its strange views from water level. At first there were looming buildings, and cranes, then the picture-postcard barges in Little Venice, selfconsciously sporting bargee-painted watering cans, buckets and pottery gnomes on their roofs, then the anxious dark of the tunnel under Edgware Road, and at last the weedy overgrowth of Regent's Park. And all the way the towpath ran alongside, snaking round bends, plunging under bridges, re-emerging reliable and unscathed. On arrival, they climbed up into the autumn sunshine. The leaves were a fandango of yellow and orange and the bright light and deep shadows disguised the tattiness of the old zoo.

'Don't you find zoos depressing?' asked Poppy, looking at a solitary bear pacing on the rocky terraces.

'Sometimes. But it's sentimental nonsense to think zoos, good zoos anyway, are cruel. The wild's much worse.'

Angelina, her face earnest as she looked up at Karl, chipped in, 'But the zebras can't gallop about like at Kaia Moya. And wild monkeys travel miles every night through the trees. It must be horrible to be shut up in a little space.'

'But nice not to be eaten by lions, don't you think? And to have big fat bananas all the year round, rather than an uncertain supply of tiny green ones?'

Angelina didn't look satisfied by this, so Karl patiently rehearsed the arguments for science, for breeding in captivity, for public education, as if he were talking to an adult. Angelina looked at him with adoration.

Karl channelled the directionless excitement of the children into concentration on the Web of Life displays: ants carrying leaves and petals along ropes to their nests and stockpiling them for others to process; tarantulas cleaning their hairy legs.

Poppy watched Karl with her children a little sadly. He was so much better with them than Eduardo. It was ages since Eduardo had taken them anywhere. When the elephant keeper assumed Karl was the children's father, Poppy was oddly pleased.

Then on Friday Poppy went shopping with Karl. He wanted presents for everyone at Kaia Moya. They ended up with dinky double-decker buses and London taxis for the camp children, Liberty scarves for the women, Aquascutum ones for the men. Hardly original, but the tourist tat was unbearable, and Poppy enjoyed the unwonted stroll down Regent Street.

Karl's interest in her opinions and his laughter at her jokes made her feel good, like a tonic. Just what the doc ordered, she thought. She would miss him. But it wasn't just that: over the last week she'd found herself stirred by his arm round her shoulders, the smell of his aftershave, his quick kiss hello or good-bye.

She was attracted to him and she was sure the feeling was mutual. He'd not said or done anything, and neither had she, but she knew they'd both felt it. Following his springy step as he weaved through the crowds, Poppy could not stop thinking how easy an affair would be. And why not? Eduardo hadn't been held back by any loyalty to her. Maybe she owed it to herself. She could do with just such an ego-boost, and where would be the harm? Karl was going back soon and then she'd be able to hug to herself the knowledge that she was still desirable, that she wasn't just a betrayed wife, that she had the courage and the verve for an adventure.

And she'd be even with Eduardo. Even if she never told him – and she never would – she'd feel less raw, less exploited. She'd have built herself some protection.

Heading home in a taxi, Karl looked at her solemn face and asked, 'Tired?' She shook her head but didn't smile. She looked ahead at the back of the driver's neck. Dandruff, she thought with a small section of her mind. The other, more important bit thought that Karl was leaving in two days, and he'd said nothing about tomorrow.

'What's up?' He put a hand round her neck and rocked her slightly.

'I was thinking that you're leaving on Sunday.' She turned her face to his. 'I'll miss you.' She liked his hand there, light but warm. She could feel the heat even when he took it away.

'I'll miss you too. The week has flown.' He frowned, suddenly serious, then said, 'I need to talk to you, Poppy.'

Her heart squeezed, then thumped. Oh God, thought Poppy, he's going to say something. Do I want him to? Yes, yes, too right I do.

'Yes?' Her eyes searched his face, ready for his. But he kept them on his shoes, and said, 'Tomorrow. Can I come tomorrow? I need more time than we've got now.' He looked up and grinned. 'I know you. You have to get home for the children's tea now.'

Poppy was tempted to say, 'You don't know me. Forget the children. Say it now.' But she didn't. Her heart was still banging in her chest.

He said, his eyes earnest, 'Can I see you alone?'

She nodded, 'Yes, of course. Come tomorrow morning. About ten?'

The taxi swung into Paddington Wharf and the next minute she was out on the pavement, giving a cheerful wave as it bore him off to his hotel.

Her mother was in the kitchen. She and Adrienne had come for tea. Oh God, I'd forgotten, thought Poppy. Just what I need. Lucille was trying to put Lorato's right shoe on her left foot. Lorato pulled her foot away and offered the right one. Lucille's face registered the familiar look of confusion and offence. She said, 'Oh, all right, if you know best. And whose smart little girl are you? One of the servants', I suppose. Are you the cook's?'

Angelina, ever patient, replied, 'Gran, Lorato's my sister. She's adopted. And we don't have any servants.'

Lucille looked from Lorato to Angelina, irritated.

'Nonsense,' she said. 'Everyone has servants. And you aren't allowed to adopt black children. It's against the law.'

What with putting her mother right about the new South Africa and explaining they were in England anyway and then helping Angelina with her project about cereals (Angelina had designated Coco Pops the commonest British crop), then getting to the theatre and through the performance, it wasn't until she got home that she could think about Karl.

Eduardo was in Spain, which helped. Poppy poured herself a whisky, sank into the sofa and stared at the ceiling. If Karl was going to make a proposition, she needed to be ready for it. Which meant she needed to know if she wanted to sleep with him or not.

It didn't take much thinking about. She knew what her answer was. Yes, an unequivocal yes. But with no strings, no commitment, no afterlife. She just wanted a carefree exhilarating affair. She was sick of being the goody-goody, sensible wife and reliable mother. She wanted sex in the afternoon and no hang-ups. She almost welcomed the fact that it was likely to be a one-night – or a one-day – stand. That way she could do something reckless, but without the danger.

Like the time Carrie had blown kisses to a young guy on the top deck of a passing bus from the safety of the top deck of their own bus going the other way.

Twenty-two

When Carrie opened the door that evening she felt sinking dismay. Karl had arrived for supper in his bush shorts, veldskoen and short-sleeved khaki shirt. It was one thing for him to look like Crocodile Dundee in Mpumalanga, or even with the Santolinis, who understood South African ways, but in front of her friends . . .? Joan and Paul Bakstansky were New Yorkers in the music business and just about as cool as you could get, Richard had the designer style of the hip and successful and even Lulu looked a knockout when not in chef's gear.

He might have tried, she thought. Even that awful suit would have been better than the shorts.

'Sweet Jesus, Karl. Do you think we are going on safari?' she said, trying to make a joke of it but not succeeding.

'Oh Carrie, I'm sorry,' he said, following her into the kitchen, where everyone was standing about, drink in hand. 'I'd forgotten you had company.'

'Had company,' she thought, dismayed. He'll be saying, 'Pardon me,' next. She introduced him to the others with: 'Karl is South African and lives in the bush. You'll have to excuse his gear. He doesn't differentiate between London in autumn and Africa in summer.'

As the evening progressed Carrie realized that, far from finding Karl a country hick, her friends really liked him. She was surprised when he talked easily about modern art with the Bakstanskys, and over the pudding Paul and Karl had a long discussion about Frank Lloyd Wright. Karl had been reading a new biography and had visited the architect's house outside Chicago. Carrie didn't even know Karl had ever been to the States.

She was also a little mortified that Lulu elicited more information about Karl's own family and childhood than she knew. Carrie had known him all her life but she did not know he'd been brought up in the Little Karoo on an ostrich farm, that his father had been drowned fishing off the rocks in Hermanus and that he'd run the ostrich farm at sixteen, only selling up when his mother died and his sister married.

As Carrie watched Karl, talking quietly and at ease, the unpleasant thought occurred to her that the reason she knew so little of Karl was that they always talked about her, never about him.

Lulu handed Karl a cup of coffee. She looks like a cat with the cream, thought Carrie. It was obvious she fancied him. She could not have made it clearer if she'd told him so. Carrie felt put out and jealous. Karl was her property.

It was a good evening, though. The food – whole

baby beetroots and slices of mozzarella with a rocket salad and balsamic dressing, with her own wholemeal bread for mopping up the juice; old-fashioned fish cakes but with a coriander and mango salsa; and gooseberry fool with ginger biscuits – had all been delicious. They'd drunk four of the six bottles of Roodeberg that Karl had brought her from South Africa, and the fifth was going down fast. They'd moved to the sitting room and now they sat on sofa and floor, contentedly passing round some very good weed provided by the Bakstanskys. Carrie noticed that when Lulu took a drag and passed the spliff to Karl, he took it carefully and passed it on to Joan without smoking it.

Karl suggested she put on a CD he'd brought her from South Africa. She didn't want to, fearing some embarrassing South African band, but Paul insisted. Karl explained that the group belonged to the Kwaito movement, a blend of African rhythms and Western music. The African beat was there, but slow. Carrie sat on the sofa, drifting peaceably.

When Richard sat down next to her on the sofa and put his arm round her, she soon got up to fetch another bottle. And when she'd topped everyone's glass up she sat down on the floor next to Karl's chair, her shoulder against his bare leg.

She knew Richard was trying to catch her eye, but she felt good where she was, and slightly resented his signals of ownership. She closed her eyes and drifted with the Kwaito.

The Bakstanskys left about midnight. When she went into the kitchen after seeing them off, she found Karl stacking glasses on the draining board. She looked at his ridiculous short shorts and the long stretch of brown almost hairless legs between them and his socks, and she couldn't resist.

She pulled the door to, and went up close behind him. She put her hands lightly on his shoulders and said, 'Karl.' He swung round, smiling.

'Hi,' he said.

Keeping her hands on his shoulders, she tilted her head back a little so she could look into his face. 'Karl, ever since I was twelve, I have been trying to get you to kiss me.'

She slid her arms round his neck and pulled his face down to hers.

She could feel his initial, quite strong resistance, but she held on. If I am going to make a fool of myself, I might as well go for it, she thought. Then suddenly he stopped pulling back, and she felt him relax, begin to sink into it. Then, in a second, he'd brought his arms round her back, almost lifting her off her feet. His kiss was urgent and hard.

He pulled back and said, 'Christ, Carrie,' his voice low and uneven. Carrie heard the door open behind her. She didn't turn round. She didn't care who it was. She just shut her eyes and cursed her luck.

Karl dropped his hold on her and said, 'Richard, this is not what you think.'

Richard said, 'I think it is.'

Carrie stayed where she was as Karl followed Richard out of the kitchen. She told herself she didn't care. She just hoped Karl would come back.

He did, but only to say he was leaving. He'd share a taxi with Lulu.

Carrie tried to protest, but he'd recovered his defences. His voice was gentle, but very firm. 'Carrie, you don't know what you want. You cannot just jump from guy to guy. Sooner or later you need to be able to bear your own company.'

It was Saturday morning. Giulia, Eduardo and the children had set off early for Manor Farm, so Poppy could set the scene for Karl.

She made her face up carefully and then put on her linen and cashmere trouser suit. The autumn days were getting cool, so she told herself she had an excuse, but when she looked at herself in the long mirror in Eduardo's dressing room, she felt a fraud. Karl would take one look at her and know she was expecting a special announcement. And presumably if he found her attractive, he'd done so when she was unmade up and wearing one of Eduardo's old shirts.

So she took the trouser suit off again and restored her jeans and sloppy sweater. She rubbed most of the lipstick off too, but left the eye make-up. It was quite subtle, and it looked good. Then she made a pot of filter coffee and put a couple of frozen Danish in the oven.

She was very jumpy. She wasn't sure that she could

go through with it. She did want to do something dramatic, to prove she wasn't completely convention-bound, and was still young and desirable. And a part of her did want revenge. But now she was scared stiff. It was one thing to fantasize. But did she really want a quick coupling with her farm manager before he caught his plane tomorrow night?

She'd been so certain she did. She'd even planned her excuses so they could meet again tonight after the last show and spend the night and all tomorrow doing what lovers did. She'd ring Eduardo and say they were called for a technical rehearsal because half the backstage staff had gone down with flu and they had to rehearse another crew. Eduardo didn't know enough of the theatre to question her. And anyway he'd believe her because she never lied.

She hadn't planned exactly where this tryst was to take place, but she had an image of a hotel bedroom. Maybe they'd go there now, drink champagne and do it. Then she'd have to go to the theatre. Maybe they'd make love in her dressing room between the shows. Then again after supper. And again . . .

When Karl walked in, she was still vacillating, but once he was sitting opposite her, his long brown fingers holding the coffee cup as though it was a mug, ignoring the handle, and his eyes steady and confident, looking into hers, she knew she'd do it. All he had to do was ask.

He wolfed down a Danish, and she poured him a second cup. There was a natural pause, a gap that elongated into a silence. Here it comes, she thought.

'Popps, I want to ask you something. I never ever talk about personal things, but I've got so close to you this week that I'd feel uncomfortable if I didn't tell you.'

Her heart lurched unevenly, then settled to a steady thumping. She didn't reply, but nodded yes, her eyes on his.

'The thing is, Popps, I'm in love with Carrie.'

The words did not go in. Did not make sense. Poppy frowned and said, 'You're what?'

Karl stood up and came close to her. He crouched down on his hunkers, put his mug down on the table and took her hand. 'I've loved her ever since you came home after your last year at that Johannesburg boarding school. She was only fifteen. The year you moved to England.'

Poppy shook her head. Her face registered disbelief and distress. Karl saw it and said, 'You don't think I'd be bad for her? Poppy. You don't disapprove, do you? Is there something wrong?' He looked into her face, his eyes demanding. She tried to look away, but his gaze held her.

'But why . . .? Why . . .?' Poppy did not know what she was trying to say, but it was enough for Karl, who launched into an earnest speech.

'It seems like I've always loved her. But at first she was far too young, and your mom was ill, and I didn't have much money. And then she went away, and I thought – I hoped – I'd forget her. But it got worse. Every time she came on holiday, I fell in love with her all over again.'

Poppy finally made a coherent response. It wasn't much, but she said, 'I never knew. I had no idea.' God, she thought, what a fool I've been. To think I . . .

'No one knew. I've never told anyone. Not even Carrie. I never touched her, I swear. Though last night . . .'

'Last night?' Poppy's voice was sharp. She'd spent most of last night tossing and turning, thinking lascivious thoughts about Karl, and all the while he and Carrie . . . She could not bear it. Oh God, was there no end to it?

Karl said, 'Last night I kissed her. I couldn't resist her.' He shook his head. 'I shouldn't have.'

Suddenly Poppy said, spitting the words, 'Why ever not? Everyone else does. In fact everyone else fucks the living daylights out of her. What makes you so different?'

Her own venom astonished her. She jumped up and pushed past Karl, hurtling towards her bedroom.

Poppy ran into Eduardo's dressing room and then into their bathroom, then turned on her heel and swung back into the bedroom. She paced about, tormented. She wanted to fling herself on to the bed and sob like a child, but she couldn't do that with Karl in the flat – he'd probably follow her in and try to comfort her. He must go. He had to go.

She could not explain her fury or her misery to him. She'd have to just stuff all that cringe-making desire down inside her again. Pretend it never happened. At least she'd not said anything. At least Eduardo didn't know.

She pushed her jaw up, raked her hair off her face with her fingers and pulled in a deep breath. Then she walked, stony-faced, back into the sitting room. Karl was on the terrace, leaning over the balcony and looking down into the canal.

She stepped out into the sunshine. At her step he turned, and came towards her, his face clouded with concern. She said, her voice buckram-stiff, 'I am sorry about that. But I don't think I can discuss Carrie with you. I would have thought I could, but it seems not.' As she said it she realized she could make Carrie's affair with Eduardo a cover-up for her own turmoil, and she continued, 'I'm still too raw about Eduardo, I guess.'

And it was true. She was raw. Raw enough to want to hurt them both, Karl as well as Carrie. She said, 'But I should at least tell you that it's no good. Carrie will never love you. She thinks you're a joke. A slightly embarrassing family friend who turns up in khaki shorts and carries a claspknife in his pocket like Crocodile Dundee. Fine as a ranger in the bush. But love you? Never.'

Karl did not say anything at once. Then he straightened his back and said, 'That's not altogether a surprise. She said much the same thing herself last night.'

His face was rigid, and he said with an effort, 'I'll go now. And Poppy, thanks for this week. And for the coffee and Danish.'

Poppy could see the damage she'd done. She could see it in the stiff formality of his speech. He was being rigidly polite, going through the motions, face of stone. A man whose dream has been cut away from him.

For a second she wanted to undo it, but he was talking again. 'Poppy, forgive me. I've been an idiot. I just wanted to tell you about me. I never thought about how you must feel about Carrie. And I never thought that's how I look to her.'

They walked back inside. His arms hung by his sides. He said, 'You're a good woman, Poppy. Eduardo is a lucky man.' And then he was gone.

I can go and blub in peace now, thought Poppy, but she knew she wouldn't. She no longer wanted to cry. She'd applied the balm of pure malice to her pain and it had pretty much worked. In spite of her humiliation and wretchedness, Poppy was conscious of a small smudge of pleasure. She had scuppered something of Carrie's.

She filled a bucket with hot water, threw a sponge into it and picked up the packet of Flash. She'd clean the terrace furniture.

As she soaped and rinsed away a summer of London grime, she let her mind free-wheel into calmer waters.

Karl's last remark, about Eduardo being lucky, came

back and cheered her. And now that they'd seen Carrie, some of the tension between her and Eduardo had gone. Maybe, as long as she gave up any fantasies of romance or revenge, they might yet be all right.

Eduardo had been complaining about the chairs and table. He'd be pleased. I could do with a bit of approval, she thought, even if it's for scrubbing.

Twenty-three

Carrie was pretty low. Richard had decamped, simply saying he was through.

And she missed Karl. She'd not heard from him in the two months since he had returned to South Africa. And he'd left England without coming to say goodbye. He'd left a message on the machine: 'It's Karl. I'm off now. Thanks for everything. And Carrie, if you want some thinking time, come to Kaia Moya. Could do you some good.' She'd resented that. Anyone would think she needed a shrink or something.

And things had not improved with Poppy. When she'd managed to get five tickets for the sell-out panto at the National she rang Poppy in triumph. 'It's my Christmas treat. We'll take the kids.'

There was a fractional pause and then Poppy said, 'I can't, Carrie. I've got a matinee.'

'No, you haven't . . .' Carrie started to say, then the coldness of Poppy's voice registered and Carrie realized her sister was lying. There was no *Filumena* matinee – Carrie had checked before she bought the tickets. Poppy just didn't want to come. She'd let her take the children, but wouldn't come herself.

Poppy's lying upset her as much as the fact that she

refused to come. She could not remember Poppy ever lying to her. Yet she knew the change in her sister was her fault. How could she object to Poppy telling her white lies when she'd lived the grand lie for months?

Feeling saintly, Carrie took Lucille instead. Her mother could only follow plays and films if the story was parked in her long-term memory, so Carrie figured she'd be okay with *Cinderella*.

But Lucille fell asleep and snored, then protested loudly that modern actors all mumbled. Then in the second act she turned to Carrie and said, 'Are you in this, dear?'

'No,' hissed Carrie. 'Poppy's the actress, not me, and if she was in it how could she be here?'

Being put right upset Lucille. Rebuffed and hesitant, she said, 'But she isn't here.' She looked like a child about to cry, and Carrie felt awful. She patted her mother's hand and said, 'Never mind, Mom. I'll explain later.'

Then, in a quiet bit with the prince mooning at Cinderella, Tom's high-pitched voice rang out, loud and clear, 'Carrie, can we turn it off now?' As the people around them burst into laughter, Lorato bounced up and down, saying, 'Turn it off. Turn it off.'

When the final curtain fell, Lucille made a beeline for the front. To Carrie's question, 'Where are you going, Mom?' she replied, 'To see you, dear. You always like friends in your dressing room.'

*

Poppy had not refused to see Carrie altogether, but the old intimacy had gone. When Carrie tried to recapture it by telling her about Richard walking out because she'd kissed Karl, Poppy brushed her off with, 'Oh Carrie, grow up. How much more shit do you think Richard could take from you before he'd had enough?' Poppy saying 'shit' rocked her. So did the uncharacteristic lack of sympathy.

When Carrie had made some reference to coming down to Oxfordshire for Christmas, Poppy had said, quite brutally, 'Carrie, I don't want you to come this year. I'm not having Mother either. We are all exhausted, I only get two nights off and I want to be as quiet as possible. With just the family.'

'Just the family' hurt. I am family, thought Carrie. But she'd said, 'Sure. Okay. No problem.'

Carrie spent Christmas with her mother, sleeping on her sofa. Adrienne was glad to shed the responsibility of Lucille for a few days and Carrie's mood as Christmas approached veered from self-pity – everyone was away skiing or tucked up with family in the country – to feeling virtuous. There was no work, nothing to do, so she might as well look after Lucille and pig out in front of the telly. She'd lay off the dope, and sleep a lot. It would be good for her.

To her surprise she enjoyed it. Her mother was much less irritating on her own, not being fussed by too much noise or made anxious by having to pretend she remembered things she didn't.

Lucille liked being spoiled, and she shared Carrie's natural extravagance. She was delighted with a Christmas lunch of nothing but hot blinis, smoked salmon and soured cream, with a bottle of Veuve Clicquot to start and finish, and one of Cloudy Bay Chardonnay in between.

'Oops, I must be tiddly,' said Lucille, as, wobbling dangerously, she sent a cascade of squeezed lemons and dirty forks off the plates.

'Hey Mom, let me,' said Carrie, taking the plates. 'You sit down. And we aren't a little tiddly. We are drunk!'

'I know,' responded Lucille. 'Fun, isn't it?' She sat down and poured the rest of the champagne into her glass.

They watched the Queen's speech, and Carrie felt a pang of real sorrow when her mother, who had faithfully listened to Queen's speeches ever since they'd come to England, said, 'Who is that woman? What *is* she talking about?'

'It's the Queen, Mom. Christmas Day speech.'

'That's not the Queen. That's an old woman. Turn her off.'

Before her mother went off for her nap, Carrie had the presence of mind to dose them both with Alka-Seltzer, then she tucked down on the sofa with the video of *Grease* and a box of Mint Matchmakers.

In fifteen minutes she could feel herself drifting contentedly into sleep, dark and luxurious as chocolate.

*

A week later, Carrie was again at Lucille's, this time for New Year's Day. My social life, she thought, is rubbish – Christmas *and* New Year with a batty old mother.

The one area of their lives the sisters still talked easily about was Lucille, although there was an unspoken but mutually understood subtext: how long would she last? They'd been told dementia patients seldom lived ten years after diagnosis, but it was nearly two decades since Lucille's illness had become obvious and they'd come to live in England. Since their father had died in '93 Lucille had got much worse, though. She was now physically as well as mentally frail.

Carrie knew that Poppy bore the brunt of caring for their mother, but she felt she'd evened up the balance a bit with her Christmas stint, and increased her Brownie point stock further with an offer to cook this lunch.

Lucille was pleased. Repeatedly pleased. For every time (about eight so far, Carrie reckoned) she asked who was coming or what the occasion was, she heard the news of a celebration afresh.

Carrie was sautéing chicken fillets in sesame oil when Lucille appeared at the door. 'Darling, I know you are cooking supper, but who is coming?'

'Lunch, not supper. It's New Year. Poppy and co. are coming.'

'Oh, how nice. I'd forgotten. Shall I lay the table?'

'You just did, Mom.' Lucille looked at the table

without noticing that Carrie had removed the tea towels she'd laid for napkins and replaced the mugs with glasses.

'So I did. How funny. You know, sometimes I think my memory is going.'

Once the Santolinis arrived, Lucille became the gracious hostess. Knowing better than to cross her, the sisters left their mother to do the honours. Having asked Eduardo what he'd like, she responded to his request for 'whisky, no water, no ice' with a brandy goblet containing gin, water, ice and a scattering of cigarette ash. Angelina's protest that she'd asked for orange not tomato juice died in her throat at a look from Carrie. Poppy pre-empted trouble with Lorato and Tom by giving them each a tumbler of orange before their grandmother could turn her attention to them.

Perhaps with a hazy memory that guests for drinks meant canapés, Lucille disappeared into the kitchen, refusing all aid.

Carrie caught Poppy's eye. Carrie shook her head. 'Leave her,' she said. 'She'll give us hell if we help.'

In a surprisingly short time, Lucille reappeared with a plate of snacks – small biscuits on which was spread some kind of pâté. Lorato, ever desperate for anything edible, reached for a canapé and ate it, her eyes already searching for the next one. Tom, less bold, put his carefully into his mouth, then promptly spat it out again. Carrie dived into the kitchen and returned with a half-empty tub of Felix, 'gourmet food for cats'.

Lucille said, 'Darling, leave the pâté in the kitchen. It's so crude to serve it straight from the tin. And I've made cocktail bits.'

Eduardo was having trouble keeping a straight face as Poppy surreptitiously gathered up the offending Felix bits. Lorato held tight to her second one, stuffing it hastily into her mouth and swallowing before Poppy could get to her.

Carrie watched as Eduardo swung Lorato up into the crook of his arm and put his other arm round his wife, saying, 'I don't suppose it will kill her.' Poppy's eyes were bright with trying not to laugh.

Carrie distracted Lucille by calling everyone to lunch and handing her the wine to pour. This proved a mistake as she filled everyone's glasses, including the children's, to the brim, but it gave Carrie time to dish up.

Halfway through lunch Lucille suddenly came to life. She'd been out of it for a while, but she came to with a vengeance.

'Oh dear,' she said, 'I'm so sorry. I really am a terrible cook.' She looked at the half-eaten plates, and pushed her own away from her. 'This stuff is truly disgusting. Don't eat it. I won't be offended. We'll just leave it and we'll go out. Get something edible in a restaurant.'

Poppy caught her sister's eye and Carrie saw something of the old sympathy and understanding there.

Poppy said, 'Mom, it's simply delicious. Did you

cook it? I would have sworn it was cooked by Carrie, it's so good.'

Lucille, her previous opinion forgotten, tasted a piece of chicken and said, 'Mmm. It is good. Did you make it, Carrie?'

Praise for the cook worked its usual magic on Carrie. After that, lunch went better than Carrie had expected. She'd barely seen Eduardo since their affair, and she'd thought she'd still be angry with him. But somehow it didn't matter any more. Nothing to do with Eduardo mattered any more.

She could see that he was still, technically, drop dead gorgeous, but he wasn't right for her. There was something weak about him. Poppy had turned out the stronger of the two, and he hadn't had the courage to leave her.

Looking at his big hands cracking nuts, one hand gripping the nutcracker, one shielding the nut to prevent pieces of shell flying, Carrie could no longer see what had turned her on so. She remembered the many times she'd felt weak with lust as she'd watched those hands hugging a mug of coffee or stroking her thigh.

She shook her head a fraction, disbelieving. It was over. Like a hurricane or a disease.

Carrie watched Poppy patiently denying Tom more chocolates, and thought how lucky Poppy's children were. Whatever the sins of the father, they had a rock-solid mother. One day, when the events of the last year were far in the past, she would mend relations with her sister.

But things went wrong over coffee.

Lucille suddenly announced, 'Carrie darling, you should get married.'

Carrie laughed. 'Who do you have in mind, Mom?'

For once Lucille was clear as a bell. 'That nice boy, Karl. Your father always hoped he'd marry one of you girls.'

Before Carrie could parry this, Eduardo chipped in, 'Not a bad idea, Lucille. Karl's a good guy. And he'd be a match for you, Carrie. Why don't you get your hooks into him?'

Carrie expostulated, 'Get my hooks into him? That's a bit rich.'

'It would make sense. He's got money now the game lodge is doing so well. If you went in with him you'd have two-thirds between you and I'm sure Poppy would sell you her third.'

'No I wouldn't,' said Poppy very quickly.

Carrie, her mouth open in astonishment, said, 'Hey, excuse me, you lot. Do I get a say in this? Or does Karl? What is this, a marriage market?'

Eduardo shrugged. 'Okay, okay, just an idea. Not serious.'

'It's a lousy idea,' said Poppy. 'Karl would never marry Carrie in a million years.'

Carrie felt the blow as if it was physical. A double blow. Why was Poppy suddenly being so unkind?

She'd been almost friendly a minute ago. And Karl liked her. She knew he did.

'Oh,' she said as coolly as she could manage, 'I dare say he wouldn't. We've never discussed it. But how come you know what Karl thinks of me?'

'Because he told me,' said Poppy, standing up and walking over to kiss her mother's cheek. 'Goodbye, Mom. Happy New Year.'

Carrie opened her mouth and closed it again. She was bursting to challenge Poppy, but the suddenness of Poppy's onslaught had taken the wind out of her, and she could not marshal her thoughts, and then Poppy had gone in a flurry of goodbyes and instructions to the children, leaving Carrie to clear up and cope with their mother, who kept putting things away before Carrie had washed them up. Christ, thought Carrie, her throat tight and her eyes pricking, who needs families?

'What is it?' said Carrie. 'A bill? Bung it in the drawer with the others, will you?' Her hands were floury from the pizza dough. Lulu could hardly expect her to open letters.

'No. You've got to read it.'

Something in Lulu's voice made Carrie turn round and look her in the face. 'Why? What's up, Lulu? What is it?'

'It's my resignation. I'm leaving.'

Carrie straightened up, her face at first blank, then astonished. She lifted her floury hands in a gesture of denial, then dropped them again. 'Lulu, you can't. I can't manage the business without you.'

'Carrie, you can't manage it with me. You used to be so great. The best. But now you are all over the place. I'm tired of bailing you out.'

Carrie felt her face flush. 'What do you mean, bailing me out?' she said, her voice rising.

'Just that, Carrie. You've lost it. Last night was the last straw.'

Carrie had an uneasy feeling about last night, and didn't want to talk about it. She said quickly, 'Look, I'm sorry about that, but . . .'

Lulu cut in, 'It's not just last night, though that was the worst. It's all the time. Last week you forgot that wedding cake and I was up all night, icing the thing, blowing the layers dry with a poxy hair-dryer . . .'

Carrie interrupted, 'But Lulu, give me a break, anyone could forget an order . . .'

'And what about the props you forgot to return and I had to go crawling to *Hot Properties* with some story about you being ill so they wouldn't charge you an extra £800?' Lulu's chin was up, her eyes accusing. 'And the millions of suppliers I have to fob off because you haven't paid them?' Lulu dropped her eyes and said, her voice flat, 'Last night was one too many, Carrie. I'm sorry, but I'm off.'

Carrie could not get her brain to focus. What had happened last night?

Lulu said, more kindly, 'You don't remember a thing, do you?'

Carrie snapped back, 'Of course I do. It was the Everton boy's twenty-first. It went off perfectly. There was a message from his mother on the machine this morning, She said it was the best party they'd ever . . .'

'Yes, because I did 90 per cent of the work, and because I managed to get you home before they found you completely out of your skull with young Everton's mates.'

Carrie turned her back to Lulu then, and washed the flour off her hands. She dried them on her apron and sat down. 'Oh God, Lulu, what did I do?'

Lulu sat in the chair next to her. 'Carrie, you've got to get some help. I don't know what drugs you were doing last night, and I don't know if you are addicted or just unhappy, but last night you ended up in a gang-bang with a bunch of twenty-year-olds.'

Carrie felt her stomach contract. Oh God, she remembered now. She'd been on such a high when the dinner was over that when the birthday boy, pissed as a newt, had asked her to dance, she'd joined in. And then . . .

Lulu said, 'Open the envelope, Carrie.' She offered it to Carrie again.

Carrie pushed Lulu's hand away. 'Why should I?' said Carrie. 'You've told me what it says. You're quitting.' Carrie took a deep breath and changed tack. 'Look, Lulu, I'm sorry. Maybe I can't blame you, but oh Lulu, don't leave now. I can't . . .'

Lulu's voice was unforgiving. 'Open it, Carrie.'

Carrie shook her head and Lulu opened the envelope herself, saying, 'It contains more than my resignation, Carrie. Look.'

She passed Carrie a sheaf of folded A4 papers. 'They were printing them out on the computer, and handing them round.'

Carrie took them, unfolding them. They were colour photographs of several very drunk young people. As soon as Carrie saw the first one, she screwed up the bundle and jumped up.

'Oh Christ,' she said, looking about as if for escape. But then she went to the work surface by the sink and flattened the sheets out again. Carrie was in three of the photographs. In the top one she was dancing wearing nothing but a single chef's clog, waving both arms above her head.

For a second Carrie's mortification was tempered by satisfaction that she looked so good – slim and willowy, with high round breasts and flat stomach, like a model – then she saw how coarse and drunk her face looked and flipped the picture over.

There were a couple of pictures without her. They were of young men, half naked, singing and leering at the camera. But there was worse to come. In one she was sitting on the lap of one of the boys, wearing her chef's trousers but without jacket or bra. The boy was wearing her chef's hat, and he had his arms round her bare tits. Another lad was pulling her clogs off, and all of them were laughing. In the third she was lying face down, bum to the world, on a bed. Her head hung over the edge of the bed, her hair sweeping the carpet. She looked asleep, or unconscious. Or dead.

Twenty-four

As Poppy stepped out into the narrow alley at 10.15 p.m. she kept her head down. The play had been on for six months now, and there were seldom any autograph hunters in the February cold, just drunks peeing in the alley, or occasional junkies.

When Carrie put an arm around her, her heart leaped with fright and she started back, flinging Carrie off.

'Christ, Carrie, what the hell are you doing?'

Then she looked into Carrie's face and saw it crumple. 'Please, Poppy, for God's sake, I've got to talk to you.'

They went to a pub. Poppy asked for two glasses of wine.

'No, I'll have a Diet Coke.'

'Coke?' Poppy looked at her sister in disbelief.

'Yes. Coke. Or water or something. I'm trying to stop drinking.'

Poppy didn't believe it. The unkind thought crossed her mind that her sister was being dramatic as usual. She said, 'If this is to warn me about the *My Mag* article, it's too late. I've seen it and I haven't the energy to care. What's a small betrayal like that after what we've already been through?'

Carrie hardly seemed to follow her. She pushed some papers across the table at Poppy, saying, 'Just look.'

Poppy unfolded the sheets and looked at the photographs. She found her face burning. It was as though it was *she* lying on the bed, *she* dead drunk, *she* dancing around stark naked, *she* arsing about with a lot of drunken youths. A little burst of anger overlaid the humiliation. Why do I take on Carrie's shame?

Carrie was gabbling on about Lulu quitting, about the money she owed, about Richard walking out. Poppy, once she'd got over the shock of the pictures, listened with changing emotions. There was the old pull of 'poor Carrie' – the familiar feeling that Carrie could not be blamed, that whatever inner weather blew Carrie off course, she could not help it. But Poppy felt tired too, wrung out. The thought flicked across her mind: I've had enough of Carrie.

Carrie was pleading, 'You've got to help me. You've always helped me.'

Poppy watched her sister's anguish but did not share it as once she would have. What she felt was weary sadness and resignation, not love, not real concern. Perhaps the horrors of the summer could never be papered over.

Still Poppy didn't answer. Carrie went on, her pale face contorted as she struggled to wring some of the old sympathy from her sister's passive one, 'I'm losing it, Poppy. I didn't even remember doing this.' She clutched at the photographs. 'Lulu had to remind me.

She says I'm a druggie. But I'm not. I know I drink too much . . .'

Poppy listened for a long time as Carrie talked. After a while she put out a hand and held her sister's forearm, holding down her violent gestures. She saw the desperation in Carrie's eyes, the drawn, hysterical look.

'Carrie, I cannot help you. You are on your own, sis. I'm sorry.'

Carrie took a taxi home, stunned. But even as she rehearsed Poppy's lack of sympathy, she understood her sister's refusal to help. How could she help? What had Carrie expected her to do?

She was going to have to get out of this mess on her own. It was tempting to give in, go to a doctor or a shrink, get on a detox programme, let the professionals take over, but Carrie knew in her heart that even with all the white-coated help in the world, things only got better if you wanted them to. Trite but true.

Then she remembered Karl's message about a stay at Kaia Moya sorting her out. Maybe he was right. Certainly she needed to get away for a bit. She'd go to South Africa, maybe take that job at *My Mag*.

The next day Carrie scrambled into action. She rang the *My Mag* editor.

'Joanna, it's Carrie.'

'Hi, Carrie, nice to hear you.' She sounded genuinely pleased. Carrie charged at her question. 'Jo, does your offer still hold good?'

'Good Lord, yes of course it does. But you turned us down flat. Why the change of heart?'

Carrie combed her hair off her face with her fingers and said, 'Oh Jo, you don't want to know. Personal stuff. I need a change of scene.'

'Works for me. When can you come?' Carrie imagined Jo pulling the diary towards her, efficiently clicking her pencil into action, already planning her induction as food editor.

The overnight flight was horrible. The rugger team in front of her kept Carrie awake most of the night and one of them spilt his lager into her sandals, which she'd kicked off under his seat. Now her feet slipped against the squashy leather. It felt disgusting, but she could hardly go through customs and the luggage hall barefoot.

Why aren't I rich, damn it? she thought. I was born to turn left into a jumbo, not right. If she took this job, she'd never get rich, that was for sure.

It took forty minutes to get through customs, and another ten until her old holdall came bumping round the conveyor belt. She lugged it into the ladies', washed her feet in the basin – to the obvious disgust of the other occupants – and changed into trainers. She considered washing the sandals, but binned them instead.

She took the airport bus to Sandton and checked with relief into the luxurious vulgarity of the Savoy Towers. As she turned on the great taps in the black marble bathroom and tipped all four of the little bottles of bath gel and shampoo into the whirling water, she thought that a glass of champagne would work wonders. I wonder if *My Mag* expenses will run to fizz? Then she pushed the thought out of her head. She must drink less, a whole lot less. No boozing until the evenings would be a good start.

Still, at least she'd made a dramatic change. She was pleased with herself for the speed with which she'd extricated herself from London. She was tempted to call Poppy, to tell her that she was in Johannesburg, that she, Poppy, need never bother with her again. For a minute she dwelled on the pleasant thought that Poppy would feel guilty, would know that her refusal to hold her hand had driven Carrie away. And then she thought that if she sorted herself out maybe Poppy would be proud of her, which would be nice. Poppy had told her often enough to grow up, drink less and sleep more. Well, maybe she would.

And *My Mag* were satisfyingly keen to have her join them. Jo had been delighted with the piece on the Santolinis and with the recipes and the pictures, and Carrie'd been writing a monthly 'Euro Food' column for her ever since. Now *My Mag* had stumped up a plane ticket. Carrie had tried for Club, but the budget wouldn't run to it, they said.

At least half of *My Mag* was food-related, so food editor was a good job, even if it paid, by British standards, lousy money. Right now, though, it felt like a lifeline. Carrie had agreed to a month's trial while she thought about a full-time job.

As she topped up the foamy water her mind turned to Kaia Moya. She was both longing to see Karl, and dreading it. She'd sent him a fax saying she'd like to come for a holiday after the Johannesburg stay, and had hoped the message would prompt him to ring her. But he'd just scribbled on her fax – '19–25 March is fine. See you then' – and faxed it back. There was no message at the hotel, though she'd told him when she was arriving, and where she was staying.

For a while, after the evening in her house, she'd been sure that kiss had meant something to him. She'd half expected a letter or an e-mail from him, and a dozen times had been on the point of writing herself. But what to say? Maybe she'd got the wrong signals. Maybe he'd forgotten the kiss by the next day. But then she'd remember the way he'd stopped resisting, and how he'd seemed to fall into her, as into a pool. The intensity of it had been real.

Then, at New Year, Poppy had blown any little fantasy about Karl right out of the water. 'Karl would never marry Carrie in a million years. He told me so.' Why would he say that to Poppy? Who said anything about marriage? Why discuss it at all?

It bugged her that she still thought of Karl's kiss. If he could shrug it off as a non-event, why couldn't she? But it wasn't just the way he'd kissed her, it was also what he'd said afterwards. 'You cannot just jump from guy to guy. Sooner or later you need to be able to bear your own company.'

The truth was that those two sentences had changed something for her. Until then Karl had just been a friend, albeit one she liked to torment a bit and flirt with. Although she admired him, she'd resented his big brother attitude, always ticking her off. Now, for some reason, she was nervous of him.

Blast him, she thought, it's no good lecturing me about independence. I want a husband, and I want children.

A month later, Carrie hired a car with air-conditioning and central locking. The air-conditioning was perhaps not vital in March, but she knew that when she dropped off the escarpment to the lowveld below, it would be much hotter. The central locking was to foil hijackers and muggers. I must be getting old, thought Carrie. A year ago I'd not have listened to scare stories, but a month in Johannesburg, where the rich lived in fortresses and the poor in slums, had taught her caution. Last night she'd been so excited about leaving Johannesburg she'd woken each time the security lights came on, which they did every time the electronic gates creaked open to admit a resident. She longed to get to Kaia Moya, where no one locked a door, and where the only security was to protect humans from animals and animals from humans.

My Mag was a good publication, with a rising readership, and the staff had been great, really friendly.

Carrie knew the job would not hold her forever, but she was tempted to take it. She'd have to make a decision by the time Joanna came back from holiday, in five weeks' time.

The roads were good, and Carrie enjoyed the drive. She'd done it dozens of times, though never alone, and she felt grown up and free.

She watched the small round kopjies of the highveld come and go, then marvelled at the colours of the escarpment: great kranses of deep brown, bright pink, cool grey, the bald rock falling hundreds of feet to wooded valleys.

Once down on the lowveld floor the thorn-spattered veld stretched mile on mile, punctuated by an occasional roadside stall offering a few hanging nets of greenish oranges. Every few miles the land was scarred by merciless erosion. It should have been ugly to her, but she'd played in just such red-sand dongas as a child and the pleasure of it came back to her. The stun gun heat, the smell of the dry grass, the sand too hot for bare feet, then the darkening of the sky, the sudden fearful lightning crack and monumental thunder roll. The first drops of rain, big as marbles splashing in the orange dust, the glorious smell of water on the parched ground. And then the rivers running red and thick as soup.

She'd loved those storms. Inside the house the racket as hail hit the corrugated tin roof was deafening. And exciting. Outside it was scarier but exhilarating. She wasn't meant to be outside of course. You could

346

be struck by lightning. But she always ran out into the warm pelting rain if she could, or failed to come in if she was already outside. It was glorious.

Once in the Manyeleti reserve, Carrie slowed down, automatically quartering the bush with her eyes. She rolled down the window and turned the air-conditioning fan off.

The smell of dust and autumn veld came through the window and Carrie stuck her head out to breathe more deeply. In the ten miles of corrugated dirt road before she came to the lodge, she saw a family of warthogs, a lone bull elephant and two giraffes. How considerate of them, thought Carrie. A happy foretaste.

Carrie pulled into the bougainvillea-covered carport at 5 p.m., and before she'd opened the boot Nelson was there.

'Sakabona, Miss Carrie.' His big head tipped shyly, both hands grasping her outstretched one.

He would not let her help, and she followed his back, loaded with both her bags, her computer and her briefcase, to reception.

Karl wasn't there. She felt a tiny wash of hurt, or disappointment. He'd taken some tourists on a game drive, and would not be back until 8 p.m.

Carrie had been given the same lodge as she'd had nine months ago. As she unpacked her stuff she frowned at the memories the little cabin contained. She and Eduardo had made hasty love on this bed.

Poppy, surveying her African purchases spread out on this matting, had berated her for being extravagant. On the little veranda outside, Maisie had told her not to lust after her sister's husband.

It seemed a long time ago. It felt like someone else's life.

At 8.15 she was sitting on a barstool on the stoep, listening to Piet telling his old tales to a French couple, his eyes narrowed as he peered back through eighty years in the bush. Carrie had heard, many times, about the ostrich that got a mouth organ stuck in his throat and forever after breathed on E flat, or the fourteen-foot crocodile that had eaten six people before he was caught, but she listened with pleasure. Piet was a great storyteller and the tales got better with the telling.

Suddenly she felt a hand on her shoulder and she knew it was Karl. She swung round to see him looking at her, smiling, surprised.

'You look great, Carrie,' he said. 'Like a schoolboy.' He ruffled her short hair with his hand, and slid on to the barstool beside her. 'Coming on the game drive tomorrow?'

It was as if he'd seen her yesterday. I must have imagined that kiss, thought Carrie. He is just the same as he's always been. Same big brother nonchalance, same indifference to the fact that I'm a woman. Schoolboy, my foot. This haircut cost an arm and a leg and is supposed to be super-feminine.

But she was relieved too. Same old Karl. He was

wearing, even in the cool of a March evening, very short shorts, a bush shirt and boots.

'And you still look like Crocodile Dundee,' she replied. 'And of course I'm coming on the drive.'

For a second Karl's forehead puckered in a slight frown, and he looked away, his jaw set. What have I said? thought Carrie. But almost at once Karl replied, 'I'll put some long pants on in a minute. It's getting cold.'

Carrie felt a rush of pleasure. It was *so* good to see him. 'It's chilly already,' she said, putting her hand on his bare leg, rubbing it above the knee. 'Look, you're all goosey, you madman.' She could feel the goosebumps, the fine reddish hairs erect against the stroke of her hand. She took her hand away with reluctance.

The French couple left the next day and a party expected from the States cancelled, too late for Karl to fill the vacancies. Carrie expressed dismay at the loss of revenue, but was secretly pleased to have the camp almost empty. An elderly pair of sisters from the Cape came on the evening drives, but not the early morning ones. The only other guests were a German couple, who mostly parked their car at one of the waterholes and waited for the game to come to them.

That left Cathy, a trainee ranger, and Carrie up for the dawn drives. Cathy drove, with Karl next to her so he could teach her, and the tracker Winston on the elevated lookout seat. Cathy was silent, listening intently, doing as Karl bid her. She drove well, her gloved hands commanding the wheel, her booted feet trampling from clutch to brake and back again as she swung the vehicle through dongas and ditches, obeying Winston's signals (slow down, go back, go forward).

When the sun came streaking over the horizon, flooding the plains with light and warmth, Karl asked Cathy to get out the breakfast stuff. She jumped down without a word, slid the bolts on the tailgate and set up her coffee stall.

Carrie thought she lacked friendliness, though. Even in camp she seldom spoke, and yet answered readily enough if spoken to. She had a quiet confidence and stillness that made one aware of her, gave her a sort of authority. You would not think she was only nineteen. Carrie could not decide if she was shy or aloof. Walking over to the waterhole at Karl's side, Carrie asked, 'How's Cathy doing? She seems keen.'

Karl's eyes were on the water's edge, tracking round where the trees met the reeds. He held his gun over his shoulder, but Carrie knew he'd have it at the ready in a second if he needed to. Without taking his eyes from their steady survey he said, 'She'll be good. She's patient, doesn't panic. Good eyes.'

For a second Carrie thought he meant Cathy's eyes were beautiful, which they were. Almost black with wide lids and long lashes. But no, he meant she could see well.

'How long has she been here?' she asked, both hands round the coffee mug.

'Er . . . Don't know. Must be six weeks. She's done a season at the Kruger Park, so she's not completely green.' He looked back towards the jeep, where Cathy was restacking the picnic things. She looked up and he signalled to her. She walked swiftly to join them, the obedient pupil.

Karl pointed at the ground, his eyebrows flicking into a question. Cathy dropped down on her haunches. Hell, they communicate in signs, thought Carrie, a little crossly. Cathy examined what to Carrie looked like an indecipherable jumble of tracks. After a minute of studying her immobile back, Carrie said, 'Go on Cathy, tell us. I'm a partner in Kaia Moya, so you'd better prove Karl's worth as a teacher.' Oh God, why had she said that? What a crass, pompous little speech.

But Cathy shot a bright smile at Karl – that's the first time I've seen her smile, thought Carrie – and said, 'It won't be Karl's fault if I get it wrong. He's brilliant.' Then she added, tracing the even twin lobes of a largish spoor with her gloved finger, 'That's buffalo. And this is elephant, of course. A really big bull.'

'How do you know?' asked Carrie, impressed.

'Because an elephant is twice as high as the circumference of one of his footprints and this one must be almost two metres.' Her hand circled the crushed-velvet pattern of the footprint. 'Which makes it a four-metre bull. Four metres to the shoulder, which is much too tall for a cow.'

Cathy stood up, and wandered to the edge of the track, her head still down, eyes on the ground. 'This is a bachelor herd. No cows and no babies.'

She kicked over a fresh pile of elephant dung. It would have filled a wheelbarrow, and was full of undigested straw. 'Yup. A pretty big boy, I guess. Thabo, do you think?' She looked at Karl for an answer and he nodded yes.

'Thabo?' asked Carrie. 'After Thabo Mbeke?'

'No.' Karl shook his head, smiling. 'Old Thabo was Thabo when apartheid was in fashion. Probably before Mandela went to jail. Thabo means happy.'

Karl turned right round slowly, checking the water, the track, the bush, near and middle distance, letting his eyes run full circle. He said. 'Thabo used to have a fair-sized harem. But he lost them to a younger rival, and now he hangs out with a bunch of young bulls. Some people say the old tuskers teach the young ones. But who knows?' He shrugged and turned back to Cathy, nodding at her to go on with her tracking lesson.

She crouched again and said, 'This long handprint is a baboon. These deep hoof prints are duiker, I think?' She looked for confirmation from Karl, who nodded.

After a while Carrie stopped listening to what she was saying and just watched her. The girl adored Karl, that was obvious. The only question was whether it was grown-up love or schoolgirl hero-worship. Carrie felt a little twist of anguish. I can't be jealous of a kid, can I? But she knew she was.

Twenty-five

One afternoon, Carrie was half asleep on a lounger by the pool. She had her eyes closed as the cicadas' incessant buzz and the soft crroo-crroo of the pigeons lulled her. Kaia Moya, she thought. It means House of the Wind. But that seemed too restless a name for it. Kaia Moya was the most restorative place on earth. No South Sea island or Caribbean hideaway could beat it.

As she drifted into sensuous semi-sleep, her sunhat covering her face, she felt a light fluttering on her legs. She opened her eyes without lifting her hat. It was Karl, carefully draping her sarong over her. She watched him through the open weave of the hat. His expression was open and tender.

She lifted the hat and smiled at him.

His face hardened. 'Sorry,' he said. 'I was trying not to wake you. But you are an idiot. If you get sunstroke it will be a right bore.'

'I'm covered in sun block.' She shifted up in the lounger, drawing up her legs to make room for him to sit down.

As he did so he said, 'Sleeping in the sun is crazy. Especially when there is no one around. Lions occasionally drink from this pool, you know.'

'I'm sorry.' She was still sleepy, and didn't say anything more.

'I've got to check the fences on the west side. Do you want to come? It's a pretty ride.'

She'd imagined they'd have a gang of fence-menders, tools and kit with them, but when she climbed into the jeep the back was empty and there was just a big coolbox between them on the front seat.

As they pulled out of the camp and on to the corrugated dirt road she tapped the box and said, 'What's in here?'

'Padkos,' he replied.

Food for the road? It was only 2.30, and they'd just had lunch, but she was pleased. This looked like an outing, a treat. And she was glad it was just her and Karl. No Cathy, no tracker, no tourists.

'If we aren't coming back for supper, who is doing the evening game ride?'

'Cathy'll take them.'

Carrie looked at him in astonishment. He took ranging so seriously. How could he be sending tourists out with a slip of a girl, a student? 'But you always take a gun. And you are so, so . . . grown up!'

Karl laughed, a big-throated full laugh. Carrie saw he wasn't laughing at what she'd said, but at her.

'Oh Carrie, you are an ass. Cathy *is* grown up. She's a lot more grown up than you in many ways. And she could drop a charging buffalo at fifty metres. She's a terrific shot.'

Carrie felt the familiar cramp of anxiety. Every time

Karl talked of Cathy it was in glowing terms. Every time Cathy looked at Karl it was with love, or something very close to it. Cathy was cucumber cool with everyone else, her stillness and self-possession creating a little barrier between her and the others, but when Karl spoke to her those ice-maiden eyes flooded with warmth.

Karl changed the subject. 'Have you decided about the magazine job?' He sounded casual, polite. Carrie wondered if it mattered to him at all.

'No,' she said. 'I like doing the monthly column. And I like the crowd in the office. But Karl, I've never liked Johannesburg. And there's much more editing and management than I'd reckoned on. I'd hoped it would be mostly writing and photo shoots, hands-on stuff.'

Karl's eyes were straight ahead. 'I've a rival proposal for you.'

'What proposal?' she asked, trying to read his profile as the truck shuddered over the corrugated road.

'Stay here and sort out the Kaia Moya kitchens. Almost all our visitors are from overseas and they don't want boerewors and steak from the braai every night. Some of the safari lodges have Californian and Mediterranean stuff now, and the punters love it.'

Carrie shook her head, thinking international fashion food was exactly what Kaia Moya should *not* serve.

Karl saw the gesture and said, 'No? Ah well, it was just an idea. You'd be good at it and . . .'

Carrie interrupted, 'I haven't said no. But it's daft, Karl. The lodge could not afford me for a start. Sixteen is the maximum number of guests, isn't it? If it was a forty-seater restaurant, maybe, but we aren't exactly in the middle of a metropolis.'

Karl did not answer at once, and she turned in her seat to look at him more squarely. He drove like most South Africans, window down and elbow leaning on it, his fingers holding the big juddering wheel lightly. He glanced at her and said, 'You're right of course, but I've got plans that I need to discuss with you and Poppy. We could build another dozen cabins at the lodge, deeper into the bush by the waterhole. And since active ecotourism is growing faster than luxury-lodge stays, we should also build a more primitive camp for sixteen or so on the western boundary, by the river. And then organize two-day safaris, with an overnight stay in the camp. The tourists would love it, and it would get them out of the lodge for a night and allow us to take more one-nighters. We could build the trek into a five-day package, but make it at the start or the end, so we don't have to pack and unpack their gear to let someone else into their rondavels.'

It was the longest speech Carrie had ever heard Karl make. She wasn't sure she'd got it all, but she felt at once how important the scheme was to Karl. In spite of his coolness and almost laid-back air, she could feel his excitement.

The more they discussed it, the more sense it made.

357

Karl had done his research and made good contacts on his trip to London, and had since had the rep from a major US travel agent come to Kaia Moya. He'd had discussions with the African Experience group of luxury hotels, and they were keen to form a marketing partnership. He'd also submitted a business plan to the Standard Bank – they'd need to borrow the capital to build the extra cabins and the new camp – and it looked like they'd get the money, albeit at very high interest rates.

'Could Poppy put up the money instead, do you think?' Karl asked. 'As I'm about to go to the Paris travel fair, I could take her the plans in person. I imagine she and Eduardo could afford it, if they wanted to.'

The introduction of the Santolinis into the conversation dampened Carrie, and she answered, 'God knows. You'd better ask them, not me.'

The terrain was changing now, becoming more hilly and wooded, greener in the riverbeds, with lumpy outcrops erupting from the grassland. They were driving steadily higher, and the road twisted and turned as they climbed. The massive stones were rounded and piled one upon each other. Perfect cheetah or baboon country, thought Carrie, narrowing her eyes as she scanned the rocks. But she could not see any animals. Too hot, she supposed. They'd all be dozing in the shade somewhere.

They inspected the fence, which was indeed trampled down over a stretch of twenty yards, two great concrete posts uprooted, the wires broken and electrics wrecked. Karl took notes. He'd come back tomorrow with a gang and the gear to fix it.

Karl swung himself into the driver's seat saying, 'Right, now I'll show you where the overnight camp will be.' Carrie felt a little flutter of excitement. She liked new projects, and she liked Karl treating her as a serious partner.

After ten minutes Karl pulled the jeep off the track and drove across the veld. They went slowly, the vehicle heaving and sighing over boulders and grassy hummocks, heading for a rocky hill with a deep ravine up one side and an apparently flat top. When they could go no further, they got out and climbed to the top on foot, Karl carrying his gun in one hand with the coolbox slung over his shoulder.

Carrie pulled herself up the last rounded rock, panting. It was hot work and the ascent had taken twenty minutes of exertion. She was sweating and the cool air on her face was delicious. She stood up, and her mouth dropped open in wonder.

So that is the meaning of breathtaking, she thought: the view blows the breath out of your body. She was silenced by its expanse and grandeur.

Finally she said, 'God, Karl. How come I've never been up here before? I lived here, damn it.'

'I guess you had your own kopjes to climb when you were kids, and this tract of land belonged to the Coetzees. We only bought it six years ago, remember?'

They were standing on a ridge looking northwest.

Immediately in front of them the rocks, red and yellow streaked with grey and black, tumbled down twenty feet to a grassy plateau, about the size of a cricket ground. Beyond that the kopje fell away steeply, a dangerous drop.

They climbed down to the grass then walked in silence to the edge. Carrie stood a few yards back, not wanting to disrupt the wonder with nervousness. Karl walked easily to the rim, and swung the picnic box off his shoulder.

Below them, way below, was the river, invisible in the green and tangled gorge, widening in a shallow meander as it flowed out across the valley floor. Now, in the dry season, it was not much more than a water-hole, but Carrie could see from the width of the riverbed how spectacular it would be after the rains. Beyond the river were the plains, vast, dun-coloured acres of veld, and in the distance range upon range of blue mountains were shimmering in the heat and disappearing into the sky.

Carrie looked at a herd of wildebeest, perhaps two miles away. They looked like tiny toys, hundreds and hundreds of them. Karl passed her his binoculars and she focused on a big bull, thinking how primitive he looked, with that outline familiar from rock paint-ings: heavy head with massive browlike horns, shoul-ders sloping to narrow hindquarters and a fly-whisk tail.

'Good place for a camp, don't you think?' said Karl. 'And there is a pool too. Come.'

Carrie followed Karl as he sprang from rock to rock, down towards the ravine. She scrambled awkwardly behind him, grateful for his outstretched arm when the jumps were too big. They could hear the sound of water splashing and sucking below them.

Soon they emerged from overhanging trees and stepped on to a wide ledge over the river. Opposite was a narrow waterfall, falling forty feet at least into the dark pool beneath. The rock face behind the waterfall was washed shiny black, punctuated with ferns and dripping creepers. Up here they were in baking sun, but the pool, only twenty feet across, was in deep shade.

'Oh God, Karl, it's magic. We've got to swim in it. But how do we get down there?'

Karl leaned the gun carefully against the rock face and wedged it upright with the picnic box. 'We dive,' he said.

Carrie shook her head vigorously. 'Not a chance. I don't know how deep it is.'

'Nor do I. But I know it's too deep to reach the bottom. I've tried.'

Karl pulled off his shirt, and bent over to unlace his boots. He twisted his head and squinted up at her, teasing, 'Come on, Carrie. I've seen you in your bra and pants before.'

Carrie knew he was referring to the photo shoot when she'd made such an ass of herself. She didn't reply.

She stood, hesitating, while Karl stripped to his

boxers. He took off his shoes and stood on his shirt – the rock was too hot for his feet. Then he dived in, an elegant, almost professional dive, hands together over his head, arms and legs perfectly straight.

As he hit the water the force of his entry pulled his boxers right down his legs, and Carrie watched his white bum winking in the limpid water as he struggled to pull them up again.

He looked up at the grinning Carrie. Gasping and laughing, he called, 'God, it's cold. Come on, Carrie. Jump.'

Carrie saw her chance. She pulled off all her clothes as fast as she could, before she could think better of it, and jumped in.

The shock of the cold water was terrifying. She plunged down, down, down, into freezing blackness, before struggling for the surface. Then her head was in the air and she was gulping, her eyes wide and scared.

Then it was heaven. She looked at her body and her long legs, brown and exotic in the Coca-Cola-clear water, then lay on her back and felt the water, silky and cool, caress her belly, her breasts, her bum. How could she have forgotten the pleasure of skinny-dipping?

She swam towards Karl, her face flushed, exhilarated. 'Come on Karl. Don't be a prude. Get your kit off.'

But he didn't answer. He swam across the pool to where the water ran over the rock lip to tumble down into a further shallower basin. He called to her, 'Here, Carrie, the next pool is in the sun. And it's shallow enough to stand in.' He climbed out of the pool, and turned to help Carrie, exactly as if she weren't stark naked.

Carrie could not believe it. He'd not even replied to her invitation to swim in the buff.

Beginning to feel foolish, she slipped as quickly as she could into the second pool and took an exaggerated interest in the ferns growing above her.

And then she had to climb out and sit with him on the dry rocks, warming up. Carrie tried not to think about her nipples, shrivelled to raisins from the cold, and the way Karl ignored them and her. He talked of his plans for the camp, and how he'd leave this pool exactly as it was. 'The camp has to be a real bush experience, tin plates round the campfire, sleeping bags under the stars, hurricane lamps and candles. No Walkmans, watches, telephones, faxes. And no swimming pools.'

Karl talked as though they were sitting fully clothed in a meeting room. If he took no notice of her nakedness, maybe he didn't find her attractive at all? But she knew she looked good. Apart from the untanned bits that gave her a white bikini, she was as evenly brown as an Ambre Solaire model. Her belly was flat, and her bum and tits round and firm. How could he just ignore her?

It must be, she thought, because he's shagging that Cathy. She wanted to go now, but she was

363

embarrassed to move, and she didn't want to ask Karl to climb up and get her clothes from the ledge.

After fifteen minutes or so, Karl did so without being asked, tossing her things to her with a smile. 'At least you've got dry underwear. My shorts have to go on top of wet ones.'

She had no option but to get dressed and pretend to herself that she always swam naked. No big deal. She hadn't done it to turn Karl on.

That night she wrote to Poppy:

Dear Poppy,

This is business, so I hope you'll reply, if not to me then to Karl.

We want to double the size of the lodge and build a safari camp for overnight game treks. The figures stack up, and the market looks good. But you need to agree.

If I had the money I'd stump up the capital for the new build. But I don't. We can borrow it from the bank, but obviously the interest means a longer payback – though it still looks viable.

Do you want to put up the money (maybe R300, 000) in return for more shares? Instead of a third each, you could have 60 per cent and Karl and me 20 per cent each, or something.

Love (and I do mean that)

Carrie

PS I'll probably take the *My Mag* job. Keep me out of

your hair, and I can help Karl with Kaia Moya. He
wants me to train the cooks. And no, before you ask,
he still wouldn't touch me with a bargepole.

Twenty-six

Through Manor Farm's kitchen window Poppy watched Karl's long legs appear out of the hire car and the rest of him unfold after them. His sun-ruined face was exactly as she thought of him, and she felt a sharp surge of pleasure. Poppy opened the door wide, and threw herself into his arms.

'Oh Karl, I'm so glad to see you. How was Paris?'

'Well, I hope that's the last time I have to man a safari stand at a travel fair. But it was worth it, I think.'

They went into the drawing room. Almost immediately Lorato appeared at the door wearing knickers but nothing else. She stood on one leg, weaving the other one round it like a snake round a pole. 'Mum, it's too hot. Tom wants a glass of water.'

Poppy laughed and said, 'You mean *you* can't sleep and *you* want some company. Is that right?' She shrugged at Karl, saying, 'Sorry. Back in a second,' and led her daughter back to bed by the hand.

While she was gone Angelina came in, headphones on, but as soon as she saw Karl she pulled them down round her neck and leaped on to the sofa next to him. 'Karl! Brilliant. Mum didn't say you were here.'

Angelina chattered excitedly until her mother

reappeared and shooed her off to finish her homework.

Karl said, 'They look well. So do you.'

Poppy handed him a glass of wine and smiled her uncomplicated open smile. 'We all are. The horrors of last summer seem far away. And I'm not working now, which means I'm fatter. And to my surprise, happier.'

Karl nodded but did not say anything. Poppy remembered that one of the great things about Karl was his ease with silence, his unhurried approach to everything.

But she didn't have much time and she felt a dip of angst. She'd embarked on this course and she must go on. 'But before Eduardo gets home – he'll be here any sec – there is something I have to tell you.'

Karl said at once, 'Look, Poppy, it's quite all right if you don't want to put any more money in. We can manage with the bank. The figures still work . . .'

'It's not that,' Poppy interrupted.

'What then?' Karl looked up at the urgency in her voice and said, 'What is it, Popps? Not more drama?'

Poppy smiled uncertainly and said, 'Could be. I hope not.' And then went on in a rush, 'Karl, the thing is, you remember I told you that Carrie could never love you? I don't know if it matters now, but I made it up. She never said it.'

Poppy swallowed and went on, her eyes on her lap, 'And I told her that you couldn't stand her either. That you'd never marry her if she was the last woman on earth.' Poppy lifted her eyes to Karl's. There, she'd told him.

She expected him to say something. To stand up, rant about, ask her what business it was of hers. Anything. But he just looked at her, confusion and pain creeping over his face.

She said, 'When she wrote to me about the new camp, she said you wouldn't touch her with a barge-pole. It made me realize . . .'

He interrupted her. 'Why, Popps?'

She'd decided to tell him the whole truth, and in fact she found it easier than she thought it would be. She told him how she'd begun to find him desirable in that week during which he'd been conscientiously mending her self-esteem.

'I suppose it was like getting hooked on your shrink. I needed you too much,' she said uncertainly. 'And I wanted to get my own back on Eduardo.'

Karl still sat there, looking stunned. She blundered on, 'I misread you completely. Of course you wouldn't fancy me. But I mistook kindness for desire. So when you came to tell me you loved Carrie, I had got it into my head you were going to fall into bed with me.'

Her throat hurt, and tears had overrun her eyes. She went on, 'I'm so sorry, Karl. So sorry . . . But you see, it was happening again. Carrie was helping herself to what was mine. As always.'

'Popps, Popps, stop.' He stood up and came across, crouching down in front of her. 'It's okay, it's okay.' He took her hands and squeezed them. 'It's fine.'

By the time Eduardo arrived Poppy was feeling surprisingly cheerful, with the lightheadedness that comes from confession. As she kissed her husband she smelt his familiar aftershave with a rare wash of desire. The pressure of his hand on her back told her that he felt it too. He said, 'Why all flushed and excited?' He turned to Karl with outstretched hand and said, 'If I didn't know you so well, Karl, I'd wonder what you two had been up to.'

They talked about Kaia Moya. Karl produced his architect's plans and detailed columns of figures to explain his business plan, but Poppy had already made up her mind. She'd put up the money. In the last six months she and Eduardo had become close – or, at least, closer – again. She knew that she'd never completely trust him, but she also knew they loved each other, and she was happy. And she wanted Karl to be too. She even thought she could bear it if Carrie was happy.

But she'd prefer Carrie to be happy in Africa.

Kaia Moya was almost deserted. They'd suspended bookings while a new cesspit was dug and both Karl and Cathy were away. Carrie was sitting on the back step with Maisie, stripping the leaves from a mountain of mielies. She liked this job, slitting the fibrous leaves of each one, pulling them away to expose the fat cob with its tightly packed rows of plump niblets. It was like treasure-hunting, with only the occasional disappointment when the seeds had not developed or some creature had got there first and eaten them.

And it was companionable. Maisie was comfy company, as she'd been when Carrie and Poppy were children. I wonder how many peas she's podded, beans she's shelled, mielies she's shucked, Carrie thought. Maisie said, a statement not a question, 'You happy now, Miss Carrie. You come home again.'

Carrie said for the umpteenth time, 'Maisie, I wish you'd call me Carrie, not Miss Carrie. And yes, it's good to be here.'

It was true. Carrie had now been at Kaia Moya for almost a month, and had long since stopped holi-daying and started working. She'd introduced the sort of bush cooking she knew was right for the guests: stir-fries that were familiar enough in flavour for Euro-pean palates but nonetheless with a whiff of the wild, crocodile with lemon grass and coriander, guineafowl with yams and cinnamon, potjies of casseroled game with figs, ostrich neck or warthog slow-cooked like oxtail with quinces, grills marinated in pomegranate or mango. She borrowed dishes from all over Africa: Moroccan lamb with apricots, Kenyan venison with sweet potatoes, Cape Malay fish with curry spices.

Her food was a great success. Tourists felt adven-turous without being overfaced by mopane worms or deep-fried grasshoppers. And it all looked so good: salad in bowls made by craftsmen in Mpumalunga, buffet dishes in hand-thrown African pottery, bread in exquisite Basuto baskets, tablecloths and napkins of local weave.

So yes, Carrie was content. She didn't miss her London life at all, and was beginning to think that whatever happened she'd sell the business to Lulu. Lulu had agreed to hold the fort while Carrie did her *My Mag* stint, and had moved into her house. She was doing well, gaining more customers. Carrie had become her landlord rather than her boss. The longer Carrie stayed in Africa, the less she wanted to go back.

Carrie still had not made up her mind whether to accept the *My Mag* job. She had a little more time to decide, but Kaia Moya was exerting an extraordinary pull. If it had been a straight choice between helping Karl with the business and working for the mag, she knew she'd stay right here, no contest.

But Carrie now knew she wanted Karl, and she couldn't bear it if Karl was in love with Cathy. She thought she'd be okay with a standoff, if Karl resisted her advances forever, but she couldn't play second fiddle to someone else. She knew she should just ask him outright, 'Are you and Cathy an item? Are you in love with Cathy?' but she couldn't. Of course she'd known him long enough to ask him anything, and she was sure he'd tell her the truth, but she feared the answer. What would she do if he said, 'Yes, we are in love, we are getting married'?

She wouldn't be able to bear it. She thought about Karl and Cathy all the time. Sometimes she told herself that of course he spent a lot of time with Cathy; he always did when training new rangers. But up to now she'd barely noticed his cadets. Most of them were raw boys, just out of school.

Suddenly she stood up. She had to know once and for all. If he loved Cathy, she'd take the *My Mag* job. It was that simple.

'I'll see you later, Maisie,' she said, and headed for the staff cottages. Karl's would be open. He never locked anything. And he wasn't due back from England for two days.

She found the evidence she needed almost at once. It was an old, leather-bound edition of *Jock of the Bushveld* lying on his desk. In the flyleaf he had written:

For C,
Who loves the bushveld a little less, I hope, than one day she'll love me.
From K

The pain was exactly as she knew it would be. She stood stock-still, staring at the words, conscious of a slowly expanding hurt inside her. So, there it is then, she thought. Now you know. She looked down again at the scuffed old volume. She opened it once more, and turned a couple of pages, past Karl's loving inscription.

And then she remembered. Even as she saw the initials D. F. on the title page she knew this had been her father's copy, the one he used to read to Poppy and her on the stoep. And then she remembered more.

Karl used to read to them from it too. Her mom must have given it to Karl after her dad died.

Anger flooded her cheeks as she thought, Bastard. *Jock of the Bushveld* had been almost a sacred text with her father. He loved that book, and she and Poppy had learned to love it too. She threw the book back on the desk, and walked back to her cabin.

The next morning Carrie stayed in her cabin, working on a piece for *My Mag*. Karl was due back the next day and she wanted to finish the article and leave for Johannesburg before his return. Cathy would be back then too, and she had no wish to see their happy reunion.

At 11 a.m. there was a knock on her door. She called, 'Come in,' absently, her mind on a recipe for ginger shortcake.

The door opened but no one said anything. Carrie was forced to swing round and look up. Karl stood in the doorway, the bright light behind throwing his face into darkness. She could not see his expression. He shut the door without turning away from her.

'Karl, hi. Aren't you back early?' she said. Good, her voice was dead cool.

'I know,' he said, 'I came home early to ask you to marry me.' He still had his hands behind him, on the door handle. He did not come any closer, but he repeated, 'Carrie, please marry me.'

She stood up then, her legs feeling very odd. 'Marry you? Me, marry you? But what about Cathy?'

Karl came towards her then, putting his arms out, tentative. 'Cathy? What about Cathy?'

Oh God, thought Carrie, this is like a bad movie. Her heart was hammering in her chest. She felt sick.

'You are in love with Cathy. I saw the book.'

He didn't seem to hear. He put his arms round her and pulled her in to his chest.

It felt wonderful. Safe. Home. How could she ever have loved anyone else? She shut her eyes, thinking, I'll just stay here and not think about Cathy.

Neither of them said anything for a long time. Then Karl said, 'What book?'

Carrie moved a fraction away, reluctantly. She didn't want to have this conversation now. She said, *Jock of the Bushveld*. I went snooping in your cottage. "For C from K".'

It took a few seconds for Karl to understand.

'Oh Carrie,' he cried, pulling her roughly to him again, 'you complete idiot!'

Carrie pushed him back, her colour rising. She insisted, 'I saw the inscription, Karl. "*For C from K*".' She wrenched out of his grasp, feeling happiness evaporating with every word.

'C is for Carrie.' He said it again, 'Darling, C is for Carrie. I was going to give you that book last July. And then I realized you were in love with Eduardo. I've kept it on my desk ever since. In hope.'

She started to laugh. A shaky laugh, near tears. 'And Cathy? You don't . . .'

'Cathy is a child. A tough, talented, good ranger. But no, I don't love her.'

He got his arms round her again, and this time she relaxed. She felt wonderfully small against him, vulnerable and cherished.

Within seconds, Carrie was having her old problem with lust. She wanted to pull Karl's clothes off. Make love to him, make him want her, prove to him that she was worth it.

She reached up and kissed him, as she had done so many months ago in her London kitchen. And again she felt his initial resistance, then his responding passion. At last, she thought, at long long last.

He pulled away. Christ, she thought, I don't believe it.

Karl said, holding her away from him, 'Carrie, wait. I promise you I'm going to screw you senseless. Fuck you like you've never been fucked before. But not here. Grab a jersey and a hat. We are going for a drive.'

She followed him out and they walked through the camp to his cottage. As he passed the kitchen he called, 'Maisie, we'll be gone all day. Do you think you could pack me a quick picnic? Just some bread and cheese and fruit. Enough for four. Put some wine in too.'

Her heart sank. They must be taking rangers or labourers with them for some job.

In his cottage he pulled a couple of blankets off the bed, threw two thick jackets to Carrie and stuffed *Jock of the Bushveld* into his pocket.

Maisie handed them a basket and a coolbox, and Carrie, as if in a dream, followed Karl to the jeep. They climbed in and Karl started the engine, driving past the staff compound without stopping to pick up anyone.

'Why a picnic for four?' she asked.

'Lunch and supper,' he said. 'We've got a lot of talking to do.'

The drive was, Carrie thought, the happiest hour of her life. Karl was going to make love to her. He was going to marry her. They'd have happy ever after, those babies, a life and business together at Kaia Moya.

Maybe, one day, she'd be friends again with Poppy. For once the thought of Poppy did not grey Carrie's skies. Rather she wished she could see her. She wanted to tell Poppy about Karl. Not to crow that Poppy was wrong about him, but because she wanted her sister to share her happiness. She wanted Poppy to be pleased for her. She wanted to tell her big sister that she'd come good after all – she was going to stop being mad and bad, and be a wife. Maybe a mom.

As if following her thoughts, Karl said, 'Poppy and Eduardo seem pretty good together again. They're going to provide the capital for the extra cabins and the camp.'

Carrie thought, This must all be a dream. Any minute I'll wake up and find that bloody Cathy is going to marry Karl. She said, 'Poppy will never forgive me. I know she won't.'

'She has forgiven you. Her problem has been forgiving herself.' And then he told her about Poppy doing her best to keep them apart.

Carrie was aghast. 'But Karl, Poppy doesn't do things like that. I do that sort of thing, not Poppy. Why would she do that? I can't believe . . .'

'Darling heart, she was jealous. She's always been jealous of you. Just as you have been of her. She's not a saint. She's a lovely woman, but she's not a saint.'

They climbed again to the ledge above the rock pool and it was like a replay, only this time the air was charged with desire and the certainty of what was to come. Karl said, 'Go on, take your clothes off again.'

She felt a moment's embarrassment as she started to pull off her tee-shirt. She giggled and said, 'Karl, this is like a B movie. I can hear the sound of soaring violins. I expect you to start beating your chest and making Tarzan noises.'

He didn't laugh. He pulled her towards him by the waistband of her shorts, and as he undid the button said very quietly into her ear, 'Last time, when you swam around that pool naked, and I pulled you out, and then sat trying to pretend that I was made of stone as the most beautiful woman in the world sat wet and slippery in front of me, I swore that if I ever did get you to love me, I'd pay you back.'

He stroked every inch of her as he undressed her, but he would not let her caress him, and he would not kiss her mouth. 'No,' he said, as her lips tried to find his, 'if I kiss you, I'll fuck you, and that's not for yet.' And he would not let her sit down, or lie down, though her legs were caving in beneath her. Oh God, she wanted him so much, the warmth of the sun and his hands on her body were more than she could bear. Her body ached, really ached, for him.

It was agony, but she was desperate for him to go on caressing her. She wanted him to use both hands, but one of them was holding her wrists together behind her back so that she could not touch him. She thought she might faint with longing.

Suddenly his arms were right round her, practically lifting her off her feet. She could feel his whole body against hers and she thought, with a little thrill of triumph, At last.

He pushed her up against the rounded wall of rock. It was smooth and hot from the sun.

'It's burning.' The words came out in a gasp of protest. But he did not release her, and she felt the heat against her thighs and bum, and then as a great blast against her back and shoulders as he pressed against her, forcing her skin against the smooth hot granite.

'Tough,' he said, and he was in her. She opened her mouth, half in ecstasy, half with the pain of the hot rock. He put his open mouth over hers, kissing her, loving her, but most of all possessing her. Her legs came up around his waist as he thumped her against the wall. Carrie was drunk, delirious.

When it was over they slid together down the smooth rock. Carrie was now oblivious of the heat beneath them, of her bruised back, of her swollen mouth. She felt nothing but an overwhelming lassitude. She was dizzy and drenched in love.

The rest of the day was a dream. They slid around each other like seals in the icy pool until desire overcame the cold and they made love again, half in and half out of the water. They ate cheese and bread with ravenous appetite, then fell asleep on their towels in the sun.

Karl woke first and smoothed suntan oil on to Carrie's scratched red back, and then continued stroking and oiling her, over her shoulders, under her armpits, between her thighs, until she couldn't bear it and she turned over, pulling him into her once more.

As the sun left the river gorge, it grew cold. They dressed and climbed to the plateau, hauling on jackets as the shadows lengthened and the game appeared at the waterhole below. They sat on the edge, Carrie's anxiety stilled by the safety of Karl's shoulder.

They watched the elephants arriving, with their shambling dignity and ponderous gait. Two cow elephants went first into the water, but didn't like it. They wouldn't drink the water stirred up by the kudu, and reversed out of the pool with careful backward steps to try another spot. Carrie loved the delicate way they explored each other with their trunks, and the efficiency with which they swooshed water under their stomachs and over their backs. She'd always loved elephants, the mothers keeping their babies between their legs, the indifference with which they felled young trees with a deliberate foot, the way they threshed a bunch of grass against their legs, winnowing out the straw and eating the green.

'Karl, I'm so happy,' she said.

Karl pulled *Jock of the Bushveld* out of his pocket and handed it to her. 'Here,' he said. 'Don't lose it. It belonged to your dad.'

Epilogue

Four years later

Poppy sat with the children sandwiched between her and Eduardo. Her eyes slid sideways along the pew and for a moment her sadness and exhaustion lifted. Angelina had her head against her father's shoulder, her blonde hair lying bright against his dark jacket as he looked down at her, doting. Poppy thought with gratitude that Lina was still kind and easy, no adolescent horrors yet. Lorato and Tom were craning round excitedly, hoping to see the promised Carrie and Karl, who had not arrived.

His voice too loud, Tom asked, 'Where's the fire, Mum? You said they were going to burn Granny up.'

Poppy bent her head and whispered, 'Tom. Lorato. Face the front and keep still. We all have to be very quiet. I'll explain anything later, but now you must sit still and you must not talk.'

The service was a nightmare. The priest provided by the crematorium was proud of his resonant voice and put it through its paces, dipping and arcing with no connection to the words. He referred to Lucille as 'Lucy' all through, and then gave a sermon about how much 'Lucy' was beloved by her friends and family and how sorely she'd be missed by all who knew her. It was ludicrous. Lucille had no friends, only carers, and all who knew her – at least during the last few years – had found her exhausting, impossible, a continuous trial.

Poppy could not concentrate. She could not even think of her mother when that travesty of a cleric called for a minute's silence in which everyone was to think of their own personal 'most loved memories of our dear Lucy'. Anguish at such bland nonsense being spouted by a stranger about her mother, and misery that she had not had the foresight to prevent it, engulfed her.

And when the moment came for the coffin to slide under the curtain it started smoothly but then stopped halfway. The singing faltered (or so it seemed to Poppy) and then the coffin gave a jerk and proceeded in undignified haste, as if yanked by invisible arms beyond the curtain.

Poppy felt the anger rising. Anger with the pompous clergyman and the amateurish mechanics, but above all anger with Carrie. How could Carrie have missed their mother's funeral?

The little clutch of mourners – a single representative nurse from the nursing home and half a dozen of the carers and neighbours who had known Lucille before Poppy had given up and put her in the Mornington – dispersed quickly with kind words and evident relief. Poppy looked round once more for Karl and Carrie, then got into the car with Eduardo and the children and drove home.

Eduardo asked, handing her a whisky, 'You okay?'

Poppy reached up for the drink. 'Oh Eduardo, I wish I'd organized it better.'

'How could you, darling? You were in Hollywood.'

'I know. But it's as though I just heaved a sigh of relief and left the undertakers to do my job. Like turning my back on poor Mom.' She took a long gulp, then went on, 'I could at least have directed the thing better. Had some decent music. Written the vicar's sermon for him.'

'Mia cara, stop it. You've been a wonderful daughter to a very difficult mother, and now it's over. There's nothing to . . .'

The phone rang and Eduardo said, 'Let the machine . . .'

But Poppy jumped up, 'No, it might be Carrie.'

It was. Her voice came gabbling out of the telephone, words falling over themselves,

'Oh Poppy, is it over? Is she cremated? I can't bear it . . .'

Poppy felt the old tug of sympathy, but she said, quite coolly, 'Where are you?'

'At Heathrow. We've just got in. We spent nineteen hours at Nairobi airport. Oh God, Poppy, that's a hellhole. Did you get my messages?'

'No. Nothing.'

Carrie let out a wailing, 'Oh no . . . oo,' then said, 'Oh Poppy, I am so, so sorry. We had engine trouble and had to land, then . . .'

Eduardo took the handset from Poppy and interrupted his sister-in-law's account of hours of waiting only to be transferred on to another plane that hit a flock of birds on take-off and had to land again. He cut in, 'Carrie. Hi. It's Eduardo. Come straight here. Giulia's making supper. We can talk then.'

Supper was delicious. Giulia's version of macaroni cheese had pieces of garlicky aubergine in it as well as an unhealthy amount of butter and pecorino. Karl, starving after thirty hours of uneatable food, had two helpings.

Carrie wondered if it was Karl's hunger, or sympathy at the loss of Lucille that made Giulia smile at her. I wonder when she last did that? thought Carrie, smiling back, and saying, 'Wonderful, Giulia, really delicious.'

It was just the sort of comforting food everyone needed, and it cheered them. Then Giulia took Tom and Lorato off to bed, and Angelina disappeared to do her homework.

Eduardo carried the wine into the sitting area, and Poppy flopped down on the sofa next to Carrie. Putting two glasses and the bottle down in front of Poppy, Eduardo said, 'Karl, let's go to the pub. Leave the women to catch up on sister talk.'

Karl said, 'Sure,' and followed Eduardo out. His

eyes met Carrie's as he passed her. He narrowed them slightly, a private signal.

Poppy caught the look, and saw Carrie's answering smile. She said, 'You really love him, don't you?'

'Yes.' There was a pause and then she said, 'You were right. I hadn't a clue what loving, or being in love, meant before.'

'I know.'

Carrie said, 'Tell me about the funeral.'

'It was awful.' She smiled bleakly. 'If it wasn't so sad it would have made a good black comedy.'

She told Carrie about Tom wanting to see flames, about the ghastly cleric, about the coffin getting stuck.

'But the worst was, you weren't there.'

'Typical of me, wasn't it? Never around for Mom.' Carrie's voice was bitter.

'I used to think that was true, but it isn't really. Mom adored you. You made her laugh. Got tiddly with her. I just bossed her about.' She sighed and put her head back on the sofa cushions, eyes closed.

Carrie looked at her sister's face, drained but somehow beautiful. She wanted to reach out and stroke her cheek.

Carrie didn't want Poppy to refer to the worst part of the past, her affair with Eduardo, but she knew one of them had to, sooner or later. It would be easier with Poppy's eyes closed.

No one said anything for a while. It was peaceful and Carrie was tempted to let the chance go. To do what she'd done for four years, politely pretend it hadn't happened. She said, 'Poppy, it's four years now. But hardly a day goes by that I'm not so, so sorry. If you seduced Karl, I'd kill you. Literally. I know I would.'

Poppy opened her eyes. 'Don't think I didn't want to kill you,' she said. Her smile was half teasing, half sad.

'But you didn't. You even let me back into your life. Until I nearly drowned Lorato. Even then, you invested in Kaia Moya. You've never done me anything but good, Poppy. Sometimes I used to hate you for it, but now I just miss you. I really miss you, Poppy.' Carrie felt her lip start to wobble, like a child's, and like a child she bit it.

Poppy said, 'I miss you too. Funny that. I even missed you when I hated you the most.'

They were silent for a minute, Carrie regaining composure, both women thinking of the other, then Poppy said, 'I did do you some harm. Or tried to. I tried to keep you and Karl apart. God knows why. He's about the only man in the world who could cope with you.'

Carrie nodded. Maybe, after all, it would be all right. Maybe not at once, but one day. She touched her sister's arm, a small hesitating gesture. Poppy put her hand over Carrie's and pressed it.

Both women smiled, and optimism ran through Carrie like a charge. She stood up. She felt great. As if she could fly. 'You haven't any oranges, have you? I'd really love an orange.'

Poppy, surprised, said, 'Orange juice do?' She pulled herself out of the sofa and headed for the kitchen, relieved that they'd closed a gap without weeping or too much talk. I'm too tired, and too old, thought Poppy, for *Sturm und Drang*.

Carrie shook her head. 'Not really.' She followed Poppy and they found two thick-skinned navel oranges.

Carrie took one and with a paring knife pulled off the skin in neat segments. Then she bent a piece of orange peel backwards so she could nibble the pith with her teeth.

Poppy watched her idly. Then the penny dropped. 'You're pregnant!'

Carrie's eyes widened. 'How on earth do you know?'

Poppy was laughing now.

'Because I did the same thing when I was pregnant. And so did Mom. She told me.'

'What? What thing?'

'Eating orange pith. Oh Carrie! How many weeks?' She stepped back to inspect her sister. 'You hardly show . . .'

'Yes, I certainly do,' Carrie cut in, indignant. She parted her long jacket to reveal a distinct bulge, which she pushed out proudly. 'And I get kicks and somersaults.'

Poppy put one hand on her sister's belly, then slid both arms round her back and pulled Carrie into a hug.

All at once it was as if there had never been dark days, as if Carrie hadn't ruined everything. Carrie closed her eyes, deep in Poppy's hug. She put her arms round her sister's comfortable frame and closed her eyes.

They went back to the sitting room and talked. Poppy told Carrie about their mother's death, how she'd heard about it in the rehearsal studio, 5,000 miles away. They reverted to the funeral. Carrie said, 'I wanted so to be there. Not for Mom, who's out of it, but for you. We should have seen her off together.'

'It's okay, it's okay,' said Poppy.

But Carrie wanted to tell Poppy everything, unleash the years of conversations she'd had with her in her head. She spoke at speed, articulate in her urgency. 'Poppy, since I've been pregnant, I've seen things so clearly. I need you so much. Not like I used to, like a limpet, expecting you to save me every minute, but just because I miss you. You've got to start coming to Kaia Moya again. Every time we change something or build something, I want you to see it. I need you to show off to.' Carrie shook her head, self-deprecating. 'I suppose I want you to see what a grown-up I am now. Oh Poppy, women need other women. A best friend who knows everything . . .' She trailed off, looking into Poppy's face. Poppy frowned.

'I've never been very good at that,' said Poppy. 'Even with you, confidences were pretty much one-way traffic.'

'Maybe we could change that. We could try.'

Poppy thought of the anguished year after Carrie left, when she watched Eduardo like a hawk, mistrustful of his every trip. When the children could not understand Carrie's desertion, and when her only release was on stage, away from her life. It would have been good to have had a friend then.

'Yes, we could try.'

Carrie tipped the last of the wine into Poppy's glass, saying, 'Besides, I want someone to bore to death about the baby, and ring up when she's sick, and ask advice about teething and tantrums.'

'She! Is it a girl then?'

'Yes. It is. It's a girl. She's called Poppy.'